VIXEN IN VELVET

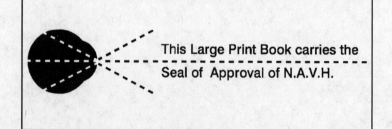

This Large Print Book carries the
Seal of Approval of N.A.V.H.

VIXEN IN VELVET

LORETTA CHASE

THORNDIKE PRESS
A part of Gale, Cengage Learning

Farmington Hills, Mich • San Francisco • New York • Waterville, Maine
Meriden, Conn • Mason, Ohio • Chicago

GALE
CENGAGE Learning®

LIBRARY OF CONGRESS CATALOGING-IN-PUBLICATION DATA

Chase, Loretta Lynda, 1949-
  Vixen In velvet / Loretta Chase.
    pages cm. — (The dressmakers) (Thorndike Press large print romance)
  ISBN 978-1-4104-8636-3 (hardback) — ISBN 1-4104-8636-2 (hardcover)
    1. Dressmakers—Fiction. 2. Nobility—England—Fiction. 3. London (England)—Social life and customs—19th century—Fiction. 4. Large type books. I. Title.
PS3553.H3347V59 2016
813'.54—dc23   2015036243

Published in 2016 by arrangement with Avon Books, an imprint of HarperCollins Publishers

Printed in the United States of America
1 2 3 4 5 6 7 20 19 18 17 16

In memory of my mother

ACKNOWLEDGMENTS

Thanks to:

May Chen: funny, wise, and understanding editor, whose patience surpasseth all understanding;

Nancy Yost: brilliant, hardworking, witty, and inspiring agent;

Isabella Bradford: kindred spirit and nerdy history co-enabler;

Paul and Carol: providers of the perfect writer's refuge on Cape Cod;

Valerie Kerxhalli: advisor in matters of French;

Colonial Williamsburg milliners and mantua makers and tailors, oh, my: experts in historic dress who continue to unlock the mysteries of clothing from the past;

Cynthia, Vivian, and Kathy: sisters, cheerleaders, confidantes, friends;

Walter: spouse, producer, cinematographer, and knight in shining armor.

CHAPTER ONE

BRITISH INSTITUTION. — ANCIENT MASTERS. This annual Exhibition is the best set-off to the illiberality with which our grand signors shut up their pictures from the public — making, in fact, *close boroughs* of their collections.
> — *The Athenaeum,* 30 May 1835

British Institution, Pall Mall, London
Wednesday 8 July
He lay naked but for a cloth draped over his manly parts. Head fallen back, eyes closed, mouth partly open, he slept too deeply to notice the imps playing with his armor and weapons, or the one blowing through a shell into his ear. The woman reclined nearby, her elbow resting on a red cushion. Unlike him, she was fully dressed, in gold-trimmed linen, and fully awake. She watched him with an unreadable expression. Did her lips hint at a smile or a frown,

or was her mind elsewhere entirely?

Leonie Noirot's mind offered sixteen different answers, none satisfactory. What wasn't in doubt was what this pair had been doing before the male — the Roman god Mars, according to the exhibition catalog — fell asleep.

If anything else was in Leonie's mind — her reason for coming here this day, for instance, or where "here" was or who she was — it had by now drifted to a distant corner of her skull. Nothing but the painting mattered or even existed.

She stood before the Botticelli work titled *Venus and Mars,* and might have been standing on another planet or in another time, so completely did it absorb her. She stood and stared, and could have counted every brushstroke, trying to get to the bottom of it. What she couldn't do was escape it.

If anybody had stood in her way, she might have throttled that person. Oddly enough, nobody did. The British Institution's Annual Summer Exhibition continued to attract visitors. It drew as well numerous artists, who set up their easels in the galleries, in order to copy the work of old masters. These artists made annoying obstacles of themselves while they desperately exercised what might be their only opportunity to copy works from private collections.

Nobody stood in Leonie's way. Nobody pontificated over her shoulder. She didn't notice this, let alone wonder why. She hadn't come for the art but for one specific reason.

A most important reason . . . which she'd forgotten the instant her gaze landed on the painting.

She might have stood transfixed until Doomsday, or until one of the caretakers pitched her out. But —

A crash, sudden as a thunderclap, broke the room's peace.

She jumped, and stumbled backward.

And hit a wall that oughtn't to have been there.

No, not a wall.

It was big, warm, and alive.

It smelled like a man: shaving soap and starch and wool. Two man-sized gloved hands, which lightly grasped her shoulders and smoothly restored her to an upright position, confirmed the impression.

She turned quickly and looked up — a good ways up — at him.

Ye gods.

Or, more accurately, ye god Mars.

Perhaps he wasn't precisely like the image

11

in the painting. For one thing, the living man was fully clothed, and most expensively, too. But the nose and forehead and mouth were so like. And the shape of the eyes especially. His, unlike the war god's, were open.

They were green, with gold flecks, like the gold streaks in his dark blond hair. And that was curly like Mars's, and appealingly unruly. Something less easily definable in the eyes and mouth hinted at other kinds of unruliness: the mouth on the brink of a smile and the eyes open a degree too wide and innocent. Or was that stupidity?

"In all the excitement, I seem to have put my foot under yours," he said. "I do beg your pardon."

Not stupid.

More important, he'd been standing too close, and she hadn't noticed. Leonie never allowed anybody to sneak up on her. In Paris that could have been fatal. Even in London it was risky.

She kept all her misgivings on the inside, as she'd learned to do eons ago.

"I hope I did you no permanent injury," she said. She let her gaze drift downward. His boots were immaculate. His valet had polished them to such a fearsome brilliance, the dust of London's streets could only stagger away, blinded.

His green gaze slid downward, too, to her footwear. "A small foot wrapped in a bit of satin and a sliver of leather doing damage? Odds against, don't you think?"

"The bits of satin and leather are half-boots called brodequins," she said. "And my feet are not small. But it's gallant of you to say so."

"In the circumstances, I ought to say something agreeable," he said. "I ought as well to produce a clever reason for creeping up on you. Or a chivalrous reason, like intent to shield you from falling easels. But then you'd only decide I was an idiot. As anybody can see, the offending object is some yards away."

She was aware of somebody swearing, about three paintings to her left. From the same direction came the sound of wood scraped over wood and the rustling of a heavy fabric. She didn't look that way. Girls who didn't keep their wits about them when gods wandered their way got into trouble. Ask Daphne or Leda or Danaë.

Today's fitful sun had decided to stream through the skylight at this moment. Its rays fell upon the gold-streaked head.

"Perhaps you were captivated by the painting," she said. "And lost track of your surroundings."

"That's a fine excuse," he said. "But as it's my painting, and I've had ample time to stare at the thing, it won't do."

"Yours," she said. She hadn't looked up the lender's name at the back of the catalog. She'd assumed the masterpiece must belong to the King or one of the royal dukes.

"That is to say, I'm not Botticelli, you know, the fellow being dead some centuries. I'm Lisburne."

Leonie collected her wits, brought business to the front of her mind, and flipped through the pages of her mental ledger, wherein she kept her private compendium of Great Britain's aristocracy as well as important tidbits from the gossip sheets and her gossipy customers.

She found the entry easily, because she'd updated it not many days ago: *Lisburne* meant Simon Blair, the fourth Marquess of Lisburne. Age seven and twenty, he constituted the sole issue of the greatly lamented third Marquess of Lisburne, whose very recently remarried widow resided in Italy.

Lord Lisburne, who'd lived abroad, too, for these last five or six years, had arrived from the Continent a fortnight ago with his first cousin and close friend Lord Swanton.

The Viscount Swanton was Leonie's reason for being in a Pall Mall gallery on a workday.

She looked back at the painting. Then she looked about her, for the first time, really. It dawned on her, then, why nobody else had stood in her way. Elsewhere on the gallery walls hung landscapes, mythological and historical deaths and battles and such, and madonnas and other religious subjects. The Botticelli had nothing to do with any of them. No preaching, no violence, and definitely no bucolic innocence.

"Interesting choice," she said.

"It stands out, rather, now you mention it," he said. "No one seems to care much for Botticelli these days. My friends urged me to put in a battle scene."

"Instead you chose the aftermath," she said.

His green gaze shifted briefly to the painting, then back to her. "I could have sworn they'd been making love."

"And I could swear she's vanquished him."

"Ah, but he'll rise again to — er — fight another day," he said.

"I daresay." She turned fully toward the painting and moved a step closer, though she knew she risked drowning in it. Again. Surely she'd seen equally beautiful works —

15

in the Louvre, for instance. But this . . .

Its owner moved to stand beside her. For a moment they regarded it in silence, an acute physically conscious one on her part.

"Venus's expression intrigues me," she said. "I wonder what she's thinking."

"There's one difference between men and women," he said. "He's sleeping and she's thinking."

"Somebody must think," she said. "And it does so often seem to be the women."

"I always wonder why they don't go to sleep, too," he said.

"I couldn't say," Leonie said. She truly couldn't. Her understanding of the physical act between men and women, while as detailed and precise as her eldest sister could make it, was in no way based on personal experience — and this was not the time to imagine the experience, she reminded herself. Business came first, last, and always. Especially now. "What occupies me is a lady's outward appearance."

She opened her reticule, withdrew a small card, and gave it to him. It was a beautiful card, as of course it must be, hers being the foremost establishment of its kind in London. The size of a lady's calling card and elegantly engraved and colored, it was nonetheless a trade card for Maison Noirot,

16

Dressmakers to Ladies of Fashion, No. 56 St. James's Street.

He studied it for a time.

"I'm one of the proprietresses," she said.

He looked up from the card to meet her gaze. "You're not the one married to my cousin Longmore?"

She couldn't be surprised he was a cousin of her newest brother-in-law. All the Great World seemed to be related to one another, and the Fairfax family, to which the Earl of Longmore belonged, was large in its main branch and prolific in its associated twigs and vines.

"That's my sister Sophy," she said. "For future reference, she's the blonde one." That was the way Society thought of the three proprietresses of Maison Noirot, she knew: the Three Sisters — sometimes the Three Witches or French Tarts — the brunette, the blonde, and the redhead.

"Right. And one of you is married to the Duke of Clevedon."

"My sister Marcelline. She's the brunette."

"How good of your parents to make you easy to tell apart," he said. "And how kind of you to explain. Were I to mistake, say, the Countess of Longmore for you, and make a stab at flirtation, her brute of a spouse

17

would try to do me a violence, to the detriment of my neckcloth. I spent fully half an hour arranging it."

Leonie was an experienced businesswoman of one and twenty, not a sheltered young lady. She examined the neckcloth in a businesslike manner — or tried to. This proved a great deal more difficult than it ought to be.

Below the finely chiseled angle of his jaw, his neckcloth was not only immaculate but so flawlessly folded and creased that it might have been carved of marble.

The rest of his dress was inhumanly perfect, too. So were his face and physique.

The inner woman felt light-headed, and thought this would be a good time to swoon. The dressmaker regarded the neckcloth with a critical eye. "You employed your time to excellent effect," she said.

"Not that it makes the least difference," he said. "No one looks at the other fellows when *he's* about."

"He," she said.

"My poetical cousin. I'm overburdened with cousins. Oh, there they are now, blast it."

She became aware of voices coming from the central staircase.

She turned that way as hats and heads

rose into view. Torsos soon followed. After a moment's apparent confusion about which way to go, the group, mainly young women, surged toward the archway of the gallery in which she stood. There they came to a halt, with only a moderate degree of unladylike pushing and elbowing. The clump of women opened up to make way for a tall, slender, ethereal-looking gentleman. He wore his flaxen hair overlong and his clothing with theatrical flair.

"Him," Lord Lisburne said.

"Lord Swanton," she said.

"Who else could it be, with two dozen girls looking up at him, every one of them wearing the same besotted expression."

Leonie's gaze took in the women, all about her age or younger, except for a handful of mamas or aunts obliged to chaperon. Near the outer edge of Lord Swanton's worshippers and their reluctant attendants she spied Sophy's new sister-in-law, Lady Clara Fairfax, looking bored. Her ladyship stood with a plain young woman who was dressed stupendously wrong.

Leonie's spirits soared. She'd come intending to add to her clientele. This was more than she'd dared to hope for.

For a moment she almost forgot ye god Mars and even the painting. Almost. She beat down her excitement and turned her attention back to Lord Lisburne.

"Thank you, my lord, for stopping me from toppling like the unfortunate artist's easel," she said. "Thank you for choosing that particular painting to lend to the exhibition. I don't care for scenes of violence, which seem to be so popular. And saintly beings are so trying. But this experience was sublime."

"Which experience, exactly?" he said. "Our acquaintance has been short but eventful."

She was tempted to linger and continue flirting. He was so good at it. Moreover, in addition to being beautiful he was a nobleman who owned a painting that, popular or not, was probably priceless. Beyond a doubt he owned several hundred other priceless or at least stunningly costly objects, along with two or three immense houses set upon large expanses of Great Britain. If — or more likely, when — he took a wife and/or set up a mistress, he'd pay for her housing, servants, carriage, horses, etc. etc. — and, most important of *et ceteras,* her clothing.

But the girl, Clara's friend, looked out of sorts and seemed ready to bolt. A prize like that didn't turn up every day. Leonie had already obtained Lord Lisburne's attention, in any event. He'd saunter into the shop one of these days, if she was any judge of men.

"It has, indeed," Leonie said. "However, I came on business."

"Business," he said.

"Ladies," she said. "Dresses." She made a brisk gesture, indicating her ensemble, which she'd spent well more than half an hour arranging for this event. "Advertising."

Then she made a quick curtsey and started toward Lord Swanton and his acolytes. She heard a muffled sound behind her, but she couldn't take the time to look back. The ill-dressed girl was tugging on Lady Clara's arm.

Leonie walked more quickly.

Eyes on Lady Clara's companion, she didn't see the canvas cloth in her way.

The toe of her brodequin caught on it and she pitched forward.

She was aware of a collective gasp, interspersed with titters, as she went down, arms flailing ungracefully.

Lisburne hadn't noticed the artist's cloth, either. He was too busy taking in the rear view of Miss Noirot, though he'd already fully employed the opportunity to study that at length — at a distance as well as at

21

improperly close quarters — while she stood before the Botticelli, oblivious to him and everybody and everything else. When she'd turned to look up at him, he'd nearly staggered, thinking Botticelli's Venus had come to life: the same — or very like — heart-shaped face and alluringly imperfect nose . . . the ripe mouth with its hint of a smile or deep thought or troublesome recollection . . . the surprisingly determined chin.

His mind might have wandered into indecorous fantasies but his reflexes were in sharp working order. He moved forward, caught her, and swept her up into his arms in one smooth movement.

Ladies' dress had only grown more extravagantly fanciful since he was last in England, nearly six years ago. It was hard to tell which parts of a girl were real and which were created for artistic effect. While he appreciated artistic effect, he was happy to discover that what seemed to be a gloriously shapely form was artificial only in the most superficial way. Judging by the warm parts with which he was in contact, her body was as lavishly rounded as he'd supposed. She smelled good, too.

He saw her eyes widen — eyes of a vivid blue that put sapphires and Tuscan skies to shame — and her plump mouth fall open slightly.

"Now you've done it," he said under his breath. "Everybody's staring."

No exaggeration. Everybody in view had stopped whatever they were doing or saying to gape. Who could blame them? Gorgeous redheads didn't drop into a fellow's arms every day.

The commotion was drawing in people from the other rooms.

This day was turning out infinitely less boring than he'd expected.

"Miss Noirot!"

Swanton thrust through his crowd of worshippers — treading on a few toes in the process — to hurry toward them. The worshippers followed. Even Lisburne's cousins, Clara and Gladys Fairfax, tagged along, though neither looked especially worshipful or even enthusiastic.

"Great Zeus, what's happened?" Swanton demanded.

"The lady fainted," Lisburne said.

He knew that a number of people had seen the dressmaker trip — those, that is, who could tear their gazes from Swanton. Lisburne glanced about, lazily inviting any witnesses to contradict him. None did so. Even those blackguards Meffat and Theaker

23

held their tongues for once.

True, Lady Gladys Fairfax did harrumph, but no one ever paid attention to her — not, that is, unless they wanted to work themselves into a murderous rage. Though she, too, had only very recently returned to London after some years' absence, no one could have forgotten her, much in the way that no one forgot the plague, for instance, or the Great Fire, or a bout of hydrophobia.

"Merci," Miss Noirot said in an undertone. Lisburne didn't so much hear it as feel it, in the general environs of his chest.

"Je vous en prie," he replied.

"It was only a momentary dizziness," she said more audibly. "You may put me down now, my lord."

"Are you quite sure, madame?" Swanton said. "You're flushed, and no wonder. This infernal heat. Not a breath of a breeze this day." He looked up at the skylight. Everybody else did, too. "And here's the sun, blasting down on us, as though it made a wrong turn on its way to the Sahara Desert. Would somebody be so good as to fetch Madame a glass of water?"

Madame? Then Lisburne remembered the elegant trade card. One generally referred to a modiste, especially the expensive sort, as Madame, regardless of her marital status.

24

And Swanton knew this particular Madame. He'd never said a word, the sneak. But no, sneakiness wasn't in character. More than likely, some poetic ecstasy had taken possession of him and he simply forgot until he saw her again. Typical.

Swanton's father had died young at Waterloo, and Lisburne's father had taken over the paternal role. That made Lisburne the protective elder brother, a position he retained on account of Swanton being Swanton.

"My lord, you're too kind," she said. "But I don't require water. I'm quite well. It was only a moment's faintness. Lord Lisburne, if you'd be so good as to let me down."

She squirmed a little in Lisburne's arms. That was fun.

Being a male in rude good health, all parts in prime working order, he wasn't eager to let go of her. Still, since it had to be done, he made the most of it, easing her down with the greatest care, letting her body inch down along his, and not releasing her until a long, pulsing moment after her feet touched the floor.

She closed her eyes and said something under her breath, then opened them again and produced a smile, which she aimed straight at him. The smile was as dazzling as

25

her eyes. The combined effect made him feel a little dizzy.

"Madame, if you feel strong enough, would you allow me to present my friends?" Swanton said. "I know they're all clamoring to meet you."

The gentlemen, beyond a doubt. They'd be wild to be made known to any attractive woman, especially in the present circumstances, when it was nigh impossible to get any attention from the lot swarming about Swanton.

But the ladies? Wishing to be introduced to a shopkeeper?

Perhaps not out of the question in this case, Lisburne decided. The three Noirot sisters had made themselves famous. He'd heard of them on the Continent recently. Their work, it was said, rivaled that of the celebrated Victorine of Paris, who required even queens to make appointments and attend her at her place of business.

Lisburne watched the dazzling gaze and smile sweep over the assembled audience.

"You're too kind, my lord," she said. "But I've disturbed everybody sufficiently today. The ladies will know where to find me: around the corner, at No. 56 St. James's Street. And the ladies, as you know, are my primary concern."

At the end of the speech, she shot a glance at somebody in the crowd. Cousin Clara? Then Madame curtseyed and started away.

The others turned away, the women first. Swanton resumed poeticizing or romanticizing or whatever he was doing, and they all moved on to Veronese's *Between Virtue and Vice.*

Lisburne, however, watched Miss Noirot's departure. She seemed not altogether steady on her feet, not quite so effortlessly graceful as before. At the top of the stairs, she took hold of the railing and winced.

Leonie was not allowed to make a quiet escape.

She heard the Marquess of Lisburne coming behind her. She knew who it was without looking. This was probably because he'd made her so keenly attuned to him, thanks to the extremely improper way he'd set her on her feet a moment ago. She was still vibrating.

Or perhaps he sent some sort of pulsation across the room, in the way certain gods had been believed to herald their arrival with strange lights or magical sounds or divine scent.

"You seem to be in pain," he said. "May I assist you?"

27

"I was hoping to slink off quietly," she said.

"No difficulty there. Everybody else is hovering about my cousin. He's spouting about *Virtue and Vice,* and they all believe he's saying something." While he spoke, he took possession of her left arm and arranged it around his neck. He brought his arm round her waist.

She caught her breath.

"It must hurt like the devil," he said. "On second thought, I'd better check your ankle before we proceed. It might be more damaged than we think."

If he touched her ankle she would faint, and not necessarily for medical reasons.

"I only turned it," she said. "If I'd done worse, I'd be sitting on the step, sobbing with as much mortification as pain."

"I can carry you," he said.

"No," she said, and added belatedly, "thank you."

They proceeded down the stairs slowly. She did sums in her head to distract her from the warmth of the big body supporting hers. It wasn't easy. She had stared too long at the Botticelli, and her mind was making pictures of the muscular arms and torso with no elegant covering whatsoever.

By the time they reached the first landing,

her usually well-ordered brain was wandering into strange byways and taking excessive notice of physical sensations.

She made herself speak. "I can only hope that people assume I was dazzled by my brief encounter with Lord Swanton," she said.

"That's what I'll tell them, if you like," he said. "But I received the impression you knew each other."

"Paris," she said. "Ages ago."

"It can't be a very long age," he said. "You're somewhat damaged but not quite decrepit."

"It was his first visit to Paris," she said.

"More than five years ago, then," he said.

When Leonie was nearly sixteen, happy in her work and her family and especially her beautiful infant niece, and reveling in the success of Emmeline, Cousin Emma's splendid dressmaking shop.

Before the world fell apart.

"Lord Swanton came to my cousin's shop to buy a gift for his mother," she said. "He was sweet-tempered and courteous. In Paris, gentlemen often mistook a dressmaker's shop for a brothel."

Those who persisted in the mistake tended to have unfortunate accidents.

One of the first rules Leonie had ever

learned was, *Men only want one thing.* Cousin Emma had taught her young charges as much about defending themselves against encroaching men as she had about dress-making. She had not, however, taught her girls anything about dealing with Roman gods. It was trickier than one would think to maintain a businesslike attitude, even though Leonie was the most businesslike of the three sisters. That wasn't saying much, when you came down to it. Marcelline and Sophy had always had their heads in the clouds: dreamers and schemers and typical Noirots, typical DeLuceys.

He smelled so clean, like the air after rain. How did he do that? Was it scent? A miraculous new soap?

By the time they reached the ground floor, the throbbing in her ankle seemed to have lessened somewhat.

"I think I can make do with your arm," she said.

"Are you sure?"

"My ankle is better," she said. "I needn't lean on you quite so much."

The fact was, she didn't have to lean at all, because he held her so firmly against him. She was aware of every inch of his muscled arm and — through all the layers of chemise, corset, dress, and pelerine —

30

exactly where his fingers rested at the bottom of her rib cage.

She let go of his neck. He let go of her waist and offered his arm. She placed her gloved hand on his, and he grasped it as firmly as he'd grasped her waist.

She told herself this was hardly intimacy, compared to his holding her along the length of his body, but the fact was, no man had got this close to her in years. Still, that didn't explain why she wanted to run away. She knew how to defend herself, did she not? She knew better than to let herself fall under the spell of a handsome face and form and low, seductive voice.

She couldn't allow panic to rule. Her ankle was only marginally better. Without help, she'd have to limp back to the shop on a hot day. Though she had only a short distance to travel, the last bit was uphill. By the time she got there, she'd have worsened the injury and wouldn't be fit for anything.

Business first, last, and always. As they passed through the door and out into Pall Mall, she set her mind to calculating his net worth, reminded herself of imminent wives and/or mistresses, and beat down unwanted emotions with numbers, as she so often did. Her clumsiness might well have put off Lady Clara's companion. This might be the

31

only new business Leonie would attract to-day.

"You said something about business," he said.

"I did?" Her heart raced. Was she speaking her thoughts aloud without realizing? Had she suffered a concussion without noticing?

"Before, when you hurried away to my cousin."

"Oh, that," she said. "Yes. Where Lord Swanton goes, one usually finds a large supply of young ladies. He'd mentioned to one of our customers his intention of visiting the British Institution this afternoon. It seemed a good opportunity to make the shop's work known to those unfamiliar with it."

"Nothing to do with his poetry, then."

She shrugged, and paid for it with a twinge in her ankle. "I run a shop, my lord," she said. "I lack the romantic sensibility." She'd worked since childhood. The young women who worshipped Lord Swanton hadn't lived in Paris during the chaos, misery, and destruction of the cholera. Grief, suffering, and death weren't romantic to her.

"It stumps me, I'll admit," he said. "I don't see what's romantic about it. But

32

then, neither do most men. The ailment seems to strike young women, with a few exceptions. Though she's at the vulnerable age, Cousin Clara looked bored, I thought. My cousin Gladys looked sour-tempered, but that's the way she usually looks, so it's hard to tell whether she's an idolater or not."

"Cousin Gladys," she said. "The young lady with Lady Clara?"

"Lady Gladys Fairfax," he said. "Lord Boulsworth's daughter. Clara's great uncle, you know. The military hero. I'm not sure what's lured Gladys back to London, though I do have an unnerving suspicion. I say, you're not well, Miss Noirot."

They'd reached the bottom of St. James's Street, and the day's extreme warmth, already prodigious in Pall Mall, now blasted at them on a hot wind, which carried as well the dust of vehicles, riders, and pedestrians. Leonie's head ached at least as much as her ankle did. She was trying to remember when last she'd heard Lady Gladys Fairfax mentioned, but pain, heat, and confusion overwhelmed her brain.

"That does it," he said. "I'm carrying you."

He simply swooped down and did it, before she got the protest out, and then it was muffled against his neckcloth.

"Yes, everyone will stare," he said. "Good advertising, don't you think? Do you know, I do believe I'm getting the hang of this business thing."

Meanwhile, back at the British Institution
Sir Roger Theaker and Mr. John Meffat, Esquire, were among the few who'd paid attention to Lord Lisburne's departure with Miss Noirot. The pair had arrived with Lord Swanton's coterie, but were not exactly part of it, even though they were former school-mates of the poet.

They were not Lord Swanton's favorite old schoolmates, having bullied him merci-lessly for nearly a year until his cousin got wind of it and thrashed them. Repeatedly. Because they were slow to catch on. They were even slower to forget.

They'd withdrawn some paces from the crowd following Lord Swanton, partly in order to maintain a safe distance from the dangerous cousin.

Theaker's gaze lingered on the stairwell. Once Lisburne and the ladybird were out of sight he said, "Lisburne's done for, I see."

"If anyone's a goner, it's the French mil-liner," said Meffat. "Ten pounds says so."

"You haven't got ten pounds," said

34

Theaker.

"Neither do you."

Theaker's attention reverted to the poet. They watched for a time the young women not-so-surreptitiously pushing to get closer to their idol, while he held forth about the Veronese.

"Annoying little snot, isn't he?" Theaker said.

"Always was."

"Writes pure rot."

"Always did."

No one could accuse them of not doing all they could to enlighten the reading public. Before Swanton had returned to England, they'd contributed to various journals half a dozen anonymous lampoons of his poetry, as well as two scurrilous limericks. Most of the critics had agreed with them.

But one fashionable young woman had ignored the critics and bought *Alcinthus and Other Poems,* Swanton's book of lugubrious verse, and cried her eyes out, apparently. She told all her friends he was the new Lord Byron or some such. The next anybody knew, the printers couldn't keep up with the demand.

Since watching the little snot wasn't much fun, Theaker and Meffat turned their attention to the unhappy artist who, having righted his easel, was trying to repair his damaged painting.

They drew nearer to offer jocular advice and accidentally on purpose knock over items he'd carefully restored to their proper places. They suggested their own favorite subjects and argued about whether a corner of the painting more closely resembled a bonnet or a woman's privates. Being pre-occupied with tormenting somebody too weak, poor, or intimidated to fight back — their usual modus operandi — they never noticed the woman approach until she'd cornered them.

And when she said, "I must have your help," they didn't laugh, as was also more usual when a person of no importance sought their aid or protection. They didn't even make lewd suggestions, which was odd, considering she was extremely pretty — fair and slender and young. John Meffat looked at her once, then twice, then seemed very puzzled indeed. He turned an inquiring look upon his friend, who frowned briefly, seeming to be struck by something.

Theaker shot him a warning look, and Meffat held his tongue.

Then Theaker broke out in a kindly smile — it must have hurt his face a little — and said, "Why certainly, my dear. Let's find us a place a bit less *public,* and you can tell us all about it."

Chapter Two

Although the Toilet should never be suffered to engross so much of the attention as to interfere with the higher duties of life, yet, as a young lady's dress, however simple, is considered a criterion of her taste, it is, certainly, worthy of her attention.

— *The Young Lady's Book,* 1829

Lord Lisburne carried Leonie up St. James's Street in the sweltering heat, past a stream of gaping faces. A couple of vehicles got their wheels tangled, and a gentleman crossing the street walked into a curb post.

Sophy would have seen this as a golden opportunity, Leonie reminded herself. She ignored the headache and throbbing ankle and made her face serene, as though this were an everyday occurrence, being carried to the shop. By a Roman god. Who didn't even breathe hard.

Darting a glance upward, she discerned a hint of a smile on his perfectly sculpted mouth.

"This is fun," he said. "Which number did you say? Right, fifty-six. Oh, look. Charming. So French. Does that boy in the breathtaking lilac and gold livery belong to you?"

"Yes," Leonie said without looking. "That's Fenwick, our general factotum."

"Does he open the door or simply stand there looking excessively decorative?"

"One of his jobs is to open the door," she said.

A stray Sophy had picked up on one of her excursions, Fenwick had been an apprentice pickpocket. Once scrubbed of layers of accumulated street grime, his exterior had proved surprisingly angelic-looking. He was a great success with the ladies. He . . .

That was when Leonie remembered. Sophy had found Fenwick on the day she'd gone to spy on a business rival. To get into Mrs. Downes's shop, Sophy had disguised herself as *Lady Gladys Fairfax.* Or what she imagined Lady Gladys looked like, given Lady Clara's description and Sophy's lurid powers of invention.

But Leonie hadn't time to think further about Lady Gladys. Fenwick had opened the door, Lord Lisburne carried Leonie in, and all the shopgirls promptly went to pieces.

There were cries of "Madame!" and little shrieks, and they ran out from behind counters and crowded about her and Lord Lisburne, then cried, "No, no, give her air!" and dashed off the other way, then came back again. They told one another to fetch water and doctors and smelling salts, and argued about it. Meanwhile, no one was paying attention to the customers, who might have walked away with half the shop, including the mannequins, while everybody else was having hysterics.

Luckily, Selina Jeffreys, their forewoman, hurried out into the showroom, sparing Leonie the need to discipline the troops through an aching head. Jeffreys briskly called them to order and directed Lord Lisburne through the door into the back of the shop. Thence Leonie directed him to her office.

He set her down in a chair. He found a footstool and, ignoring her assurance that she was capable of moving her own foot, knelt, and gently lifted the injured limb onto it. The touch of his hands traveled like a magnetic current up her leg and spread everywhere, including parts some women didn't even expose to themselves.

"I believe a restorative is in order," he said as he rose.

He looked perfectly cool. She needed an ice bath.

"Have you any objections to brandy?" she said.

"I meant for you," he said. "You're looking peakish."

"I made a cake of myself in front of London's latest craze in poets," she said. "I tripped twice in the same room, and everybody will say I was drunk. The second time, I tripped so clumsily that I turned my ankle. The Marquess of Lisburne has been carrying me about St. James's, to the entertainment of the multitudes and the mental derangement of my employees. I ache at top and bottom, and I'm in a sweat despite not having done anything but let myself be carried. Of course I look peakish. And I'm cross besides, or I should have said thank you before launching into the complaints."

"No thanks required, I assure you. It was the most fun I've had since Swanton and I came back to London." He pulled off his gloves. "Where do you keep the brandy?"

She told him. He poured out a drink for her and a drink for him. Then he walked about the office as though he owned the place. Nothing odd in that. Aristocrats

41

always owned the place, whether, techni-
cally, they did or didn't, since they owned
England.

But then he started *touching her things.*

Lisburne was fascinated.

Along one wall, ledgers stood perfectly
straight and exactly aligned on three gleam-
ing shelves. Likewise polished to within an
inch of its life, the desk held, in addition to
an inkstand, a tray of pencils, all sharpened
to lethal points. On the other walls, French
fashion prints and a few Parisian scenes
hung precisely straight and equidistant from
one another. Whatever else the office contained must be secreted in the firmly closed
drawers and cupboards.

He tipped his head to read the spines of
the ledgers, then pulled one out to look at
the front. He flipped through the pages.
Scrupulously ruled columns held concise
descriptions of transactions. Alongside them
marched, in the same rigorous order, columns of numbers.

"Not a blot anywhere," he said. "Do you
do this? How do you write all these numbers
and such and never blot?"

"My lord, that is private financial information." The faintly accented voice climbed a
degree in pitch.

"Your secrets couldn't be safer," he said. "It's all hieroglyphs to me. I could read it for days and come away none the wiser. No, that's not quite true. I do know what the red ink signifies. My agent has pointed it out often enough. That is to say, he did, until I left such matters to Uttridge, my secretary. He warns me when I'm stumbling into red ink territory."

"Your secretary manages your funds?" she said, her horror plainly audible. "You don't look at the books at all?"

What entertaining handwriting she had! So precise and orderly yet purely feminine.

"The trouble with looking into the books is, it throws a fellow's inadequacies in his face," he said, adroitly sidestepping the boring truth. "I note very little in the way of red here, Miss Noirot. And do you do all this yourself, without any Uttridges or agents or such? Simply write down every accursed item and what it costs, and what somebody pays and what the total is and somehow make everything come out right at the end?"

"That's my job," she said. "The Duchess of Clevedon specializes in designing clothes. Lady Longmore is in charge of keeping Maison Noirot in the public eye. I manage the business."

"You keep track of the money, you mean."

"That's part of it. I hire and dismiss the seamstresses, attend to their various crises and hysterias, pay everybody's wages, and oversee all purchasing."

He closed the book and looked at her for a time. It was a great deal to take in. Her extraordinary face, for one thing. The immense blue eyes and soft mouth and uncompromising chin.

The chin went with the columns of neat numbers and no blots.

The dress belonged to some fairyland.

White ruffles and lace cascading to her waist like ocean foam. Below the lace swelled sleeves as plump as bed pillows. From her dainty waist a skirt billowed: white embroidered with what seemed like thousands of tiny blue flowers. It was deliciously, madly feminine and it made a man want to rumple her, just to hear the rustling.

Well, not *only* for that reason.

What a treat to carry all that up St. James's Street!

He looked at the face and the dress and thought about the neat numbers in their precisely ruled columns.

He put the ledger back.

She made a little sound.

44

"Are you all right?" he said. "Your foot is paining you? More brandy?"

"No, no, thank you," she said. "My lord, I must detain you no longer. You've been so kind, so chivalrous."

"It was my pleasure, I assure you." He moved on to inspect her desk. "I had expected another dull afternoon of listening to Swanton being emotional."

He picked up one of the alarmingly sharp pencils and stuck it into the end of his index finger. It made a tiny indentation. Probably not lethal, unless one stabbed ferociously, which he felt certain she was capable of doing. He examined her meticulously sharpened pens. As he put each object back, he was aware of her breathing erratically, in little huffs.

"Are you feeling overwarm, Miss Noirot?" he said. "Shall I open a window? Or will that only let in more of the day's heat?"

She made a small strangled sound and said, "If you must pry, my lord — and I realize that noblemen must do as they please — can you not at least put my belongings back in the same order in which you found them?"

He stepped back from the desk and folded his hands behind his back. Not because he was abashed but because he was so sorely

45

tempted to disarrange everything, including, most especially, her.

He looked down at the pencil and the pen, then at the ledgers once more. "Er, no. That is, I could try, but it mightn't turn out as we hope. That's the reason Uttridge intervenes, you see. I grow bored very quickly, and things go awry." That wasn't entirely untrue. Once he'd fully mastered a thing, he grew bored.

"Your dress is immaculate," she said.

He glanced down at himself. "Odd, isn't it? Don't know how I do it. Well, there's Polcaire, of course, my valet. Couldn't do it without him."

He contemplated his waistcoat for a moment. It was one of his favorites, and he was fairly sure he looked well in it. Some perspicacious genie must have whispered in his ear this day.

No, that was Polcaire.

Polcaire: But milord cannot wear the maroon waistcoat to this occasion.
Lisburne: Swanton is the occasion, which means all the girls will look at him. No one cares what I look like.
Polcaire: One never knows whom one will meet, milord.

Which proved that Polcaire was not only a genius among valets, but an oracle, too.

Lisburne looked up from his waistcoat at Miss Noirot.

The palest pink washed over her cheekbones like a little tide, coming and going. It was delicious.

"Shall I risk trying to get it all straight again?" he said. "My work may not be up to your standards — and I have a strong suspicion that you're going to leap up from the chair, and . . ." He thought. "Stab me with the penknife?"

He was aware of her forcing herself to be calm. It wasn't easy to discern. Her face ought to be in a dictionary, under *inscrutable.* Though she was a redhead, her complexion was strangely parsimonious about blushing. Still, whatever other faults he had, he wasn't unobservant, especially of women. In her case, he was paying hawklike attention. The way she relaxed her pose wasn't unconscious at all. He watched her arrange her features and bring her shoulders down.

"The thought crossed my mind," she said. "But corpses are the very devil to get rid of, especially aristocratic ones. People notice when noblemen disappear."

The door having been left partly open, he became aware of the approaching footsteps an instant after he saw her posture grow more alert.

Following a quick tap and Miss Noirot's *"Entrez,"* one of the young females who'd thronged the showroom entered.

"Oh, madame, I am so sorry to interrupt you," the girl said, or at least, that was what he made of her excessively mangled French, before she gave up on a bad job and went on in English, "But it's Lady Clara Fairfax and . . . another lady."

"Another lady?"

Miss Noirot's face lit, and she bounded up from the chair, momentarily forgetting the injured ankle. She winced and swore softly in French, but her eyes sparkled and her face glowed. "Send them up to the consulting room, and bring them refreshments. I'll be there in a moment."

The girl went out.

"*Up* to the consulting room?" he said. "Are you meaning to mount stairs in your condition?"

"Lady Clara has brought Lady Gladys Fairfax," she said. "Did you not see her?"

"Of course I saw Gladys. One can no more fail to notice her than one could overlook a toppling building or a forty-day flood. I pointed her out to you."

"I meant her dress," she said.

48

"I looked away immediately, but not soon enough. It was a catastrophe, as usual."

What Gladys lacked in good nature she made up in bad taste.

"It was," Miss Noirot said, her tell-nothing face radiant with an excitement as incomprehensible as it was breathtaking. "She needs me. I would get up those stairs if I had to crawl."

Blast.

And this afternoon had been going so well, too.

Leave it to Gladys to barge in like the Ancient Mariner at the wedding feast.

"What nonsense you talk," Lisburne said. "You can't crawl up the stairs. You'll wrinkle your dress."

He crossed to Miss Noirot and offered his arm before she could attempt to stagger to the door.

"I'd carry you in," he said, "but if she spots us, it'll only make Gladys sarcastic. More sarcastic. And she'll make your afternoon disagreeable enough as it is. Are you sure you want to see her? Couldn't you send one of those multitudes of girls?"

"Fob her off on an inferior?" She took his arm. "Clearly you have a great deal to learn about business, my lord."

"And you've a great deal to learn about

49

Gladys. But there's no helping it, I see. Some people have to learn the hard way."

He got her up to the next floor, but retreated when he saw the open door and heard Gladys's voice. It had reached the peevish stage already.

He had a nightmarish recollection of the first time he'd seen her, waiting at the house after his father's funeral. A spotty, surly, sharp-tongued fifteen-year-old girl who oughtn't to have been let out of the schoolroom. And her father! The famous military hero, who'd tried to bully a grieving widow into betrothing her son to that obnoxious child. Lord Boulsworth had acted as though Father had been one of his officers, struck down in combat, over whose regiment Boulsworth must assume command — as though other people's wives and sons and daughters existed merely to march to his orders. Lisburne had encountered her a few times since his return to London. Apart from a remarkably clear complexion, he'd seen no signs of Gladys's improving with maturity. On the contrary, she seemed to have grown more like her father.

"Sorry to play the coward and cut and run," he said, "but I'll do you no favors by hanging about. Clara's well enough, of course. Gladys is another article. Let's simply say that she and I won't be exchanging pleasantries. Seeing me will only put her in a worse humor, if you can imagine that, and I'd rather not make your job any more difficult."

Forty-five minutes later
"Are you blind?" Lady Gladys said. "Only look at me! I can't have my breasts spilling out of my dress. People will think I'm desperate for attention."

She glared at the three women studying her, her color deepening to a red unfortunately like a drunkard's nose.

She sounded furious, but Leonie discerned the misery in her eyes. Her ladyship was difficult: imperious, rude, impatient, uncooperative, and quick to imagine insult. Normal client behavior, in other words.

At present, Lady Gladys stood before the dressing glass, stripped to corset and chemise, thanks to Jeffreys's able assistance and Lady Clara's moral support. Even so, reaching this point had been a battle. Meanwhile, Leonie's ankle hurt, and so did her head, and neither of these things mattered, any more than Lady Gladys's obnoxious behavior did.

This was the opportunity of a lifetime.

"My lady, one of the basic principles of

51

dress is to emphasize one's assets," Leonie said. "Where men are concerned, your bosom is your greatest asset."

"*Greatest* I can't quarrel with, if you mean immense," Lady Gladys said. "I know I'm not the sylph here." She shot an angry glance at Lady Clara, who was too statuesque to qualify as a sylph. She did qualify as impossibly beautiful, though: blonde and blue-eyed, gifted with a pearly complexion and a shapely body. And brains. And a beautiful nature.

Nature had not gifted Lady Gladys with any form of classical beauty. Dull brown hair. Eyes an equally unmemorable brown, and like her mouth too small for her round face. A figure by no means ideal. She had little in the way of a waist. But she had a fine bosom, and acceptable hips, though at the moment, this wasn't obvious to any but the most expert observer.

"That doesn't mean you don't have a shape," Leonie said.

"Do you hear her, Gladys?" Lady Clara said. "Did I not tell you that you were hiding your good parts?"

"I don't have good parts!" Lady Gladys said. "Don't patronize me, Clara. I can see perfectly well what's in the mirror."

"I beg to differ," Leonie said. "If you

52

could see perfectly well, you'd see that your corset is wrong for your ladyship's figure."

"What figure?" Lady Gladys said.

"Well, let's see what happens when we take off the corset."

"No! I'm quite undressed enough. My dressmaker at home —"

"Seems to have a problem with drink," Leonie said. "I cannot imagine any sober modiste stuffing her client into this — this sausage arrangement."

"*Sausage?*" Lady Gladys shrieked. "Clara, I've had quite enough of this creature's insolence."

"Jeffreys, kindly assist Lady Gladys with her corset," Leonie said firmly. The modiste who let the client take charge might as well close up shop and earn her living by taking in mending.

"You will not, girl," Lady Gladys snapped. "You most certainly will not. I refuse to be manhandled by a consumptive child who speaks the most disgusting excuse for French to assault my ears in a city grossly oversupplied with ignoramuses."

Jeffreys had grown up in a harsh world. This was motherly affection compared to her childhood experience. Undaunted, she moved to the customer, but when she tried to touch the corset strings, Lady Gladys twisted about and waved her arms, practically snarling.

Like a cornered animal.

"Come, come, your ladyship is not afraid of my forewoman," Leonie said.

"Jeffreys can't possibly be consumptive," Lady Clara said. "If she were, she'd be dead, after the ordeal of wrestling you out of your frock and petticoats."

"I told you this would be a waste of time!"

"And I told you I was tired of a certain person's sly remarks about remembering your dresses from your first Season. And you said —"

"I don't care what anybody says!"

"*Ça suffit,*" Leonie said. "Everybody go away. Lady Gladys and I need to talk privately."

"I have nothing to say to you," Lady Gladys said. "You are the most encroaching — no, Clara, you are not to go!"

But Lady Clara went out, and Jeffreys followed her, and gently closed the door behind them.

Lady Gladys couldn't run after them in her underclothes. She couldn't dress herself, because, like most ladies, she had no idea how. She was trapped.

Leonie drew out from a cupboard an excessively French dressing gown. The color of cream and richly embroidered with pink buds and pale green vines and leaves, it was not made of muslin, as ladies' nightdresses usually were. This was silk. A very fine, nearly transparent silk.

She held it up. Lady Gladys sniffed and scowled, but she didn't turn away. Her gaze settled on the risqué piece of silk, and her expression became hunted.

"You can't mean that for me," she said. "That is suitable for a harlot."

Leonie advanced and draped it over her ladyship's stiff shoulders.

She turned her to face the looking glass. Lady Gladys's mutinous expression softened. She blinked hard. "I-I could never wear such a thing, and you're wicked to suggest it."

Leonie heard the longing in her voice, and her hard little dressmaker's heart ached.

Lady Gladys wasn't a beauty. She'd never been and never would be, no matter how much of the dressmaker's art one applied.

Yet she could be *more.*

"I'm not suggesting you purchase it," Leonie said. "Not yet. It will be more suitable for your trousseau."

"Trousseau! What a joke!"

"Here's what we're going to do," Leonie said. "We're going to rid you of that monstrosity of a corset."

"You are the most managing, impudent —"

"I'll provide you with something more suitable until I can make up exactly what you need." Corsets were Leonie's specialty.

"I will not . . . You will not . . ." Lady Gladys blinked hard and swallowed.

"Your ladyship is never to wear ready-made stays again," Leonie went on briskly. It never did to become emotional with clients. They could manage that sort of thing more than adequately themselves. "They don't provide proper support and they make you shapeless."

"I am shapeless. Or rather, I have a fine shape if you like b-barrels."

"You do have a figure," Leonie said. "It isn't classical, but that isn't important to men. They're not as discriminating as young women think. You're generously endowed in the bosom, and once we get that ghastly thing off, you'll see that your hips and bottom are in neat proportion."

Lady Gladys looked into the mirror. Her face crumpled. She walked away and sank onto a chair.

"Let us review your assets," Leonie said.

"Assets!" Lady Gladys's voice was choked.

"In addition to what I've enumerated, you

own a clear complexion, an elegant nose, and pretty hands," Leonie said.

Lady Gladys looked down, surprised, at her hands.

"Of course, the décolletage is of primary importance," Leonie said. "Men like to look at bosoms. In fact, that's where they usually look first."

Gladys was still staring at her hands, as though she'd never seen them before. "They don't look," she said. "They never look at me. Then I say things, and —" She broke off. A tear rolled down her nose.

Leonie gave her a handkerchief.

"Your first Season didn't go well," Leonie said. She remembered Lady Clara mentioning it — or was that Sophy? In any case, she didn't know the details. She didn't need to.

Gladys blew her nose. "There's a fine understatement! You know. All the world knows. I was a colossal failure. It was so ghastly that I slunk home to Lancashire and never came back."

"Yet here you are," Leonie said.

Lady Gladys colored, more prettily this time. "It's nothing to do with the Season," she said hurriedly. "It's nearly over, in any event. But I'd read in the papers that Lord Swanton would be giving a series of readings from his work and some lectures on poetry. It's — it's purely literary. The reason I've come. Nothing to do with — that is, I won't run that gantlet again. The balls and routs and such."

"A young lady's first Season is like a prizefight or a horse race, I always thought," Leonie said. "A great lot of girls thrust into Society all at once, and it's all about getting a husband, and they don't fight fair. Your rivals might not take a whip or spurs to you as you run alongside, but they use words in the same way."

Lady Gladys laughed. "Rivals! I don't rival anybody. And there I was, making my debut with Clara, of all people. Aphrodite might have stood a chance. Or maybe not."

"I understand the difficulty," Leonie said. "Still, let's bear in mind that you made your debut before my sisters and I became established in London. You were not properly prepared." Among other things, Lady Gladys's governesses and dancing masters had served her as ill as her dressmaker had done. Her ladyship didn't walk; she lumbered. And her walk was only one unfortunate trait. "Certainly you weren't properly dressed."

"Oh, yes, that explains everything. If you'd had the managing of things, I'd have been the belle of the ball."

Leonie stepped back a pace, folded her arms, and eyed her new client critically. After a long, busy moment while her mind performed complicated calculations, she said, "Yes, my lady. Yes, you would have been. And yes, you can be."

Early evening of Friday 10 July
"You hateful little sneak! I always attend her!"

"Always? Once, two months ago."

"It was only last week I waited on Miss Renfrew, while you was flirting with Mr. Burns."

"I never was!"

"Maybe he wasn't flirting with *you,* but you was trying hard enough."

Leonie had heard the raised voices, and was hurrying from her office into the workroom at the same time as Jeffreys, on the same errand, was running that way from the showroom.

By the time they burst through the door, Glinda Simmons had got hold of Joanie Barker. They scratched and kicked and slapped and pulled each other's hair, screeching the while. The other girls shrieked, too. In a matter of minutes, they'd tumbled bolts of costly fabric, boxes of ribbons, flowers, feathers, and other articles hither and yon.

Leonie clapped her hands, but no one was paying attention. She and Jeffreys had to move in and forcibly separate the two girls. This didn't stop the screaming. The combatants called for witnesses to various crimes perpetrated by the opposing party, and the noncombatants took that as an invitation to express their own grievances against this one or that one.

It took nearly an hour to restore full order. Having warned the girls that they'd all be dismissed without notice or a character if they indulged in another outburst, Leonie hurried upstairs to change out of her workday dress. Jeffreys followed her.

"You'd better send Mary Parmenter to help me dress," Leonie said. Mary had been left in charge of the showroom when Jeffreys came to stop the war. "You keep an eye on the seamstresses. You're the best at managing these battles."

This was only one of the reasons Selina Jeffreys, despite her youth and apparent frailty, was their forewoman.

Jeffreys ignored her, and started unfastening Leonie's pelerine. "You're going to be late, madame," she said. "And you know Parmenter gets nervous and clumsy when she feels rushed. I don't."

Late wasn't good enough, in Leonie's opinion. *Never* would be preferable. She was not looking forward to this evening's engagement.

Lord Swanton was hosting a poetry lecture to raise funds for the Deaf and Dumb Asylum. This was the sort of activity at which Sophy shone. She would put in an appearance, then slip away and write all about it for London's favorite gossip sheet, *Foxe's Morning Spectacle.* The account would include detailed descriptions of what every Maison Noirot customer was wearing.

Leonie looked forward to the writing much in the way a French ancestor had looked forward to making the acquaintance of Madame Guillotine.

Misinterpreting her frown, Jeffreys said, "Please don't worry about the girls, madame. They'll be all right now. It's that time of the month, and you know how it is with girls who're always together."

They all had That Time of the Month at the same time.

"It's worse this month, and we both know why," Leonie said. Marcelline had married a duke and Sophy had married a future marquess. Though any other women would jump at the chance to quit working, Marcelline and Sophy weren't like other women. They might give it up eventually, but not without a fight.

The girls didn't understand this, and it wasn't easy to prove, since neither sister was much in evidence at present. Marcelline, who was having a miserable time with morning sickness, was abed a good deal, on her doctor's orders. Sophy had had to go away to give Fashionable Society time to forget what the French widow she'd recently impersonated had looked like.

That left Leonie, who could do what the other two did, but not with their brilliance and flair. Each sister had her special skills, and Leonie was missing her sisters' talents acutely. And their company.

And she was more worried than anybody about what would become of Maison Noirot. She'd put everything she had into the shop — mind, body, soul. The cholera had killed Cousin Emma and wiped out their old life in Paris. Emma had died too young, but here in London her spirit and genius lived on in their hearts and in the new life they'd so painstakingly built.

"The girls will be better when my sisters are in the shop more regularly," Leonie said. "Routine and habit, Jeffreys. You know our girls need not merely to be kept busy, but to have order in their lives." Many had ended up in charitable institutions. Their lives before had been hard and chaotic. "But matters are bound to change, and everybody needs to adapt." For these girls, adapting wasn't easy. Change upset them. She understood. It upset her, too. "We'll have our work cut out for us, getting them used to a new routine."

"You don't need any more work," Jeffreys said. "You need more rest, madame. You can't be three people."

Leonie smiled. "No, but with your help, I might be nearly that. But do let us make haste. I must get there before it's over."

Later that evening
Leonie hurried into the conversation room adjoining the New Western Athenaeum's lecture hall —

— and stopped short as a tall, black-garbed figure emerged from the shadows of a window embrasure.

"I thought you'd never come," Lord Lisburne said.

He was not, she saw, dressed entirely in black. In addition to the pristine white shirt and neckcloth, he wore a green silk waistcoat, exquisitely embroidered in gold. It called attention to his narrow waist . . .

thence her gaze wandered lower, to the evening trousers that lovingly followed the muscled contours of his long legs.

Leonie took a moment to settle her breathing. "Did we have an appointment?" she said. "If so, I must have made it while concussed, because I don't recall."

"Oh, I was sure you'd be here." He waved a gloved hand at the door to the lecture hall. "Swanton. Young ladies in droves." He waved at her dress. "Advertising."

For this event, she'd chosen a green silk. Though a dress for evening, exposing more neck than day attire did, it was simple enough to suit a public lecture. No blond lace or ruffles and only minimal embroidery, of a darker green, above the deep skirt flounce and along the hem. The immense sleeves provided the main excitement, slashed to reveal what would appear to be chemise sleeves underneath — a glimpse of underwear, in other words. Over it she'd thrown, with apparent carelessness, a fine silk shawl, a wine red and gold floral pattern on a creamy white ground that called attention to the white enticingly visible through the slashing.

"I meant to arrive earlier," she said. "But we had a busy day at the shop, and the heat makes everybody cross and impatient. The customers are sharp with the girls in the shop, who then go into the workroom and quarrel with the seamstresses. We had a little crisis. It took longer to settle than it ought to have done."

"Lucky you," he said. "You missed 'Poor Robin.' "

" 'Poor Robin'?" she said.

He set his hat over his heart, bowed his head, and in a sepulchral voice intoned:

When last I heard that peaceful lay
   In all its sweetness swell,
I little thought so soon to say —
   Farewell, sweet bird, farewell!

All cloudy comes the snowy morn,
   Poor Robin is not here!
I miss him on the fleecy thorn,
   And feel a falling tear.

"Oh, my," she said.

"It continued," he said, "for what seemed to be an infinite number of stanzas."

Her heart sank. One must give Lord Swanton credit for using his influence to raise funds for a worthwhile organization. All the same, if she had to listen to "Poor Robins" for another two hours or even more, she might throw herself into the

Thames.

"Lord Swanton seems to take life's little sorrows very much to heart," she said.

"He can't help himself," Lord Lisburne said. "He tries, he says, to be more like Byron when he wrote *Don Juan,* but it always comes out more like an exceedingly weepy version of *Childe Harold.* At best. But happily for you, there's no more room."

No room. Relief wafted through her like a cooling breeze. She wouldn't have to sit through hours of dismal poetry —

But she hadn't come for her own entertainment, she reminded herself. This was *business.* Where Lord Swanton appeared, Maison Noirot's prime potential clientele would be. Equally important, Lady Gladys would be here.

"All the better if it's a crush," Leonie said. "And a late entrance will draw attention."

"Even if you deflated the sleeves and skirt, you couldn't squeeze in," he said. "I gave up my place and *two* women took it. The lecture hall is packed to the walls. That, by the way, is where most of the men have retreated to. Since they're bored and you're young and pretty, you might expect to encounter a lot of sweaty hands trying to go where they've no business to be."

Leonie's skin crawled. She'd been pawed

before. Being able to defend herself did not make the experience any less disgusting. "I told Lady Gladys I'd be here," she said.

"Why on earth did you do that?"

"It's business," she said.

"None of mine, in other words," he said.

She had no intention of explaining about Paris and the night she'd been hurrying home, to warn her sisters of the danger, and found herself in a mob of men, being groped and narrowly escaping rape.

This wasn't Paris, she told herself. This was London, and the place did not contain a mob. It was merely crowded, like so many other social gatherings. She walked to the lecture hall door.

He followed her. "A hot, stuffy room, crammed with excitable young women and irritated men, and Swanton and his poetic friends sobbing over fallen leaves and dead birds and wilted flowers," he said. "Yes, I can understand why you can't bear to be left out."

"It's *business*," she said.

She cracked open the door and peered inside.

She had a limited view, through a narrow space the doorkeepers had managed to maintain in front of the door. Primarily women occupied the seats on the ground floor, and they were so tightly squeezed together, they were half in one another's laps. They and a few men — fathers and brothers, most likely — thronged the mezzanine and upper gallery as well. The latter seemed to sag under the weight. Men filled every square inch of the standing room. The space was stifling hot, and the aroma of tightly packed bodies assaulted her nostrils.

Meanwhile somebody who wasn't Lord Swanton was reading, in throbbing tones, an ode to a dying rose.

She retreated a step. Her back came up against a warm, solid mass. Silk whispered against silk.

Lord Lisburne leaned in to look over her shoulder, and the mingled scents of freshly pressed linen and shaving soap and male wiped out the smell of the crowd and swamped her senses.

"Aren't you glad you were late?" he said. "You might be sitting in there." His breath tickled her ear. "And you wouldn't be able to get out until it was over."

She'd be trapped, listening to poetic dirges, for hours. She closed her eyes and told herself it was *business,* then took a steadying breath and opened them again. She would go through this door. She —

His large, gloved hand settled on the door

inches from her shoulder. He closed the door.

"I have an idea," he said. "Let's go to the circus."

Chapter Three

Never warn me, my dear, to take care of
  my heart,
When I dance with yon Lancer, so fickle
  and smart;
What phantoms the mind of eighteen can
  create,
That boast not a charm at discreet
  twenty-eight.
  — Mrs. Abdy, "A Marrying Man," 1835

Miss Noirot turned quickly. Since Lisburne hadn't moved, she came up against him, her bosom touching his waistcoat for one delicious instant. She smelled delicious, too.

She brought up her hand and gave him a push, and not, as you'd think, a little-girlish or flirtatious sort of push. It was a firm shove. While not strong enough to move him, it was a clear enough signal that she wasn't playing coquette.

He took the message and retreated a pace.

"The circus," she said, much as she might have said, "The moon."

"Astley's," he said. "It'll be fun."

"Fun," she said.

"For one thing, no melancholy verse," he said. "For another, no melancholy verse. And for a third —"

"It's on the other side of the river!" she said, as though that were, indeed, the moon.

"Yes," he said. "That puts the full width of the Thames between us and the melancholy verse."

"Us," she said.

"You got all dressed up," he said. "What a shocking waste of effort if you don't go out to an entertainment."

"The circus," she said.

"It's truly entertaining," he said. "I promise. Actors and acrobats and clowns. But best of all are the feats of horsemanship. Ducrow, the manager, is a brilliant equestrian."

For all his careless manner, Lisburne rarely left much to chance. In her case, he'd done his research. Her given name was Leonie and she was, as she'd said, the businesswoman of Maison Noirot. One sister had married a duke, the other the heir to a marquessate, yet she went to the shop every day, as though their move into the

71

highest ranks of the aristocracy made no difference whatsoever. This was an odd and illuminating circumstance.

The seamstresses, he'd learned, worked six days a week, from nine in the morning until nine at night, and her own hours seemed to be the same or longer. This, he'd concluded, greatly increased the odds against her having time to spend at Astley's or any other place of entertainment.

She gave a little shake of her head, and waved her hand in an adorably imperious manner, signaling him to get out of her way.

He knew he stood too close — that was to say, as close as one could get without treading on her hem, women taking up a deal of space these days, in the arm and shoulder area as well as below the waist. In her case, he tested the boundary more than usual. Still, he was a man of considerable, and successful, experience with women.

He obediently moved out of the way to walk alongside.

"Here's the thing," he said as he accompanied her across the conversation room. "We can take a hackney to Astley's, watch the show for an hour or so, and still get back before this funeral is over. By that time, the crowd's bound to have thinned out. The girls are all here with chaperons. A good many girls, I promise you, will be dragged home earlier than they like, because there's a limit, you know, to how much a brother, say, will sacrifice for his sister. Same for Papa and Mama and Great Aunt Philomena."

They'd reached the door to the lobby. He opened it.

She sailed through, in a thrilling swish of silk.

"I know you're unlikely to find the sort of clientele you prefer in a place like Astley's," he said. "But I thought you might enjoy the women's costumes."

"Not half so much as you will, I daresay," she said. "Skimpy, are they?"

"Yes, of course, like a ballerina or nymph or whatever it is Miss Woolford will be playing," he said. "She's a treat. But the whole show is wonderful. The performers stand on the horses' backs, and go round and round the ring. And the horses perform the cleverest tricks. As good as the acrobats."

She looked up, her blue gaze searching.

He bore the scrutiny easily. A boy born beautiful becomes a target for other boys, and the schools he'd attended never ran short of bullies. He'd learned very young to keep his feelings out of sight and out of reach unless he needed to use them.

You are like a diamond, one of his mistresses had told him. *So beautiful, so much light and fire. But when one tries to find the man inside, it's all reflections and sparkling surfaces.*

Why need anybody see more?

True, he wasn't the shattered young man he'd been nearly six years ago, when his father died. The loss had devastated all the members of the tight-knit little family Father had created. That family, comprising not only Lisburne and his mother but her sister — Swanton's mother — as well as Swanton, had fled England together. Still, it had taken a good while, far away from London and the fashionable world, to recover.

Few, including the many who'd respected and loved his father, understood the magnitude of the loss. Not that Lisburne wanted their understanding. His feelings were nobody's business but his own.

All the same, he knew what true grief was, and mawkish sentiment made him want to punch somebody.

He couldn't punch Swanton or his worshippers.

Much more sensible to set about what promised to be a challenging game: seducing a fascinating redhead.

"You'll like it," he said. "I promise. And I promise to get you back here before the lecture is over."

She looked away. "I've never seen an equestrian," she said.

And his heart leapt, startling him.

Astley's was crowded, as always, but the multitude seemed not to trouble Miss Noirot as much as the crowd at Swanton's lecture had done. Perhaps this was because the space was so much larger and more open. In any event, Lisburne took her to a private box, where she wouldn't be jostled, and from which she'd have a prime view of both the stage and arena.

They arrived too late for the play, which was a pity, since it usually featured fine horses and horsemanship and stirring battle scenes. They were in good time for the entertainment in the arena, though. He and Miss Noirot settled into their seats as the crew members were shaking sawdust into the ring.

It had been an age since he'd entered the premises, and Lisburne had thought it would seem shabby, now that he was older and had lived abroad and watched spectacles on the Continent.

Perhaps the place awoke the boy in him,

75

who'd somehow survived life's shocks and lessons and had never entirely grown up or become fully civilized. He must be seeing it through a boy's eyes because Astley's seemed as grand as ever. The lights came up round the ring, and the chandeliers seem as dazzling, the orchestra as glamorous as he remembered.

Or maybe he saw it fresh through her great blue eyes.

He'd observed the small signs of apprehension when they'd first entered and the way the uneasiness dissolved, once she'd settled into her place and started to take in her surroundings. She sat back, a little stiff, as a clown came out and joked with the audience. She watched expressionlessly when the ringmaster appeared, carrying his long whip. Her gaze gave away nothing as he strode about the ring and engaged in the usual badinage with the clown.

Then the ringmaster asked for Miss Woolford. The crowd erupted.

And Miss Noirot leaned forward, grasping the rail.

The famous equestrienne walked out into the arena, the audience went into ecstasies, and Miss Noirot the Inscrutable drank it all in, as wide-eyed and eager as any child, from the time the ringmaster helped Miss

Woolford into the saddle, through every circuit of the ring. When the performer stood on the horse's back, Miss Noirot gasped.

"So marvelous!" she said. "I don't even know how to ride one, and she stands on the creature's back — while it runs!"

When, after numerous circuits, Miss Woolford paused to rest herself and her horse, Miss Noirot clapped and clapped, and cried, *"Brava! Bravissima!"*

The pause allowed for more play between the clown and ringmaster, but Miss Noirot turned away from the clown's antics — and caught Lisburne staring at her.

For a moment she stared back. Then she laughed, a full-throated, easy laugh.

And his breath caught.

The sound. The way she looked at this moment, eyes sparkling, countenance aglow.

"How right you were," she said. "Much more fun than dismal verse. How clever she is! Can you imagine the hours she's spent to learn that art? How old do you think she was when she first began? Was she bred to it, the way actors often are — and dressmakers, too, for that matter."

The eagerness in her voice. She was so young, so vibrantly alive.

"I reckon, even if they're bred to it, they

fall on their heads a number of times before they get the hang of it," he said. "But they must start young, when they're less break-able."

"Not like dressmaking," she said. "Sooner or later would-be equestrians have to get on the horse. But we mayn't cut a piece of silk until we've been sewing seams for an eter-nity and made a thousand handkerchiefs and aprons. What a pleasure it is to see a woman who's mastered such an art! The equestrians are mostly men, aren't they?"

"That does account in part for Miss Wool-ford's popularity."

"But she's very good — or does my total ignorance of horsemanship show?"

"She's immensely talented," he said. "A ballerina equestrienne."

"This is wonderful," she said. "My sisters are always telling me I need to get away from the shop, but Sunday comes round only once a week, and then I like to spend time with my niece, or outdoors, preferably both. Sometimes we go to the theater, but this is entirely different. It smells different, certainly."

"That would be the horses," he said.

"Beautiful creatures," she said.

He caught the note of wistfulness. He considered it, along with her reactions to

Miss Woolford, and filed it away for future reference.

The second part of the equestrian performance began then, and she turned back to the stage.

He looked that way, too, outwardly composed, inwardly unsettled. She'd changed before his eyes from a sophisticated Parisian to an excited girl, and for a moment she'd seemed so vulnerable that he felt . . . what? Ashamed? But of what? He was a man. She was a woman. They were attracted to each other and they played a game, a very old game. Yet along with the thrill of the chase he felt a twinge of something like heartache.

And why should he not? Hadn't he endured an hour of death and dying in rhyme? And was he not obliged to go back to it?

It seemed to Leonie a very short time before she and Lord Lisburne were in a hackney again, traveling along Westminster Bridge Street, back to the "obsequies," as he had put it a moment ago.

He'd been true to his word.

But then, she'd felt certain he would be, else she wouldn't have come with him.

Yes, she'd been aware of his watching her during the performance when he thought she wasn't paying attention to him. As

79

though one could sit beside the man and not be aware of him, even if a host of heavenly angels floated down to the stage or a herd of elephants burst into the arena. And when she'd turned and caught him at it, he'd looked so like a boy caught in mischief — a boy she wanted to know — that her logic faltered for a moment, and something inside her gave way.

But only for a moment.

Now he was the charming man of the world again, and she was Leonie Noirot, logical and businesslike and able to put two and two together.

"You don't care for his poetry, yet you came back with Lord Swanton to London for the release of his book," she said. "That's prodigious loyalty."

He laughed. "A man ought to stick by his friend in hours of trial."

"To protect him from excited young women?"

"That wasn't the original plan, no. We'd prepared for a humiliating return. The reviewers were savage. Didn't you know?"

"I'm not very literary," she said. "I look at the reviews of plays and concerts and such, but mainly we're interested in what the ladies are wearing. I rarely have time for the book reviews."

"He'd had a few of the poems published in magazines before *Alcinthus and Other Poems* came out," he said. "The reviewers loathed his work, unanimously and unconditionally. They lacerated him. They parodied him. It was a massacre. Until he saw the reviews, Swanton had been on the fence about coming back to London when his book was unleashed on the general public. After that, the choice was clear: Return and face the music or stay away and be labeled a coward."

"I had no idea," she said. "I was aware that his lordship had returned to London when the book came out because everybody was talking about it. Certainly our ladies were. I haven't heard that much excitement since the last big scandal." The one Sophy had precipitated.

"We're still not sure what happened, exactly," he said. "We arrived in London the day before it was to appear in the shops. We had a small party, and Swanton was a good sport about the rotten reviews — he doesn't have a high opinion of himself to start with, so he wasn't as desolated as another fellow might have been. We made jokes about it at White's club. Then, a few days after we arrived, we had to order more copies printed, and quickly. Mobs of young women were storming the bookshop doors. The booksellers said they hadn't seen anything like it since Harriette Wilson published her memoirs."

Harriette Wilson had been a famous courtesan. Ten years ago, men had paid her *not* to mention them in her memoirs.

"Lord Swanton seems to have struck a chord in young women's hearts," she said.

"And he's as bewildered as the critics." Lord Lisburne looked out of the window.

At this time of year, darkness came late, and even then it seemed not a full darkness, but a deep twilight. Tonight, a full moon brightened it further, and Leonie saw that they must have crossed Westminster Bridge some while ago. She saw, too, the muscle jump in his jaw.

"Sudden leaps to fame can be dangerous," he said. "Especially when young women are involved. I should like to get him back to the Continent before . . ." He trailed off and shrugged. "That crowd tonight troubled you. The one at the lecture."

"When I see so many people crowded together," she said slowly, "I tend to see a mob."

A moment's pause, then, "That's what I see, too, Miss Noirot. I should have remained and stood guard. But . . ." He paused for a very long time.

"But," she said.

"I had a chance to steal a pretty girl from the crowd, and I took it."

Leonie and Lord Lisburne arrived in time for the concluding event of the poetic evening when, according to the program, Lord Swanton would debut one of his recent compositions.

As Lord Lisburne had predicted, the crowd had thinned. Though the hall remained full, the men had moved out of their cramped quarters along the walls and into seats in the back rows. The galleries no longer seemed in danger of collapsing.

While she and Lord Lisburne paused in the doorway, looking for a place to sit, what looked like a family group bore down on them. He drew her back and, either out of courtesy or because he wasn't in a hurry to join the audience, made way for the departing family. When the other gentleman thanked him, Lord Lisburne smiled commiseratingly and murmured some answer that made the other man smile.

That was charm at work, charm of the most insidious kind: humorous, self-deprecating, and disarmingly frank and confiding.

Leonie well understood that type of charm. Her family specialized in it.

She of all people knew better than to let it work on her. The trouble was, it truly was insidious. One was drawn closer without realizing. One believed one had found a true intimacy when what was there was only a masterful imitation.

She lectured herself while he led her in the direction the group had come from, to the recently vacated seats at the far end of the rearmost row.

Though she'd prefer to sit closer to a door, for an easy escape, this was preferable to any place she'd have found for herself earlier. With reduced crowding, air could circulate, and when the doors opened for departing audience members, cooler night air drifted in.

Having a large, strong male nearby — even the kind who was dangerous to a woman's peace of mind — helped keep her calm, too.

Since she truly didn't want to listen to the poetry, and it was unintelligent to dwell too much on the large, strong male, she let her attention drift about the room. She counted twenty-two Maison Noirot creations. That was a good showing. Maybe writing the article for *Foxe's Morning Spectacle* wouldn't be so difficult after all.

Among the ladies in Maison Noirot dresses were Lady Clara and — Oh, yes! Lady Gladys Fairfax had worn her new wine-colored dress! A victory!

Leonie smiled.

Her companion leaned nearer. "What is it?" he whispered.

She felt the whisper on her ear and on her neck. Thence it seemed to travel under her skin and arrow straight to the bottom of her belly.

"An excess of emotion from the poetry," she murmured.

"You haven't heard a word Swanton's uttered," he said. "You've been surveying the audience. Who's made you smile? Have I a rival?"

Like who, exactly? Apollo? Adonis?

"Dozens," she said.

"Can't say I'm surprised." But his green gaze was moving over the crowd. She watched his survey continue round the hall, then pause and go back to the group sitting in the last row, as they were, but to their right, nearer to the doors.

"Clara," he said. "And Gladys with her. I never saw them when we came in, thanks to the gentleman desperate to drag his family away. But there's no more room on that side, in any event, and so we're not obliged to join them — oh, ye beneficent gods and spirits of the place! Well, then . . ." He tilted his head to one side and frowned. "Not that I should have known Gladys straightaway."

He turned back to Leonie, his green eyes glinting. "She isn't in rancid colors for once. Is that your doing?"

Leonie nodded proudly.

He turned back again to look. "And there's Valentine, roped in for escort duty, poor fellow."

Lord Valentine Fairfax was one of Lady Clara's brothers. Unlike Lord Longmore, who was dark, Lord Valentine was a typical Fairfax: blond, blue-eyed, and unreasonably good-looking.

"He's been here the whole time, unfortunate mortal," Lord Lisburne said. "Whiling away the hours weaving luscious fantasies of killing himself, I don't doubt. Or, more likely, Val being a practical fellow, his dreamy thoughts are of ways to kill Swanton without getting caught."

"If the men dislike the poetry so much, why do they come?" she said.

"To make the girls think they're *sensitive.*"

She smothered a laugh, but not altogether successfully or quickly enough. A young woman in front of her turned round to glare.

Leonie pulled out a handkerchief and pretended to wipe a tear from her eye. The girl turned away.

The audience wasn't as hushed as it had been earlier in the evening, when Leonie had peeked through the door. Though many occupying the prime seats on the floor sat rapt — or asleep, in the men's case — others were whispering, and from the galleries came the low hum of background conversation that normally prevailed at public recitations.

The increased noise level didn't seem to trouble Lord Swanton. Someone had taught him how to make himself heard in a public venue, and he was employing the training, his every aching word clearly audible:

. . . Aye, deep and full its wayward torrents
    gush,
Strong as the earliest joys of youth, as
    hope's first radiant flush;
For, oh! When soul meets soul above, as
    man on earth meets man,
Its deepest, worst, intensity ne'er gains its
    earthly ban!

"No, dash it, I won't hush!" a male voice boomed over the buzz of the audience.

Leonie looked toward the sound. Not far from the Fairfaxes, a well-fed, middle-aged gentleman was shooing his family toward the door.

"A precious waste of time," he continued. "For charity, indeed. If I'd known, I'd have sent in twice the tickets' cost and stayed at home, and judged it cheap at the price."

His wife tried to shush him, again in vain.

"Give me Tom Moore any day," he boomed. "Or Robbie Burns. Poetry, you call this! I call it gasbagging."

Lord Lisburne made a choked sound.

Other men in the vicinity didn't trouble to hide their laughter.

"It's a joke, it surely is," the critic went on. "I could have gone to Vauxhall, instead of wasting a Friday night listening to this lot maunder on about nothing. Bowel stoppage, I shouldn't wonder. That's their trouble. What they want is a good physicking."

Gasps now, from the ladies nearby.

"I never heard anybody ask your opinion, sir," came Lady Gladys's musical voice. "None of us prevented your going to Vauxhall. Certainly none of us paid for a ticket to hear *you*. I don't recollect seeing anything on the program about ill-educated and discourteous men supplying critiques."

"Glad to supply it gratis, madam," came the quick answer. "As to *uneducated* — at least some of us have wit enough to notice that the emperor's wearing no clothes."

Lord Valentine stood up. "Sir, I'll thank you not to address the lady in that tone," he said.

"She addressed me first, sir!"

"Blast," Lord Lisburne said. He rose, too. "Leave it to Gladys. Valentine will be obliged to call out the fellow, thanks to her."

Men were starting up from their seats. Lord Swanton became aware of something amiss. He attempted to go on reading his poem, but the audience's attention was turning away from him to the dispute, and the noise level was rising, drowning him out.

Leonie became aware of movement in the galleries. She looked up. Men were leaving their seats and moving toward the doors. A duel would be bad enough, but this looked like a riot in the making.

Images flashed in her mind of the Parisian mob storming through the streets, setting fire to houses where cholera victims lived . . . her little niece Lucie so sick . . . the tramp of hundreds of feet, growing louder as they neared . . .

Panic swamped her.

She closed her eyes, opened them again,

and shook her head, shaking away the past. She counted the rows in the hall and estimated the audience size, and her mind quieted.

This was London, an altogether different place. And this was a different time and circumstance. These people were dying of boredom, not a rampaging disease.

"Ladies and gentlemen, if I might have your attention," Lord Swanton said.

"You've had it these three hours and more!" someone called out. "Not enough?"

Other hecklers contributed their observations.

By this time Lord Lisburne had reached his cousins and the irate gentleman, who was growing more irate by the second, if the deepening red of his face was any clue.

Meanwhile, the audience grew more boisterous.

Leonie reminded herself she was a Noirot and a DeLucey. Not nearly as many of her French ancestors had got their heads cut off as deserved it. Hardly any relatives on either side had ever been stupid or incompetent enough to get themselves hanged. Or even jailed.

Marcelline or Sophy could have handled this lot blindfolded, she told herself.

She swallowed and rose. "Thank you, my

lord, for your kind invitation," she said, pitching her voice to carry. "I should like to recite a poem by Mrs. Abdy."

"More poetry!" someone cried. "Somebody hang me."

"Hold your tongue, you bacon brain! It's a girl!"

Lord Swanton cut through the commentary. "Ladies and gentlemen, Miss Noirot — that is to say, Madame, of Maison Noirot — has kindly agreed to contribute to our poetic mélange."

Leonie had dressed for the occasion. She knew she'd get the men's attention because she was young and not unattractive, and the women's because her dress was beautiful.

She was aware of the argument continuing to her right, and more aware of how hard her heart pounded, and how she couldn't stop her hands from shaking. She told herself not to be ridiculous: She performed every day, for extremely difficult women, and she got *them* under control.

She began, " 'I'm weary of a single life —' "

"Why didn't you say so?" someone called out. "Come sit by me, my poppet."

"Oh, stifle it!" somebody else said. "Let the lady say her piece."

Leonie started again:

I'm weary of a single life,
   The clubs of town I hate;
I smile at tales of wedded strife,
   I sigh to win a mate;
Yet no kind fair will crown my bliss,
   But all my homage shun —
Alas! my grief and shame is this,
   I'm but a Second Son!

A burst of laughter.

That first sign of glee was all the encouragement she needed. Anxiety and self-consciousness washed away, and the DeLucey in her took over.

She went on, this time with dramatic gestures:

My profile, all the world allows,
   With Byron's e'en may vie,

[— she turned her head this way and that]

My chestnut curls half shade my brow,

[— she toyed with the curls at her ears]

I'm almost six feet high;

[— she stretched her neck, to laughter]

And by my attitudes of grace,

Ducrow is quite undone,

[— she mimicked one of the equestrian's elegant poses]

Yet what avail the form and face
    Of a poor Second Son?

Amid the men's laughter she heard women giggling.
She had them.
She continued.

For an instant, while the angry gentleman grew more incensed, his complexion darkening from brick red to purple, Lisburne had felt sure the only outcome would be pistols at dawn. The only hope he had was for a riot. Once men started knocking one another about and women commenced screaming, Valentine and the other fellow might stop making asses of themselves.

When he heard Miss Noirot call out to Swanton, Lisburne had wanted to shake her. Was she mad? To offer more of the poetry that was driving every rational man in the hall to distraction? And to taunt them now, when he hadn't a prayer of getting to her fast enough?

All hell should have broken loose.

But he'd reckoned without . . .

. . . whatever it was about her: the quality, so obvious, and so hard to put a satisfactory name to. The same power of personality that had attracted and held captive his attention at the British Institution seemed to work on a general audience.

Add that compelling quality to her appearance, and the men could hardly help responding. She was exceedingly pretty and a redhead besides, and the green silk dress, insane as it was, was voluptuous.

But the women, too?

Ah, yes, of course. The green silk dress.

Furthermore, Mrs. Abdy had written, along with the usual sentimental claptrap, a number of comic poems, which Swanton would give a vital organ to replicate.

London's favorite poet was smiling. He gently prompted Miss Noirot as she faltered for a stanza. It was a longish poem — not half so long as some of Swanton's, but still a good bit to get by heart.

And she'd said she wasn't literary, the minx.

Even the irate gentleman was smiling. "That's more like it," he said.

"It isn't," Gladys said. "It's an amusing bit of doggerel, no more."

"We must allow for differences of taste,"

Lisburne said. "Is that a new dress, Cousin? Most elegant."

To his amazement, she colored, almost prettily. "I could hardly wear last year's dress on such an occasion."

"There, that explains," Lisburne said to the irate gentleman. "She wore her new dress and you mentioned the emperor's new clothes. A bit of confusion, that's all."

Gladys huffed. "Lisburne, how can you be so thick? But why do I ask? You know perfectly well —"

"I know you're eager to leave before the crush," Lisburne told the irate gentleman. "Bon voyage."

The man's wife took hold of her spouse's arm and said something under her breath. After a moment's hesitation — and another moment of glaring at Valentine — the man let himself be led away.

From the lectern came Swanton's voice. "Thank you, Miss Noirot, for your delightful contribution. Perhaps somebody else would like to participate?"

Crawford, one of Longmore's longtime cronies, stood up. "I've got a limerick," he said.

"If it brings a blush to any lady's cheek, I'll gladly throttle you," Swanton said with a smile.

"Lord Swanton is so good," Gladys said, her voice soft for once. "A *perfect* gentleman."

"Who likes a ribald limerick as well as the next fellow," Lisburne said. "If Crawford contrives to keep it clean, he'll be the last one to do so. Fairfax, I suggest you take the ladies home while everybody's still on good behavior."

"You ever were high-handed," Gladys said, in a magnificent example of pot calling kettle black. "The lecture isn't over, and I'm sure we're not ready to leave."

"I'm sure we are," Clara said. "My head is aching, not to mention my bottom. Val, do let us go."

"Finally, after hours of misery and tragedy, we get a little good humor, and you want to leave," Valentine said.

"Yes, before you're tempted to challenge anybody else over a *poem,*" his sister said.

Meaning, *before Gladys could cause more trouble,* Lisburne thought. Leave it to her to turn a poetry lecture into a riot.

A riot the redheaded dressmaker had simply stood up and stopped with a handful of verses.

He left his cousins without ceremony. More of the families and groups of women were leaving now, delaying his progress to the place where he'd last seen Miss Noirot standing in all her swelling waves of green silk, reciting her amusing poem as cleverly as any comic actress.

When he got there, she was gone.

Lisburne pushed through the departing throng out into the street. Nary a glimpse of the green silk dress or cream-colored shawl did he get. By now, hackneys and private carriages had converged outside the entrance. Drivers swore, horses whinnied, harnesses jangled. The audience jabbered about the poetry and the near riot and the modiste in the dashing green dress.

And she'd slipped away. By now she was well on her way to St. James's Street, Lisburne calculated.

He debated whether to go in that direction or let her be. It was late, and she would be working tomorrow. He would like to keep her up very late, but that wasn't going to happen tonight. He'd made progress, but not enough. Pursuit this night would seem inconsiderate, and would undo what he'd achieved.

He returned to the hall and eventually ran Swanton to ground in one of the study rooms.

The poet was packing papers into a portfolio in a desperate fashion Lisburne recognized all too well.

"I see you made good your escape," Lisburne said. "No girls clinging to your lapels or coattails."

Swanton shoved a fistful of verse into the portfolio. "The damnable thing is, that fellow who was shouting? I couldn't have agreed more. It's rubbish!"

"It isn't genius, but —"

"I should give it up tomorrow, but it's like a cursed juggernaut," Swanton went on. "And the devil of it is, we raised more money in this one evening than the Deaf and Dumb Asylum sponsors have raised in six months, according to Lady Gorrell." He paused and looked up from crushing the poetry so many girls deemed so precious. "I saw you come in. With Miss Noirot."

"She tried to get in earlier, but there wasn't room. And so I took her to the circus instead."

"The circus," Swanton said.

"Astley's," Lisburne said. "She liked it. And as a consequence of her brain not being awash in grief and sorrow when we returned, she had the presence of mind to save your bacon."

Swanton's harassed expression smoothed into a smile. Then he laughed outright. "I remembered Miss Leonie, of course. From Paris. Who could forget those eyes? And the mysterious smile. But I'd forgotten how quick-witted she was. That was no small kindness she did, turning the audience's mood."

"You don't know the half of it," Lisburne said. "Your poetical event wasn't the only thing she saved. My cousin Gladys almost got Valentine in a duel."

"Was your cousin Gladys the girl who gave the noisy fellow what for?" Swanton said. "I couldn't see her. Men were standing up, and she was behind a pillar. And I couldn't hear exactly what she said. But her voice is splendid! So melodious. A beautiful tone."

Lisburne had never thought about Gladys's voice. What she said was so provoking that one never noticed the vocal quality.

"Gladys is best heard at a distance," he said. Lancashire, he thought, would be an acceptable distance at present.

Swanton closed the portfolio, his brow furrowed. "I'll have to thank Miss Noirot. No, that's insufficient. I need to find a way to return the favor. Without her, we should have had a debacle. That will teach me to let these things run on for so long. An hour, no more, in future."

"But the girls want you to wax poetic all

day and all night," Lisburne said. "Half of them had to be dragged out of the lecture hall. If you give them only an hour, they'll feel cheated."

Swanton was still frowning. "Something to do with girls," he said. "They take in charity cases or some such."

"Who does?"

"Mesdames Noirot," Swanton said. "Somebody told me. Did Miss Noirot mention it? Or was it Clevedon?"

"I know they took in a boy they found on the street," Lisburne said.

Swanton nodded. "They do that sort of thing. I'd better look into it. I might be able to arrange an event to raise funds for them." He grimaced. "But something less boring and . . . funereal."

"I'll look into it," Lisburne said. "You've got your hands full, fending off all those innocent maidens whose adulation you're not allowed to take advantage of. I'm the one with nothing to do."

CHAPTER FOUR

SYMMETRICAL PERFECTION. — Mrs. N. GEARY, Court Stay-maker, 61 St James's street, has the honour to announce to the Nobility and Gentry, that she has returned from the Continent, and has now (in addition to her celebrated newly-invented boned "Corset de toilette") a STAY of the most novel and elegant shape ever manufactured . . . totally exterminating all that deadly pressure which has prevailed in all other Stays for the last 300 years . . . two guineas, ready money.

— *Court Journal,* 16 May 1835

Monday 13 July
"A steady routine is of first importance," Leonie heard Matron explain. "Four hours of lessons, four hours of work, two hours for exercise and chores, half an hour for meals. As your lordship will see, the Milliners' Society for the Education of Indigent

Females is a modest enterprise. We can take in but a fraction of the girls who need us. But this is only the beginning. The Philanthropic Society, as you may be aware, began in a small house on Cambridge Heath and currently accommodates some two hundred children in Southwark. We, too, expect to grow, with the aid of charitable contributions as well as sales of our girls' work, which I will be pleased to show you."

From where Leonie stood in the corridor, no one in the workroom could see her. However, even with only a view of his back, she had no trouble recognizing the gentleman Matron was falling all over herself to accommodate.

Ah, yes, undoubtedly Lord Lisburne would like nothing better than to look at needlework.

Leonie debated for a moment. Not about what to do, because she was seldom at a loss in that regard. She did wonder, though, what had brought him here, of all places. She knew he was bored in London. He'd said he wanted to return to the Continent. In the meantime, he seemed interested merely in amusing himself, and she seemed to be one of the amusements.

Very well. Easy enough to turn that to her advantage. Business was business, he was rich, and he was *here.*

She swept through the open door.

"Thank you, Matron, for undertaking tour duty," she said. "I know Monday is a busy day for you. I'll continue Lord Lisburne's tour, and you may return to your regular tasks."

Matron relinquished Lord Lisburne with poorly concealed reluctance. And who could blame her? All that manly beauty. All that charm.

Unfortunately, all that manly beauty and charm must have turned Matron's brain. Otherwise she'd have known better than to bring him into the workroom. Many of the girls in the bright, airy room stood on the brink of adolescence if not well in. Putting a stunning male aristocrat in front of them was asking for trouble.

Most sat in a stupor. Three had stuck themselves with their needles and were absently sucking the wounded fingers. Verity Sims had overturned her workbasket. Bridget Coppy was sewing to her dress sleeve the apron she was making.

They'd be useless for days, the lot of them.

Even Leonie was aware of a romantic haze enveloping her brain. Last night he'd sneaked into her dreams. And today he'd plagued her as well. Her mind made pictures of him as he'd been at Astley's Royal Circus, the tantalizing glimpses she'd had of the openhearted boy he might have been once upon a time.

Nonetheless, she briskly led his lordship out of the workroom and into the corridor.

"We're somewhat cramped, as you see," she said.

"Yet what efficient use you've made of the quarters you have," he said. "Given your penchant for order, I oughtn't to be surprised. Still, it's one thing to write numbers and such neatly in a ledger and quite another to organize a poky old building into something rather pleasant and cozy."

Though she had her guard up, she couldn't squelch the flutter of gratification. She and her sisters had worked hard to make the most of what they had. They hadn't much. Their financial success was only very recent, and she knew better than to take it for granted. In the dressmaking business, failure could happen overnight, from natural catastrophes or merely the whims of fashionable women. With the Milliners' Society, they'd proceeded cautiously, incurring no expenses they couldn't cover with ready money.

They'd done it because of Cousin Emma, who'd given to three neglected children a real home and an education. She'd taught them how to make beautiful things and she'd saved them from the pointless, vagabond life of their parents.

And she'd died too young, with only the first taste of her own success.

Leonie thanked him calmly enough and said, "All the same, we'd prefer rather less coziness. We should like to expand into the house next door."

"I daresay. Always room for expansion."

By this point they'd moved out of the others' hearing range.

"Very well, I'm stumped," she said. "Did you merely stumble upon the place and decide to look in, or is this all part of a master plan?"

"Master plan," he said. "Swanton charged me with finding out your charity. He wants to raise funds for you while everybody still loves him. You know how fickle the public can be, especially the female part of it."

"He charged you," she said.

"To be strictly accurate, I volunteered," he said. "Eagerly. This is because I have two uses at present. One, I can watch and listen to him make poetry. Two, I can hang about him, ostensibly to shield him from poetry-maddened females, but actually to do very little and enjoy the edifying experience of being invisible to the females."

"Despair not," she said. "You weren't invisible to Matron or the girls in the workroom."

"Be that as it may, I had a good deal more fun looking into your activities," he said.

Inside her head, a lot of panicked Leonies ran about screaming, *What? What did he find? What did he see? Why?*

Outwardly, not so much as a muscle twitched, and she said, "That sounds tedious."

"It proved far more difficult than I expected," he said. "You and your sisters are strangely quiet about your philanthropy."

The inner Leonie settled down and said, *Oh,* that's *all right, then.*

She said, "It isn't much to boast about."

"Is it not?" He glanced back toward the room they'd left. "I've lived a sheltered life. Don't think I've ever seen, in one room, so many girls who've led . . ." He paused, then closed his eyes and appeared to think. "Let us say, unsheltered lives." He opened his eyes, the green darkening as he studied her for one unnerving moment. "You keep getting more interesting. It's rather a trial."

"It's business," she said. "Some of the girls turn out to be more talented than others. We get to pick the crème de la crème as apprentices for Maison Noirot. Too, we've trained and educated them ourselves, which means that we know what we're getting. We're not as disinterested as your duchesses and countesses and such. It isn't pure philanthropy."

"The fact remains, you pluck them from the streets and orphanages and workhouses."

She smiled. "We get them cheaply that way. Often for free."

She led him into the small shop, where the girls' productions were on display. "If your lordship would condescend to buy a few of their trinkets, they'll be in raptures," she said.

She moved to a battered counter and opened a glass display case.

He stood for a moment, gazing at the collection of watch guards and pincushions and handkerchiefs and sashes and coin purses and such.

"Miss Noirot," he said.

She looked up. He was still staring at the display case's contents, his expression stricken.

"The girls made these things?" he said. "The girls in that classroom?"

"Yes. Remember Matron telling you that we raise funds by selling their work?"

"I remember," he said. "But I didn't . . ." He turned away and walked to the shop's one small window. He folded his hands behind his back and looked out.

She was baffled. She looked down into the display case then up again at his expertly tailored back.

After what seemed a long time, he turned away from the window. He returned to the counter, wearing a small smile. "I'm moved," he said. "Perilously near to tears. I'm very glad I came on this errand instead of Swanton. He'd be sobbing all over the place and writing fifty-stanza laments about innocence lost or abused or found or some such gobbledygook. Luckily, it's only me, and the public is in no danger of suffering verse from this quarter."

For a moment, she was at a loss. But logic swiftly shoved astonishment aside. He might feel something on the girls' account or he might be feigning great-heartedness and charitable inclinations, as so many aristocrats did. Philanthropy was a duty and they performed it ostentatiously but they didn't really care. If even half of them had truly cared, London would be a different place.

But it didn't matter what he truly felt, she told herself. The girls mattered. And money was money, whether offered in genuine compassion or for show.

"It would seem that your friend's poetry has infected you with excessive tenderheartedness," she said.

"That may be so, madame, yet I wonder how any man could withstand this." He waved his hand at the contents of the display case. "Look at them. Little hearts and flowers and curlicues and lilies of the valley and lace. Made by girls who've known mainly deprivation and squalor and violence."

She considered the pincushions and watch guards and mittens and handkerchiefs. "They don't have Botticelli paintings to look at," she said. "If they want beauty in their lives, they have to make it."

"Madame," he said, "is it absolutely necessary to break my heart completely?"

She looked up into his green-gold eyes and thought how easy it would be to lose herself there. His eyes, like his low voice, seemed to promise worlds. They seemed to invite one to discover fascinating depths of character and secrets nobody else in the world knew.

She said, "Well, then, does that mean you'll buy the lot?"

Swanton gazed at the objects Lisburne had arranged on one of the library tables — after he'd cleared off the heaps of letters and the foolscap covered with poetic scribbling.

After what seemed to be a very long time, Swanton finally looked up. "Did you leave anything in the shop?"

"I found it hard to choose," Lisburne said.

"Yet you claim I'm the one who's always letting himself be imposed on," Swanton said.

"Miss Noirot didn't impose," Lisburne said. "Like a good businesswoman, she took advantage of me during a moment of weakness."

He wasn't sure why he'd been weak. It wasn't as though he'd never visited a charitable establishment before. With his father, he'd attended countless philanthropic dinners and visited asylums and orphanages and charity schools. He'd watched the inmates in their distinctive uniforms and badges standing stiffly at attention or parading for their benefactors' inspection or singing the praises of deity or monarch or benevolent rich people.

He was used to that sort of thing. Yet he had wanted to sit down and put his face in his hands and weep for those girls and their dainty little hearts and handkerchiefs embroidered with pansies and violets and forget-me-nots.

Confound Swanton for planting him in his poetic hotbed of *feelings*!

"I suppose you didn't realize quite how canny she is," Swanton said.

"I did not," Lisburne said. "She's the very devil of a businesswoman."

After she'd torn his heart to pieces and cleaned out the display case as well as his purse, she'd very charmingly got rid of him.

"I'm glad you weren't there," he told Swanton. "It might have killed you. It nearly killed me when she said, 'They don't have Botticelli paintings to look at. If they want beauty in their lives, they have to make it.' "

Swanton blinked hard, but that trick rarely worked for him. Emotion won, nine times out of ten, and this wasn't the tenth time. His Adam's apple went up and down and his eyes filled.

"Don't you dare sob," Lisburne said. "You're turning into a complete watering pot, worse than any of those deranged girls who follow you about. Pull yourself together, man. You're the one who proposed to raise funds for Maison Noirot's favorite charity. I found out all about it for you. I've

111

brought you abundant evidence of their work. Do you mean to compose a lugubrious sonnet on the occasion, or may we discuss practical plans?"

"Easy enough for you to talk about pulling oneself together." Swanton pulled out his handkerchief and blew his nose. "You're not the one who's afraid to put a foot anywhere lest he step on a young female. I have to be careful not to hurt their tender feelings, and at the same time not say anything too kind, lest it be construed as wicked seduction."

"Yes, yes, it's a hellish job," Lisburne said. "If you want to go back to Florence or Venice tomorrow, I'll go with you happily."

He might as well. What had he to do here but try to keep Swanton out of trouble with swooning girls? Though a grown man, supposedly capable of taking care of himself, the poet tended to be oblivious at times. This made him easy prey for any of a number of unpleasant women, like Lady Bartham's younger daughter, Alda.

As to Miss Leonie Noirot . . .

If Lisburne did return to Italy tomorrow, would she notice he was gone, or would she simply find another fellow to intrigue while she set about picking his pockets?

Swanton took up one of the pincushions

that had stabbed Lisburne to the heart.

"That's Bridget Coppy's work," Lisburne said. "Miss Noirot says the heart shape is traditional for pincushions. But instead of the usual red, the girl exercised her imagination and made it in white with a coral trim, to set off the colorful flowers. The cord attaches to the waist."

"The flowers are charming," Swanton said. "So delicate."

"Bridget is becoming a skilled embroiderer," Lisburne said.

"My mother would like this," Swanton said.

"Then by all means let us deliver it in person. I see gifts aplenty here for my mother as well. And her new husband. They would both be enchanted."

His mother had chosen her second husband as wisely as she'd done her first. Lord Rufford was a good, generous man, who made her happy. He'd made a friend of his stepson, too, no easy feat.

"You're in a devil of a hurry to return," Swanton said.

Lisburne laughed. "Perhaps I am. I'm supposed to be such a cosmopolitan fellow, yet I let a redheaded French milliner get the better of me. Perhaps I want to slink away in shame."

113

"That I beg leave to doubt," Swanton said. "I believe you're so far from wishing to leave that you're even now puzzling over how she did it, so that you can plan how to prevail at your next encounter."

Lisburne looked at him.

"She's the only woman you've taken any particular notice of since we came to London," Swanton said. "And I know you. As well, that is, as anybody can know you."

"As though there were anything of great moment to know," Lisburne said. But Swanton was a poet. He imagined everybody had hidden depths. If Lisburne did have them, he wasn't interested in exploring them, and he certainly wouldn't encourage anybody else to do so. "What about you? Do you feel compelled to stay?"

"I feel I must," Swanton said.

"Do you? I'd as soon be stalked by wolves as by a lot of gently bred maidens."

"They'll grow sick of me soon enough," Swanton said. "In the meantime, I should be a coward to run away when I can do so much good. It would be unworthy of your father's memory, in any event."

"Yes, yes, stab me with my father, do," Lisburne said.

"I know it isn't fair, but it's the only way I know to win an argument with you," Swanton said.

"Very well," Lisburne said. "We stay until they turn on you. Then we pray we can get away in time."

He glanced at the piles of correspondence he'd flung onto one of the library's sofas a short time earlier. "Meanwhile, does your secretary need a secretary? The heaps of letters have only grown higher since yesterday." Remembering what Swanton had said moments ago, he added, "Begging letters, you said. One of the perils of rank and wealth. Everybody puts his hand out, and somebody has to decide who's deserving and who isn't."

"That's the least of it," Swanton said. "Today alone I received two claims for child support and one extortionate note threatening a breach of promise suit."

To anybody who knew Swanton, the claims were absurd. Yet they oughtn't to be taken lightly.

Fame aroused envy and greed and, generally, the worst instincts of some people. Too many would be willing to believe ill of him.

"Show me the letters," Lisburne said.

Evening of Tuesday 14 July
Had Lisburne not been so deeply engrossed in his cousin's unpleasant correspondence,

115

he might have got wind of the other matter sooner. Or maybe not.

Though he'd been to White's often enough, he hadn't looked into the betting book in days. Why bother? So many of the wagers were witless, arising from boredom. How long a fly would crawl about the window before it died or flew away, for instance.

Lisburne, for the present at least, wasn't bored. Watching women moon about Swanton had been tiresome, and even the possible dangers of the situation hadn't made life exciting. But then Miss Leonie Noirot had entered the picture, and London had become far more interesting.

Since she was everything but boring, Lisburne wasn't shocked to find her at the heart of the latest gossip.

He and Swanton had attended the Countess of Jersey's assembly, where the ladies made the usual fuss about the poet. While the younger women were fluttering about Swanton, Lisburne drifted toward the card room. As he was about to enter, Lady Alda Morris detained him, in order to whisper something behind her fan.

Maison Noirot
Wednesday 15 July

Lady Gladys stood before the dressing glass, her face pink.

Four women — Leonie, Marcelline, Lady Clara, and Jeffreys — watched and waited.

Today, for the first time, Lady Gladys wore the corset Leonie had designed especially for her.

Unlike the one they'd hastily adapted last week to replace the monstrosity she'd brought from home, this one employed all of Leonie's knowledge of mathematics, physiology, and physics. Until this moment, she hadn't been allowed to enjoy her accomplishment, because Lady Gladys had refused to come out and show herself in the corset. She said she would not cavort about in her undergarments to be gawked at.

That, however, was before she'd seen the gold evening dress.

When they'd first shown it to her, she'd made a face and said the color would make her look as though she had a liver disease. But by Lady Gladys's standards, the protest was feeble. A moment later she said she might as well try it on. Then she'd insisted on Jeffreys — the allegedly consumptive speaker of vile French — attending her in the dressing room.

Ladies were nothing if not capricious, but this lady had apparently devoted her young life to making everybody about her want to throttle her.

"Well," she said at last.

One word, but Leonie caught the little bubble of pleasure in it. Lady Gladys had a beautiful voice, as expressive as an opera singer's.

"I never thought I could wear this color," she said.

"So you made abundantly clear," Lady Clara said. "I thought we should have to stupefy you with drink to get you to try on anything today."

"That isn't true. I didn't make a fuss about *trying on* the corset. I only didn't want to prance about in my underwear while everybody stared at me."

She smoothed the front of the dress though Jeffreys, naturally, had made sure every seam lay precisely in place.

"The corset is comfortable," Lady Gladys said. "I'm not sure what you did, but . . ." She trailed off, studying herself. "You did something," she said.

Leonie had done a great deal. She'd designed the stays to support her ladyship's generous embonpoint. The corset's shape smoothed her waist in a way that made it seem smaller, though the compression was minimal.

Her figure remained much fuller and less shapely than the fashionable ideal. But fashionable ideals were only that. What was important was making a lady look as beautiful as it was possible for her to look. And the gold satin was as much a surprise to Leonie as it was to Lady Gladys.

As usual, Marcelline had imagined the dress entirely in her head. This time, though, she'd relied solely on Leonie's detailed description of their new client.

Yet from her sickbed, and in spite of near-constant nausea, Marcelline had designed a miracle of a dress. Gold satin trimmed in black blond lace. Simple yet dramatic. The pointed waist created the illusion of a narrower waistline, and the black languets that fastened it in front enhanced the effect.

Pointed waists had supposedly fallen out of fashion, but Marcelline never concerned herself with what she considered petty fluctuations of taste.

This dress would bring pointed waists straight back into style, Leonie calculated. The black lace mantilla, attached to the tops of the sleeves, not only added drama but drew the eye upward, toward Lady Gladys's ample bosom. It was, perhaps, not quite the thing for an unwed young lady, but Lady Gladys would look ridiculous in the types of dresses that suited the average maiden.

She brought her hand up to the edge of the bodice. "It's very low-cut," she said.

"But of course, my dear," Marcelline said. "You have a beautiful bosom. We want to draw the eye to it."

"I'll feel naked," Lady Gladys said.

"What's wrong with that?" Lady Clara said. "You'll feel naked and still look perfectly respectable."

"Hardly *perfectly* respectable," said her cousin.

"It's all right to look tempting," Lady Clara said.

"Will you stop it!" Lady Gladys snapped, her vehemence startling everybody. "Stop being *kind.* I can't tell you how provoking it is. No, wait, yes I can. You've only to crook a finger to have any man you want. You have no idea what it's like to be — to be — *not* to be beautiful and sweet-natured!"

"I'm not sweet at all," Lady Clara said. "People only think that because of my looks."

"That's the point! You can say anything!"

"No, I can't," Lady Clara said sharply. "I can't be myself. There's Mama, looming over me all the time. You don't know how

120

suffocating it is."

"Oh, yes, all those men crowding about you, clamoring for a smile."

"They only see the outside. They don't know who I am, or care particularly. You know me — or you ought to know. And you know I'm on your side and always have been, in spite of how difficult you make it."

Lady Gladys went scarlet and her eyes filled. "I don't know how to behave!" she cried. "I don't know how to do *anything*! You complain because your mother is always at you. But at least you have one. You've had women about to teach you how to be *womanly.* Look at me! My father's a soldier, and I might as well have been raised in an army camp. He treats me like a regiment. He gives orders and then off he goes, to smash some Foe of England." She flung away and stormed back to the dressing room. "Jeffreys! Get this thing off me!"

With a panicked look at Leonie, Jeffreys trotted after her.

Lady Clara stomped to a chair and flung herself onto it.

Marcelline looked at Leonie.

Leonie lifted her shoulders and mouthed, *I have no idea.*

"What on earth is the matter?" Marcelline said to Lady Clara.

"I don't know," Lady Clara said.

"I can tell you what's the matter," Lady Gladys said from behind the curtain. "I'm not going to Almack's tonight, no matter how they cajole. I told them I wouldn't do that sort of thing ever again, yet Clara won't stop plaguing me about it. And now you've given her this curst dress for ammunition!"

"You look very well in it, but you're too obstinate to admit it!" Lady Clara cried.

"I don't care if I look well. They should never have made it, because I'll have no occasion to wear it. I don't want it! I wish I'd never come to London!"

Lady Clara sighed, braced her forehead with one hand, and stared at the floor.

From behind the dressing room curtain came a choked sob.

Other than that, the consulting rooms were silent, apparently peaceful.

That was when Mary Parmenter came in, all flustered, to report that Lord Lisburne and Lord Swanton had arrived. They had business with Miss Noirot, they said. Should Mary ask them to wait in the showroom or in the office?

"We're busy," Leonie said. "You may tell them to make an appointment."

She heard a gasp from behind the curtain. Then, "You can't make Lord Swanton *wait,*" Lady Gladys called out shakily. "You're not busy with me anymore. You might as well see what the gentlemen want."

"Tell them to make an appointment," Leonie told Parmenter.

Then she sent the others away and walked behind the curtain.

Leonie found Lady Gladys sitting on the edge of the dressmaking platform, head in her hands.

"I'm not talking to you," her ladyship muttered. "You're like a human thumbscrew."

"One of the secrets of our success is knowing our ladies' minds," Leonie said. "We squeeze it out of you one way or another. You might as well tell me and save us both energy we can employ more happily elsewhere."

"Happy!"

Leonie dropped onto the platform beside her.

Lady Gladys lifted her head. "You only pretend to be my friend. You only want me to order more clothes."

"I haven't got to pretending to be your friend yet," Leonie said. "But I do want you to order more clothes. Why else be in business?"

"It hasn't occurred to you that I might put you out of business? All of London knows you've taken me in hand. They're already betting on the outcome."

In truth, of all the matters that might be making Lady Gladys irrational, this hadn't been the first to cross Leonie's mind — probably because of the large mental distraction known as the Marquess of Lisburne.

Still, the betting didn't surprise Leonie. Members of the ton, men and women alike, gambled, mainly because they were bored and idle. And whether they made bets or not, the women would be deeply interested in the results of Lady Gladys's visits to the shop.

Leonie knew this. It was, in fact, part of what had propelled her toward Lady Gladys. Once Maison Noirot succeeded in showing her ladyship at her best, all the fashionable world would be pounding on Maison Noirot's doors.

But her ladyship did have to cooperate.

"Aristocrats wager about everything," Leonie said briskly. "Naturally, you find it galling —"

"Especially when Lady Bartham's irritating daughter takes great pains to explain the terms," Lady Gladys said. "As will not surprise you, the phrase 'silk purse from sow's ear' came up more than once."

Lady Bartham was a close friend and venomous social rival of Lady Clara's mother, Lady Warford. Leonie didn't understand why anybody would make friends — or having made them in ignorance, continue — with an adder. She was aware that one of Lady Bartham's daughters, Lady Alda, was equally toxic.

"Some people are either so ignorant, self-centered, or deeply unhappy that hurting others makes them feel good," Leonie said. "It's perverse, but there it is. The best way to fight back is to find a reason to laugh or to feel pleased. It will confuse and upset them. A good revenge, I think."

Lady Gladys scowled at her. "Tell me what's amusing. Tell me what I ought to feel pleased about."

"Why should she go to so much trouble to insult and hurt you unless she's trying to undermine your self-confidence? Maybe she's afraid you'll turn into competition."

Lady Gladys gave Leonie a you-need-medical-help look.

"Only imagine," Leonie said, "if you had patted her hand reassuringly and said, 'Oh, my dear, I'm so sorry to worry you, but I promise to try not to steal any of your beaux, if I can help it.' Then you could laugh. You have such a pretty laugh. And she would go away a good deal more upset than you."

"A pretty laugh?" Lady Gladys said. She turned away to stare at a French fashion print on the opposite wall.

"A beautiful voice altogether." Leonie rose. "Please stop wishing to look like your cousin. It makes you blind to your own assets. You'll never look like Lady Clara. But she'll never have your voice."

"That hardly makes us even!"

"The biggest army, even in the smartest uniforms, doesn't always win the battle," Leonie said. "Did his lordship your father never tell you that cleverness and luck come into it?"

Shortly thereafter

At this time of day, when ladies of fashion were dressing for the parade in Hyde Park, Lisburne had expected to find the shop relatively quiet. Otherwise he wouldn't have let Swanton come with him. The shop was quiet enough. The showroom held a few shopgirls restoring order after their most recent customers. They were putting ribbons and trinkets into drawers, reorganizing display cases, straightening hats their clien-

126

tele had tipped askew, and rearranging mannequins' skirts. The only remaining customer was an elderly lady who couldn't make up her mind among several shades of brown ribbon.

Swanton was pacing at one end of the showroom when the girl returned to inform them that they needed to make an appointment.

"They must be busy with an important client," Lisburne told him. "Why don't you toddle up to White's? The club will be free of women, and you can compose your turbulent mind with the aid of a glass of wine or whiskey."

Swanton had stopped pacing when the girl returned from her errand. Now he looked about him as though he'd forgotten where he was. "White's," he said.

"Yes. The young ladies can't get to you there."

"And you?"

"I'm going to wait," Lisburne said. "I'm perfectly capable of carrying out our errand on my own. And I can do it in a more businesslike manner if you're not mooning about."

"I need to write half a dozen new poems in less than a week!" Swanton said. "You'd be in a state of abstraction, too."

"All the more reason for you to go away to a quiet place, where the women are not giggling and blushing and making up excuses to get close to you."

Naturally Swanton didn't realize what was going on about him. The shopgirls would have to hit him on the head with a hat stand to get his full attention. Still, unlike the young ladies of the ton, they were mainly excited to have a celebrity in their midst. They probably hadn't time to read his poetry — if they could read. Their interest wasn't *personal,* in other words.

Swanton looked about him, seeing whatever hazy version of reality he saw. "Very well," he said. "I can take a hint."

No, you can't, Lisburne thought.

With any luck, Swanton would manage to cross St. James's Street without walking into the path of an oncoming carriage. If not, and if he seemed headed into danger, a sympathetic female would rush out and rescue him, even if she was one of the two people in London who didn't know who he was. Because he looked like an angel.

In any case, Lisburne wasn't his nursemaid. Furthermore, he'd wrestled with enough of the poet's problems in the past two days.

He was in dire need of mental relief.

128

Such as Miss Leonie Noirot.

Who was too *busy* to see him.

He walked about the shop, studying the mannequins and the contents of the display cases. He even allowed himself to be consulted on the matter of brown ribbons.

He was solemnly examining them through his quizzing glass, trying to decide which had a yellower cast, when Gladys hurried out into the showroom, then swiftly through the street door. Clara followed close behind. Neither noticed him, and he didn't try to attract their attention.

"I wonder if Miss Noirot will see me now," he said to the girl who'd told him to make an appointment.

The girl went out.

She returned a quarter hour later and led him to Miss Noirot's office.

CHAPTER FIVE

The management of a dispute was formerly attempted by reason and argument; but the new way of adjusting all difference in opinion is by the sword or a wager: so that the only genteel method of dissenting, is to risk a thousand pounds, or take your chance of being run through the body.

The Connoisseur, 1754

When Lisburne entered, he found Miss Noirot straightening her ledgers with excessive force.

Since she'd spent more than an hour with Gladys, he diagnosed pent-up rage. No surprise there.

He was, however, distracted by the stormy picture Leonie Noirot made, in a maniacally feminine concoction of white muslin: the swoosh of the billowing sleeves and the way the overdress — robe — whatever it was — lifted and fell against the dress underneath and the agitated flutter of lace. Her bosom rose and fell, the embroidery and lace like white-capped waves on a tumultuous sea.

It was only a woman in a pet, by no means an unfamiliar sight. All the same, he had to take a moment to slow his breathing to normal and drag his wits out from the dark seas into which they were sinking.

"I sent Swanton up to White's, but I thought it best to wait," he said, his voice a shade hoarser than it ought to be.

She took up the little watch at her waist and opened the case. "An hour and twenty minutes," she said.

"But I was waiting for *you*," he said. "The time was as nothing. And it allowed me to perform deeds of mercy without much trouble."

"Deeds of mercy," she said. "Have you been helping my employees lose their wits? Or were you mercifully wafting sal volatile at the customers after you made them swoon?"

He adopted a hurt expression. "I helped somebody's great-grandmother choose ribbons."

"You ought to be careful, plying your 'mercy' upon elderly persons," she said. "Their constitutions may not withstand the

131

onslaught of so much manly beauty and charm. You may not realize how bad it is for business when ladies go off into apoplexies in our showroom." She put the watch away, folded her arms, and donned a blankly amiable expression.

As though he were any other customer.

He squelched the prickle of irritation and told himself not to act like an oversensitive schoolboy. Careful to keep his voice smooth, he said, "Thank you for the reminder, madame. In future, I'll take care to inflict my beauty and charm only on big, strong wenches."

"I know you can't help it," she said. "You were born that way. But some of my best customers are the older ladies, and I don't wish to send them off before their time."

"I promise to try not to murder any elderly ladies by accident," he said.

"Strictly speaking, it isn't murder if it's an accident," she said. "Or if it looks like one," she added, as though to herself. He saw her gaze shift to the desk . . . where she kept her penknife and probably other instruments of mayhem, like sharp scissors. Dressmakers always had sharp things about them — scissors, needles, pins. He had an odd sensation of having wandered inadvertently into danger. No doubt because the

132

atmosphere seemed to vibrate with the passion she was having so much trouble suppressing.

He was very badly tempted to push, to see — experience — what happened when her control slipped.

"I have customers waiting, my lord," she said. "I believe Parmenter said that you and Lord Swanton had come on *business.*"

He caught the note of impatience. What next? Would she throw things?

"So we did," he said. He put two fingers to his right temple and pretended to think.

The air about him throbbed harder yet. "Perhaps it would be best for you to join Lord Swanton at White's. Perhaps if the two of you put your heads together, you'll remember what it was that was so desperately urgent."

She started toward the door.

"Oh, yes, now I remember," he said. "It's to do with the girls you've taken under your wing. Swanton and I want to help."

She paused. "My girls," she said.

Her girls.

"The Milliners' Society," he said. "The poetic genius and I came to tell you about our brilliant idea for raising funds."

She wanted him to go to the devil. She wanted funds for her girls. The struggle

133

between these opposing desires was so well concealed that he would have missed it had he not been watching her so closely.

She couldn't altogether calm herself, but she mastered the impatience.

"I shouldn't have plagued you today, especially when it's clear you're so extremely *busy*," he said. "The trouble is, we need to do it quickly, and I wasn't sure I could get an appointment soon enough."

She folded her hands at her waist. "It was very good of you and Lord Swanton to think of the Milliners' Society," she said.

"I should like to know how we could avoid doing so, when I brought home the shop's entire contents," he said. "We can hardly stir a step in the library without tripping over pincushions and purses and who knows what. Having to plan prevented Swanton from excessive weeping. I was so glad I didn't bring him to the shop with me. He'd have wanted weeks to recover. And I very much doubt we have weeks, young women being famously fickle."

"You said you had a plan," she said, womanfully crushing her impatience.

"Ah, yes. The plan." He went on to describe it. In detail. With various detours and contingencies.

If he'd hoped for an explosion, he'd

underestimated her.

She moved to her desk, took up a pen, and took brisk notes.

While she wrote, he talked and wandered seemingly aimlessly about her office, gradually drawing nearer, until he paused beside her to watch her write.

She had compressed his meandering verbiage amazingly: a charity fête at Vauxhall during the grand gala on Monday night. Swanton to read new poems in one of the smaller theaters. An additional five-shilling fee for admission to the poetry reading. A small percentage of proceeds to Vauxhall's proprietors for use of the hall. The rest to the Milliners' Society for the Education of Indigent Females.

He was aware of the words but more aware of the sounds. Everything upon her person fluttered and billowed, so that even nearly still, only writing, she made a sort of murmuring sea of sound, audible below the pen's scratching. Mingling with the sibilance was her scent, light and clean, of lavender.

His mind conjured nights in the Tuscan mountains, high in a villa overlooking a tiny village . . . glowworms flickering in the darkness of the terraced vineyards below . . . and the scent of lavender, carrying his first intimations of grief easing and a possibility of peace.

He was aware of a stabbing in his chest, and of heat, in so sudden a surge that it startled him, and he drew back a fraction.

She looked up at him.

"What a knack you have for . . . reducing the thing to its essentials," he said.

"I've had plenty of practice," she said. "My sisters are geniuses, but they're not concise." Before he could comment she went on, "Monday night is rather short notice. Most of the ton will be engaged already."

"While Swanton's star is in the ascendant, people will make time," he said. "We start early, which allows his admirers to listen to him for an hour, then go on to their other amusements. But it will be all new poetry, always a draw. Well, then, will it do?"

She put her pen back into its place. "Certainly. This is most generous of his lordship."

"You rescued his lecture the other night," he said. "And then there were the things the girls made. Very touching."

"Yes, I daresay." She straightened away from the desk, getting away from him so smoothly that he didn't realize it until she'd done it, and the tantalizing scent was gone. "I expect you shall want one of the patronesses of the Milliners' Society to put in an appearance."

He resisted the urge to draw near again. He oughtn't to have been breathing down her neck in the first place. He knew better than to be so obvious.

"And she ought to make a little speech," he said. "To solicit additional donations. Men are more likely to empty their pockets if an attractive woman is onstage, asking them."

"It will have to be me," she said. "Marcelline's unwell and Sophy's away. But I'm good at talking about money and getting it out of people, so that's all right. Well, then, my lord." She set down her pen and stepped back from the desk. "I do thank you, indeed. Will there be anything else?"

The dismissal couldn't have been clearer.

He told himself he wasn't provoked and certainly needn't provoke in retaliation, like a child. Yet he took his time. First he reread her notes, then he looked over the items on her desk.

"Did you forget a part of your plan?" she said. "Mistake the time? The entrance fee?"

"No, it's all in order." He stepped away. "All in order."

But she wasn't. She was still smoldering away.

Because of Gladys.

Then he remembered the whispery voice behind the fan.

"There was only —" He broke off. "But no, I'm sure it's of no possible interest to you. Idle gossip."

He sensed rather than saw her come to sharp attention. He knew little about dressmaking but he understood business far better than he let on. For business people, gossip was seldom truly idle. If Sir A was on the brink of bankruptcy or Lord B was growing tired of his mistress or Lady C was hiding gigantic gambling debts from her husband, their tradesmen wanted to be the first to know.

"Well, then, I shan't keep you," she said cheerfully.

He ought to go. Her business errors weren't his problem — and she couldn't wait to be rid of him. He started for the door.

One, two, three paces. He was reaching for the handle when Lady Alda's blue and pink fan fluttered in his mind's eye and he heard her whisper, all feigned concern.

Could someone not counsel dear Lady Gladys? It is a great shame she's put herself into such hands. I shall not say those women are unscrupulous, *precisely. And yet . . .*

He stopped and turned back to her. "No, I can't do it. I can't go without knowing. Miss Noirot, I'm perishing of curiosity. Tell me you didn't tell Gladys you'd make her the belle of the ball."

She blinked once.

"You've blinked," he said. "In you that can only be a sign of tremendous shock. Perhaps I ought to have broken the news more gently."

"No, no. I was only taken aback at the change of subject." She shook her head. "I'm not at all shocked. I'd heard they're already placing bets."

"They were all tittering about it at Lady Jersey's assembly last night," he said. "Are you saying it's true? The belle of the ball? *Gladys?*"

She donned the politely amiable smile. "You seem to find it inconceivable that Lady Gladys has unfulfilled potential. To you it may seem impossible that anybody not born beautiful and charming could ever win anybody's heart. Or do I misunderstand?"

"We're not talking about anybody," he said. "We're talking about *Gladys.* You can't be serious."

"A young woman's hopes and dreams are no joking matter to me," she said. "My livelihood depends on helping her achieve them. In this case, I have every expectation of accomplishing our mutual aims, and all is well in hand. By the time Maison Noirot is done with her, Lady Gladys will need only to crook her finger to have any beau she wants."

Leonie wanted to choke him.

How dare he? That poor girl!

"This is deranged," he said. "I thought you were a sensible woman of business."

"Pray don't trouble yourself," she said. "I know what I'm about, my lord."

"No, you don't know what you're about," he said. "You don't know Gladys."

"I know her better than you do," she said.

"She has a talent for making trouble wherever she goes," he said. "The other night she nearly got Val into a duel. She has somehow provoked you to a challenge impossible to meet, and led you in far over your head."

"Led me?" she said with a smile. "Led *me*." The notion of any Noirot being led was hilarious.

"You'll become a laughingstock," he said. "Your business will suffer. And my cousin Gladys will never be grateful for any efforts you exert on her behalf. She won't thank you for any sacrifices you make for her.

What she'll do is blame Maison Noirot for not doing what is completely impossible to do!"

"You underestimate me," she said. "You wouldn't be the first."

There was a short, taut silence.

He eyed her up and down.

Sizing her up.

She was used to arrogant men looking her over. But he might as well have put his hands where his glittering green gaze went. She grew hot and confused. And so she made a mistake.

She returned the favor.

A very stupid mistake, given the perfectly sculpted face and dangerous green eyes and the powerful torso . . . tapering to a taut waist and then the view downward . . . looooong, muscled legs. She felt a wave of dizziness, which she resolutely ignored.

"By the time you're done with her," he said slowly, as slowly as he'd let his gaze run up and down over her like hands. "That's conveniently vague. This strikes me as a life's work."

She was going to make him pay. The pride of the Noirots and DeLuceys demanded it.

"Let me see," she said. She put two fingers to her temple the way he'd done before, pretending to be an idiot. "What is today?

The fifteenth. She'll have gentlemen at her feet by the month's end."

She leaned over the desk to reach for a pencil that had shifted a degree out of alignment with its fellows. The position, she was aware, placed her backside prominently on view. A not so subtle taunt. But then, subtlety was usually wasted on men.

"At her feet," he said. His voice had dropped and grown rougher. "In a trifle over a fortnight's time."

"Yes."

"Anybody she wants," he said.

"Yes." She fiddled with the pencil, waiting.

He said, "Would you care to make a wager?"

She swallowed a smile.

Madame took her own sweet time placing the pencil in the tray, aligning it with the others.

He was aware of his hands clenching. She'd taken that pose on purpose, to disorder his wits.

It worked, too.

The back of her dress was almost as elaborate as the front: Delicate lace touched the nape of her neck. Thence descended rows of finely pleated muslin alternating with embroidered rows of the same material, in the shape of a V whose point rested on her waist. From under the lace cap, stray tendrils of garnet-colored hair drifted near her ears, as though her coiffure was coming undone.

He knew it wasn't. The arrangement was for effect, and most effective it was. He wanted to make a wild disorder, of her, of everything. He wanted to make her ledgers crooked and put her pencils where the pens ought to go. He wanted passionately to leave the stopper off the inkwell. He wanted to sweep everything from the desk and bend her over it . . .

She straightened and came around to face him, making a pretty flurry of white muslin and lace.

She was a dressmaker, he told himself. She knew how to wield clothes as a weapon. And it worked all too well, like a club to the head.

She gave him the enigmatic smile, so like the one Botticelli's Venus wore. "A wager," she said.

"Everybody else is doing it," he said. "Why shouldn't we?"

"Because you'll lose?" she said.

"Oh, but I'm sure you'll lose," he said. "And my mind is wandering over an interesting range of forfeits."

"Mine, too," she said. "Money means nothing to you, so I must use my powers of imagination."

"I had higher stakes in mind," he said. "Nothing so ordinary as money. Something significant."

She set her hands on the edge of the desk and leaned back.

He couldn't exactly see her calculating. She was too good at not showing what she was about. Yet he knew she was weighing and measuring, and so he calculated, too.

He sensed the moment when she'd worked out her answer. Yet she waited one moment. Another.

Playing with him, the vixen.

Drawing it out, pretending to deliberate.

She was fascinating.

He waited.

Then, "I know," she said. "The Botticelli."

He heard his own gasp, one quick, involuntary intake of breath. He smoothed his face, but he suspected he was too late.

Whatever else he'd expected, it wasn't this. Yet it should have been the first thing. The *very first thing.*

"You said high stakes," she said. "I don't know what it's worth, but I do know it's irreplaceable." She gazed at him with limpid

144

innocence.

For a moment, the air between them crackled.

Then he laughed. "I've grievously underestimated you, madame. High stakes, indeed. Let's see. What will you put up against my Botticelli? What's irreplaceable to you? Time. Profit. Business. Your clients." He paused for a heartbeat, two. "Well, then, will you stake a fortnight?"

"A fortnight," she repeated blankly.

"With me," he said. "I want a fortnight."

Her blue gaze sharpened then.

"Of your exclusive attention," he said. "At a place of my choosing."

He couldn't be sure — she was so skilled at concealment, she seemed even able to control her blushes — but he thought a hint of pink washed her cheeks before it faded.

"You do understand, don't you?" he said.

"I'm not naïve," she said.

What he'd seen must have been a blush, because it had washed away completely, leaving her pale. With fear? Good gad, what did she think he'd do to her? With her. But she was a milliner and beautiful. Countless men must have made themselves obnoxious.

He wasn't that sort of man, yet he felt as though he'd stepped wrong, and he was aware of heat stealing up his neck — the disagreeable, embarrassed kind of heat.

"I don't ravish women, if that's what you're thinking," he said.

"Oh, no," she said. "I had supposed that women stood in line waiting for you to relieve them of their virtue."

Then why had she paled?

Or had he only imagined it? Her color seemed normal now.

"I want two full weeks of your undivided attention, that's all," he said.

"That's all?"

"I should like a fortnight of not taking second or third or eighteenth place to *business*."

"And?" she said.

He smiled. "You cynic, you."

"And?" she said. "Not that it matters, because you'll lose, but I'm interested to hear what, precisely, you have in mind."

"Precisely?" he said.

"Yes."

He gazed at her for a moment, his head tipped to one side, considering.

Then he advanced.

Lisburne clasped the edge of Leonie's shoulders, just above the sleeve puffs.

She stood very still, her heart racing, her gaze fixed on his blindingly white, perfectly tied, folded, and creased neckcloth.

"Madame," he said.

She looked up. That was a mistake.

She saw his beautiful mouth, turning upward at the corners, turning into a dangerous curve of a smile. She saw his eyes, as green as the sea must have been between Scylla and Charybdis, here and there catching the sun in glints of gold. Dangerous waters, and she — the responsible one — wanted to leap in.

Then the smile vanished and he bent toward her and kissed her.

A touch of his lips to hers. Only that, and the world changed, grew infinite and warm, offering a glimpse . . . of something. But it was over before she could tell what it was she glimpsed or felt.

He started to draw back, then "Blast!" he said.

It would have been wise to pull away, but she was lost and wondering, unable to be wise.

He brought his hands to her waist and lifted her straight off the floor, until they were eye to eye. He kissed her again.

It was more than a touch of his lips, this time. So much more. The sheer physical power of him, the way he lifted her up as easily as he might pluck a flower. He pressed his mouth against hers, firmly this time, like a dare, and she took the dare, though she didn't know what to do. She'd thought she knew, but the feel and taste of his mouth was sweet and dangerous and entirely beyond the little naughtinesses she'd once called *kisses.* This was like an undertow.

She lifted her hands to his shoulders and held on while the world tumbled away. Something pressed against her heart and set feelings into flight, like flocks of startled birds, wings beating as they darted away.

Only a moment, and it was over. Only a moment like years passing, a lifetime between Before and After.

He set her down on her feet. She let go of him, and she could still feel the texture of his coat against her palms. The room tilted, like a ship in heavy weather.

He stared at her for a moment. She stared back while she tried to get her brain back in balance and the crowd of little Leonies in her head cried, *Don't you dare faint!*

"Er, that sort of thing," he said.

"I thought so," she said.

"Did you?"

"I'm not naïve," she said.

"Really? I could have sworn —"

"Not *experienced,*" she said, too hotly. She was not in control. She'd slipped out of control so swiftly that her head was still spinning. But he'd done things to her or she'd done something to herself.

One thing was painfully clear: She'd made a mistake. No great surprise. She was a Noirot-DeLucey, and being the most sensible one of them all still didn't count for much. "There's a difference. Not that it matters either way, because you'll lose."

"I think not," he said. "And I'm looking forward to furthering your experience."

Whatever else Lisburne had expected, he hadn't expected her to be . . . surely not *virginal*?

No, no, that was too absurd. She was a French milliner. From Paris. She was one and twenty, hardly a child. Her sisters had swept two of London's most sophisticated men off their feet.

Inexperienced, she'd said. Not quite the same. And yet . . . the tentative way she'd held herself at first and the hint of uncertainty before she'd let go and kissed him with something like assurance, and . . . feeling.

Perhaps, after all, it was nothing more than uncertainty about a man she scarcely knew. He hadn't had time to tell, really. So brief a kiss.

He shook off his doubts and watched her stroll back to the desk in a flutter of ruffles and billowing muslin.

"We ought to be specific about the terms," she said, brisk and businesslike once more, while he was still trying to find his balance. "I've made general statements, open to interpretation. What would you take as proof?"

"Proof?" he said.

"Of Lady Gladys's conquest of the beau monde."

"The entire beau monde?" he said. "I shouldn't dream of disputing your genius, madame, but I believe that would be a great deal to accomplish in half a month's time, for any young woman who isn't Lady Clara Fairfax."

She stiffened. The temptation was almost unbearable, to cross the room and kiss the back of her neck until she melted.

But he'd already rushed his fences.

He never rushed his fences.

His patience was prodigious. He enjoyed the game of pursuit as much as the conquest.

Yet he'd been so hasty and clumsy.

He made himself think, as he ought to have done earlier. He tried to remember what she'd said.

Gladys. She'd become so emotional about Gladys.

"What do you believe *Gladys* would wish to accomplish?" he said.

"That is not a sensible question." She walked round to the back of the desk, as though she knew what he'd been thinking about her neck and wanted a large piece of furniture between them. "You know perfectly well Lady Gladys would be happy if people stopped behaving as though she were one of those horrid little dogs some ladies take everywhere with them."

For a moment he couldn't take it in. Surely Gladys took no notice of others' reactions to her, any more than she gave a thought to what she said and did to offend and hurt them.

"Anybody in need of the lady's goodwill pretends it isn't foul-tempered, ill-bred, and ugly, and regards it with a pained smile," she said. "Lady Gladys believes a pained smile is the most kindly reaction she can expect. I aspire to a great deal more than that, my lord. I mean for gentlemen to want her company. I mean for her to receive offers of marriage. I mean for her to have dancing partners who ask her of their own free will, not because their relatives order them to. I mean for her to be invited to not

151

one but several country house parties."

He reminded himself how insufferable Gladys had been at a time when he was trying so hard to be the man of the family and not give way to the black misery engulfing him. And her father!

Lisburne was shaken, all the same, and acutely uncomfortable.

"It's easy enough to ascertain when a young lady is popular with gentlemen and when she isn't," he said. "If we fail to see it, the scandal sheets will point it out. Let's say that if my cousin Gladys acquires a following by the end of the month, you win. Will that do?"

She looked up at him. "You're making it too easy, my lord. She'll acquire a following in a matter of days."

She exuded confidence.

Enough to make him doubt himself.

But no, she had to be out of her mind. In this regard, at any rate. One of the perils of her trade. Like mad hatters.

Still, she wasn't completely insane. She couldn't have been more lethally precise in choosing the Botticelli. Of all his possessions, the loss of that one would hurt deeply. On the other hand, it would go to a good home, to a young woman he had no doubt appreciated it as much as, perhaps even more than, he did. And she'd probably share it with those indigent girls of hers.

But losing the fortnight in which he might educate Leonie Noirot at delicious length? Now that he'd had a taste of what he could look forward to?

Out of the question.

"What then?" he said. "Shall we say half a dozen beaux? An offer of marriage?"

"But not by anybody in financial straits," she said. "Lady Gladys's dowry, I estimate, is something between twenty-five and fifty thousand pounds. No obviously mercenary offers."

"Are you *trying* to lose?" he said. "I'm flattered, madame."

"Half a dozen beaux," she said. "Either men hang about her or they don't, and that's easy enough to judge. Social success is measured by invitations, too. She'll have at least three invitations to country house parties. And, yes, at least one offer of marriage."

"All by the thirty-first of July," he said.

"Yes. Is there anything else, or would these three conditions satisfy you?"

"I have every expectation of being satisfied," he said. She rolled her great blue eyes.

He wanted to laugh. He wanted to kiss her witless. What a treat she was!

153

She took out from a desk drawer a sheet of paper.

He approached the desk.

She folded the paper in half, took up a pen, and wrote out their agreement twice. She signed her name twice. She handed him the pen. "Here and here," she said, pointing.

He signed.

Using a ruler, she tore the sheet into two precisely equal halves. She gave one copy of the signed agreement to him, and bid him good day.

The following morning, Lisburne was at breakfast, reading *Foxe's Morning Spectacle,* like nearly every other member of Fashionable Society.

And like everybody else that day, he found himself reading the account of the previous night's assembly at Almack's twice. Because, like everybody else, he didn't believe what he'd read the first time.

The ball on Wednesday was numerously attended, there being present upwards of 500 persons of distinction. Weippert's band filled the orchestra, and dancing continued until four o'clock. One of the more notable among the brilliant assembly

154

was Lady Gladys Fairfax, who wore a dress of an altogether new style, in gold satin, ornamented with black blond, a creation by Maison Noirot's talented mantua-makers. We are informed that her ladyship regaled a small group of the attendees with her delightful recitation of a comic poem, her own adaptation of Aristophanes's naughty *Lysistrata,* which her ladyship had composed, she said, in response to a Member of Parliament's declaring that women had no rights.

A ghastly image was painting itself in his mind's eye when he became aware of Swanton plunking down his breakfast plate on the table.

"You look ill," the poet said. "Has that rascal Foxe found out about the hundred pincushions you bought?"

"My cousin Gladys has been reciting poetry," Lisburne said. "In public."

"Is that the girl with the melodious voice? I should like to hear her recite some of mine. Maybe she can make it sound intelligent."

Lisburne put down the paper and looked across the table. *"Lysistrata,"* he said. "She wrote a poem about it."

Swanton's pale blue eyes widened. "But

155

that's the one — the one about the women. The Peloponnesian War — and the women banding together to stop the fighting by refusing to —" He made the universally understood gesture for coitus. "It's obscene. How on earth did she get hold of it? Surely it isn't part of a lady's curriculum. Or have I been away from England for too long?"

"Her education wasn't feminine," Lisburne said. "And her father was rarely at home. She learned Greek and Latin and probably read whatever she pleased. I can't believe she did this. Is she *trying* to be ejected from Society?"

Yes, of course he had to win his wager with Miss Noirot. That didn't mean he wanted Gladys to humiliate herself. Again. He hadn't been in London for her debut, but Clara's mother, Lady Warford, who'd sponsored her, had written to Lisburne's mother, in despair and at length. A host of others had written, too, not so compassionately, because Gladys had, in a few short months, contrived to make everybody loathe her.

Every year, flocks of girls made their social debut. Naturally, not all of them were successful. By all accounts, Gladys's failure had been so spectacular as to set a new standard.

"Let me see." Swanton snatched the newspaper from him and swiftly read the entry. "It doesn't sound scandalous. She 'regaled' the company and the recitation was 'delightful.' Obviously, her version must have been highly expurgated. If she'd shocked and offended everybody, the *Spectacle* would be thrilled to say so." He gave back the paper.

"Maybe not. The *Spectacle* might have decided that the better part of valor is discretion. Her father is Boulsworth. You remember him, don't you? At my father's funeral?"

"Who could forget?" Swanton said. "He was terrifying. I reckoned that was the secret of his military success. At the mere sound of his voice, the enemy fled, screaming like girls. I certainly would. Your cousin Gladys is his daughter? The poor thing! Or perhaps not so downtrodden as one might suppose. A girl who can compose a poem based on *Lysistrata* — and recite it — at Almack's — sounds like a girl of spirit."

Lisburne stared at him. "Sounds like? You've met her, on more than one occasion. How can you not recall? The general brought her to my father's funeral with him."

Swanton shook his head. "Those days are a haze of misery. But the general stands out

157

vividly. A personality like a charging bull."

"She was at the British Institution the other day," Lisburne said, striving for patience. How could anybody who'd ever seen Gladys forget her, even if he wanted to? "With Clara. Surely you remember. You must have spoken to them. And I'm sure we've encountered them elsewhere."

Swanton lifted his shoulders. "There seem always to be so very many young women. Their faces become a blur." He shook his head. "But your cousin Gladys can't have spoken to me. Had I heard her voice before, I could not have forgotten." He looked down at his plate, and seemed to recall what it was there for, because he picked up his cutlery and began to eat.

A day earlier, Lisburne might have dropped a hint to his cousin about Gladys's being unforgettable in less than agreeable ways. But Miss Noirot's remarks silenced him on that subject.

Her father, however, was fair game.

"Even Tom Foxe might decide against stirring up the wrath of Boulsworth," Lisburne said.

"If your cousin Gladys stirred up the wrath of Almack's patronesses, everybody will know about it. Hard to believe Foxe would ignore such a juicy story." Swanton chewed in silence for a moment. Then he said, "Only one way to find out whether or not she's made herself persona non grata. She's staying with the Warfords, is she not? Let's pay a call at Warford House."

If Gladys had made no impression on Swanton in person, Lisburne preferred to keep it that way. While he couldn't believe she'd suddenly become alluring to men, he could believe that Swanton sometimes saw what he wanted to see. He wasn't the best judge of women. He was softhearted and too easily imposed upon. This made it not entirely impossible to imagine Gladys effecting, through sheer force of personality, a capture.

The prospect of Swanton trapped by Boulsworth and his daughter, and having his sensitive soul crushed beyond recovery, was too horrible to contemplate.

Wager or no wager, sporting or not, in this case Lisburne had no choice but to intervene.

"You don't have time for social calls," he said. "You were the one who was moaning yesterday about having to write half a dozen poems in less than a week. I'll call at Warford House this afternoon, after Clara's adoring hordes have come and gone. I'll report to you when I return."

CHAPTER SIX

How often do we see the same countenance change its expression, according to the influence of the feelings! And how many are the transformations of beauty when under the magic power of Fashion's variegated wand! Inexhaustible in her resources, she rules over the female part of the human species with peculiar despotism.

— *La Belle Assemblée,* 1827

Later on Thursday afternoon
Lisburne had had an earful this afternoon, at Warford House and elsewhere. He still didn't believe what he'd heard. He had to see it for himself.

Driving in an open carriage to Hyde Park, he couldn't help but be aware of the sky's unpromising grey complexion and the air's increasing oppressiveness. But this was a distant perception. He was aware in the same way of the streets on which he drove and the vehicles, animals, and people who cluttered the route. This afternoon they cluttered it more than usual. His mind, though, was mainly on the phenomenon those four hundred acres contained this day.

It was no great journey from St. James's Street to the park. The trouble was, at this time of day everybody — meaning Everybody who was Anybody — traveled in the same direction. Even though the Season neared its end, the ton could produce carriages and riders enough to take possession of the park during what they considered to be their time. Today, especially, everybody wanted to be there, because Lady Gladys Fairfax was driving with her cousin Lady Clara.

And everybody wanted to know what she was wearing, according to both Lady Warford and the shopgirls at Maison Noirot.

People wanted to see what *Gladys* was wearing, not Clara.

When Lisburne reached Hyde Park Corner, he realized that word had traveled even unto the lower ranks. Not only was the entrance to the park in the stage of conglomeration more commonly seen on Sundays, but a wall of onlookers lined the railings of the roads.

161

Once he'd disentangled himself from the mob near the Triumphal Arch and was able to look about him, he spotted her easily enough.

Not Gladys.

Leonie Noirot.

She stood surrounded by men at the railing, a short distance from the statue of Achilles.

She wore a dress of deep blue, adorned with a frothy piece of white ruffles and lace that spread like a cape over her shoulders and tucked into her belt, to reappear beneath it in two flowing tails. A narrow green scarf draped the garment's neck, drawing the eye upward to the matching green flowers and bows of her bonnet.

Though she seemed not to notice all the fellows ogling her, Lisburne hadn't the slightest doubt she'd taken an exact count of those vying for her attention, assessed their bank accounts, and could make a reasonable estimate of their property holdings.

He halted his curricle, to the audible annoyance of the other drivers. His tiger, Vines, jumped down from his perch at the rear of the vehicle and went to the horses' heads.

Lisburne alit.

162

"Drat you, Lisburne!" someone shouted. "You're blocking the road."

The road here was wide enough to allow several vehicles to ride abreast. Today, however, too many were trying to squeeze in. The place reminded him of Paris, especially Longchamp during Easter week.

"Gentlemen, I must beg your indulgence for a moment," he called. "A moment only, if luck is with me."

He sauntered to the rail where Miss Noirot stood. In his usual lazy way he let his gaze travel over the crowd surrounding her.

The men moved away.

"Miss Noirot," he said. "This is a pleasant surprise."

"My lord," she said, with a polite nod that set the ruffles aflutter. "Is it?"

"Pleasant but probably not a surprise, since I was told you'd be here," he said.

"I'm waiting for Lady Clara and Lady Gladys," she said. "I thought this would be the best place to wait, since all the park roads meet here."

"Confound it, Lisburne!" someone behind him shouted.

"Had we but world enough, and time, dear lady," he said, "I should linger here for days and converse. A hundred years should

163

go to the innocent pleasure of contemplating a great mind and prodigious wit in a beautiful package. But at my back I always hear those louts in the road, who are in a perishing hurry to cover ground. I seem to be in their way. Will you join me — in the carriage I mean," he said, leaning closer and dropping his voice. "The other connection will come, I hope, later . . . at a place of my choosing."

She didn't blush, exactly. He saw only a hint — more of a promise, so faint it was — of color washing over her cheeks. He wondered what it would take to make her blush fully.

"In the carriage," she said. "A drive?"

"That is what, in my clumsy way, I was trying to say."

He watched her blue gaze flicker to his cattle, a fine matched pair. He remembered her reaction at Astley's, to the horses, and the note of longing he'd detected in her voice.

"Are those good horses?" she said.

"They are not permitted to go wherever they please at any rate of speed they choose," he said. "They are not allowed to rear up when the whim takes them or bite each other or anybody who looks at them in a way they don't like. You'll be quite safe."

"That isn't what I meant," she said. "They seem unusually beautiful to me. I only wondered whether I'd judged correctly."

"As always, madame, your taste is impeccable," he said. "The question remains, Will you allow me to take you round the park? I'll let you hold the ribbons."

Her eyes widened before she caught herself. "You're only trying to tempt me," she said. "I may know nothing about horses, but I know how men feel about women driving their carriages. In any event, the point is moot, because I'm on this side of the railing, and you're on the other, and I'm not going to — oof — no! Don't you —"

Lord Lisburne picked her up and lifted her over the rail.

Leonie had not seen it coming.

"That isn't what I meant," she said, her voice not completely steady.

"Now we're on the same side," he said as he set her on her feet. "Moreover, we've given the fashionable set something to talk about besides my cousin Gladys."

Now, drat him, Leonie was reeling with physical awareness. The expert tailoring and almost foppishly perfect style hugged a body, she was hotly aware, of solid muscle.

As was not the case with other big, strong men, the muscle did not extend to his brain, unfortunately. He was entirely too perceptive.

She didn't have time for this. She had a young woman's future to save, not to mention her shop. She couldn't afford to have her mind cluttered with Male. Big, strong, male, smelling of male things — starch and shaving soap and leather and mingled with it, the tantalizing scent of horses.

While she was trying to put her wits back into order, he found the part of her arm not encased in stuffing — her lower arm — took hold of it, and led her to the carriage. In other words, like every other aristocrat, he did as he pleased, leaving others to cope with the consequences.

England belonged to them, and so, naturally, she belonged to him.

She'd noticed the way he'd given the latter message to the men standing near her.

Oh, very well, she'd felt a thrill, stupid she, because this splendid man had given other men possessive signals about her, and she was human, not made of wood or stone or steel, as would be infinitely more practical. Meanwhile, there were those beautiful creatures. He'd promised to let her hold the reins because she'd given herself away in some manner, and he knew how much she wanted to.

She climbed into his carriage and wondered whether one of his ancestors had been a Noirot or DeLucey.

He took his seat and the ribbons again, and his groom leapt to the rear of the carriage. The onlookers applauded.

Lord Lisburne threw her a little smile, and set the carriage in motion. And all of it, from the moment he'd stopped the vehicle and come to the railing, he'd done with effortless grace. So smooth, so elegant, and so charming that he made it all too easy to forget how dangerous he was.

Last evening she'd dined at Clevedon House, and the duke had told a story about Lord Lisburne — Lord Simon Blair at the time — at Eton. A group of boys had been bullying Lord Swanton. Young Blair had taken on the lot of them. He'd walked away from the melee with a few cuts and bruises. "The rest of them lay broken and bleeding on the ground," the duke said. "Lisburne was like a berserker — if you could picture a cold, quiet, and methodical one."

She could easily picture it. Wolves and tigers were beautiful and graceful, too. She'd known from the start he wasn't harmless. Those Roman gods never were.

He'd picked her up, not once but three times now, as easily as if she'd been a kitten. *His* kitten. To play with, she reminded herself. To him it was a game. And he was too damned good at it.

"This is excellent," he said when the carriage was in motion. "We've created a diversion."

"Is that why you came?" she said. "To create a diversion?"

"Certainly not. I came because the girls at your shop said you'd be here, and I had to know what you were up to."

"I wanted to treat myself to the sight of my newest client in a becoming carriage dress," Leonie said. "I was too late to see her entrance, but I overheard some men speaking in a complimentary way about it."

"I'm not entirely surprised," he said. "Her father would never tolerate slovenly horsemanship."

"Lady Gladys is so clever," she said. "I had only to drop a hint — and she created an entirely new strategy."

Out of the corner of her eye she caught the sharp glance he sent her.

"I've heard that Lord Boulsworth was a brilliant strategist," she said. "She said he treated her like a regiment. That accounts for some of the traits people find so obnoxious. She's a young woman who's been trained more or less in military fashion. Now she's finding the bits that work to her advantage. She's thinking like an officer."

"What bits? Reciting obscene verse at Almack's?"

"Hardly obscene," she said. "You seem to be hysterical."

"I nearly fainted when I read it in the *Spectacle,*" he said.

"Do try to consider this in a rational manner," she said. "If her ladyship had behaved in any way improperly, she would have been ejected. His lordship her father may be a great hero and, I'm told, a most intimidating one, but Almack's patronesses fear nobody. They once refused the Duke of Wellington admittance because he arrived too late."

"Miss Noirot, do you know what *Lysistrata* is about?"

"Of course," Leonie said. She knew nothing about horses, but the rest of her education had been as good as and in some cases better than many ladies' schooling. She knew something about the Peloponnesian Wars and rather a good deal about Aristophanes's play. "But she must have used the premise in a clever way, because a number of the older ladies, especially the married ones, were amused. As you know, in respectable society it's no good winning over the men if you can't get some women on your side."

"She seems to have got away with it," he said. "If it's a strategy, though, it's a risky one."

"Conventional methods don't work for her, because she isn't like other young ladies," she said. "She wasn't taught to be missish or defer to men or keep her opinions to herself. She's had a degree of freedom other girls haven't. Because no one taught her to walk gracefully, she walks like a man. All this makes her seem unfeminine. On the other hand, she drives like a man, too. Wearing a handsome carriage dress, with her pretty cousin by her side, she must make a rather exciting picture."

"Exciting, like attacking cavalry?"

"Here she comes. Let's see."

As Lady Clara's carriage approached, the situation became happily clear.

Several gentlemen on horseback escorted the vehicle, and Mr. Bates, one of Lady Clara's admirers, was talking animatedly to Lady Gladys. She looked amused. Thanks to that and the splendid green carriage dress Marcelline had designed for her, her ladyship's not-beautiful face wore a becoming glow.

Keeping her own face schooled to give nothing away, Leonie watched Lord Lisburne's profile.

He didn't give much away, either. One tiny flicker of surprise before his handsome countenance became as smooth as a marble statue's.

As Lady Gladys drew nearer, he saluted her, and she returned the acknowledgment.

When she passed, he was the only one who didn't turn his head to watch her departure. He seemed to concentrate on a small gap in the vehicle parade. This looked very small indeed to Leonie, yet a moment later he'd entered it. In no time, the greater part of the crowd was behind them, all straining for a glimpse of Lady Gladys Fairfax.

"You're going to lose our wager," Leonie said.

He laughed. "You're leaping to conclusions. Yes, I saw the entourage of gentlemen. Yes, I saw Bates talking to Gladys. But all the men know Clara has a soft spot for her prickly cousin, and they're trying to curry favor with Clara. For all the good that will do. She keeps them about for show or, more likely, defense. Safety in numbers. No one is favored. No one's encouraged, either. They all hover about her, living in hope, poor fools."

Leonie didn't so much as raise an eyebrow.

Inside, though, the Leonies were looking at each other and saying, *What? How did he know?*

Except for Leonie and her sisters, no one, even those closest to Lady Clara, had an inkling of the game her ladyship played. Young ladies were not allowed to sow their wild oats, as young men were, but she was determined to enjoy as much freedom as she could for as long as she could. As the Member of Parliament had said, women had no rights. This was the one time in Lady Clara's life when she had any real power over men, and she meant to make the most of it.

Somehow, though he spent little time with his Fairfax cousins, Lord Lisburne had caught on.

Somewhere on his family tree, a DeLucey must have skulked.

"To my thinking, if Mr. Bates was conversing so amiably with Lady Gladys, she's made rapid progress," Leonie said. "He wasn't wearing the pained smile."

"I don't care about them," Lord Lisburne said. "The road's clearing ahead of us, and you're going to have a driving lesson."

They had been traveling along the stretch of park road running parallel to Park Lane. Now the marquess halted the carriage under a stand of trees near the reservoir. His groom jumped down and took charge of the horses, and Lord Lisburne stepped down from the carriage and walked round to the other side. He waved to the astonished Leonie to move over. Excitement warred with anxiety as she moved into his seat.

It was still warm with the heat of his body.

Lady Gladys disappeared from Leonie's mind.

He settled into the passenger seat, then proceeded to give her charge of the whip and the reins. This was a complicated business. One must hold the reins in both hands and they must go around the fingers in a certain way and one must hold the whip as well and one's hands must be just so. This process left no room in her mind for anything but him and what to do with her hands.

"The seat's tailored to me, so it's a bit high for you," he said. "But we're going only a short distance. In any case, it's good to learn how to drive any vehicle."

"About as useful as learning to steer a

yacht," she said. "It's not as though I'll be having my own carriage, or joining the Four-In-Hand Club."

"You never know," he said. "You might be out driving with a gentleman someday, and he might faint from the heat or excessive drinking the night before or the unbearable happiness of being near you."

"Yours is a lively imagination," she said.

"When it comes to you, yes," he said. "I often imagine other fellows being with you and meeting with illness or injury. Right now, for instance, I'm picturing one of my friends toppling out of his seat beside you and falling on his head in the road. Such thoughts brighten the endless hours while I await my fortnight with you."

Her imagination came vividly awake at that moment, and the images it created sent jittery sensations up and down her spine. "I thought you were going to teach me to drive," she said.

"You need to learn to drive and flirt at the same time," he said.

He went on to basic principles of starting and stopping, the delicate pressure one ought to apply, the importance of keeping the horses' heads straight, the proper use of the whip, and about ten thousand other details.

Luckily, Leonie had a head for details. Too, she'd seen other ladies drive. If they could do it, so could she. What she couldn't do at present was shut away her feelings toward him, or erase the memory of that kiss. And now it was worse because she had gratitude to contend with as well.

"No, elbows a little closer to your hips, madame. Wrists a little bent. Yes, like that. Well, then, enough theory. All right, Vines, I think we're ready."

The groom stepped away from the horses and returned to his place at the back of the vehicle. At this point, Leonie realized that the only thing controlling the immense, not-very-tame-looking creatures was her hold on a few strips of leather.

Her heart sped to triple time.

"Call them to order," Lord Lisburne said. "Pull them together. You want them at a complete stop before they start. Good. They'll start when you say, 'Walk on.' Tell them in the same way you'd tell one of the shopgirls to straighten the mannequin's bonnet. Calm, clear, firm. Confident, in short, because you know what you're about."

Heart thudding, Leonie checked her posture and her hands once more, then said, "Walk on."

And they did. Slowly and calmly as though they didn't know a complete neophyte held the ribbons.

A thrill went through her, and her chest heaved. It was all she could do not to cry. For all her life she'd wanted to do this: to be near horses, to drive or ride. But there had been too much else to learn and do. She and her sisters had been trained to be ladies, because aristocratic blood ran in their veins. Unlike ladies, though, they'd had to learn a trade as well. And before Cousin Emma had put her foot down, there had been intervals of living with Mama and Papa, and learning to live by one's wits, on the streets of what seemed like a hundred different towns, in England and abroad.

She bit her lip and made herself concentrate, preserving outward calm, keeping her hands the way he showed her, not leaning forward, not pulling. She was distantly aware of riders and vehicles coming and going, but they might as well have been in Madagascar. Her mind was overwhelmingly occupied with her hands and the horses and the road ahead and Lord Lisburne's low voice, quietly correcting.

"I wonder how you keep from grabbing the reins from me," she said.

"I can't grab the reins because I'm required to appear to have absolute confidence in whatever I do," he said. "The animals need us to be calm as well. These are very good cattle, but even the best-trained beasts can react badly to surprises. What we don't want is a large, powerful animal with a not over-large brain getting the idea it needs to run away."

"Then I'd better not do anything stupid."

"I didn't say that," he said. "Only think, if you do something stupid, I shall have to save you in some heroic manner. I haven't yet had a chance to be heroic for you, Miss Noirot."

"You saved me at the British Institution," she said. "But then, you're probably so busy rescuing damsels in distress that it slipped your mind."

"You have grossly underestimated my powers of recollection," he said. "Every moment of that encounter is branded into my memory. Not to mention you've a paltry idea of heroism."

"It's unsporting to be seducing me when I'm preoccupied with trying not to get us killed," she said.

"Am I seducing you?" he said. "I hadn't realized I'd got to that part yet. How amazingly clever I am. But here, pay attention. We're coming to the Cumberland Gate."

He was telling her how to guide the horses round the turn, in order to continue on the road westward along the park's northern edge, when he broke off, looked up, and "Blast," he said.

That was when the world went dark.

Lisburne had been so deeply engrossed in getting her smoothly through the vehicles, riders, and walkers clustered at the Cumberland Gate that he was only indistinctly aware of the rapidly changing atmosphere. Then he saw people running toward them from the footpaths. He looked up and swore. In an instant, the sky went from leaden grey to black, and the skies opened up.

Though the greater part of the beau monde had departed, the park was far from empty, especially today, when so many had turned out to watch the Gladys show. Stragglers in carriages and on horseback hurried to the shelter of trees or raced toward the gates and home. Heedless of horses and vehicles, pedestrians ran along the footpaths and across the road.

Meanwhile, the rain fell in blinding sheets. It beat on his hat and dripped from the brim, and it was in the process of flattening Leonie's bonnet — because he'd been in too great a hurry when he left Maison Noirot to let Vines raise the hood.

Leonie stopped the horses without waiting for instructions, and Lisburne was reaching for the reins when a small figure burst out from a footpath, ran straight at the horses, and fell.

They shied, and Leonie cried, "Oh, no! The child!"

She threw the reins to him, and without regard for the dancing animals, leapt down from the curricle.

He got the startled horses under control, not the easy feat it ought to have been, because she darted at them to take hold of the child. She snatched up the limp little body and carried it to the side of the road to the shelter of a tree.

Leaving Vines in charge of the carriage, Lisburne went after her. The rain fell in torrents, turning the world into a blur. She was thoroughly drenched, her bonnet sagging limply on the back of her head.

"That was a stupid thing to do," he said.

"What did you want me to do, run over her?"

"I did not want you to — blast! It's breathing, I take it."

"Yes, not that you —"

"Here, give it over." He held out his hands.

"*It* is a girl."

On closer inspection he saw that it was female, and well dressed, not a street urchin like those who roamed the parks, picking pockets. Well fed, too.

"So it is," he said. "Give her over. She's too heavy for you."

Her arms must be aching because she didn't argue about handing over her burden. He'd no sooner collected the child than its eyes opened wide, and so did its mouth. It let out a piercing wail.

"Noooooo! Let me go! Let me go! I'm wet! I'm wet!" She started pummeling him, kicking and wriggling while she screamed. She was too small to do any hurt, but it was deuced annoying. He was strongly tempted to put her down as she demanded. In the nearest puddle.

"Stop your noise," he said. "Nobody's hurting you."

"I'm wet!"

"It's raining. If you didn't want to get wet, you oughtn't to have run about in the rain."

She went into a high-pitched crying fit.

"You'd better to give her back to me," Leonie said above the uproar.

"She must weigh close to four stone," he said. To the girl he said, "Stop your noise. You've no reason to take on in that ill-bred

180

way. Nobody's hurting you. And we're going to give you back to whomever you belong to as soon as possible. I'm Lisburne. What's your name?"

She went on crying, kicking, punching.

"This is tiresome," he said.

"Vines!" he called. "Stop fooling with the hood and find the umbrella!"

Vines dug out the umbrella, delivered it, and ran back to the carriage.

"Miss Noirot, if you'd be so kind as to hold the umbrella over us, we shall set out and attempt to deliver this Satan's spawn to its caretakers," Lisburne said.

It was still raining, but not quite as hard as before. In any event, they were already soaked. Had a hurricane commenced, he would have set out in it to get rid of this accursed child.

"She came from one of the footpaths," he said. Two footpaths met at the Cumberland Gate. He nodded toward one. "That one?"

"Yes," Leonie said. "If she'd come up from behind me, I wouldn't have seen her until she was in the road."

She'd been paying attention, as he'd told her to do. She'd had the good sense to stop the carriage promptly. She'd panicked over the child, but she hadn't lost her wits entirely.

On the other hand, she had panicked over the child and nearly got herself killed, rescuing the little beast. Not to mention, the beast had covered Madame's beautiful dress in mud.

"Look at what you did," he told the wailing child, who paid him no attention whatsoever. "You spoiled Miss Noirot's beautiful dress."

"Nooooo! Put me down! I'm wet!"

"I'm a dressmaker," said Madame above the shrieking. "I'll make another one."

"But it won't be the same," he said. "It'll be in *tomorrow's* style. And I like this one."

"You weren't expecting me to wear the same dress *twice*?"

"I hate you! I want to go home! I'm wet! Let me go!" More wailing, kicking, pummeling.

Maybe he could drop her by accident.

"Oh, Lady Sarah!"

The voice turned out to belong to a sodden nursemaid hurrying toward them, carrying an enormous umbrella. "Oh, my goodness, I was at my wits' end, you naughty child."

"This belongs to you, I take it?" he said.

"No! No! No!" Lady Sarah screamed. "Hate you! Mean, mean witch!"

"I'm so sorry, sir," the maid said. "I'll take her."

"No!" As he tried to dislodge her, Lady Sarah grabbed his neckcloth. "No! I won't go!"

"You didn't like me much before," he said. "Now you can't bear to part from me? *Women.*"

"I'm so sorry, sir." The nurse tried to take hold of her charge, who kicked out, striking the nurse on the chin.

It took the three of them to detach the child, and then not easily. In the struggle, she kicked the umbrella out of Leonie's hand and dislodged his hat, which fell into a puddle. When they finally got her off, she left behind a torn neckcloth, mangled lapels, and large dollops of mud. He glanced at his hat, then kicked it aside.

The servant didn't attempt to carry her young charge, but set her on her feet. Her ladyship promptly sat down in the footpath and kicked and screamed. When the nurse-maid tried to lift her up, the girl wriggled, kicked, and punched, wailing all the while.

Lisburne was about to intervene — though he wasn't sure how to control the child except by knocking her unconscious — when Madame spoke.

"That's quite enough, young lady," she

said in French. "You are too big a girl to carry on like a baby. Furthermore, ladies do not scream at the top of their voices and pummel their elders. You will stand up — *now* — take your nursemaid's hand, and go along with her. It's past your teatime. Not that you deserve tea. If I were Nurse, I should send you straight to bed, you naughty child."

At some point in the course of this speech, the little girl became quiet.

"Up," Leonie said, gesturing. *"Now."*

The child stared at her. Leonie regarded her expressionlessly.

Her ladyship rose and went to her nurse and took her hand.

They walked away.

Lisburne had no idea he was in a temper until it exploded. This happened as soon as the nurse and demon child were out of earshot.

He turned to Leonie, who was as wet and filthy as he was.

"What in blazes were you thinking?" he said. "You could have been trampled!"

She turned sharply toward him, and her blue eyes flashed. "So could she. In case you failed to notice, she fell — and she was out of her senses momentarily."

"She is out of her senses permanently," he said.

"She was terrified and she threw a fit," she said. "Children don't always behave logically. Mainly they behave illogically. Like some men I could mention."

"Talk of illogical," he said. "You'd already stopped the horses. They weren't going anywhere. You'd only to hold them."

"You said they didn't like surprises!"

"And so you thought it was a good idea to run at their legs?"

"She'd already run in front of them! You were the one who told me horses have small brains. I was terrified they'd think something dangerous was at their feet. And they did! They became agitated — you saw!"

"They were a little nervous, that's all."

"They wouldn't keep still, even for you!"

"Because you'd jumped out, you mad creature!"

"What would you have done, Lord Know-It-All?"

"Why didn't you let me do it? You could have been killed! What if you'd been kicked in the head? No, come to think of it, that might improve matters. It would stop your calculating, for once."

"A moment ago, you were accusing me of not using my head."

"Because you didn't."

"Make up your mind what you want!" she shouted. And stormed away.

He caught up with her in two strides and moved to stand in her way. She tried to walk around him. He caught her by the wrist and stopped her.

"Don't you manhandle me," she said. "You have no rights over me. I am not your property and I'm not one of your servants. You have no power over me whatso—"

He pulled her up against him and wrapped his arms about her and kissed her.

CHAPTER SEVEN

Obedience is so much demanded in the female character, that many persons have conceived it was the one virtue called for in woman . . . If man, as the guide and head of woman, were himself a perfect creature, this would, unquestionably, be true; but as a being, accountable to her Creator, and endowed by him with reason — unqualified and implicit obedience to a creature like herself, liable to many errors, cannot, consistently, be required.
— *The Young Lady's Book,* 1829

Maybe it wasn't wise. Maybe, worse, it was the sort of clichéd male reaction Lisburne abhorred. He was too intelligent — not to mention inventive — to resort to such histrionics. But at the moment, it was all he could think of.

Then, once his lips met hers, he couldn't think of anything else.

She tasted like rain.

She tasted, too, like nobody else on earth. He'd had only a hint yesterday, but it was enough to keep him sleepless for half the night. Now night seemed to have fallen on the universe, and he was half in a dream and half wildly awake.

She tasted sweet like innocence and sweet like sin. She was wet, and all her elegant frills and furbelows drooped. Yet she seemed so light and frothy in his arms and so full of life, making a struggle for a moment and then no struggle at all, but meeting him headlong, her mouth pressing to his and parting at the first urging. And when he deepened the kiss, she followed his lead. An instant's hesitation, then her tongue was coiling with his in an erotic dance, and the taste of her deepened and heated.

Like the surprisingly fine brandy he'd sipped the first day he'd entered her lair, it was sweet and fiery. He'd marveled at her then: so delicate and feminine and apparently fragile even while he was aware, excitedly aware, of banked fires and danger.

He ought to be aware of danger now. He ought to realize he was falling into a place he might not easily get out of. But he wasn't thinking, except in a dreamlike way. Only his senses were at work, telling him of the warmth of her body and the shape of it, and the way she fit under his hands and the way her mouth fit against his.

He was aware of damp muslin and lace fluttering about him and wet bonnet ribbons tickling his chin. He was aware of his hand at the back of her neck and the bonnet sliding downward, against his hand. He was aware of her hair, like silk, under his hand, and the velvety skin of her neck and the scent of her: lavender and Essence of Leonie. He couldn't get enough of it. He wanted to drown in it.

He slid one hand downward, to her waist, and moved the other hand lower, to her hip, and pulled her closer.

In his dreamlike consciousness he was aware of fragility and innocence. A distant voice wailed something about trespassing, but he couldn't make logical sense of it. What use was logic when he drank kisses like brandy, hot and sweet? What good could warnings do when he was already intoxicated? And besides, she'd reached up to grasp his shoulders and her body was pressed to his and stirring up trouble down below.

He drew her nearer still, and slid his leg between hers, pushing against layers of petticoats.

She gasped, and pulled her head back, and looked up at him, blue eyes wide and dazed. "No," she said. She pushed him away, with force.

Taken unawares, he staggered. Or maybe he staggered because he was dizzy.

But that was absurd. Mere kisses had not made him dizzy since he was a boy, stealing one from the very first girl of his dreams.

Then he'd been so excited, he had to summon every iota of masculine pride not to swoon.

Now?

Well.

Exciting, yes. But that was . . . heat. Lust. Frustrated lust.

The blue eyes flashed at him. "That is so typical!" she said breathlessly. "You can't win the argument logically, so you resort to seduction."

"I wasn't *resorting*," he said, also breathless for some reason. Probably on account of lugging that raging child about, and having to exercise so much restraint *not* to toss her into the nearest shrubbery. "And don't pretend you weren't participating."

"I was fighting you on your own ground," she said. "You think you know everything."

"That was a fight?" he said.

"Yes," she said. She untied her bonnet ribbons — not without a battle, for they were wet — planted the sagging bonnet back onto her head, and retied the ribbons with great energy. "I may be inexperienced but I learn very quickly, and whatever I learn to do, I am determined to do *extremely* well. You think you can distract me from my mission with your masculine wiles, but I have wiles you've never dreamed of. And how dare you do *that,*" she added with a furious glance at the thigh he'd pressed, for one delicious instant, as close to her womanhood as eighty-five layers of petticoats and frock and whatnot would let him get. "Did you think to have me against a tree in Hyde Park? On a public footpath?"

"I was not exactly thinking," he said. "And how could you expect me to, under the onslaught of you?"

She rolled her eyes and turned away and marched down the footpath. "I can't believe you're playing injured innocence. Did I throw myself at you, my lord?"

"No, and it's extremely inconsiderate of you not to, when I've taken such great pains to make myself attractive to you. Why must I always be the one to make advances? Why can't you make a little more effort?"

"I'm busy!" she said. "I don't have time to roam London, seducing innocent gentlemen. I have a shop to run and ladies to make beautiful."

"You wait," he said. "Two weeks, madame. Then we'll see what you can do when you're not *busy*."

Damn me damn me damn me.

Leonie wanted to knock her forehead against the nearest lamppost.

She had lost control completely. In about three seconds. All he had to do was touch her, and she went up in flames. And the first thing to burn away was her brain.

It was a wonder she'd had the wit to stop when she had. That, she supposed, was only because of the surprise of finding a muscular male limb between her legs.

The next time, though, she wouldn't be startled, and like all the Noirots and DeLuceys before her, she'd go merrily to ruin — which wouldn't be so bad if she weren't sure she'd go, far less merrily, to heartbreak, too.

He was getting under her skin. He was making her *want*.

She — the sensible Noirot sister, the one with both feet planted firmly on the ground — had somehow let him turn her into a moony idiot.

"What have you done with the umbrella?" he said.

She'd had it kicked out of her hand and she'd forgotten all about it, between the argument and being so desperately eager to get her hands — both hands — on him.

"I don't know," she said. "I don't care. At this point, do you think it'll make us *less* wet?"

"I was merely curious. I've lost my hat, too. That is to say, I know where it is, but I'll be hanged before I'll retrieve it."

She looked up at him through the haze of a steady drizzle. His hair glistened. Though it had plastered itself to his skin and neck, this only enhanced the effect of the obviously natural curls.

And why not? Roman gods weren't like mortal men. Even sopping wet, they'd magically make themselves unbearably beautiful.

She looked away. They'd neared the carriage road. She saw his curricle waiting, its hood now raised. Vines stood at the horses' heads, stoically indifferent to rain as well as capricious masters.

"We'll have to continue your driving lesson another day," Lord Lisburne said. "While it's unlikely you'll take cold in this warm weather, it can't be comfortable to lug about so much wet clothing. Like carrying a basket of wet laundry, I imagine."

"Something you've had a good deal of

experience with, I'm sure."

"And you're dirty," he said. He let his gaze range over her, and she was amazed that steam didn't rise from her skin.

Irate, she gave him the same study. This was the first time she'd ever seen him looking less than perfect. Yet he contrived not to look imperfect at all. His neckcloth was a mud-spotted wet rag, his coat a larger wet, drooping rag, and his trousers clung to the muscles of his legs like silk stockings, leaving nothing of those muscled limbs to the imagination — including the upper area that had been in excessively close contact with her most private part.

She was wet and dirty. He was glamorously disheveled.

She wished she still had the umbrella, so that she could hit him with it.

"Very dirty," he said, his voice dropping. "I'm strongly tempted to take you home and give you a bath."

Her toes curled inside her wet half-boots.

Her mind raced ahead, to the end of July.

A fortnight with him. Alone. The things he could do to her.

"It's my business to be tempting," she said. "Just as you must always seem completely confident of what you do, I must always appear irresistible in some way, even when disarranged. However, I shall have to make do with bathing myself this day, my lord. I need to get back to work."

Without question it had been worth seeing her mouth fall open and her eyes glaze over in the too-brief instant before Madame collected herself. Yet by the time they'd climbed into the carriage Lisburne wished he hadn't mentioned bathing her. Now he couldn't get the idea out of his head, and it was deuced inconvenient to pretend to be perfectly at his ease while he was battling to keep the brain in his skull in charge of the little one lower down.

She was wet and dirty and adorably bedraggled and cross.

Being soaked through, her garments clung where normally they puffed out, thereby revealing more of her natural shape than was ordinarily visible.

It was not a sight calculated to rouse the male intellect to perform even basic thinking tasks.

Being closely confined with her behind the carriage apron and under the hood didn't make the exercise any easier.

Still, keeping his feelings to himself and presenting a smooth exterior was more or less second nature. True, she'd knocked him on his beam ends for a moment or two, but the circumstances had been exceptionally trying.

By the time he'd taken up the ribbons and given the horses leave to start, Lisburne was his urbane self again. On the outside, in any event.

He made light conversation and flirted in the usual way, and she responded in kind with no visible effort — as though nothing had happened and the earth hadn't trembled on its axis and he hadn't got turned upside down and inside out and made an inexcusably crass error, the sort of mistake overheated schoolboys made, not worldly men of seven and twenty.

In a way, when they reached the shop, he was relieved. He needed time to put himself in proper order again.

Yet as he watched her step through the door, he was strongly tempted to lunge at her and drag her back again.

He returned to the carriage and drove home.

Friday

As a consequence of trying to distract himself at parties until five o'clock in the morning and then still not sleeping well, Lisburne was late coming down to breakfast. Swanton, for once, had preceded him. He had not, by the evidence, made any progress with his meal, however. Though his plate sat in front of him on the table, the contents were congealing while, dragging his hands through his hair, he stared at *Foxe's Morning Spectacle.*

"What's Gladys done now?" Lisburne said, moving to the sideboard. "It must be extreme, to shock even you."

"It isn't your cousin," Swanton said, hollow-voiced. "It's me."

"You?" Lisburne hauled his mind to order. "Now what have you done?"

"Oh, it isn't what I've done. It's what I've *not* done, the scurvy, insinuating scandalmongers." Swanton laid the paper on the table and pointed.

Lisburne leaned over him and read:

We do not know where or how these ridiculous rumors start, but we are informed on very good authority that there exists no basis whatsoever for stories currently flying through Fashionable Society that a certain nobleman of poetical inclinations has been named in a breach of promise suit. As those who understand such matters will readily agree, nine out of ten such suits are merely attempts at extortion or quests for notoriety. Undoubt-edly, this is the case with his lordship. Those familiar with the gentleman's affairs have assured us that the rumors are completely unfounded, and these same parties confess thorough mystification as to the origin of this strange story.

"Nothing like beating everybody over the head with denials," Swanton said. "Nothing like making every gossip in the ton decide, 'Methinks thou doth protest too much.'"

Lisburne pushed the paper aside and returned to the sideboard, though he'd lost his appetite. "One of your petitioners is merely gambling that you'll settle quietly to protect your reputation," he said.

"I'm not going to settle," Swanton said. "I've not led anybody astray, and I won't have anybody think I have — which is what they'll think if word gets out of a settlement. And you know it'll get out. There will be no such thing as 'settling quietly.' If Foxe got hold of this, he can get hold of anything."

That one of the women who'd applied to Swanton for money had gone so far as to contact *Foxe's Morning Spectacle* was surprising. Normally, the kinds of creatures who attempted such frauds gave up at the first rebuff, and crawled back under whatever rock they'd crawled out from. They had no legal standing. Swanton hadn't been in the country for five years and more. A curt letter from one's secretary ought to suffice.

"We can only wait to see whether one of your imaginary brides-to-be writes a second time," Lisburne said. "Then we'll let Rowntree deal with it. Once we bring in the solicitor, she'll have to give up. He'll remind her of the law of *scandalum magnatum*." The law imposed fines and imprisonment on anybody who made scandalous statements — true or not — about a peer of the realm. "That'll encourage her to find another dupe."

"You can't fine rumor," Swanton said. "You can't put rumor in prison."

"She wants money," Lisburne said. "One doesn't give money to rumor, either. If she wants it, she'll have to come forward. We have the advantage, cousin. Put her out of your mind."

Saturday morning's *Spectacle* brought yet another denial. This time it wasn't true that "a well-regarded poet of the upper ranks" had seduced "a respectable young Englishwoman" in Paris a year ago, "the consequences usually attending such occasions having been confided, we are told, to the

199

care of an orphanage maintained by holy sisters."

Though Rowntree promptly sent a strongly worded note to the *Spectacle*'s publisher, he explained to his employers that very little could be done. The *Spectacle* not only named no names but did not, in fact, accuse Lord Swanton of any ill-doing.

"They're clever," he said.

"Yes, and they'll hang me with denials," Swanton said.

"Mr. Foxe will trip over his own cunning in time," Rowntree said. "And your lordship may be sure we shall deal with him then, and summarily — as half the ton have longed to do this age."

"In time, in time," Swanton said. "Meanwhile my name is dragged through the mud with 'It isn't true!' " He turned to Lisburne. "You did well to tell me to make haste with our charity event. At this rate, my reputation will be in shreds before another week is out."

"Not if somebody else makes a bigger scandal," Lisburne said. "Which I'll do, if necessary."

"Why should you get into trouble, because some vile-minded creature is determined to make a fool of me?"

"It isn't trouble but a diversionary tactic,"

200

Lisburne said. "And I should do it because, firstly, I should have to exercise my imagination, which is deplorably out of practice. And secondly, because I suspect it will be great fun. Stop fretting about these rumors that aren't rumors. Some jealous scribbler's behind it, I don't doubt. Let's let Rowntree go on about his lawyerly tasks while you and I settle a few last bits of business for Monday. Then I'll carry the results to all necessary corners of London, leaving you at leisure to throw yourself back into your verse."

Later on Saturday
One necessary corner of London was Maison Noirot.

It was a good thing Lisburne had a scandal to think about, because he found he was obliged to cool his heels in Maison Noirot's showroom. Madame, he was told, was busy with customers in the consulting rooms.

He had kept away on Friday because, after all, he wasn't a moony schoolboy. He was a gentleman with other things to do besides hang about a girl, waiting for her to take notice of him.

He had, along with Swanton's trials and tribulations, the poet's personality to deal with. Getting him to concentrate on practi-

201

cal or logistical matters when he was in the throes of composing verse was, even at the best of times, like trying to hold the undivided attention of a dog when a squirrel chittered nearby. The whispering campaign or whatever it was made him more shatter-brained than he was normally.

No one in his right mind would send Swanton to the shop in such a state, and not on a busy Saturday, when he'd cause more than the usual uproar.

In other words, Lisburne had excellent reasons for being there.

So, unfortunately, did Gladys, who turned up shortly after he arrived. She came with Clara, whose maid Davis trailed after them as she always did. But there was Bates as well, part of the entourage.

Since Gladys's voice made its entrance shortly before her person did, Lisburne wasn't taken unawares. The showroom at this point was crowded. He ducked behind one of the mannequins elevated on pedestals. Given the wide skirts, ballooning sleeves, and enormous hats adorning the figures — not to mention the customers swarming about them — it was very good odds his relatives wouldn't notice him.

Because his cousin's allegedly "melodious" voice carried as well as an opera singer's, he had no trouble hearing her above the general chatter.

"No, Parmenter, I do not object in the least to waiting," she said. "My eyesight being in excellent order, I can see this is a busy day. Everyone and her great aunt Theodosia must be wishing to have a new dress for Vauxhall on Monday. You must be run off your feet. But it's all in a worthy cause. And so I must be patient and you must be strong."

Bates said something.

"Do try not to be excessively inane, sir," said Gladys. "While I support Lord Swanton in his literary endeavors, I should not patronize every charity case strictly on his say-so. For one thing, you know I'm as softhearted as a curbstone. For another, sadly enough, I'm a good deal less naïve than I ought to be. That's the trouble with always having military men lounging about the place."

Bates laughed, and Clara said something and he answered.

"My cousin exaggerates not at all," Gladys said. "I dragged Clara there because I wanted to see for myself. The Deaf and Dumb Asylum is one thing. Everyone has heard of that. But whoever heard of the Milliners' Society for the Education of Indigent

Females? No, no, of course I must see the place with my own two beady eyes. And having seen, I have put my name down as a sponsor, and Clara very kindly did the same, to indulge me — or perhaps out of fear I'd sit on her."

Clara said something and laughed.

Bates said something.

Gladys said, "Oh, there you are, Lisburne."

He looked to his right, and found her looming there. For a large girl, she walked quietly — more quietly, certainly, than he recalled her doing. She wore a handsome rose-beige promenade dress and an excessively feminine bonnet that ought to have looked ridiculous on her, but in fact became her round, plain face shockingly well.

She'd looked well in Hyde Park yesterday, he recalled, but he'd had only a passing awareness, Leonie occupying the front of his mind. Now he saw how grossly he'd underestimated Maison Noirot's skills. Had he been a superstitious man, he'd have suspected witchcraft.

"Playing with mannequins?" she said. "Or come to play with the seamstresses and shopgirls?"

"Business with Madame," he said.

"I daresay," she said, eyebrows aloft.

"The charity event on Monday," he said. "Were you not speaking of it a moment ago? You can't be surprised that Swanton and I have details to settle with one of the Milliners' Society's founders."

Her expression softened. "Oh, yes, of course. Lord Swanton cannot be expected to attend personally to tiresome practical matters. The poetic imagination is not always coupled with a pragmatic nature. It is so with many artists. Someone must act as his representative. I quite understand."

She turned to Bates. "While it would be stretching a point to commend my cousin Lisburne for making a *great personal sacrifice* in attending to this particular matter, we're obliged to admit he has a point. I'm afraid we'll have to save teasing him for another time. What a pity. I had composed at least three silly puns the instant he said, 'business with Madame.' "

"But my dear Lady Gladys, I was looking forward so much to teasing him," Bates said.

"You'll have to make do with teasing me, as unrewarding as that is," she said. "Or Clara, if you dare. Or both of us, if you're feeling especially reckless."

She wandered away to examine a mannequin. A number of women watched her every move.

Clara went with her but Bates lingered behind.

"In case you were wondering," he said, "I've got fifty pounds riding on your cousin, and I'm keeping an eye on my dark horse."

"Not trying to influence the outcome, by any chance?" Lisburne said.

"As though I had any influence," Bates said. "No one cares what I do. Having neither funds nor title, I'm no marital prize, and no one's ever mistaken me for a leader of fashion. The fact is, those two ladies, especially together, are more interesting than any ten other people I know. I began hanging about in curiosity. I continue because it's so deuced entertaining."

Until a moment ago, Lisburne had found Gladys as entertaining as a toothache. Though Leonie's analogy of the ugly dog was burned into his brain, that didn't explain how Gladys had disarmed him today. The kindly reference to the Milliners' Society? The understanding of Swanton's nature and the job it was to look after him? The jokes at her own expense?

Or it might simply have been the becoming bonnet.

"She did tell me I was a damned fool, throwing my money away on her," Bates went on when Lisburne, momentarily pre-occupied with working out the riddle, failed to answer. "At first I was amazed she'd heard about the betting."

"Then, when you thought about it, you weren't so amazed," Lisburne said.

"Cats," Bates said. "I can guess which one told her, too."

So could Lisburne. Lady Alda Morris, Lady Bartham's fair-haired younger daughter, who had made it her business to enlighten Lisburne at Lady Jersey's party the other night.

At that moment, the back of his neck prickled.

"No, no, I'm content to wait, madame," came Gladys's voice from somewhere behind him. "Here's my cousin Lisburne on important literary business. You'd better see him first. He has nothing to do but hide behind mannequins, hoping he won't be accosted by annoying women, while Clara and I have this shawl to argue about, and I was on the brink of demolishing her with my logic."

A heartbeat later, Madame appeared at Lisburne's side.

"My lord," she said coolly. "Be so good as to come this way."

Lisburne found Leonie's office this day not

as painfully neat as previously. Papers strewed her desk and one of the ledgers had fallen half an inch out of alignment with its mates. He walked to the shelf and adjusted it.

"I don't know how you retain your sanity," he said. "A hundred women must be swarming in the showroom, all of them talking at once. My head is still vibrating."

"Eighty-seven, not counting my employees," she said. "It's wonderful. And it's all thanks to Lord Swanton and you."

"Not me," he said. "I'm merely the pragmatic fellow who executes his brilliant ideas."

"Ideas are useless without execution," she said. "Someone has to keep his feet on the ground. Someone has to see to everyday boring details."

"And someone gets not enough sleep, I can see," he said, advancing on her. Of course she didn't retreat. Her chin went up and her blue eyes grew brilliant, challenging. Yet they were shadowed, and her face was taut.

"You're working too hard," he said. "What you need is a fortnight away from the shop. With me."

"The unlikelihood of that occurring increases by the day," she said.

"Don't get too excited about Bates," Lisburne said. "He hasn't a feather to fly with, which disqualifies him from the marriage stakes."

"But he likes Lady Gladys," she said. "He qualifies as a follower. Furthermore, he stands to inherit an earldom."

"Only if two healthy young male relatives of his, one recently wed, take it into their heads to die early and childless."

"I'll admit he makes poor odds as a marital candidate," she said. "Still, he's a follower."

"You need only five more. Half a dozen, you said. I have it in writing."

"I'm not in the least anxious," she said.

"You needn't be," he said. "You'll find me generous — to a fault — in victory."

"And in defeat?" she said.

"Defeat is highly unlikely," he said.

"Yet not as unlikely as you originally believed," she said. "Admit it."

"I'll admit you've exceeded my expectations regarding Gladys," he said. Since he'd expected a catastrophic failure, it hadn't taken much.

She smiled a deliciously self-satisfied smile.

"I'll admit to a concern, not previously existing, regarding our fortnight together,"

209

he said. "But it's merely the smallest quiver of uncertainty. Only enough to lend a degree of excitement to the intervening days. The faintest hint of suspense where before there was none."

Her smile only broadened, and he became aware that he was starting to lean in toward that wicked curve.

He walked away from her and back to the shelf of ledgers.

He didn't trust his hands to stay where they ought, which was provoking. He disliked, immensely, the ease with which she eroded his self-control without losing her own.

Those were merely his own difficulties. More troubling was how ill and tired she looked. He wanted to do something about that, but there was nothing he could do at present, only observe and fume.

"I know I'm not to keep you," he said more briskly. "Gladys had an appointment, and I doubt you have time to spare between clients. I only wanted to let you know what the arrangements are for Monday evening. For a number of reasons I won't waste your time with, we'll have to start at ten. But we'll have the small theater for a full hour, and since we won't be competing with any major social events elsewhere in London, we ought to fill the seats."

He went to the desk, removed a folded sheet of paper from his breast pocket, and tossed it onto a pile of papers there.

She hurried to the desk, snatched up his addition to the heap, and neatly rearranged the others. Then and only then did she unfold his document and read it.

He swallowed a smile. "The program," he said. "For Monday night. All that remains is to make Swanton stop changing his mind about the order in which he'll present his new works. Too, he keeps adding stanzas. Since our time is limited, and we need to leave room for speeches and pledges and such, we'll either have to cut them or eliminate at least one poem."

She looked up at him. "Speaking as one who has two artistic sisters, I recommend you not leave it to him. Steal one of the poems, and don't let him find out until the event is about to begin, then push him out onto the stage."

He thought of all the swooning girls to whom each word was sacred, and he laughed. "Merely steal one of the poems," he said. "How do I judge which one?"

"Does it matter?" she said.

"No, my dear, it doesn't, but only you would say so."

He saw her face change, but it was only for an instant — the smallest flicker of emotion — before she was businesslike again.

She folded up his note and set it on the desk. "Very efficient and orderly," she said. "For a gentleman who claims to live in a sort of chaos moderated only by secretaries and men of business, you have a remarkable grasp of logistics."

"When there's a real prize in sight, I can set my mind to anything," he said.

A hint of color came and went in her too-pale face. "Improving the lot of unfortunate young women is a worthy goal indeed," she said. "I'm happy to know you've exerted yourself on their behalf."

"Right," he said. "Them, too."

"Well, then, if that is all, my lord." She came out from behind the desk, and folded her hands at her waist. The wicked smile he'd seen before had vanished without a trace and the curve of her mouth now was the professional one: amiable, patient, polite.

"Nearly all," he said. He crossed the room to her in a few quick strides. "One last thing I forgot to write down." He made to reach for the program. She put out her hand, instinctively, to protect her neat heap of papers. He caught her hand and brought it to his mouth and kissed it. She inhaled sharply, but before she tried to pull her hand away he'd let it go, and wrapped his arms about her waist and lifted her onto the desk.

"Don't you —"

He cupped her face in his hands and stopped whatever she was going to say with one long, fierce kiss.

Then he backed away and turned away and strode to the door. "On second thought," he said, "best not to write it down."

"Oh, no, you don't," came her voice from behind him.

Leonie leapt down from the desk and ran across the room. Before Lord Lisburne could walk through the door, she slammed it shut.

He turned to her, surprised, for once.

She took hold of his lapels — never mind damaging their perfection — and pulled.

"Come here," she said, face upraised. "I'm not done with you."

She saw the wariness in his green eyes, and knew she ought to be wary, too, of what she was doing, but she was too angry. She pulled, and he bent his head. She reached up, caught his face in the way he'd caught hers, and brought his mouth to hers.

My dear, he'd said, so casually, and her heart had tied itself in knots.

She kissed him as fiercely as he'd kissed her, holding nothing back. He'd made her hot everywhere, inside and out, in an instant. She would *not* be casually set on fire and made to ache for more, then be cast aside, so that he could make a pretty exit.

My dear, he'd said.

She'd make him pay.

This wasn't the best reasoning Leonie had ever done, but it was all she had at the moment.

Then he wrapped his arms about her, and reasoning no longer mattered. His arms were strong, holding her tight, and he was warm, and these were simple things that couldn't explain the soaring happiness she felt, like being drunk, but better and *more.* He smelled like himself, like a man, but clean and crisp as so many men were not. Under her hands, his jaw was smoothly shaven, almost like marble, like a perfect sculpture. Yet it was warm and alive, carrying the masculine scent so unmistakably his own, tinged with hints of shaving soap and clean linen.

It was nothing, merely the scent of a man, but it made her drunk in this not-drunk way, and so happy, even while she raged.

He kissed her in the way she wanted him to do, the real thing, not a tease. His mouth pressed to hers, slanting, coaxing, demanding. And she yielded, of course, to get more, and to give more, and . . . to show him. She could tease, too, and play with him, and recklessly provoke him further. If she couldn't keep herself under control, she'd make sure he couldn't be in full control, either.

He wanted her. It was no secret. And if he was determined to make her want him, then she would make him want her *more.*

He'd thought he could walk away so coolly, but she wouldn't let him. She goaded, urging him to kiss her more sinfully. She slid her hands to his neck, then wrapped her arms around his shoulders, and her body lifted with the motion and pressed closer to his.

She felt the shudder run through him, and she tasted as much as heard the groan against her mouth. He slid his hands down her back, down over her bottom, and pulled her hard against him. Even through all the layers of her dress she felt his arousal, and the sensation sent a stream of heat rushing upward and outward from the place. Yet along with the heat, she felt triumph, too —

over him and his too-easy control of her. But stronger than any other feeling was the wanting.

She hated it.

She wanted it.

She wanted to be free of wanting him and thinking about him and the craving to touch him, because these thoughts and wishes were too strong, and they made her feel helpless and lost.

She wanted at the same time to let herself drown in the longing, to be drunk with it, to go freely, recklessly, where it took her.

Yet somewhere on a far horizon of her consciousness, she was aware as well of business, of where they were, and of the shop, filled with ladies and the splendid opportunity to dress them for the Vauxhall event.

She broke the kiss and pushed herself away from him, even though she wanted to scream at having to stop, and even though, for one appalling instant, she wished all the ladies and their accursed clothes to perdition.

"There," she said breathlessly. "*Now* I'm done."

He didn't let go immediately, and he was breathing hard, too.

Good.

If he was going to make a wreck of her, she was going to make him at least slightly discomposed.

"You wicked girl," he said. His voice was very low, very deep.

"I told you I learn quickly and well," she said.

"Yes," he said. "This grows more interesting by the minute."

"And speaking of minutes," she said as nonchalantly as her wit and will would let her, "I ought not to keep Lady Gladys waiting any longer. Good day, my lord."

His eyes, whose color had deepened to the dark green of a forest, seemed to bore into her soul. Not that, being half DeLucey and half Noirot, she was at all certain she owned a soul.

Then he shrugged and laughed. "Very well, madame, have it your way. For now. *Au revoir.*"

And out he went.

Very gently and carefully she closed the door behind him.

She sagged back against it. She took six slow, deep breaths before she opened it again and went out into the corridor and into the showroom to collect Lady Gladys.

CHAPTER EIGHT

Simpson, Vauxhall's Corinthian column!
To speak thy praise would take a volume,
Or rather, were each dingy leaf
On Vauxhall's trees a real folio,
I fear me all would prove too brief
Of thy deserts to give an olio.
— *Fraser's Magazine for Town and Country,*
1833

Royal Gardens, Vauxhall
Evening of Monday 20 July
Lisburne wanted to strangle her.

He'd come within a gnat's eyelash of tripping over his own feet as he left Leonie on Saturday. Then, even after a glass or three of wine at White's, and extensive perusal of every single newspaper in the club, he'd found it difficult to settle down. To anything.

He'd spent Sunday driving from one park to another, expecting to see her, and he'd seen everybody else instead.

He'd remembered her telling him she liked to spend Sundays with her niece. He knew of only one niece, daughter of the sister who'd married Clevedon. Lisburne knew the duke well. They'd been at school together. They'd spent time together on the Continent. He might have called at Clevedon House with no excuse but to visit a friend.

Lisburne almost did it. He was powerfully tempted. But at the last moment, his pride balked, and he told himself not to be a nitwit.

He'd made a small error of judgment, not entirely his fault.

He'd never thought he and Swanton would remain in London for more than a week or two. But no, it turned out the stay would drag on for who knew how long. Then Lisburne had met Leonie Noirot, and he'd imagined a brief affair with a sophisticated, interesting young woman would compensate for the boring bits.

He'd got the "sophisticated" and "interesting" parts right.

He was not bored, certainly.

But she was turning out to be difficult, in ways he didn't fully understand — though he suspected that her genius for making herself a walking distraction had something to do with it.

Only look at her!

Lisburne stood to one side of the theater's stage, behind the curtains. She stood before him, dressed in what he'd initially taken for maidenly white. The dress was not so maidenly, it turned out. For one thing, it wasn't pure white, for it boasted, among numerous other adornments, pink and green embroidered something-or-others. Neither was it so very virginal, given the depth of the bodice's neckline.

She'd thrown a pale blue flimsy nothing of a shawl — what the ladies called a *mantilla* — over her shoulders. This, too, only invited a man to examine her velvety skin more closely. Lace adorned her neckline and wrists and the flounces of her skirt, and pale yellow ribbons and bows fluttered over the frothy creation, the bows dancing on the skirt's flounces and on her sleeves, which weren't enormous single puffs but multiple smaller ones.

A fine topaz brooch drew attention to the center of the low, lacy neckline, a topaz necklace circled her smooth neck, and matching topaz earrings dangled below the deep red curls clustered at her ears. Higher up, sprigs of flowers sprouted from the elaborately braided topknots springing from her head.

He looked her up and down not once but three full times. It ought not to require so much willpower to *not* sweep her up into his arms and carry her away to someplace very private, where he could disorder her at his leisure.

"You've outdone yourself," he said.

"The ladies will be breathlessly awaiting Lord Swanton," she said. "Obtaining their full attention demands special exertions."

"You look delicious," he said. "Like a delicate French cake."

Though numerous lamps lit the theater, they stood in shifting light and shadow, and he couldn't tell if he'd made her blush in that way she had of barely blushing.

She fanned herself. "Handsomely said, my lord. If only all the other gentlemen will feel the same, and if only the sensation will compel them to empty their purses, I'll consider my ensemble a triumph."

"You've sold every last ticket," he said. "The seats are all taken and we've still some minutes to starting time."

"We were lucky in the weather," she said. "And in your organizing abilities — or those of your secretary, if you refuse to take credit. You made sure everybody knew we'd start exactly on time, and you know the young ladies won't want to miss a word, even though they'll have to listen to me before they get their poetry."

"You're not nervous about having to face them first," he said. "If you are, you make an excellent pretense of being fully at ease."

"I'm used to dealing with ladies," she said. "And when it comes to money, I know precisely what I'm about. Most important, I believe in the Milliners' Society with all my heart."

Swanton joined them then. Unlike Miss Noirot, he suffered his usual pre-performance nerves. Or maybe they were simply everyday poetic nerves.

"Swanton hates taking the stage," Lisburne told Madame. "He'll be all right once he starts, but beforehand he tends to become agitated."

"I never meant to be performing," Swanton said. "I'd supposed, if I happened to be fortunate, people might read my work to each other if not silently to themselves. Sometimes I feel like a curst Punch and Judy show."

"Poetry needs to be heard," she said. "That's what I was taught."

"It seems not all of mine will be heard tonight," Swanton said. "One's gone missing."

"I daresay you threw it on the fire in a fit of abstraction," Lisburne said, careful not to look at Leonie. She'd told him to steal one, and he'd done so, and hidden it under a heap of invitations.

"It's July," Swanton said. "I know this is London, but we haven't lit a fire since we came."

"You'll find it in a pocket later," Leonie said. "I was always finding ladies' bills and orders for ribbons or embroidery silks or such in Sophy's apron pockets, and sometimes in her undergarments."

Swanton stared at her. Despite the fitful light, it was easy enough to see his romantically pale countenance redden.

"Well done, madame," Lisburne said. "Your sister's undergarments will take my cousin's mind off his poetic nerves."

Swanton's expression eased, and he laughed.

In the theater, the chattering began to subside.

Lisburne took out his pocket watch and glanced at it. "I believe it's time," he said.

"Don't keep them waiting," she said.

He went out and made his brief speech introducing her. He'd felt certain she was completely at her ease. Yet as he started to leave the stage for the shadows again, he saw the change come over her as she prepared to face the audience: the slight lift of her head and the small motion of her shoulders.

When she took his place at center stage, the ladies and gentlemen went completely still. Her presence alone did that, some force of personality, for she didn't speak or gesture. Then she curtseyed, and it was like a moving work of art or a dance. She sank down, and the ribbons and bows and lace fluttered, and the theater's lights danced over them. It was only a curtsey, a polite gesture to her listeners, yet he heard people catch their breath. And why not? It was the most beautiful curtsey in the world.

And when she rose, she was smiling the dazzling smile, and Lisburne could have taken an oath that her blue eyes had grown more brilliant, as though lit from within by a thousand lamps.

Then she began to speak.

Later

Madame had been right enough about the weather, Lisburne thought. The day had dawned overcast and oppressively warm but began to brighten by late afternoon. A moment ago, when he'd looked outside, the nighttime skies were about as clear as they

224

ever got over England, and the day's humid warmth had subsided to the sort of mild summer temperature more often encountered in poetry than in reality.

As to the poetry, that had gone as well as usual. As had happened at the New Western Athenaeum, a majority of the men stood at the back, many of them with arms folded and chins upon their chests, in various attitudes of sleep.

The young ladies, however, were desperately awake and listening with all their might. Lamplight glistened in a legion of tear-filled eyes raised to the lectern as Swanton recited in low, aching tones:

Oh! late I view'd her move along, the idol of
    the crowd;
A few short months elapsed, and then — I
    kiss'd her in her shroud;
And o'er her splendid monument I saw the
    hatchment wave; —
But there was one fond tear which did more
    honour to her grave.

A warrior dropped his plumed head upon
    her place of rest,
And with his feverish lips the name of
    Ethelinda prest —
Then breathed a prayer, and check'd the

> groan, the groan of parting pain;
> And, as he left the tomb, he said — "Yet
>   we shall meet again."

Lisburne had to stifle his own groan, because the poem's end met with a prodigious silence, broken here and there by choked sobs. Then the ladies burst out, clapping and clapping, so that in spite of their gloves the walls of the theater shook, and Vauxhall's fireworks would have to look sharp to outdo the row these girls made.

Still, even he had to admit that "Ethelinda" was one of Swanton's more intelligible efforts.

Not that Swanton could hold a candle to Leonie Noirot's performance, in Lisburne's opinion — and no doubt the opinions of all the other gentlemen in the audience. Following the devastating curtsey and smile, she had launched into her short, shockingly effective appeal, telling the audience at the outset that she knew they hadn't come to hear her but Lord Swanton. Yet her five-minute speech had her listeners laughing and weeping by turns. Lisburne had even seen that cynic Crawford brush a tear from his eye.

That was only what she said. She'd presented as well a display of neatly dressed girls, a sampling of her organization's beneficiaries. Between the speech and the three waiflike girls she'd chosen to represent the "indigent females," Madame obtained results very like those she'd wrung from Lisburne when he'd entered the little shop at the Milliners' Society.

The girls distributed slips of paper for writing down pledges, and supplied pencils for those who hadn't brought their own writing instruments. After collecting the papers in their prettily decorated baskets, the waifs turned the contents over to Lisburne's secretary, Uttridge. Seated in the wings, he'd marked the pledges down in a notebook, as Lisburne had recommended. It was as well not to leave money matters to the faulty memories of the bon ton.

It only remained for Swanton to step out into the audience and allow himself to be congratulated and petted.

He hated that even more than he hated the moments before he was obliged to read his work aloud, but he knew his duty and did it. In the same dutiful spirit, Lisburne had resisted the impulse to escape the theater and the depressing verse and go watch acrobats and jugglers and ballet dancers instead. He'd sat through the whole dratted thing, and had the small comfort of knowing that Madame hadn't been able to escape, either.

But in a little while, the Duty part would be over, and then . . .

He smiled.

He had plans, delicious plans.

Leonie and Matron had gathered their poetry-dazed charges and were leading them to the door while the rest of the audience surged toward Lord Swanton. As Leonie reached the door, Lord Lisburne stepped into her path.

"Ah, there you are, madame," he said. He nodded at Matron and the girls. "Ladies. Splendid work."

Matron beamed. The girls played with their baskets, too shy to look up at him.

"They did beautifully," Leonie said. "Although I suspect they found the poetry something less than comprehensible, not one of them yawned, even once."

The girls looked sheepishly at each other. "But it was so interesting to look at the fine ladies and gentlemen, madame," one of them said softly.

"I think we can do better than a lot of confusing poetry tonight," Lord Lisburne said. "Madame, if you would be so kind as to give your permission, Mr. Simpson would like to take Matron and these hardworking girls on a tour of the gardens. Ah, here he is, right on cue."

At that moment an old-fashioned-looking gentleman of sixty or thereabouts entered, holding his hat high above his head and bowing in the way that had been made famous in countless caricatures. Thanks to his frequent appearances in print shop windows and handbills, even Leonie recognized Vauxhall's famous Master of Ceremonies, Mr. C. H. Simpson, Esquire.

It would have been cruel to deny them the treat — as Lisburne well knew, the manipulative wretch — and Leonie hadn't the heart to protest, or even a good excuse, beyond being annoyed with Lisburne's making arrangements for her girls without telling her. But even if she'd had an excuse, she hadn't time to say a word before Mr. Simpson launched into one of his flowery speeches of welcome.

A moment later, he was leading Matron and the girls away.

Then what could Leonie say? Vauxhall's famous Master of Ceremonies was taking them on a tour of one of London's most magical places. He'd bowed to them. He'd made them feel like princesses. It would be the grandest time they'd ever had in all their short, wretched lives.

She looked up at Lisburne. "Thank you," she said.

"Don't be absurd," he said. "You know my motives were selfish and ulterior."

"That doesn't matter to them," she said. "Even Matron will be thrilled."

"Never mind them," he said. "Now you're not *busy*. We've endured an hour of flowers and birds and young men and women dying before their time in rhyme. And now it's time —"

"How could you?" a woman's voice soared above the chatter behind them. "How could you be so unkind, nay, so *cruel,* my lord? After all we've been to each other, to abandon me . . . and our child?"

Leonie threw Lisburne one startled look, which he returned. Then, as one, they turned back, toward the theater's interior.

"Why must I debase myself in this way?" the voice went on. "Was it not enough for me to give you that which is a woman's most precious gift?"

The audience, parts of which had been departing, paused. In the next moment, they were all moving, as inexorable as a tide, in the direction of the woman's voice.

"Tell me you don't remember the beautiful

weeks we shared in Paris. Can you have forgotten all you said then and all we were to each other? Is our time together gone from your mind, swept away like rubbish after a fête?"

The woman went on in this vein while Leonie and Lord Lisburne tried to make their way through the crush of spectators.

Leonie had an easier time, because she entered the part of the crowd where the men had gathered, and they made way for her. No one needed to move nearer to hear the woman. Her voice carried across the theater — and probably out of the open doors into the gardens.

As Leonie neared the scene, though, she found a pack of young ladies in her way, partially blocking her view. Fortunately, they didn't keep still. When they elbowed one another and rose on tiptoes and otherwise strained for a better view, Leonie caught glimpses, between their elaborate evening headdresses and fluttering fans, of a disheveled blonde dressed in black. Her bonnet was sliding down the back of her head.

"You *promised*," the woman in black cried. "Forever, you said. Yet you left me, even when you knew I was —" She broke off, dodging somebody who was trying to pull her away.

Leonie nudged her way into a better viewing position, next to an older lady and the girl she seemed to be chaperoning.

The wailing woman had taken hold of Swanton's coattails and was sinking to the ground in an attitude of supplication.

No small acrobatic feat, considering her other hand grasped that of a small child. The child was crying piteously.

"Madam, I don't know who you are, but —" Swanton began.

"Not know me! Not know me! We were *everything* to each other! And there is your daughter, your very image!"

The little girl, who might have been about Lucie's age or possibly younger, was fair. So was her mother. So were a great many other English men and women. Though Leonie had no illusions about men, she had as well no illusions about most things. The scene might as easily have been false as true. Either way, it was well played and couldn't have been worse timed.

Leonie didn't need to know the truth to see disaster looming — for the Milliners' Society, for her shop. And for Swanton, too, curse him.

"Now, now, madam, that will be quite enough of that," came a firm voice nearby.

It wasn't Lisburne, who was still trying to

make his way through a knot of ladies. It was another gentleman, who looked vaguely familiar. He pushed through the crowd like a policeman or soldier, and the women gave way, though not without exclaiming to each other about his lack of courtesy and What was Vauxhall coming to? and Who did he think he was?

He ignored their complaints and went straight for the blonde woman. "See here," he said. "A joke's a joke, but this has gone far enough."

"A joke!" the woman shrieked. "Ruination! Abandonment! A joke!"

The man took hold of her elbow and said something Leonie couldn't hear. The woman seemed to sag with weariness. She let go of Swanton's coat and rose. Still weeping, and stumbling a little as though emotionally depleted, she let the unknown gentleman lead her away. The child's wailing subsided to sniffs as she went along with the adults.

The audience had remained more or less silent throughout. Some were dumbfounded by shock, others speechless with rapture about the juicy tale they'd tell their friends. For a short time, the silence continued. Then the whispering started, like a wind hissing through the theater. It built to a hum of excited chatter.

The older woman near Leonie took hold of her charge's arm, muttering, "This is disgraceful. I won't stay another minute." Ignoring the younger woman's pleas, she led her away.

Leonie went out, too.

The scene's ending rendered Lisburne as dumbstruck as everybody else.

Theaker? Coming to Swanton's rescue?

Theaker? Playing justice of the peace instead of riot instigator?

Then the whispering started. And grew louder, swiftly driving Theaker to the back of Lisburne's mind.

"Did you hear what she said?"

"A drunken woman. She ought not to have been let in."

"Must have been a prank. Somebody's idea of a joke. In very bad taste, I must say."

"Can you credit it? Carrying on about *unfortunate women* and abandoning one he'd made unfortunate, the wretch — leaving her to make shift for herself and his natural child?"

"Shocking scene! But I blame myself. The instant I saw that creature on the stage — like a ballet dancer! — I had my suspicions. I should have taken you away directly. Milliners' Society, indeed!"

"But Mama, I'm sure it was a mistake. I heard someone say the woman was drunk."

"Where there's smoke, there's fire."

"How dare they harangue us for funds, when he lets his own child go begging, the horrid hypocrite!"

And so the mills of the beau monde began to grind away at reputations — Swanton's, Leonie Noirot's, and the Milliners' Society itself.

Lisburne tamped down his anger. He wanted to hit somebody, but that was the trouble with episodes like this: no proper target.

Realizing the show was over, the crowd swiftly made for the doors. Naturally they couldn't wait to share the news.

The clumps of women having melted away, he reached Swanton at last.

"No time to try to mend it now," Lisburne said. No time to get to Theaker and the woman, either. By now they were long gone. "The jugglers come on in a moment. We have to get out of here."

Swanton met his gaze. "But can it be mended?" he said. "This isn't like the letters. She spoke of that year in Paris. You remember the state I was in. It's all a muddle in my mind, those weeks." He rubbed his forehead. "Simon, what if it's *true*?"

"Then we'll have to make it right," Lisburne said. "On a host of counts. The Milliners' Society. Maison Noirot."

Swanton fell back as though he'd taken a physical blow. "Good God, I'd forgotten," he said. "Not only me, is it? Madame. Her girls. And it's worse for them, isn't it? This is a nightmare."

"Yes." Lisburne looked about him. "And I've lost Madame."

Given Leonie's eye-catching attire, not attracting attention wasn't the easiest task. On the other hand, she was a DeLucey and a Noirot. Until Cousin Emma had obtained control, Leonie's parents had let their children run wild in the streets, where they learned less-than-honest ways of making their way in the world. Though limited, the experience had been educational.

Leonie knew, for instance, how to carry herself so as not to attract notice.

She knew how not to look furtive. And if she wanted to do murder at present, nobody could tell by looking at her.

In any case, she wasn't yet sure who needed killing.

She followed her quarry along the southern covered walk past the Gothic Piazza and on out through the Kennington Lane entrance.

For all this time the gentleman appeared to be ex-postulating with the woman, and now and again the child recommenced weeping.

Was he threatening them with the authorities or critiquing the performance?

By the time they reached the coach field they appeared to be arguing, and the gentleman made as though to drag the woman somewhere. Then he looked about him, up and down New Bridge Street. A moment later, a hackney pulled out from the cluster of vehicles at the coach field. The gentleman waved it down.

Leonie swore under her breath. She ought to be able to determine whether what she'd seen was real or a hoax, but she was at a disadvantage. The dramatic scene had been so unexpected. Though she was good at reading faces and even better at discerning frauds and fakes, she hadn't had a clear view. Now she was uncertain, a state she hated.

Maybe the scene in the theater had been exactly what it appeared to be, and this vaguely familiar gentleman was one of Swanton's friends quietly dealing with an unpleasantness, as aristocratic men were known to do for their friends. Maybe the woman was drunk or deranged. Maybe the gentleman meant to take her to the nearest magistrate. Maybe he was warning or bribing her to go away.

Maybe, maybe, maybe.

Not that it made a particle of difference what the truth was, Leonie reminded herself. The damage was done. She'd have to devise a way to undo it — which, at present, she hadn't the faintest idea how to do. Dealing with scandal was Sophy's forte. But even Sophy couldn't devise a counterattack without having at least an inkling of the true state of affairs.

This was why Leonie had followed the trio. She'd no assurance she'd learn much, but it had to be more productive than attacking Swanton, and taking him apart, piece by piece.

And so she remained. And watched.

Then, at last, the hack drew up, and she saw him.

The sun had set and the moon hadn't yet risen, but thousands of lights illuminated Vauxhall. It was as poetic and romantic a scene as Lisburne could wish — and no earthly use, after what had happened.

He stood in the walkway in front of one of the piazzas, only half listening to two of Longmore's longtime friends, Crawford and Hempton, argue about whether Theaker was trying to get himself into Swanton's good graces or was up to his old tricks of tormenting him.

Meanwhile, Leonie had vanished.

After a quick search of the theater, he'd hurried out here, where he could keep an eye on the entrance. She wouldn't have left without her girls, he was sure, and he'd sent a friend to look after them. Now he needed only to keep an eye on this corner of the gardens.

He was debating whether he'd done the right thing in sending Swanton to hunt for her rather than sending him home when, looking toward the entrance for the hundredth time, Lisburne saw her.

She approached in her usual style — a graceful flutter of ribbons and bows, and unassailable self-confidence — but something in the way she carried herself gave him the sense of being borne down upon.

Naturally he went on the offensive, striding to meet her. "Where the devil have you been?" he said.

"Backstage," she said.

"You were nowhere near the stage," he

239

said. "I looked. I've searched everywhere, and made Swanton hunt, too, to take his mind off that appalling scene."

"Do *not* scold me," she said. "Do not play the overprotective swain, either, because —"

"Overprotective! *Swain!*"

"That show of possessiveness thrills other women no end, I'm sure, but I'm not thrilled," she said. "I'm in no mood to be overborne and ordered about and lectured. I realize your nature is protective —"

"It most certainly isn't!"

"Don't be absurd," she said. "You make yourself a sort of Praetorian Guard for Lord Swanton, and try to do all his thinking for him, as though he were mentally deficient. I've seen no signs of that. He seems to me a perfectly normal, healthy, man — certainly not lacking in virility, if what that woman said is true."

"Damnation, you don't know anything about —" He broke off, aware of heads turning their way. "We can't stand here arguing — and most certainly not about Swanton's *virility.*" And he needed to calm down. "I understand you're upset," he went on, very very calmly. "You've more than sufficient reason. But can we discuss this in a rational manner in a less public place? Crawford and Hempton are gaping at us and trying to draw nearer to listen without making it obvious."

She threw Crawford and Hempton a dazzling smile, and the pair of hardened rogues and gamesters looked abashed. They promptly turned away and began talking in an animated manner.

"We're not *discussing* anything at present," she said. "I need to find my girls and send them home before a jokester decides to humiliate them with Swanton's folly. Someone's bound to subject them to ghastly puns that will go over their heads. But we can expect more obvious and obscene jokes as well. We need to get them out of here."

"I've sent Geddings after them," he said, naming one of his cousin Clara's numerous hopeless suitors. "His lordship is familiar with Simpson's tours. Since they follow an established pattern, he'll find them easily enough. Equally important, Geddings is a large fellow whose setdowns are famously deadly. Between his standing guard and Simpson's talent for making trouble go away, your girls will be able to enjoy their evening unmolested. That's one worry you can put out of your mind."

She regarded him expressionlessly for a moment.

"A waiter is holding a supper box empty

for us," he said. He'd bribed the waiter to do so. He gestured. "This way, if you would be so kind, madame. And, yes, I know I deserve no kindness, but I'm counting on your charitable impulses."

That won him a narrow look, which was marginally more encouraging than the blank stare.

"I realize you'd rather not be seen with me," he began.

"On the contrary, I like being seen with you," she said. "Your attire always sets mine off to advantage. I chose this dress because I've noticed that your valet often favors a dash of green to complement your eyes — an emerald stickpin, or a green waistcoat, or green embroidery on a white waistcoat. This is most convenient, because a redhead often looks well in greens and yellows few other women can carry off."

He caught the tremor in her voice. She was furious. And why not?

"Thank you," he said. "My humiliation is complete."

"*Yours?*" she said. "My girls have been reduced to l-laughingstocks. My shop may n-never recover —"

"I'll mend it, I promise," he said. "You're upset. You have every reason. Hate me all you like. Hate Swanton, too. But I must

242

urge you to hate us in a less public place. And I must beg you to take some food and drink. You're trembling."

"With rage," she said. She lifted her chin and blinked hard, once.

"You need to sit down," he said. "You need a drink."

"I don't," she said.

He gave her a little push. "Over there," he said. "Don't make me carry you."

If Lisburne carried her, she would go to pieces.

Leonie let him take her arm and escort her to the supper box.

She sat, trying to summon her composure — and wondering at having lost it in the first place — while Lisburne gave the waiter an order.

The waiter had hardly gone when Lord Swanton turned up. And instantly launched into apologies.

She put up her hand. "Don't," she said. "Not a word."

He looked at Lord Lisburne. "Sit," he said. "Not a word."

The poet sat. He looked wretched.

But what did she care? For him this was a temporary ailment, to which his lawyers would apply the infallible cure: money. For her and for her girls, it was a catastrophe.

"I do *not* understand," she said. "Hadn't you the slightest inkling?"

Swanton shook his head. "I swear —"

"No hint that you might be called to account publicly?" she said. "Because I recall one or two mentions of woman problems in *Foxe's Morning Spectacle.* It never occurred to you that these might be warnings, rather than the usual random scandalmongering?"

Swanton pinched the bridge of his nose. "I don't know. Lisburne can tell you. I get letters nearly every day from somebody claiming I promised this or that, including marriage."

"But those were either typical begging letters or incompetent attempts at blackmail," Lisburne said. "The writers seemed ignorant of Swanton's having only recently arrived in London. He couldn't possibly have formed the sort of 'attachments' they claimed. Or done any wooing. He hadn't time. I can vouch for that."

"Then the woman's lying?" Leonie said. "It was a performance, meant to discredit you, no more?"

Lord Swanton looked at his cousin.

"Which is it?" Leonie said. She wanted to scream, but they'd all received quite enough attention. "The Milliners' Society has lost at the very least a hundred pounds in pledges this night, because we're instantly tainted by association. I can't counteract this without knowing the truth."

Lisburne began, "My dear, I promise —"

"Don't," she cut in. No *my dears*. Not now. Not ever. "For the same reason, it's more than likely I'll lose customers as well. I'll be weeks, possibly months, undoing the damage. The least you *gentlemen* can do is answer me straight."

"I wish I could," Lord Swanton said. "The trouble is, I don't know."

Chapter Nine

A thousand faults in man we find —
Merit in him we seldom meet;
Man is inconstant and unkind;
Man is false and indiscreet;
Man is capricious, jealous, free:
Vain, insincere, and trifling too;
Yet still the women all agree,
For want of better — he must do.
        A.A., *The Literary Gazette,* 1818

For once Leonie Noirot wasn't hiding much.

For once her face mirrored her feelings, and Lisburne well understood them.

She stared at Swanton in patent disbelief.

"The little girl," Swanton said. "The woman said she was not five years old. She said it happened in Paris. It might have happened."

"Might have," she repeated.

"He doesn't remember," Lisburne said.

"And it's no use trying to make him remember."

"Are you claiming amnesia?" she said. "Because otherwise . . ." She closed her eyes briefly. When she opened them again, her mask was back in place. "It takes a great deal to shock me, Lord Swanton." Her voice was nearly steady now. "Yet I'll admit I'm a trifle taken aback. Were there so many women in your life in Paris at the time that you *lost track*?"

Swanton's face reddened.

No help for it. He'd only jabber on inarticulately. Explanations would fall to Lisburne, as usual. "It was a difficult time," he began. "After my —"

"Correct me if I'm wrong, Lady Alda," came a familiar feminine voice from somewhere in the vicinity. "I had always thought — at least the general my papa said so, and as we all know, he's always right — but where was I? Oh, yes, I had always thought that in this greatest of great nations of ours, a man was innocent until proven guilty."

Everyone at Lisburne's table went still.

The red faded from Swanton's face, which settled into the frown of concentration he usually applied to composing verse.

"Yes of course, anything is possible, or so some will believe," Gladys went on. "People believe in hobgoblins, too. Perhaps you weren't aware, my dear, that Vauxhall is notorious for attracting strange characters, especially those desperate for attention. There was that fellow — What did he call himself? The Great something. What was it? About ten years ago, I believe. I read about it in one of Mr. Hone's books. Do you know to whom I refer, Mr. Bates?"

A masculine voice answered. Not Bates. *Flinton?* That timid fellow, who lived in terror of his great aunt? Talking to *Gladys?*

Swanton turned his head this way and that, trying to locate the speakers.

The voices seemed to come from behind their supper box, but Lisburne couldn't be sure. So many voices. And the orchestra was playing. Gladys's voice wasn't really louder than anybody else's. It simply carried, or soared, like a songbird's.

Which was a strange image for Gladys, admittedly.

"Yes, thank you, Lord Flinton," Gladys said. " 'The Aerial.' That was the name I wanted. Sometimes styled as 'The Great Unknown,' as you said. He believed his beauty was without equal in all the world. He would prance among the audience right there, in front of the orchestra, handing out cards, and challenging the spectators to produce anybody who could match him."

Bates's voice responded this time. Then Lady Alda Morris said something.

Gladys laughed. "That would have been more amusing, certainly," she said. "And only think, my dear, if I had been there, to see the expression on his beautiful face when I took up his challenge!"

Yet another masculine voice entered the conversation. The fellow uttered only a word or two, not enough to enable Lisburne to identify him.

The voices began to drift away.

Swanton jumped up from his seat, looking wildly about him. "Where is she?" he said. "That voice!"

"It's only Gladys," Lisburne said. "A pity she couldn't go on the stage. She projects so —"

"Is it she? That voice!"

"Yes, perfectly audible," Lisburne said.

"I must find her!"

"I recommend you don't."

"She defended me!"

"Only to vex Lady Alda, I've no doubt. Confront Gladys, and you risk becoming the target of her wit. Be warned: She has a fine, skewering way with words."

"Then let her do her worst," Swanton said. "I half wish somebody would." And away he went.

Leonie watched him go. "Is he insane?" she said.

"He's overwrought," Lisburne said. He rose. "It's unwise to let him go on his own. He's completely distracted."

She waved a gloved hand. "Go," she said. "I'm not keeping you."

She was overwrought, too, though she hid it well.

He looked in the direction Swanton had gone, then back at her. "You'd better come with me. You can't stay here alone."

Her smile was cool. "I strongly doubt I'll be alone for very long."

Too true. At least a hundred men here tonight would happily take his place. Maybe two hundred.

He sat down again. "To the devil with him, then."

"I doubt he'll come to harm," she said. "If he wants to talk to Lady Gladys, he'll have to push his way through her throng of admirers. You might have been too pre-occupied to notice how many gentlemen accompanied her."

"I counted only three masculine voices," he said. "She had Lady Alda and Clara with her as well. The three men could be anybody's followers."

"Tomorrow's *Spectacle* will tell us," Leonie said. "If, that is, there's room, once they're done demolishing Lord Swanton, Maison Noirot, and the Milliners' Society."

Though she spoke coolly, he detected the undercurrent of anger and grief.

"We'll make it up to you," he said. "I give you my word."

"That and the Botticelli, if you please."

He was trying to decide how to respond to this when she glanced about her, then leaned in, wafting toward him a tantalizing scent of lavender and Leonie. That didn't help in the Intelligent Reply Department.

Dropping her voice, she said, "He doesn't *remember*?"

Lisburne leaned toward her, careful to avoid the things sprouting from her coiffure. "He was distraught," he said, keeping his voice low, too. "After my father died." It was hard to get the words out. He hated speaking of that time. "When we first arrived in Paris, we sought distraction in the way young men often do. Swanton hasn't the stamina for dissipation. He fell ill. When he recovered, he had only a confused memory of the previous weeks."

She sat back again. She lifted the tips of her fingers to her temple.

"I know it sounds ridiculous," he said. "At

251

best. You'll wonder at the depths of depravity to which we must have sunk."

"When it comes to men, I rarely wonder at anything," she said.

"We tried to be completely dissolute," he said. "We began by attending certain exclusive parties, where gaming, drink, opium, and women — expensive women — were in plentiful supply. Two weeks of that nearly killed us. Maybe the opium destroyed his memory. Or maybe it's just him. His mind's like a roiling ocean, and some things sink to the bottom, like ships lost in storms."

"You'd think he'd have some recollection, however dim, of seducing an innocent young woman," she said.

"Especially since it's so foreign to his nature," he said. "It could only have happened during those two weeks, and I'm having trouble imagining where and when he would have encountered any innocents during that interval."

"But we don't *know*," she said. "I will not call the woman's credibility into question unless I'm positive. Too many women end up with the Milliners' Society or on the streets because it's always the woman's fault. And now we mayn't have a Milliners' Society for th-them."

He was appalled. He'd never seen her so

near breaking, or even approaching breaking. He remembered how confident she'd been, the grace with which she'd taken the stage, the way she'd held the audience in the palm of her hand, her radiant expression when she returned backstage, confident she'd triumphed.

In a moment she'd lost all she'd won.

No, the damage extended farther than undoing this night's achievement. He'd looked into the Milliners' Society. He knew when it had been founded and how it was supported. He knew she and her sisters had put money into it when they hadn't much to spare from the shop's earnings. He remembered her expressing hopes of expanding into the building next door. If the support they'd so painstakingly built fell away, they could lose everything they'd achieved. And if the shop lost customers as well . . .

No point now in reviewing the *if*s. It was a nightmare, as Swanton had said, and he didn't know the half of it.

"I'll get to the bottom of this," Lisburne said. "I promise. And I'll make it right."

She turned away, blinking, and gave a short laugh.

The waiter appeared with their supper.

■ ■ ■ ■

The waiter's arrival jolted Leonie back to her present surroundings.

She looked up and saw, behind him and everywhere about him, a land of fantasy. Stars twinkled in the heavens and lights twinkled among the trees and on the buildings. Coming down the covered walk to the supper box, she'd seen the orchestra building with its multicolored lamps, a structure that might have been conjured from *The Arabian Nights' Entertainments.* From it came the sound of real music. An orchestra played and people danced. It wasn't homemade music or organ grinders on the street.

Her girls would hear real music this night, perhaps for the first time in their lives. They'd see Vauxhall's wonders, too: the paintings and sculptures, the Gothic and Chinese temples, the Eagle fountain and the Submarine Cave, the hermit telling fortunes, the jugglers and dancers and acrobats. And the fireworks. Above all, these were gardens, a pretty place out of doors, instead of dingy streets and poky rooms.

She thought of the cramped building she and her sisters had taken pains to make into a comfortable and attractive home for unwanted girls. She thought of Cousin Emma, who would have been so proud of what they'd done. A weight pressed on Leonie's chest.

She watched Lisburne peel off his gloves. For some reason, the sight of his bare, aristocratic hands made her want to cry.

She stared hard at the food on her plate and took off her gloves, though she didn't see how she could swallow a morsel.

"When did you last eat?" Lisburne said.

"Midafternoon," she said. "I meant to dine before I came here, but I was too — too —" She swallowed. "Excited." She blinked hard. "The opportunity."

He gazed at her for a moment, his face taut. "I'll make it right," he said. "I promise. But you must eat something. A bite of ham. Look." He cut a piece from the ham on his plate and held it up. "Vauxhall's ham is famous. It's so very thin, you'll think you haven't swallowed anything so gross as meat. No, you'll think you're inhaling a gossamer confection made by fairies."

He mimicked Swanton at his most earnestly and dramatically poetic, and she laughed because she couldn't help it. Yet the weight pressed, and she was terrified she'd burst into tears.

Don't think about tomorrow, she told her-

255

self. *Don't think about failure. You've played worse hands than this. All the Noirots and De-Luceys have.*

But she was so tired of playing bad hands. So tired of losing everything and starting over again. And now she wasn't sure she could count on Marcelline and Sophy to help her start over.

"Never mind," he said. "I should have realized: You've borne enough punishment for one night. I'm going to take you home."

Lisburne paid for their uneaten suppers and took her away. She was too demoralized to put up any real fight about abandoning the Milliners' Society girls, so he had to assure her only three times that Simpson would send Matron and her charges home in a hired carriage, and it had all been arranged beforehand, and she couldn't seriously be proposing to take them away before they saw the fireworks?

Since it would be hours before Vauxhall closed, and since those of Swanton's audience too indignant to remain had gone by now, Lisburne was able to get his curricle from the coach field quite quickly.

If Vines was surprised at the early departure, he was too disciplined to show it or evidence any confusion at seeing Miss

Noirot climb into the vehicle instead of Swanton.

During the journey, she told him what she'd been doing when she disappeared. Though he could actually feel his hair standing on end, Lisburne called on all his willpower not to rage at her for endangering herself. He didn't point out that dressed as she was, she'd invited trouble. Nothing terrible had happened, he told himself. And it was too late to take a fit now.

All the same, he fretted and, when she'd finished, had to exert his self-control to the utmost in order to say only, "It must have been Meffat in the hack. He and Theaker have been a matched pair since their schooldays. I'm not surprised. When I saw Theaker take her away, I knew they were involved. They think it's a fine joke, I daresay. They always did enjoy tormenting Swanton."

She looked up at this. "Are those some of the boys you thrashed at school?"

He swallowed his surprise. "Somebody had to," he said. "How did you learn of that?"

"Clevedon," she said. "But knowing they're involved doesn't tell us whether they put her up to playing Woman Wronged or simply encouraged and helped her embarrass Lord Swanton in public."

"Does it not strike you as an unlikely co-incidence, their simply happening upon possibly the only woman in the world Swanton might have wronged during two weeks of his entire life? In Paris?"

She turned away, seemingly watching the passing scene. But he knew she was thinking. It was in the way she held herself and in the tilt of her head and the arc of her neck.

"Not entirely unlikely," she said at last. "I was trying to recall where I'd seen Theaker before. It was at the British Institution. When you picked me up, and —"

"I remember," he said. "Vividly."

He remembered the way she'd stood rapt with the painting so many others had shunned.

He remembered the silk and lace and ribbons and the warmth of her body in his arms. He remembered the low, delicious murmur of perfect Parisian French when she'd thanked him and the enticing hint of Paris in her otherwise flawless English speech. He remembered her scent, simple and fresh and utterly beguiling.

"I noticed them, Theaker and his friend," she went on. "They seemed to be with the others though somewhat apart. Obviously they were gentlemen. If the Mystery Woman was hovering in the background, looking for a way to get to Swanton, she might have noticed them and approached them. Or they might have noticed her."

Lisburne dragged himself back to reality and the infuriating truth. A beautiful summer night ruined because of Theaker and Meffat. When he got his hands on them, he'd kill them. Slowly.

"Since she's young and attractive, they wouldn't hesitate to approach," he said. "Though probably not if she'd had the child with her. It's hard to say. It's certainly possible that they encouraged her to include the child this night, as a heartrending scene prop."

They were cunning enough to think of such a thing. Theaker was, in any event. And if, instead of creating a complete hoax, they'd merely leapt at the chance to help the woman embarrass Swanton, was it unsporting to kill them on general principles?

"I can imagine the crowd about Swanton intimidating her," Leonie said. "She might have felt desperate, but unsure how to approach him. And if she seemed vulnerable, these sound like the sort of men who'd approach, thinking she was easy prey."

She nodded, satisfied with this possible scenario, and the flowers sprouting from her head bounced, an incongruously happy movement. "I knew I needed to follow them," she said. "Then, when I saw her get into the hackney and not seem alarmed because another man was already inside, I was sure they were all in it together, whatever it was." She smoothed her gloves. "Yes, that's better."

"All sorted, then?" he said.

She looked up at him.

He smiled. "You've neatly narrowed the harrowing scene and its hundred possible interpretations into two lines of inquiry. I can picture the ledger in your mind — or perhaps, when you get home, you'll make a ledger page. One column for Theory A. One column for Theory B."

"Somebody," she said, "has to be the organized one. Somebody has to keep her feet on the ground."

"I know," he said. "Believe me, I know."

Her house was dark when they arrived. Lisburne found this less than reassuring.

"Where are the servants?" he said, as she unlocked the private door at the rear of the building.

"In bed," she said. "I try not to make them wait up for me."

He couldn't imagine how she would

undress herself without a maid's help. Probably two maids. But then his mind started exploring the process of undressing her, and that led to his exploring the ways he could assist.

He wiped that train of thought from his mind.

There was no point in indulging the fantasy. It would only add to his frustration. The undressing wouldn't happen tonight. Or ever, if he didn't mend matters.

Not all the charm in the world would win her over after this disastrous night.

"One of them will have to be roused," he said. "You need to eat something."

"I can find food belowstairs," she said. "I'm used to looking after myself, you know. We moved to this grand building only a few months ago. In the past we made do with only a housemaid. There was a time, in fact, when we hadn't any servants, and looked after ourselves."

"If you go downstairs in your present state, you've an excellent chance of stumbling and breaking your neck," he said. "The odds of your survival improve if you go upstairs, holding the rail firmly. I'll wake somebody and have them assemble a meal of some kind from the larder." He waved at her. "Go."

"Fenwick might be awake," she said. "He's not fond of early bedtimes. He didn't grow up in an orderly world."

"I'll find him," Lisburne said.

The building was a tall one, but like many others in London, it was narrow. Buildings of this type tended to adopt the same layout. He knew enough, in any event, to envision the servants' quarters here as a good deal smaller than those in his town house in the Regent's Park. True, he never ventured belowstairs, because the master of the house simply didn't, and violating this rule would throw any self-respecting set of servants into a tizzy. A household was a delicate and complicated mechanism. Tizzies could be disastrous.

All the same, he had a clear image in his mind of the floor plan. He understood each of his houses. He knew who worked where and what they did and what it cost. He'd lived abroad, but that didn't mean he'd abandoned his property and those who worked for him. With rank, power, and wealth came responsibility. That was one of the first lessons his father had taught him.

Somebody had to be organized. Somebody had to keep his feet on the ground. Somebody had to take charge, ready or not.

A short time later

The Marquess of Lisburne had made sandwiches. For *her.*

Leonie stared at the tray in his hands, then at his face, wondering if she'd fallen asleep and entered a dreamland of marvels and miracles.

"The boy was half asleep, and I could understand almost nothing of what he said," Lisburne said. "I know several languages, but Cockney is not among them. I stumbled about the place on my own. I found half a loaf of bread and ham and cheese and mustard. I found a very good bottle of wine. I know how to open a bottle of wine. I even know how to make a sandwich."

He set the tray down on the table.

She hadn't yet made it to her dressing room to undertake the tedious process of undressing, beyond discarding her mantilla. She hadn't advanced beyond the sitting room. Entering it, she'd seen one of Sophy's notebooks on a table. Leonie had opened it and looked at the so-familiar handwriting. And she wept. But only for a moment. She was happy for her sister. For both sisters. Truly. They'd fallen in love and the men had married them, in spite of finding out they were Dreadful DeLuceys as well as Noirots, the DeLuceys' French counter-

263

parts. That was miraculous and wonderful. They were happy. She wanted her sisters to be happy.

Her trouble was, she was tired, and the night had been difficult and discouraging, and she hadn't eaten, and so yes, she was . . . emotional.

She knew all that. She'd pulled herself together.

Then he'd walked through the door, carrying sandwiches he'd made for her with his own aristocratic hands.

At that moment, she gave up fighting and fell in love with him.

"I hope you're meaning to join me," she said as crisply as she could. "You can't possibly expect me to eat all that."

"I intended for you to invite me," he said. "I'm famished. Unlike Swanton, I'm crudely lacking in delicate sensibilities and unable to live on *feelings.*" He transferred the plates and glasses and bottle to the table from the tray, leaned the tray against the nearest wall, and set about serving.

He took Marcelline's chair, not quite opposite, but not beside Leonie, either.

"Eat," he said. "I slaved over this meal."

"You're obsessed with food," she said.

"You work too hard to skip meals," he said. "You need your strength. The girls need your strength. I need your strength. We've a mystery to solve, and we need to do it quickly." He raised his wineglass. "But not tonight. Tonight we calm our turbulent spirits and sustain our bodies with food and drink. Tomorrow we go on the hunt."

"We," she said.

"We both have a problem," he said. "It's in our best interests to solve it together. I'll never solve it with Swanton. I need your brain. The one that narrowed our choices to two. That one. I love that brain."

Her heart skipped. Twice. She raised her glass. "To justice, then," she said.

"Yes," he said. "Tonight, just us."

Disturbingly enough, it was only the two of them. Disturbing because Lisburne could feel her sisters' absence. He wasn't a fanciful man. This feeling had nothing to do with sensing anybody's spirit in the house. It was the little signs about the sitting room: an open notebook whose handwriting was feminine, but not hers . . . a sketchbook that must belong to the Duchess of Clevedon . . . three chairs at the table . . . odds and ends betokening other personalities. The room itself had been arranged for three people.

This sense of somebody missing troubled

him, but while they ate, he kept the talk to easy channels. Fenwick was a good choice. Leonie was teaching him, Lisburne learned, and the boy was a quick learner. His speech had already improved, she said, and he had learned the alphabet as well as how to write his name. He could recognize a fair number of words, especially on printed materials. He'd advanced remarkably, though she'd been able to work with him at odd times and only for a few weeks. But when he was tired or excited, she said, the Cockney consonants and vowels and slang crept back, and yes, it was difficult to discern his language's relationship to English.

"Have you any idea what possessed your sister to pluck him from the streets and bring him home?" he said.

"Sophy decided that so much criminal intelligence would be far too dangerous let loose in the streets, and much more useful to us," she said.

"I've only ever seen him open doors for customers," he said as he refilled their glasses.

"He has a strong affinity for horses and an extensive knowledge of carriages," she said. "He makes friends with all the grooms and coachmen and hackney drivers. We gain a great deal of useful information that way.

His former associates and other connections have helped us more than once already with certain problems. And our ladies seem to like him. Some have made a pet of him. But no, as you seem to be wondering, we don't make it a habit to rescue boys from the streets. We chose to put our efforts into women."

More than two years' effort . . . which a pair of aristocrats had undone in minutes.

He needed to make it right. Which meant he needed to get his head clear first. He needed to think.

They'd finished eating, and he hadn't any excuse for lingering. It was past time he left.

He rose, meaning to make his adieus, but he put it off, again. Because she seemed so utterly alone, sitting at the table meant for three. He could so easily picture the three heads — brunette, blonde, and red — bent together to share confidences, complaints, jokes.

And so he looked about him and said, "Please tell me you've someone living with you besides the servants."

"Selina Jeffreys has moved in, at Clevedon's insistence," she said. "You haven't seen her because she'll have gone to bed hours ago."

"I should have thought Matron would be

more suitable," he said. "An older woman."

"As a chaperon?" She lifted an eyebrow. "I'm not a lady. Shopkeepers don't require chaperons."

"Perhaps not, but most women have a man about the place, for safety, if nothing else."

"My sisters and I are not most women," she said. "You sound like Clevedon. He wants me to move to Clevedon House. Can you imagine?"

He could. It would be the proper, not to say wise, thing to do.

It would be deuced inconvenient.

"I should have a footman dogging my steps every time I left the house, as Marcelline does," she said. "I don't know how she tolerates it. But then, she's been ill, and not entirely herself lately. In any case, I know it's only a lure to get me away from here. He wants us to stop working at the shop. He has other plans for us. I'm not . . . ready."

Lisburne thought, and it took some thinking, because women in his world didn't work, and he found it difficult to perceive her as a woman not of his world. Whoever had had charge of her upbringing had brought her up as ladies were brought up. She was a lady. It was there in her speech, her manner, her walk. It wasn't acting. There was no mask to slip.

Yet she wasn't a lady.

He walked about the room, admiring the collection of prints hanging on the walls. A dozen beautifully colored French fashion plates. And, surprisingly, a set of Robert Cruikshank's satirical prints. Each dealt with fashion excesses and absurdities.

"You'd be bored, I suppose," he said. "With nothing to do. When you didn't grow up in that way, it must seem an empty life. Oh, this is brilliant." He paused in front of a print titled *A Dandy Fainting or — an Exquisite in Fits.* Cruikshank had set the scene in an opera box. The images were hilarious, the speech balloons equally so. Lisburne couldn't help laughing.

She rose and moved to stand beside him. "I think the gentlemen are so sweet."

" 'Mind you don't soil the dear's linnen,' " he read. "Says another, 'I dread the consequence! That last Air of Signeur Nonballences — has thrown him in such raptures' — Ha ha! I see myself. And Swanton, of course."

"You are exquisite, beyond a doubt," she said. "We may blame Polcaire, yet the result is the same. The print pokes fun and makes them seem precious and effeminate. But it exaggerates greatly for comic effect. The reality is rather different. So many of the dandies I've encountered are manly men — quite as *virile* as Lord Swanton, certainly."

He looked at her. She was looking at the print and smiling.

Her spirits had risen, clearly. He'd done the right thing in making her take food and drink. They'd cleared the plate of sandwiches and emptied the wine bottle.

Now he must do the intelligent thing and go home.

"It would seem I've done my job," he said. "You no longer bear the smallest resemblance to the poor, fainting dandy. Still, you must get some sleep, else you won't be much good to me tomorrow — and you ought to expect me first thing."

"Noonish, you mean," she said.

"Thereabouts, yes." He looked about the room for his hat.

"You can leave the tray and dirty dishes and cutlery for the maid to deal with," she said. "I'm aware that gentlemen assemble their own sandwiches on special occasions. However, I strongly doubt your aristocratic nerves can withstand the shock of clearing away and washing up."

"Hat," he said. "Only looking for my hat. Now I recall. Downstairs. Left it on the table near the door."

"I'd better let you out," she said. "If Fenwick was actually sleeping when we arrived, I'd rather not wake him again."

"Obviously you're not a lady," he said. "No lady would trouble herself with a servant's lack of sleep."

Stop putting it off, he told himself.

He walked to the door and opened it. She went past him, ribbons and lace trembling, silk whispering.

He followed her down the stairs, relieved to see she was steadier on her feet now and more like her usual self.

At the door, he found his hat. He said, "I meant this to be a perfect evening. I'm sorry it was the opposite."

"The first part went well," she said. She gave a soft laugh. "And the supper, too. Thank you. It was very kind of you."

She drew near and rose on tiptoe and kissed him on the cheek.

He, surprised at her approach, turned his head at the exact instant her mouth was there. His mouth touched hers and the next he knew, he had one hand cupping the back of her head and the other drawing her close, and he was kissing her back with all the ferocity he'd been stifling all this long night.

CHAPTER TEN

Piety, integrity, fortitude, charity, obedience, consideration, sincerity, prudence, activity, and cheerfulness, with the dispositions which spring from, and the amiable qualities which rise out of them, may, we presume, nearly define those moral properties called for in the daily conduct and habitual deportment of young ladies.
— *The Young Lady's Book,* 1829

She'd acted on impulse, that was all.

There he stood, the hall's lamplight casting a glow upon his curling dark gold hair. At that moment romantic fantasy simply overwhelmed reality and practicality and logic, and Leonie did what another girl would do, after a man had made her sandwiches and made her talk and laugh and stopped her from sinking into a slough of misery and self-pity. She kissed him.

The trouble was, she wasn't like other

girls. Her impulses came from a deep and narrow place, where she'd stuffed years and years of secrets.

At the first touch of his lips the vault's trapdoor sprang open, like the lid of Pandora's box. The secrets of her heart flew out, and swarmed over her sensible brain and swamped it, and she went into Lisburne's crushing embrace without a second's hesitation or the smallest qualm.

She was the one with her feet on the ground. She was the logical, organized one, yet she fell headlong and recklessly, the way all her kind did.

She threw her arms round his neck and arched her body to fit against his. She kissed him back with everything she had, and that seemed to be an eternity of pent-up longing.

They had one tender meeting of lips before tenderness gave way to a wilder urge she hadn't a name for, didn't understand, and hadn't the right armor or weapons to fight. Whatever it was, wherever it led, it was irresistible.

She'd been kissed before, and not innocently, either, and she'd liked it. With him she entered another realm. To call what he did to her a kiss was to call the ocean water. She lost herself in it. She sank into the strange joy of it, and the wild sensual pleasure of it: his muscled torso's warmth, his arms' possessive pressure, the fine linen and wool softly brushing her face and neck. The erotic tangle of taste and scent and movement engulfed her.

She wanted to stay in this place, this world within his arms, forever.

A warning drummed at the edges of her awareness, but she refused to listen.

He slid his hand down her back over her bottom and pressed her against him. Too much stood in the way. The layers of her dress, its adornments, and all her undergarments were like a featherbed wedged between them. Her life was about clothes, but at this moment she wanted skin to skin.

He broke the kiss, his breath coming fast. "I need to leave," he said. "Now."

"Yes," she said, and told herself to be sensible.

In a corner of her brain, on a peaceful island amid the churning seas of feelings, her intellect went on working. It reminded her of what had happened earlier in the evening and all she stood to lose, and what those who depended on her and on her shop stood to lose. Lisburne's brilliant plan had got her into trouble, and she had to get herself out, as usual. She hadn't time for falling in love and breaking her heart.

She stood for a moment, her head bowed, her forehead resting below the folds of his neckcloth, and fought with herself. She needed to find her well-ordered world again, the stable place where she could live in peace. She knew this. She tried to put the knowledge at the front of her mind, but his linen distracted her.

So crisp and so painstakingly arranged and tied when the evening had begun, it now hung limp and creased. The last time she'd seen him rumpled was in Hyde Park. In the rain. When they'd kissed and when, she realized, he'd taught her to want more from him than kisses.

She let her fingers creep up toward the knot. She wanted so much to untie it and touch her fingers to his naked throat.

He covered her hand with his.

"I need to leave," he said.

"Yes," she said. She twisted her hand to tangle her fingers with his. Skin to skin. His hands were warm. Their twined hands rested against his heart. She could feel it beating. Or maybe not. Her own was beating so hard, she couldn't tell.

"I'm going to leave now," he said, gently disentangling her hand from his. "We'll talk tomorrow, when we're . . . calmer."

She didn't want to be calm.

"Yes," she said, and made herself take one step back, away from him, away from the feel of linen and wool and the big, warm body, where she'd felt so safe when she wasn't safe at all.

He reached for her and pulled her back to him again, and kissed her again, raking his hands through her hair, demolishing her coiffure, scattering pins and flowers and ribbons.

Some sensible part of his brain must have been working, because he let her go at last.

She retreated a pace and told herself this was best. Somebody had to resist temptation, and she no longer had any idea how.

He reached for the door handle.

Then, "My hat," he said. "Dammit. My hat."

She wanted to stamp her foot, preferably with the accursed hat under it. She had a rampaging horde of desires and disappointments to beat into submission. She had to shove them back into the narrow little strongbox in her heart. She needed to get away to a quiet place away from him, and stop being a fool.

But no. She had to stay and pretend she was completely calm and sensible and only waiting to lock the door after him.

Meanwhile, there he was, all elegant grace while he peered into the light and shadow of the entryway. There he was, in exactly the place where the lamplight could cast a halo-like glow upon the top of his head, highlighting the dark gold curls. Like the neckcloth, they weren't in perfect order anymore, but tousled as though he'd risen from his bed moments ago. She remembered the feel of the thick curls when she'd pushed her fingers through them. She could almost feel them now, against her hands.

Botticelli's painting rose in her mind's eye, and she saw the goddess of love putting her hands on the god of war, on naked skin. She saw Mars putting his hands on Venus, in places where some women didn't even touch themselves.

Leonie folded her hands at her waist and waited. She watched his head go still and the curls settle into place when he spotted his hat at last, on the floor where he'd dropped it.

He swept it up and set it on his head and grasped the doorknob and opened the door and walked out.

Not a minute later, before she'd had time to shake off disappointment and mortification and start for the stairs, in he walked again, slamming the door behind him, throwing his hat at the table and sweeping her into his arms, all in one storm of motion.

He kissed her, raking his hands over her, along her arms, her back, and crushing her against him. She dug her fingers into his back and tried to get closer still.

His mouth left hers and he drew back.

She pushed him away and started to turn away, to let him go — to the devil, for all she cared. But he caught her arm, and the next she knew she was pressed against the wall and he was leaning over her and saying, his voice low and harsh, "Dammit, Leonie," and she said, "I'm not *Leonie* to y—" and his mouth stifled her angry retort.

She was supposed to stop him. She was supposed to injure him if necessary.

She didn't even pretend to struggle. The best she could do was remain as she was, the palms of her hands pressed against the wall while he dragged her into the dark place again, his mouth and tongue teasing and demanding by turns, until she teetered on the edge of what felt like a turbulent sea whose waves rushed to drag her under.

She was aware of his hands pressing against the wall as well, on either side of her face. His long body hovered mere inches away, boxing her in, and his scent, spicier and darker than before, filled the narrow space. His taste was in her mouth and swirling in her head, mingling with the dizzying man-scent. She couldn't find her balance, and her legs wanted to give way, and if she didn't take hold of him, she'd slide down the wall.

He broke the kiss.

She was lifting her hand to strike him, because she was drowning, and he was toying with her, when he touched his lips to her cheek.

She sucked in her breath.

Then he was kissing her, all over her face, tender kisses that made her ache and want to weep.

Lust she could cope with.

Not this sweetness.

She couldn't move. She stood enchanted, dissolving, while kisses fell like slow summer rain on her face. She remained so, putting up no fight at all, while he trailed kisses down her neck and along her shoulders and while everything melted, and she didn't know whether she was standing or falling.

She stood, lost, while he took his hands from the wall to cup her face then move downward slowly over her shoulders, over her breasts, while she had to teach herself another way to breathe, above or below or through the great onrush of feelings.

Longing and pleasure tangled together and somewhere among them, below them, and driving them, seethed a craving beyond anything she had words for.

His voice, husky and deep, was at her ear. "Tell me to stop."

"I won't," she said.

"Don't leave it to me," he said. Between words he was kissing her neck.

"I will," she said. If he wanted to stop, let him. He knew what he was doing. She was a novice, and weak in the morals department besides. Let him make up his mind.

"Leonie."

The sound of her name, the way he said it, tied knots in her heart. It wasn't fair that he could do this to her. What did he want? Why wouldn't he take what was so obviously his for the taking?

She reached up and grasped a fistful of neckcloth. "Go," she said. "Who prevents you? Why do you keep coming back? Do I beg you? Do I hold you here?"

"You don't make me stop," he said.

He left it to her — the one who'd fallen in love and whose heart he was going to break, the one who knew nothing of lovemaking after all, only the mechanics — and that knowledge was *useless.*

"Very well," she said. "Stop playing with me." She let go of his neckcloth, summoned what stray bits of willpower she could find, and pushed him away, as hard as she could. Then she stalked away and started up the stairs, pushing her tumbled hair out of her face.

He was a man. He was supposed to want One Thing.

How difficult was this supposed to be?

Marcelline should have —

"Aren't you going to bolt the door?" came his voice from behind her.

"When I'm sure you're gone," she said.

"It isn't safe."

She kept walking.

Not safe. What was the matter with him?

As she left the landing, she heard the bolt slide home, with force.

Her heart thudded.

She walked faster, up the remaining stairs and into the consulting room. She repositioned a mannequin and straightened the pattern books. It didn't matter if he came back and left again. She'd survived devastation in Paris and a catastrophe in London. She'd survived her sisters' marrying aristocrats. At some point he'd make up his mind. And she'd survive that, whatever happened.

Meanwhile, she'd go through the entire

establishment, if necessary, putting everything into perfect order until *she* was in perfect order.

She heard his footsteps in the passage and sensed his pausing on the threshold. She didn't turn around.

"You know I can't leave when there's no one to bar the door after me," he said.

"That's a good excuse," she said.

"Come here," he said.

Her blood boiled. For a moment, the world turned red. She wanted a weapon. A rusty ax would do admirably.

She turned. " 'Come here'?" she said. " *'Come here'?* What is *wrong* with you?"

"I tried to go," he said. "But I can't leave you like this." He gestured vaguely about him.

"You can't leave me in my own house?"

"I don't want to . . . I didn't realize . . ." He trailed off, his brow knitting. "You're angry, and it isn't safe —"

"You don't know anything about me," she said.

"If you're trying to tell me you can take care of yourself, I know that isn't true," he said. "You should have slapped me or kicked me or stabbed me with a hatpin. You didn't do anything!"

She hadn't thought it possible to get any

hotter without erupting into flames, but she felt her cheeks take fire, and the fire spread everywhere: embarrassment and frustration and an immense, chaotic rage.

"I didn't want to stop you!" she burst out. "And how dare you blame *me* when you know exactly what you're doing when it comes to women. Do *not* pretend you haven't been working on seducing me since the minute we met. You and your ridiculous wager. It doesn't matter to you whether you win or lose our bet, because you mean to win the thing you really wanted. When it comes to seduction, you surpass any other man I've ever met — and possibly ever will meet, though I reserve judgment. Well, you've succeeded. And you're surprised? Indignant? You *object*?"

"That isn't what I meant."

"Do you know what you meant?" she said. "Because I suspect not. I think you're like other men, especially aristocratic men, who grow bored more quickly than most. You want what you can't have, then when you get it, you lose interest. Very well. You've lost interest."

"I have *not*. That isn't —"

"Funny thing," she said. "I have. I'm bored now. I want you out of my house. I wish I could tell you to get out of my life,

283

but that would be impractical, and I'm nothing if not practical and hardheaded and orderly. You've made anarchy of my work, my responsibilities, my life — you and your fool of a cousin, who can't remember impregnating a young woman, though he notices every wilting daisy and every sparrow that may or may not be suffering from a fatal c-catarrh." To her horror, she burst into tears.

He started toward her. She picked up the nearest object — a pincushion — and threw it at him.

"Leonie."

She hurried toward the door, trying to stifle the sobs that wanted to tear her chest apart.

He caught her before she reached the door and swept her off her feet and into his arms.

"No!" She struck his chest and kicked wildly. "Put me down! Go away! I'm done with you!"

He carried her to the chaise longue, as though she were one of her ladies, about to faint from an excess of sensibility or delicacy, when it was the opposite, and she wanted to do something violent. He didn't lay her down but sat holding her in his lap while she fought him and the grief that threatened to suffocate her.

"I hate you," she choked out. "I hate you and your idiot cousin. You've ruined everyth-thing!"

Her head sank onto his shoulder and she gave up and wept. She was miserable — embarrassed, disheartened, angry. She had reason to weep. The life she'd so laboriously constructed was falling apart. She'd fallen in love with a Roman god, and everyone knew where that sort of thing led.

Lisburne couldn't leave her here, alone, crying.

He couldn't leave her in any event, could he?

Now she was in his lap and she was warm and weeping and disheveled, her hair coming undone, literally, the false braids slipping from their moorings. And so, to give himself something to do while he tried to decide what to do, he set about disassembling her coiffure.

He unpinned flowers and carefully detached a false braid wound with ribbons. He unpinned the Apollo knots at the top of her head, and gently loosened her hair, there and at the sides. The clusters of curls at her ears softened and loosened as well, tumbling to her shoulders.

While he worked, she quieted. By the time

he'd removed the last pins, she'd lifted her head from his shoulder to sit, her eyes closed, her head turned away from him.

He looked at her smooth neck and he knew he wouldn't be leaving anytime soon.

You've succeeded, she'd said, and he hadn't known how to explain, because he wasn't at all sure what had made him behave as he'd done. If he hadn't taken her in his arms, he might have made sense of it. But he'd lost control and kissed her and held her close. Then, every time he tried to leave, it was far too difficult, and it seemed as though leaving made no sense whatsoever.

He couldn't possibly think now. All the turbulence — the passion and anger and whatnot — seemed to be with them still, throbbing under the surface, and the turmoil kept his mind from clearing.

He held a beautiful woman in his arms, and she smelled so good and she was warm and shapely and he'd wanted her for what seemed an eternity and he'd undone her hair and it fell in glossy waves over her shoulders and down her back.

He wanted to see those garnet curls against her naked back.

He found the hook and eye at the back of the dress's neckline and began unfastening the dress. She took in a quick breath and let it out, but said nothing. She sat so very still, waiting.

He said nothing, either. He couldn't think well. The risk was too great of saying the wrong thing.

Concentrating on the hooks and eyes, he made his way down the back of the dress. He was aware of his breath coming faster as the dress's two sides slid apart, and he could see the beautiful stitchery of her stays, the lines and swirls of thread cording the satiny cotton. Her fine linen chemise peeped out between the corset's back lacing and at the very edge of the neckline.

He kissed the back of her neck above the necklace, then below it, and continued downward, making a path of soft kisses to the teasing bit of chemise.

He heard her draw in a breath and let it out, the exhale shaky.

He wasn't altogether steady, either, as he unfastened the two larger hooks at the back of her waist. The dress fell open, well below the waist where a long slit had lain hidden under a fold of the skirt. Even with the extended opening, getting the dress's upper half down was a complicated business, especially the sleeve puffs he needed to untie and extract. Yet he did it efficiently enough, considering that a man rarely took the time to deal with such details, or needed to. Experienced women found ways to arrange matters beforehand. More usually, one simply didn't bother with shedding much clothing.

This was different, though he couldn't have said why or how.

He simply made a plan, as he usually did. He had a general idea of how the parts went together. Moreover, he'd been studying her clothing and planning how to disassemble it this age.

He told her to stand, which she did without looking at him. He knelt and untied her shoe ribbons and slid her feet out of the shoes. He rose, taking the hem of her dress with him. He reached under the dress and untied the corded petticoat that kept it puffed out. He slid the petticoat down and away. He lifted the dress over her head and dropped it onto the floor, where it subsided with a faint hiss.

He said, "I've been wanting to do that forever."

She looked down at herself.

Layers remained. Corset, chemise, drawers, garters, stockings.

Then skin. The soft parts and pink parts.

He was growing very impatient.

He turned her so her back was to him, and reached under the chemise and untied her drawers. They slid to the floor. She closed her eyes and swallowed and stepped out of them.

His heart beat frantically, like a boy's heart, the first time.

He drew her close again and bent his head and kissed her neck along the arc of her shoulder. She trembled. He trembled, too, his pulse at a gallop, his hands not as steady as they ought to be as he started on the corset strings. The ties lay over the slope of her beautifully shaped bottom. For all the artificiality of her dress, her shape was real, sweetly curved.

Perfect.

Her scent floated everywhere now. Lavender and Leonie imbued her undergarments, the fragrance so much richer because they lay so close to her skin. His heart drummed, fast and uneven.

He wanted to go fast, too. He made himself unlace her corset as steadily and soberly as he'd undone her hair and her dress. He wasn't a boy but a man of the world, and he knew one didn't hurry women unless they made it clear they wanted to be hurried.

The corset was falling open, and her

hands came up, to hold it over her breasts. The gesture, so innocent, made his throat tighten.

He started kissing her back while he loosened the strings of her chemise. Still she held the corset, covering herself. He made paths of kisses along her upper arms, her naked arms, which he'd never seen before. He grasped them, his palms curving round warm, silky skin, while he kissed behind her ears, first one, then the other. She made a little sound, a laugh or a sob, he wasn't sure.

He covered her hands with his, and lifted hers away from the corset. It slid downward. When she reached for it, he brought his hands over her breasts. She gasped. The fine linen was warm with the warmth of her skin. He cupped her breasts and squeezed them and "Oh," she said.

He kissed her neck and her ears while he caressed her, and she let go of the stays, and let them fall. She was trembling again, her breath hitching.

If he had been thinking, he might have hesitated. He might have considered what her reactions meant. But he was beyond putting two and two together. The closest he came to thinking was pondering her clothing and skin and what he needed to do to get what he wanted. The difference between a girl of limited experience and a girl with none didn't occur to him.

He turned her around and kissed her full on the mouth, and wrapped his arms about her, and this time there was no indecision or doubt. The armor was gone and she was so soft and warm and perfectly shaped in his arms, his Venus. There was no more deciding what was right or wrong or best or worst.

Deep kisses made him drunk. Her skin was velvet under his hands. He pulled off the chemise and threw it aside. He cupped her breasts and kissed and suckled them. He caressed her belly, and slid his hand down, to the feathery copper curls between her legs. When he touched her there, she gasped.

He paused. "Am I hurting you?"

"No." She opened her eyes, so blue. "My stockings," she said, her voice thick.

The sound sent heat surging through him, threatening to blast the last particles of his self-control. He managed to say, "I want to leave them on."

She shivered. "And you?"

"I'll take off my coat."

She looked up at him, eyes wide and dark. "More," she said. She lifted her hands to

291

his neckcloth and clumsily untied it, her hands as unsteady as his. She unraveled it from his neck and let it drop to the floor. She hurriedly unbuttoned his waistcoat, then undid the button of his shirt. It fell open.

"There," she whispered. And she kissed him, at the base of his throat. And more kisses, moving lower, the way he'd done to her.

If he didn't act quickly, he'd disgrace himself.

He pushed her down onto the chaise longue.

He'd planned to take his time, but he'd done that, the endless time of undressing her, of caressing so gently, as though she were a bird he needed to tame. He'd reckoned without her voice and her eyes and her touch.

He shed the rest of his lower clothing — shoes, stockings, trousers — in a flurry, as though he hadn't a moment to lose, as though the bird would fly away. His shirt concealed his breeding parts, but not his arousal, and he was dimly aware of her drawing back slightly, her eyes wide.

If anything could have alerted him to the truth, that would have done it, but he was past that level of thinking.

He pulled the shirt over his head and threw it aside.

"Mon Dieu," she said.

The blood was pounding in his ears but he paused at that small, shocked sound. She was studying him, her wide-eyed gaze going up and down, lingering on his swollen cock.

Then she drew in a long breath and let it out, saying in French, her voice shaky, "You are very handsome. Come here." And she put her arms up and he went to the chaise longue and into them.

Leonie was terrified, but she wouldn't stop.

Marcelline hadn't explained a fraction of it: what a touch could do . . . the feel of his mouth on her skin . . . the shocking pleasure when he took her breasts in his hands and caressed them . . . and now, his long beautiful body arched over hers, his unruly curls tickling her chin as he showered kisses over her neck and downward . . . the shock of his lips closing over her nipples and suckling, and the way heat raced from there to the pit of her belly and made her squirm and arch her back and utter sounds she'd never made before.

There was no explaining this in words: the way one couldn't keep still, couldn't stop touching . . . the way she had to bury her face against his skin, because she couldn't get enough of the way he felt, the way he smelled, the way he tasted.

No one could explain the need, the force that carried one along, like a raging current.

No one needed to explain anymore.

He slid his hand down over her belly and downward, to the place between her legs where he'd touched her before. She'd known he would, but it had surprised her all the same. Now he moved downward altogether, and then his mouth was where his hands had been, and he was kissing her there. Her body arched and twisted, and he added his thumb, and the pleasure was beyond anything. It built and built until she couldn't bear it, yet she did, somehow, because she couldn't stop, and if he stopped she'd die.

Then she lost any sense of what he was doing, because her body had taken charge. She could feel her blood rushing in her veins and pounding in her head. Everything was vibrating, her legs, too, until all the feelings shot upward, like an explosion inside, and she let out a little shriek, and dug her fingers into him, to hold on, to keep from flying into the ceiling.

Then she felt him rise, and in the instant

she opened her eyes to see what he was doing, he pushed into her.

Ouch.

She'd known it would hurt, at least a little, but that was when she had a brain and now she hadn't, and she was surprised and unhappy and uncomfortable.

He said, "Dammit, Leonie."

She looked up at him. The godlike being was sweating like a mortal, and looking dazed and wild.

"I didn't know," he said. His voice was hoarse.

She could barely find hers. When she spoke it sounded like a drunkard's. "Didn't know what?"

"This is your first time, isn't it?" It was an accusation.

"I've been *busy*," she said.

One long, pulsing moment. Then he let out a thick laugh and shook his head, and bent and kissed her.

"It's pointless to stop now," she said when he raised his head.

"I'm not stopping," he said. "It's too damned late for that."

He settled back onto his haunches, and hooked her legs over his arms. She felt the place where he was wedged give way a degree, and the squeezed feeling eased. He moved inside her, and her muscles relaxed a little more. And soon the moment of disturbance passed. The feelings flooded back, and the heat and pleasure and excitement of having him inside her, of being joined, smothered qualms and fears.

He went on moving inside her, slowly, and her body gave way, accommodating him. The heat built, and she was vibrating again, the way she'd done before, only this was more feverish and powerful. He thrust into her again and again, and her body answered his rhythm. It was like dancing in a storm, like riding ocean waves. She forgot discomfort, forgot everything but him and this rapturous joining.

Once again, the feelings pulsed inside and seemed to carry her upward, as though some god carried her to Olympus. On and on, the mortal world hot and pulsing, and feelings, the great storm cloud of feelings, swirling about her and inside her. At last she reached her destination, a long, soaring moment of pure joy, and then release. Then he sank onto her and kissed her, and she drifted down to the world again, her hands tangled in his hair.

CHAPTER ELEVEN

There is a most scandalous story about a certain English Mr. H. at Paris, and two orphan children of a German baron by an English wife: we shall wait to hear if it has reached our correspondent's circle.

— *Lady's Magazine & Museum,*
March 1835

The chaise longue was narrow, not meant for two people. But when Lisburne moved to take his weight off Leonie, she turned in his arms and tangled her legs with his and fit herself against him as easily as though they'd practiced for years. Then they had room enough, all the room they needed, which was to say none at all between them, though he was no longer inside her.

He was cooling and calming, and a part of him was sliding into sleep, one hand resting so comfortably on her hip. Yet a fragment of his being clung to wakefulness. That was the part where his conscience was working itself into a frenzy — now, when it was too late, after it had lain about in a stupor during all the time when it might have made itself useful.

He said, "Are you all right?"

She had her face nestled against his shoulder, and the words came out slightly muffled. "Now I know why Venus wore that look. She was thinking, 'What just happened? Am I all right? How can he sleep at a time like this?' "

It wasn't remotely like any answer Lisburne had expected. Tears, shame, fear, guilt — weren't those the usual reactions?

He should have known better. This was Leonie, who'd stood motionless for at least a quarter hour in front of his painting. She'd done it because, he now understood, she had been trying to organize and arrange it in her mental ledger.

"He sleeps," he said, pushing aside his qualms for the moment, "because he feels as though he's performed all the labors of Hercules in the space of a few minutes. In the most enjoyable way possible. But still . . ."

"It takes a lot out of a man," she said. "I understand that now."

Now she understood. Thanks to him.

Other men, he knew, delighted in virgins and paid high prices for them. Those men were not Simon Blair, the fourth Marquess of Lisburne. His father had told him that a true gentleman had intimate relations with only one virgin, and that was his bride, on the wedding night.

Lisburne had only himself to blame for what had happened. Leonie was a novice. No matter how sophisticated she seemed, she was inexperienced. Lisburne, who had abundant experience, was the one responsible. He ought to have known better. He ought to have seen. But he'd been willfully blind.

Now, when it was too late, he remembered the clues: the tentative way she'd first kissed him, the sense he'd had of her learning as she went along. Gad, hadn't she told him?

I may be inexperienced but I learn very quickly, and whatever I learn to do, I am determined to do extremely *well.*

Inexperienced. He'd made the word mean what he wanted it to mean. He'd barely acknowledged the possibility she was an innocent. He'd dismissed it as highly improbable. She was one and twenty. She was a milliner who'd lived in Paris. She was sophisticated, and it was a deeper sophistication than the mere Town bronze debutantes acquired after a Season or two.

Yes, that made virginity unlikely. It didn't make it impossible.

His intellect, in whose logic he took so much pride, must have logically allowed for the possibility. But he'd let desire and vanity overwhelm his judgment. He'd refused to see the clues.

"You've labored mightily, yet you're not going to sleep," she said.

"I'm thinking," he said.

He felt her tense.

"That you made a mistake?" she said.

"That I did something I know is wrong," he said.

"Oh, your *conscience*," she said.

"My dear —"

"I don't have one," she said. "I only understand them theoretically. I don't have morals, either. I'm not a lady."

"It doesn't matter. This was your first time."

"My first time would have happened a long time ago, if I'd had more time — or made more time — for men," she said. "If it hadn't been you, it would have been somebody else, eventually. I wanted it to be you. I knew you'd make it pleasurable, and you did. It was . . . very nice. I can almost forgive you for ruining my life."

300

He kissed her shoulder again. "I thought it was more than very nice."

"I have no basis for comparison," she said.

"I don't, either."

Her head came up and she drew back to give him a hard stare.

"You're my first maiden," he said, and in spite of his unhappiness with himself, he couldn't help enjoying the view of lush curves and the creamy skin that made a perfect frame for her hair. Titian would have swooned. Botticelli, too.

"Are you roasting me?" she said. "Not even when you were a boy?"

Except within the close bounds of his family, he disliked talking about his father. Even now, the sense of loss made it difficult to speak. Time had lessened the sorrow. It hadn't erased it. No one but close family members understood how it was.

Yet he came up onto one elbow, like some ancient Roman settling to dinner conversation, and explained. The rules. What a gentleman did and didn't do. The whys and wherefores. She listened, her blue eyes sharply focused, completely attentive. She was thinking it over and organizing it into neat files and marking it down in the columns of her private account book, he knew.

He felt *more* naked.

When he'd finished, she brought her hand to his cheek. He turned his head to kiss the palm of her hand.

She swallowed and said, "Not the clearest judgment either of us has ever exercised," she said. "But to be fair, Lord Lisburne —"

"Simon," he said. "I think when two people are naked, sharing a narrow piece of furniture, a degree of informality is permissible."

She shook her head. "I'm not ready for informality. I'm not sure I'll ever be ready. I think you should call me Miss Noirot when we're naked. Especially when we're naked. At a time like this, when . . ." She trailed off, her gaze turning inward, her eyes widening. "Oh, Gemini, what have I done?"

She was off the chaise longue in an instant, and hurrying away while he was still trying to find his balance and sit up. She scurried across the room, one of her stockings sliding down her leg. "What time is it? What have I done?"

"Leonie."

She scrambled among the discarded clothing on the floor and various other surfaces where odds and ends of their attire had landed. She found her lacy handkerchief and hastily cleaned herself with it. She snatched up her chemise and pulled it on.

"How could I be so stupid?"

"Leonie, there's no need to —"

"You'd better go." She disappeared behind a curtain — a dressing room, it seemed to be.

"I most certainly won't," he said. "I expected tears. And hysteria. But I expected that sooner. You said —"

He broke off as she burst through the curtain, now wearing a nearly transparent, completely obscene dressing gown over a chemise made of mist. "Of course I'm hysterical!" she said. "Tonight, of all nights, I forgot about Tom!"

She ran out of the room.

It took Lisburne a moment to find his shirt and throw it on. He was confused and alarmed, but preserved sufficient presence of mind to avoid shocking any innocent maidservants lurking about the place.

The thought of servants gave him pause. Gossip . . . yet more scandal spreading about Leonie and about her shop . . .

And if she bore a child . . .

A child, a child. Leonie carrying his child.

No, no, he wouldn't think of that now. He'd enough to deal with at the present moment. One problem at a time, and right now, her panic was paramount.

Since she hadn't closed the door behind her, he caught the muted sound of stockinged feet on the stairs. He hurried out of the room, looked down the stairwell then up. He caught a glimpse of the filmy dressing gown.

When he reached the passage on the second floor, he saw light spilling from the doorway of the sitting room. He found her there, placing foolscap and an inkstand on the table where they'd supped.

"I cannot believe that Tom — whoever he is — will expire of grief if you fail to write a love letter this night," he said.

"Don't be ridiculous," she said. "Who has time for love letters? It's business, my lord —"

"Simon."

"It's business, *mon cher monsieur.*"

"Very well, I'll accept *my dear sir,*" he said, "because you say it precisely like a Parisian."

"I grew up mainly in Paris," she said. "Being the youngest, I spent the greatest percentage of my life there. Please don't make me think about anything else. This is hard enough as it is. Maybe you ought to go home. Or . . ." She sank into a chair and stared at the sheet of paper. "Or maybe you would fill a large glass of brandy for me. I hate this!"

He moved to the table and looked down at the empty page.

She looked up at him. "Have you any notion how difficult it is for a girl to think when a nearly naked man looms over her?"

It was hard to think while looming over a nearly naked woman who smelled and tasted and felt delicious. What he wanted to do was sweep the paper and inkstand and everything else from the table and lift her onto it, and teach her some new things.

He said, "What do you need to think about at this time of night? Midnight came and went ages ago."

"I know! And he must have it before five o'clock, if I hope to have any chance of its being inserted."

"Madame, what, pray, are you talking about?"

She looked up at him. "Tom Foxe. The *Spectacle.* If I don't send in my report about Vauxhall, the world will read only what the other correspondents have contributed, and they're sure to make the shop and the Milliners' Society look like swindlers and degenerates. But I don't have the knack. Sophy has the knack. But she's — she isn't here!"

He drew a chair close to hers and sat down. He took the pen from her and replaced it on the inkstand. He took both her hands in his. "Here's what we're going to do," he said. "You're going to take a moment to calm yourself. Then you'll explain your problem to me in your usual orderly fashion. Then I'll bring you drink or try to help or do whatever seems the most useful thing to do."

Leonie looked at their joined hands and told herself this was most unwise. She couldn't confide in him merely because they'd had an extremely intimate interlude. She didn't want to see him as someone she could turn to when she was in difficulties, because once he was gone, she would miss him all the more. Only look at the wreck she was without her sisters!

But she was in a great difficulty, and sometimes simply explaining a problem helped one discern the solution.

And he was practically naked. And the way the light fell on him made him look like a golden god, and he was holding her hands and it was very hard to be wise.

She explained that Maison Noirot was one of the *Spectacle*'s several Anonymous Correspondents. "Mainly we report what our customers wear to such and such an occasion. Tom combines that with whatever his gossip sources tell him happened at the event, to make as lively a story as possible. But Sophy had her own gossip sources, and she'd combine the stories and the clothes descriptions so beautifully to draw attention to our shop."

Leonie paused. The world must never discover that Sophy visited these fashionable social gatherings in disguise, in order to spy on the beau monde and report what everybody did and said. She passed on to Tom Foxe exclusive gossip in exchange for prime real estate in his immensely popular scandal sheet. "Sophy would find a way to turn tonight's fiasco to our advantage, or to make people think twice."

"The way Gladys did?" Lisburne said.

She looked up. She could see *everything* through his shirt. It didn't matter that she'd seen paintings, engravings, and sculptures of naked men. None of those images had made her blush from the top of her head all the way down to her toes.

"Gladys?" she said, and tried to remember who that was.

"The way she deflected her listeners from Swanton without obviously doing so," he said. "She talked of Vauxhall attracting odd sorts, then obliged her listeners to turn their minds to pinning down the Ariel's identity.

Once she had their attention on his story, she went on to tell it. An interesting way of defending Swanton without seeming to be defending him. Instead of saying, 'I don't believe it' or 'It can't be true' as some of the besotted girls would do, she used a diversionary tactic."

In spite of an extreme level of anxiety, Leonie smiled. She'd briefly referred to military strategy and the general's daughter had taken hold of the idea brilliantly. Her ladyship had realized she didn't need a complete metamorphosis. She'd discerned the way to make the most of her "good parts," and to turn the less appealing aspects of her personality into assets. She was no longer at the mercy of the Lady Aldas of the world.

"I should describe Lady Gladys's dress," she said. "I should give it the most words, because it was splendid and because lately everybody's curious about what she's wearing."

"We could say she was 'overheard to mention' the strange sorts who appear at Vauxhall," Lisburne said. "Then we could say we're awaiting further information from correspondents. That way, the scene everyone witnessed would appear to be a mystery needing solving, instead of a foregone conclusion."

This sounded like something Sophy would do, though she tended to enhance the drama. Leonie nodded slowly. "That's . . . very good."

He released her hands.

She took up the pen. She stared at the paper.

He said, "Perhaps I could write it under your supervision. You provide the clothing details, and I tell the story. Or shall I dictate my part and you do the writing?"

She looked up at him. "I notice that you've offered two choices, both of which mean you're involved."

"The sooner we get this done," he said, his voice deepening and darkening, "the sooner we can attend to less *mentally* strenuous matters."

She put down the pen. "I'll get the brandy," she said.

With Lisburne assisting, the task took a fraction of the time it would have done otherwise, with results superior to anything Leonie could have produced on her own. This she easily admitted. She was good with numbers, not the written word.

In about half an hour he'd dictated a clever, rather amusing piece, which included three gossip items Leonie hadn't heard. He even polished her descriptions of the Maison Noirot dresses. He had a way with adjectives she hadn't. But best of all was the part about Lady Gladys. Considering how much he seemed to dislike the lady, he described her ensemble as well as her comments with generosity and gentleness. He was almost lyrical.

But then, he was trying to save Lord Swanton, and Leonie understood how Lisburne felt. She would gladly sacrifice personal feelings to rescue her sisters or niece.

The brandy they consumed during the writing assignment made personal sacrifices less painful. Too, it forced Leonie to slow her pace as she hurried down the stairs with the precious news item.

She wasn't drunk, exactly. It would take more than a few glasses of wine and a glass of brandy. Still, the world had grown softer around the edges, and her balance wasn't perfect. Warm though it was, the night air that rushed in when she opened the rear door sent her reeling backward a pace. She quickly recovered, placed the message in the box where Tom's messenger would pick it up, and stepped back into the house.

She had closed and barred the door and was turning toward the stairs when she saw

Lisburne's hat. It lay on the floor near the table he'd aimed it at. She picked it up, and brushed it with her hand. She started to set it down on the table. She changed her mind and put it on her head.

She became aware of movement on the floor above. She remembered then that he didn't live here, and would be going home. Of course he would be getting dressed. She debated whether to return the hat to the table. But it was too large for her, and that made her smile, and it smelled like Lisburne, and she wasn't quite ready to let go of him or anything to do with him.

She took her time climbing the stairs, making the pleasurable feelings last as long as possible. When she reached the top of the stairs, she paused to prepare herself for the goodbye, much in the way she might prepare herself to face a difficult customer, or to step out onto a stage in front of half the ton and ask them for money.

She walked to the sitting room. And stopped in the doorway.

Evidently the sounds she'd heard had been Lisburne collecting their clothing from the consulting room on the first floor. He was in the process of sorting their garments into piles of his and hers. He looked up from his work and stared at her.

She lifted her chin and straightened her shoulders and folded her hands at her waist and gave him a devastating DeLucey smile.

He threw down the waistcoat in his hand and said, "I was going to do the sensible thing and go home, but I must have been insane to think I could be sensible when you were about. *Cherie,* I think you're drunk."

"Certainly not," she said.

"You have almost no clothes on and you're wearing my hat," he said. "What do you call that?"

She'd forgotten about the hat. How could she forget the hat? There it was on her head.

"Never mind what you call it," he said. "I call it fetching. Come here."

He held out his arms. This time she didn't argue. She walked straight into them, her heart soaring.

Under cover of night, Lisburne had told himself, he might leave by the back way, sneak out of the court and through the passage out into the street. He'd leave undetected except perhaps by any servants who hadn't slept through the recent tumult.

Anyone who spied him in St. James's Street at that hour would probably not recognize him as more than one of the

312

gentlemen making their way to or from Crockford's Club or any other of the numerous gaming establishments in the neighborhood.

Leaving well before dawn was the wisest course. After that, the fashionable types would be returning from their engagements. In daylight, they'd easily identify him and notice his rare state of dishevelment. They wouldn't need any more clues to decide where he'd been and what he'd been doing there.

Then Leonie appeared in the doorway, wearing the dazzling smile and his hat and not very much else, and that was the end of being sensible.

She walked into his arms and he closed them about her and held her tight, knocking the hat askew. Once he'd inhaled his fill for the moment, and savored the warmth and softness of perfectly curved body, he drew back and tried to recover his wiser self. But the hat had tipped over one blue eye and she wore such a naughty, teasing smile as she looked up at him.

He picked her up and carried her to the table and set her down there, one arm wrapped about her while with the other he swept the table clear of paper and pens and pencils and inkstand.

Paper flew hither and yon and bottles crashed and he didn't care. He was pushing the hat off her head and kissing her forehead, her nose, her cheeks, her lips. He was kissing her neck and tugging at the dressing gown ribbons. She covered his hands with hers and pulled his away from the ribbons. Swiftly she untied them while he dragged his mouth back to hers, and lost himself in the taste of her mouth and the scent of her skin, while he pushed away her flimsy garments and captured her beautiful breasts. They fit his hands perfectly, the way her mouth fit his perfectly, and the way her kisses answered his with the same teasing and beckoning, tongues coiling in a sinful dance to which only they knew the movements.

She caught hold of his shirt and dragged it up and splayed her hands over his chest, then dragged them down over his belly and hips. She caressed him in the easy way of one who knew what was hers and wasn't shy about enjoying it. The confident touch of her hands was like the touch of a candle flame to a pile of straw.

She let her fingers slide to his erection, her touch tentative and curious. He reached for her hand to hold her there and to show her how to curl her fingers around him more firmly. She said, "You like that?"

His heart pumped like an over-fueled steam engine, thunderously pushing blood through his veins.

He'd made a mistake, underestimated what she could do to him.

"Yes," his voice was a mangled whisper.

"Show me," she said.

"Later," he gritted out. He was holding on to his control by the thinnest of threads. "I like it too much." He moved her hand away and thrust into her, and she let out a little cry.

His head was pounding, and everything in him wanted to explode, but he paused.

"No, don't stop," she said breathlessly. "It's *very nice.*"

Very nice.

In spite of himself he let out a choked laugh. "Leonie," he said.

"Miss Noirot, if you please, my lord. Or madame."

"Madame," he said. He raised her legs in the way she'd found more comfortable before, and it was a wonder he could think of that, a wonder he could remember anything. Yet somehow he did, even while he pushed into her, and his body found a rhythm with hers. This time she was surer — *I learn quickly,* she'd said — and she lifted

315

herself up onto her elbows and shifted her body to move with him and take him deeper.

She was beautiful, her blue eyes half closed, a half smile curving her lips. She'd learned quickly, as she said, and she was sure of herself and sure of him. The instinctive motion, the quick understanding, the sureness of her — it made him ache and it made him wild and witless and carried him past any thought. What remained was a mad, mad need and his senses' messages: the scent and softness of her . . . the way it felt to be inside her . . . the way it felt to move inside her, to feel her muscles tighten about him in this most intimate of all lovers' games.

Intimate as it was, he needed to be closer still. He bent toward her, and she arched up and kissed him boldly and flung her arms about him. She held him as the rhythm of their joining took them to a pulsing crescendo. She held him as the heat of coupling gave way to piercing happiness. And still she held him, while the world slid into darkness.

When Leonie recovered — to the extent she'd ever recover — the first thing she was aware of was his breathing, deep and steady. He'd slumped into a chair and his head rested on her thigh. She trailed her fingers through his hair. Some sound from outside made her look up, and that was when she noticed the change in the light. Her gaze went to the window, and the rectangle showed the darkness fading, promising dawn.

It took her lust-damaged brain time to work out what this meant, beyond morning's swift approach. Then the busy moments before the debauchery on the sitting room table flooded back into her mind. Tom. The article for the *Spectacle.*

What time was it?

She had no idea where her watch was, but the insufficiently dark window told enough of a tale. She gave Lisburne a little shake. And when he grumbled and turned his head the other way, she shook him again.

He lifted his head. "What?" Then he seemed to realize where he was because he turned to kiss her thigh. Her entire being seemed to liquefy. But she heard sounds outside, not so much of London waking up as of one part of London heading for bed: the sound of carriages.

"Wake up," she said. "The sun will be up soon, and you can't be here."

" 'It is not yet near day,' " he murmured, kissing her thigh again. " 'It was the nightingale, and not the lark.' "

"I wasn't talking about nightingales," she said.

" 'It was the nightingale, and not the lark,/ That pierced the fearful hollow of thine ear,' " he said. He kissed her knee. *"Romeo and Juliet."*

She'd seen the play, more than once. Yet she remembered only snatches of phrases. She was more familiar with the ancient Greeks and Romans, whose stories she'd read in French and English.

"I'm sure it's beautiful," she said, "but Shakespeare speaks a version of English I find difficult to understand."

"I'll teach you," he said softly.

"No, you will not. We haven't time. You must go away, now — before the *Spectacle*'s messenger arrives. They're supposed to print the gossip we write for them, not discover and write their own about us."

He sat back fully then, and shook his head. He raked his fingers through his hair, and somehow managed to make himself even more attractive than before.

But that was all in her head. She couldn't see him in any other way but beautiful and desirable; witless, hopeless she!

To resist temptation, she slid down from the table. "You must make haste," she said, turning her gaze to the window. The rectangle had grown a shade lighter than a moment ago.

This was awful. She didn't want him to go. No one had explained about the way one felt after so deep an intimacy. No one had told her she'd wish to keep him by her, or how a bleak place opened in her heart at the idea of his leaving, and everything being over . . .

She knew about consequences, and she'd worry about that later, no doubt, but at this moment, the consequence was the ache of separation.

Romeo and Juliet . . . the scene he'd quoted from . . . now that she knew where the words came from, she remembered the scene, when Juliet had tried to persuade Romeo it wasn't morning yet. Now Leonie understood why Juliet couldn't be sensible, and let her lover go.

It was silly, she knew. Men wanted One Thing, and once they got it, they left.

She knew this. She knew women were the ones who had to deal with the consequences.

It made no difference.

She didn't want him to go.

She made shooing motions. "Make haste, make haste!" she said. "I hear carriages, and in a few minutes the light will be —"

"I know," he said.

He rose, and not ten minutes later, he'd made himself something like presentable, and then he was gone.

Later, at Lisburne House

Lisburne was starting up the stairs to his bedroom when he heard Swanton come in.

Only then did Lisburne remember he'd left his cousin to find his own way home from Vauxhall.

Lisburne paused while he tried to decide what to say.

"There you are," Swanton said. "No one seemed to know where you'd got to, but they didn't know where Madame was, either, so I assume you looked after her?"

"Yes."

"How ghastly for her!" Swanton started up the stairs after him.

Lisburne continued upward. "It was," he said. "Though I might have reduced the damage somewhat. But you? Did you find Gladys?"

Swanton said nothing.

Lisburne looked at him. The poet's face was scarlet.

"She was not as friendly and forgiving as you'd hoped?" Lisburne said.

"I couldn't find her," Swanton said. "Now and again I heard her voice — but so faint and faraway, I might have missed it altogether were it not so distinctive. I'm certain I heard it among some of our acquaintance who were dancing. But I couldn't find her. All the world was dancing, it seemed, and —" He broke off, brows knitting. "I believe she isn't as tall as Clara?"

"Not many women are as tall as Clara," Lisburne said. He thought Gladys broad enough not to be missed in a crowd. On the other hand, she seemed to have lost weight. Either that or her new garb made her seem a degree slimmer. Still, it was only a degree. One could never call her slender.

"In any event, it was impossible to be quite sure which one she was, and after what had happened this night, I hesitated to accost any woman without knowing for certain it was the right woman." Swanton rubbed his forehead. "And perhaps I had second thoughts about accosting her. And so . . ." He paused, his color deepening. "I occupied myself with listening for her voice, and by and by Crawford stopped to talk. Said the whole scene with the woman was ludicrous. No one would believe it of me. Then Hempton turned up, and *he* said people will believe anything scandalous.

They argued about it, naturally. I vow, they're never happy but when they're contradicting each other, because that's an excuse to bet on who's right and who's wrong. Then I lost track of the beautiful voice, and couldn't find it again. I reckon your cousins left Vauxhall while Crawford and Hempton were bickering, because the next time I saw Bates and Flinton, the ladies weren't with them. That is to say, they were with other women, and . . . well, it would have been embarrassing to ask about your cousins."

"They would have roasted you fearfully, I daresay," Lisburne said.

They'd reached the top of the stairs, and he felt a hundred years old. It was so unfair that Swanton, so sensitive, should be placed in this humiliating position. Had an unknown woman accused any other man of fathering and abandoning a child, the Great World would have shrugged. But the world loved to topple an idol. In Swanton's case, the ton would break him into pieces, and drag the fragments through the mud.

But worst of all — because Swanton would survive this, and recover eventually — was the damage to Leonie. And her girls. And her shop.

Still, it was no good brooding about that,

any more than it made sense for Lisburne to brood over his own breach of honor. Or the fact that he wasn't as upset about it as he ought to be. He'd wronged her, and yet . . .

He was happy. Her image floated in his mind — nearly naked, wearing his hat — and though he could suppress the smile, he couldn't squelch the gladness.

In any event, he and Leonie had done what they could to moderate the scandal. Gladys had done her part, too, whether intentionally or not.

There was nothing more he could do at present — nothing intelligent, certainly, until he'd had a good night's sleep.

"Get some sleep," he told Swanton. "We'll all do better for it."

CHAPTER TWELVE

Ros. There is none of my uncle's marks
upon you: he taught me how to know a
man in love; in which cage of rushes, I
am sure, you are not prisoner.
Orl. What were his marks?
Ros. A lean cheek; which you have not: a
blue eye, and sunken; which you have
not . . . Then your hose should be
ungarter'd, your bonnet unbanded, your
sleeve unbuttoned, your shoe untied,
and every thing about you demonstrating a careless desolation.

As You Like It, Act III, Scene II

Tuesday 21 July

Lisburne tried to sleep, but that didn't go
as well as it ought, considering how weary
he'd been when he fell into bed. He tossed
and turned and now and again came full
awake in a sort of frenzy, certain that alarm
bells had gone off or the roof was falling in,

and he had to run and warn people and Do Something.

Though he gave up hoping for sleep by the time the sun had climbed a short distance from the horizon, he remained in bed. Arms folded under his head while he stared at the canopy, he relived his time with Leonie, especially the last few hours of that time.

Eventually he heard Polcaire creep in as he always did, to make all ready before his master thought of stirring. This morning the master stirred, to the valet's annoyance. He wasn't any happier when the master bathed, shaved, and dressed with indecent haste, and went down to breakfast.

Swanton was eating. *Foxe's Morning Spectacle* lay folded for easy reading at the edge of his plate.

"The news can't be completely ghastly, if you still have an appetite," Lisburne said.

"I'm hoping to find a clue to the truth," Swanton said. "A name, a word I might have missed — something, anything, that might rouse dormant memories. I'm pretending the *Spectacle* talks about somebody else. It might as well, since Foxe has included three conflicting reports. The most intelligible one deals in exhausting detail with what everybody wore." A pause. "Especially what your cousin Lady Gladys wore. And what she said. In this article, she gets more column inches than Lady Clara." He looked up at Lisburne. "I did wonder whether you'd written the piece, but then I couldn't picture you rhapsodizing about your lady cousins, even Lady Clara, whom everybody seems to agree is the most beautiful woman in London. Falling into raptures about a woman isn't your style. I'm not sure I've ever seen you fall into raptures about anything. And what do you know about women's clothes, beyond the quickest way to get them off?"

It was true that Lisburne wasn't inclined to be poetical about women. He hadn't done so since he was a schoolboy in the throes of his first infatuation.

Yet he'd quoted Shakespeare to Leonie — from a lovers' scene in *Romeo and Juliet,* no less.

Not that Swanton needed to know that.

"You aren't even attentive to your own clothes," Swanton said.

Lisburne looked down at himself and frowned.

A scene from *As You Like It* rose in his mind's eye: Rosalind describing how to recognize a man in love.

Then your hose should be ungarter'd . . .
your sleeve unbuttoned, your shoe untied,
and every thing about you demonstrating
a careless desolation.

But that was drama and poetry — Swanton's line — and Lisburne was *not* in love. He'd simply been too tired and irritated to want to spend the usual eternity dressing.

Swanton was saying, newspaper in hand, "You always leave your appearance to Polcaire. Maybe he can translate this for us. 'Sleeves with double bouffans and lace sabot'? 'Corsage half high mounting'? Have you the least notion what any of this means?"

Lisburne shook his head and moved to the sideboard. He stared at the covered dishes for a time before he realized his mind wasn't on food. It held only Leonie. Wearing his hat and some bits of gossamer. Wearing nothing but the half smile . . . caressing him . . . sure of him . . .

Very well. He liked her excessively. He lusted for her, perhaps more than was entirely comfortable. But he wasn't *in love.* He was aware such a thing existed. His parents had been deeply in love. But they were exceptions, from all he'd seen.

"I see you're as stumped as I am," Swanton said. "I suppose the word is meant to be *bouffant,* but I'm at sea as to where this bouffant is on the sleeve and how it's doubled — vertically or horizontally — and how this is accomplished."

"I'll ask Madame when I speak to her," Lisburne said. "*If* she'll speak to me."

"Did you not part on good terms last night?"

Before Lisburne's weary brain could compose a discreet reply, Swanton fell back in his chair and smote his forehead precisely in the way a poet ought to do. "But how stupid of me! How could you part on good terms, after what's happened? And there was I, looking like the most thoroughgoing idiot when she asked me about the child. Did you see her expression when she asked me if I was claiming amnesia? By gad, a man ought at least have an inkling as to whether he's fathered a child! I was too agitated to examine the little girl — but had she the look of me, do you think?"

"From the little I could see, she had the look of you and thousands of other Englishmen," Lisburne said.

He threw food on his plate without heeding what it was, and returned to his place and sat down. He ate because food was necessary to sustain a man, and he needed sustenance because he had a great deal to do today. He couldn't afford to be romantically languishing, caring nothing for such banal matters as food. He wasn't a poet. Let Swanton keep his head in the clouds. Lisburne was the one with his feet on the ground.

They ate in silence, Swanton poring over the *Spectacle* as though he were an antiquarian perusing a scroll newly dug from the ashes of Pompeii.

By the time they finished breakfast, Lisburne had decided what to do. One decision was to tell Swanton as little as possible. Another was to pay a visit to Maison Noirot, though he wasn't sure what he'd do or say when he got there.

He made the mistake of mentioning the projected Maison Noirot visit to Swanton. Then he had to spend an irritating amount of time convincing his poetic cousin of the likelihood of disastrous results, should he come along.

"But Lady Gladys might be there," Swanton said.

"If you want to see her so badly, go to Warford House," Lisburne said. "It's absurd to hope for a chance encounter at Maison Noirot. How often do you imagine women visit their dressmakers? Even the vainest don't make it a daily exercise."

"The family isn't at home on Tuesdays," Swanton said.

Lisburne stared at him.

Swanton's ears and neck became tinged with red. "I overheard somebody say something about calling there today, and somebody else said the family doesn't receive visitors on Tuesdays," he said. "Not that they'd receive me, in any event. You can't suppose I'd want to show my face to Lady Warford the day after I've been exposed as a debaucher of innocent young women and a getter of bastards whom I deny and abandon."

"Then I recommend you loiter in Hyde Park during the promenade hours," Lisburne said. "When Gladys drives by, run out into the road, pretending to be in some sort of poetic agony. But do give her time to stop the carriage, unless you'd like to be trampled and die with a stain, possibly undeserved, on your escutcheon."

Swanton gave him a piercing look. "You're strangely whimsical today."

"I'm obliged to exercise my imagination," Lisburne said, "since yours seems to have deserted you at Vauxhall. I can't believe I need to tell a man of five and twenty how to further his acquaintance with a girl. I can't believe you resort to skulking about pleasure gardens eavesdropping. I don't understand why you can't approach her in a straightforward manner."

He left the room and went upstairs, where a greatly relieved Polcaire put his unsentimental and not-at-all-in-love master into proper attire.

Maison Noirot
Later that afternoon

"We'll have to send for Sophy," Marcelline was saying. "The piece in the *Spectacle* was so clever. I know how much you dislike that sort of thing. Yet you did a fine job, and I'm sure it smoothed matters quite a bit. Unfortunately, 'quite a bit' is insufficient. Clevedon and I have talked until we're blue in the face, and neither of us knows how to do it as it needs to be done. We need Sophy."

"The fact is, no one knows how Sophy does it," the Duke of Clevedon said.

The three stood in the showroom, which was empty of customers. A paucity of clients wasn't unusual at this time of day, when the ladies were at home, dressing for the promenade or resting before dressing for the evening. However, the ladies had kept away all day. Even Lady Clara had sent a note apologizing for not coming to show her support — but her mama had not thought it advisable for her to visit the shop quite yet. Lady Gladys, according to the note, had made a brilliant argument in favor of the shop, but as everybody knew, it was nigh impossible to get round Clara's mama once she'd made up her mind. Only Sophy could do that, and Sophy wasn't here.

"We can't bring her back," Leonie said. "It's too soon. People will recognize her, especially now, when we'll all be under extra scrutiny."

"That nitwit Swanton," Clevedon said. "I should like to tear his head straight off his neck. I'm not the only one. Don't delude yourself, Leonie. When Longmore gets wind of this — which he's bound to do in a matter of days, if not hours — he'll race back to London to break Swanton into pieces. And Lisburne as well, for not keeping his flighty cousin under proper restraint."

"I don't understand why people expect Lord Lisburne to control his cousin," Leonie said. "Lord Swanton is a grown man. And I daresay he was man enough five years ago, in Paris."

Fortunately or unfortunately, she'd had direct experience of what Swanton might or might not have done with the woman in black. Though her hair was red, her coloring wasn't a typical redhead's. Leonie lacked freckles and the tendency to easy blushing. Yet she felt hot, and she was aware of a tingling in a place below her waist that didn't normally tingle.

"It's no good playing propriety with us, *chéri,*" Marcelline said to her husband. "We all know what you were doing in Paris, only six months ago. Englishmen go there to debauch."

"That isn't the point," Clevedon said. "The point is, everybody knows Swanton is a dreamer. He needs minding. Lisburne, of all others, knows this."

"I do not see why Lord Lisburne's life must always revolve around Lord Swanton's," Leonie said. "It's one thing to look after a younger, weaker cousin when they're boys at school. But Swanton is quite old enough to look after himself. Or if this is beyond him, he ought to hire a bodyguard."

Marcelline looked at her.

Later, Leonie mouthed.

She always told Marcelline everything. But she hadn't had time to share the momentous news. Marcelline had come with Clevedon. While Leonie liked and respected him, she was not about to confide in her sister while Clevedon was present. Not only present but furious with Lord Lisburne and his impractical cousin.

"This would not be a problem," Clevedon said, "if the three of you weren't directly involved with the shop at present. If you were ordinary dressmakers, no one would blink. But you're not ordinary dressmakers anymore —"

"We never were," said his wife. "*Ordinary,* indeed! I cannot believe you said that."

"You're a duchess," he said. "Sophy's a countess. No one cares what dressmakers do. Everybody minds what duchesses and countesses do. Great Zeus, Marcelline, you were presented to the Queen! Can you not understand the implications? You may care nothing for Society —"

"What nonsense. I care everything for it. Society is my clientele."

"Those people form your *social acquaintance,*" he said. "It's too ludicrous, your hosting a dinner for ladies you must wait on the next day in the shop."

Leonie had no doubt this quarrel had been going on for some time. Initially, Clevedon had let Marcelline go her way without interference, because he appreciated her passion for her work. He understood that she was an artist, and her work was part of who she was. Too, he couldn't see how to stop her. That would demand extreme measures, like violence or confinement, and he wasn't that kind of man.

But now she was pregnant, and the pregnancy had made her ill, and he worried.

The plain fact was, he was right, in all the essentials. Logic told Leonie that the present state of affairs couldn't continue and oughtn't to. A duchess had responsibilities, and the social responsibilities mattered. Great hostesses wielded political as well as social power. Marcelline had the potential to be a great hostess. She had all the DeLucey and Noirot charm. She was clever. She could do more good as a duchess than as a dressmaker.

But she would be wretched if she couldn't design clothes. She was an artist. She needed her art.

Logic had not yet shown Leonie how to resolve the conflict.

"Most certainly we need to talk about that," she said. "But at present it would be more productive to deal with the immediate problem. Why don't we adjourn to my office? It's no use hanging about here, waiting for nobody to come in."

The shop bell tinkled. All three heads turned toward the door.

Lord Lisburne sauntered in.

■ ■ ■ ■

"Lisburne."

"Clevedon."

An exchange of cool nods.

Lisburne's heart might be going faster than it needed to, but that had more to do with anticipation regarding Leonie than with any fear of Clevedon. Lisburne wasn't afraid of any man, even this one, who was as large and strong as he was, and who seemed larger still, because he was almost visibly swelling with anger.

Lisburne made himself larger, too.

"Come to buy some dresses?" Clevedon said. "Because nobody else has."

Lisburne looked at Leonie, who did not seem overjoyed to see him.

"Not one customer, all day," she said.

He'd supposed it would be bad. He hadn't guessed it would be this bad.

"Have you any idea what my wife and her sisters have been through in the last few months, while you and Swanton idled abroad?" Clevedon said. "While your cousin was in Venice, murdering the English language —"

"I shouldn't call it murder," Lisburne said. "Flesh wounds, no more. You give him

336

too much credit. And it was in Florence, not Venice, that he composed his latest batch of verse. In a pretty house overlooking the Arno."

"You'd be well advised not to provoke a man whose wife is in the family way," Clevedon said, growing bigger yet. "Her Grace is ill enough without the intolerable anxiety of losing everything she and her sisters have worked for. All because Swanton is — what? Too delicate to remember whether or not he seduced a young Englishwoman in Paris? Too busy dallying with the muse to respond to requests for help from his child's mother? By gad, Lisburne, *you* know what's owing in these cases, even if his mind is in the clouds. How the devil could you let it come to this?"

"Clevedon, do try to be rational," Leonie said. "Swanton isn't a child. Why do you blame Lisburne for his cousin's errors?"

"As easily as I should blame Longmore if one of his brothers behaved so stupidly," Clevedon said. "These two have been the same as brothers since they were children. And Lisburne has sufficient intelligence to defend himself without your leaping to his aid. I know all the women swoon over him, and think he can do no wrong, but you at least I should have thought had more sense

337

than to be taken in by a pretty face."

"I never knew you to be so pompously wrong-headed," Leonie said. "Marcelline's only pregnant, not in the last stages of a galloping consumption. And if she weren't so nauseated at the moment —"

"I'm bored, not nauseated," the duchess said.

"Is my face pretty?" Lisburne said. "I'm glad to know somebody thinks so, even if it's only Clevedon."

"Don't be provoking," Leonie said.

"But my dear —"

"Your *dear*?" Clevedon said. "Your dear *what*?" His green gaze went from Lisburne to Leonie. She colored a very little. "Damn you to hell, Lisburne! You've debauched my sister!"

He lunged at Lisburne, who pushed back. In the next instant they were at each other's throats. They fell over a chair and crashed to the floor, bent on murder.

"Stop it!"

"Not in the shop!"

"Get up! Stop it!"

The men heard nothing. They went on trying to throttle each other, first one then the other gaining the advantage.

The seamstresses heard, though.

338

At the sounds of battle, they rushed into the showroom, along with Selina Jeffreys, who tried in vain to herd them back to the workroom.

They arrived as the men scrambled to their feet and started throwing punches in earnest.

They were well matched, and excellent boxers, and Leonie liked a good fight as well as the next blood-thirsty woman. But not in the shop. They knocked over a hat stand, then a mannequin. The girls screamed and one of them fainted.

Leonie grabbed a vase of flowers, and flung the contents at the men. "Stop it! Now!" she shouted. She threw the vase itself at Lisburne's back. He didn't seem to feel it, but when it landed with a loud crash on the floor and shattered to pieces, he paused.

She rushed at him and grabbed the back of his coat and pulled him away. Marcelline pulled her husband back, too.

Both men wrenched free and started for each other again.

"Enough!" Marcelline cried. "I'm going to be sick!"

That stopped Clevedon in his tracks. Then Lisburne had to subside, too.

"Out," Leonie told the seamstresses. They ran out again. It took Jeffreys a moment to get the fainter on her feet and drag her away, but they soon followed the others. The door closed behind them.

Leonie regarded Lisburne and her brother-in-law the same way she'd regarded her quarreling seamstresses not many days earlier. "This is ridiculous," she said.

"Brawling," Marcelline said. "In the *shop*. Clevedon, you're impossible."

He did not look abashed. He still looked as though he wanted to murder Lisburne. Which, in a way, was rather sweet.

When Clevedon had married Marcelline, he'd taken on the whole family. Her sisters were his sisters. Her daughter was his daughter. Yes, it was aristocratically possessive of him, and it could be annoying at times to have an older brother when one had got along perfectly well without one for all one's life. Still, it wasn't disagreeable to know that somebody other than one's sisters cared about one's well-being — and one's virtue, when it came to that. Not that any Noirots ever cared about the last article themselves.

"I refuse to beg his pardon," Clevedon said. "Unless I've wronged him, which I greatly doubt. He ever was a seducer of the first order."

"What I do you may criticize and mock

all you like," Lisburne said. "But you seem not to notice that you call Miss Noirot's behavior into question as well."

"Were you both defending my honor, then?" Leonie said. "How thrilling! I've not the least objection to a brawl, in any case. Marcelline is more squeamish, especially now, but I love the sight of men pummeling each other. You're welcome to continue the fisticuffs in the court behind the shop or — better yet — in St. James's Street. It will give London something new to talk about. If Sophy were here, I'm sure she'd encourage it."

Lisburne smiled at her then, and the world seemed to open and brighten. Her life was in dire straits, yet his affectionate smile was like sunbeams breaking through a gloom she hadn't realized was there.

"As always, you go straight to the heart of the matter," Lisburne said. "We've a scandal to undo, and I'll be happy to pound Clevedon into oblivion if you think that will help."

"If anyone's going to be pounded, it's you," Clevedon said. "And I'll be honored to undertake the task."

"No, you will not," Marcelline said. "I've had enough fighting for one day, and the seamstresses will spread the news quickly enough. Diversionary tactics are all very well, but that's Sophy's specialty, and she isn't here."

"And I have a plan," Leonie said.

"Of course you do," said Lisburne, still smiling.

If one wanted to believe a man was besotted, he wore precisely the look one would use for evidence. But it was a look any Noirot or DeLucey would have mastered, and Leonie knew better than to trust such flimsy evidence, merely because it fit her fantasies.

True, last night she'd believed her fantasies. To a point. But he'd made sandwiches for her! And now she was much more clearheaded. And not tipsy, certainly.

"We can discuss it in the consulting room," she said.

It would be difficult to return to that room with Lisburne, remembering what had happened there. But the chances of being overheard were smaller there than in her office on the ground floor. In any case, Clevedon and Marcelline would be with them. And so the meeting wouldn't be . . . fraught. Not that Leonie would allow herself to display any signs of confusion or awkwardness. She'd grown up in Paris, after all. She was a Noirot. And a DeLucey.

She used the speaking pipe to summon

Mary Parmenter to look after the show-room. The shop would remain open during the usual hours, even though Leonie expected no customers. Closing early would look like surrender. In any event, thieves were as likely to turn up today as any day. They didn't care whether a shop was under a cloud.

But this, and a quick stop at her office took time, and when Leonie reached the consulting room, her sister and brother-in-law weren't there.

"I did not murder them and hide the bodies," Lisburne said when Leonie came in, holding a sheet of paper. "Her Grace was ill. I saw her turn white, then a curious shade of green. She darted into a little room at the back of the passage. Clevedon went with her. When they came out, he said he was taking her home. They went out the back way. We're to meet with them at Clevedon House."

"Meet them?" Leonie looked about the consulting room, exasperation clear in every feature.

That, he realized was unusual. She was always so guarded. Except in lovemaking.

"I can't leave the shop!" she said. "Not today, of all days. It will look as though we've abandoned it."

"Never mind that your customers have abandoned you," he said.

"He doesn't understand," she said. "He tries. He understands to a point, but he never had to work for a living. He doesn't —" She shook her head. "He lives his life as a duke, that's all, and he assumes we'll live as a duke's family. Did he hurt you much?"

"A glancing blow, no more," Lisburne said. He caught himself before he tested the sore place on his jaw where His Grace had made contact — and where he might have done substantial damage had Lisburne been an instant slower to dodge. "We're too evenly matched, and we hadn't time to assess each other's weak points. Still, I noted a slight redness at the top of Clevedon's right cheekbone. With any luck, it'll turn into a black eye. But speaking of injuries" — he pointed to the place in his jaw — "I detect some throbbing, after all. Perhaps you could kiss it and make it better."

Leonie moved away. "Not during business hours."

He glanced at the chaise longue and away and suppressed a sigh.

"Well, then, business," he said. "I'd just as soon not have to argue with Clevedon over every detail of what's to be done. He can be intolerably overbearing. Ducal, as you said. If you'll tell me your plan, I promise to listen attentively and be as good as gold."

If he stood too close, he'd catch her scent. Then he wouldn't be as good as gold.

He moved away to the looking glass and examined himself. Nothing horribly out of order. Everything buttoned and tied properly. His boots gleamed. His hair was a trifle disordered and his neckcloth wasn't right, thanks to the contretemps with Clevedon. But he discerned no signs of *careless desolation.*

He heard a little giggle, quickly smothered. He turned.

Her expression was sober, but he knew she was amused to see him playing Narcissus — he who always left it to his valet to fuss over his appearance.

She looked down at her piece of paper.

"Have you made two columns?" he said. "Drawn with a ruler?"

"Yes, of course," she said. "For one thing, I had to weigh the pros and cons of summoning Sophy. The cons outnumber the pros. I won't bore you with them. She'd find a way to turn the furor to our advantage, I don't doubt. But we have strong reasons against her returning quite yet. And so I believe the best way for all of us to recover is find out the truth. Shall I explain my reasons?"

He wondered why Sophy, who seemed so important to the shop, needed to stay away. He'd heard stories about her and Long-more, but nothing, apart from a bridal trip, that explained an enforced absence.

He knew it was no good asking. Leonie could be amazingly direct and open. If she wasn't, she wasn't, and that was the end of it.

"I want the truth about Swanton's mystery woman, too," he said. "But my reasons are obvious. I'd like to hear yours."

"They're simple enough," she said. "If we discover that Lord Swanton is in the wrong, he'll make amends. This is good for us. Since Maison Noirot and the Milliners' Society are now associated with him, we'll be associated with doing the right thing. People love confessions and redemption."

"They like hangings, too."

"I hope it won't come to that, even if we discover a fraud," she said. "But first we have to find out which it is."

He hadn't the least doubt she'd enumer-ated possible courses of action for every possible outcome.

"I'll be happy to beat the truth out of Theaker and Meffat," he said. "While I don't require help, I believe Clevedon would be overjoyed to assist. That would present a good way of — er — mending our fences. I don't like to be at odds with him."

He hated it. He especially hated knowing he'd deserved Clevedon's attack.

"He's tetchier these days because of Marcelline," she said. "But I should prefer to reserve beating for a last resort. I'd rather find the woman."

"Except for Theaker and Meffat, nobody knows who she is," he said. "She might be anywhere. We don't know her name. I didn't even get a good look at her."

"I got the number of the hackney," she said.

He blinked once, surprised. Then he saw how stupid he was to be surprised. She was logical and orderly and good with numbers. She'd had the presence of mind — or the recklessness — or both — to follow Theaker and the woman, while Lisburne and Swanton had dithered, chasing their own tails.

"Do you know how many hackneys ply the London streets?" he said. "Over a thousand. They might be anywhere at any time of the day. Or night."

"Fenwick knows most of the hackney coachmen," she said. "I'm sure I mentioned this."

He remembered then. Her sister Sophy had found Fenwick on the streets. The boy liked horses, and made friends with grooms and hackney coachmen. Leonie had told him this. Last night.

Before the *very nice* interlude.

"We still don't know much about Fenwick," she said. "He's a clam about his past. But we do know he's well acquainted with London's less elegant population. I sent him out to track down our woman in black."

"You sent the boy who wears the gorgeous livery, who speaks his own peculiar version of English," he said. Lisburne's mind wasn't working as well as it ought. It drifted to the chaise longue. It wandered upstairs, to the sitting room. He remembered undressing her. The delicious forever it had taken. The touching gesture of modesty when she'd held the corset over her beautiful breasts . . . the complete lack of modesty and self-consciousness afterward.

"The people he'll be talking to understand him well enough," she said. "This won't be the first time he's helped us find a missing person. We must hope he does it quickly. Almack's last assembly is tomorrow night. People will remain in Town after that, but by the end of the month, they'll be scattering."

"Ten days," he said.

"We can't afford ten days with no customers," she said. She paused and moved away, to pick up a bit of ribbon from a chair. Since she'd had no customers today, it must be debris from last night.

Last night. Last night.

He could close the door. No customers. Her employees worked on the floor below. He could take her behind the curtain . . .

"I may be forced to sell the Botticelli," she said.

Lisburne's face was a picture.

His mind had been elsewhere, Leonie knew, and she had a good idea where. Her mind wanted to go there, too. Her body, actually. Straight into his arms. More of what they'd done last night. She'd dreamed such beautiful, wicked dreams.

But this was full day, a dreadful day, and dreams were for the night, like lovemaking. Dreams, like lovemaking, were for escaping.

She couldn't escape now. She had an immense, dangerous problem to solve. If she didn't solve it, she'd lose everything that mattered, everything she and her sisters had worked and risked and struggled for. She'd lose all that Cousin Emma had given them, and it would be like seeing her die again.

Leonie had to keep her mind on business.

Lisburne was pleasure. No, to her he was a great deal more. She'd fallen in love and given herself gladly, and she'd do it again and again until he was done with her. Or until some miracle occurred and she was cured and was done with him.

But business came first, last, and always. She had a disaster to recover from, and not a minute to lose.

"The Botticelli," he said.

"Our wager?" she said. "Lady Gladys? Beaux and proposals and invitations by the end of the month? Do you recollect?"

His green gaze narrowed. "I recollect. Two weeks with you. Your undivided attention. No *business.*"

"If matters continue as they are, I'll have no business," she said.

"How the devil do you propose to win, if the ladies won't come to the shop?" he said. "Gladys resides with Lady Warford, you know, while her father the great general is abroad, getting soldiers killed somewhere. It doesn't matter if you're related by marriage. If you were Clara's own sister, and had got yourself into a scandal, Lady Warford would send you away to live with the sheep on a desolate island off the coast of Scotland, and Clara would be forbidden to even write to you."

"Lady Gladys must come to the shop," she said. "We've two promenade dresses, a ball dress, and a dinner dress for her. And Joanie Barker has made a splendid hat. Sophy is a genius with millinery, and Joanie is her protégée."

"Where the devil is Sophy, then, if she's so indispensable?"

"Where she needs to stay," Leonie said. She remembered what Clevedon had said about Longmore racing back to London to kill Swanton. It couldn't happen within hours, though. They were in Scotland at present. "I'd better write to her, and send it express. I'll tell her everything is in hand, and she's not to come and complicate matters."

She started toward the door. Lisburne caught her by the arm, an easy light grasp. But she felt the warmth and pressure everywhere, especially in the place where they'd come together last night.

"I haven't the least expectation of losing my Botticelli," he said. "But I want you to have a sporting chance. Do you want me to write to Longmore? Or talk to him, if that's feasible."

What could she do? She brought her hand up to his cheek. He turned his head and kissed the palm of her hand. "I want to help," he said. "And I don't want to sit about waiting for Fenwick to report. Shall I present myself to Longmore so that he can attempt to kill me?"

"You're more useful alive and undamaged." Leonie drew her hand away. "If I write, Sophy will listen, and she'll manage him — or render him unconscious if necessary. I need you here in London."

"That sounds so promising," he said. "But I have a feeling you mean something other than what I'm thinking."

"I need a spy," she said.

"Does that mean I report to you, in disguise, in the dead of night?"

It was the low, insinuating voice. It was the hint of a smile. It was the way he drew nearer and the way his head bent and the way he seemed aware of nothing else in the world but her.

She could not have him come here again in the dead of night. She couldn't risk it, not at present.

She was a businesswoman, first, last, and always.

But she was as well, like all her kind, a gambler.

"Don't let anybody see you," she said.

CHAPTER THIRTEEN

Almack's. — The ball on Wednesday evening closed a most brilliant season. Dancing commenced, a little after eleven o'clock, to Collinet's fine band, with Musard's quadrilles 'Les Gondeliers Venetiens,' which were followed by the waltzes 'le Soufle du Zephir,' and the favourite 'Les Souvenirs de Vienne.' In the course of the evening 'Les Puritans, Rome,' &c., were performed in admirable style. At four o'clock the ball terminated, when the band struck up 'God save the King.'

> — *Court Journal,* 25 July 1835

Almack's
Early Thursday morning

Though by now he'd observed enough of the new Gladys to be past shock, Lisburne was nonetheless taken aback to see her dancing with Crawford. One of the Earl of

Longmore's hard-living cronies, and owning neither a sharp intellect nor much in the way of wit, Crawford was nonetheless popular with women, because he was one of London's best dancers.

He was dancing with *Gladys,* of whom Lisburne recalled somebody writing, during her first Season, "she puts one painfully in mind of a dancing bear decked out in silks, lace, and a king's ransom in jewelry."

Crawford had engaged her for a quadrille, and he was smiling, and so was she, moving as easily through the figures as any other young woman. Lady Alda stood not far away, avidly watching, her head turning this way and that, and occasionally disappearing behind her fan when she whispered one of her barbed comments to whoever was at hand.

When the steps brought Crawford and Gladys together, Gladys said something and he smiled. Then he said something. She laughed, and a great many gazes turned that way, Lady Alda's included. Lisburne noticed a number of puzzled looks and some appreciative ones. Lady Alda's expression soured.

Gladys had a pretty laugh, surprisingly warm, Lisburne realized. Not a titter. Not trying for a tinkling sound. Not feigned in any way. It came from within, a happy sound, and it seemed to make its hearer happy.

A voice, he knew, could be a powerful tool.

He'd learned to use his to command servants, to be taken seriously by men twice and thrice his age, and of course to win over women. Certainly Gladys's seemed to have captured Swanton's imagination. But he was extreme in everything. Lisburne found it agreeable, no more.

Leonie's voice was another story altogether. There was the brisk, businesslike tone he found so perversely arousing. But even more delicious was her private voice, the one not everybody heard. The low, suggestive chuckle wasn't for public consumption. Neither was the way she'd look at him from the corner of her eye, a ghost of a smile curving her lips . . .

And he couldn't let himself dwell on that, even though he hadn't seen her since Tuesday afternoon.

As he'd done at Lady Eddingham's ball last night, at various clubs this day, and at dinner at Lady Gorrell's not many hours earlier, he was here to gather information. Clevedon was doing the same, but elsewhere. Lisburne hoped the duke was having better luck, in both senses, at Crockford's

355

and whatever other gaming establishment he meant to visit this night.

Lisburne had never acquired a taste for gambling. A game of cards now and again was good fun, but gaming hells held little allure.

Tonight he'd undertaken Almack's duty instead. His job was to flirt and dance with the foremost gossips. Next on his list was a waltz with Lady Alda Morris.

He watched Crawford lead Gladys back to her place, where Lady Warford presided as chaperon. Thence Geddings returned Clara. Several men loitered in the vicinity. Crawford lingered, talking to Gladys. Flinton advanced to claim his dance with . . . Gladys. Someone else led out Clara. Herringstone.

It was hard to be certain, but Crawford, Flinton, and Geddings seemed to be in Gladys's circle. Or at least dividing their time between her and Clara.

All Gladys needed was six beaux, three invitations to country houses, and one marriage proposal, and the Botticelli would have a new home after the exhibition.

But the odds were still in Lisburne's favor. Gladys had only eight days to meet the wager's conditions. Meanwhile, she seemed to be doing well enough socially, a success

Lisburne didn't begrudge her.

But he would very much begrudge losing his two weeks with Leonie. Her undivided attention . . .

. . . which wouldn't be undivided if they couldn't put the Vauxhall incident to rest before then.

And so he made himself fix his mind on Lady Alda, whose acidic look vanished when he came to lead her out.

"How sorry I'll be to see the Season end," she said when they'd begun dancing. "Lady Gladys has enlivened it so."

"Has she, indeed?" he said. "I've seen her only in passing lately." He paused. "Though, like everybody else, I've kept up with her doings and sayings, thanks to the *Spectacle.*"

"There's no predicting what astonishing thing she'll say," Lady Alda said. "I know some say it's pert and unladylike to express opinions so forcefully. But we may acquit her of the charge of being *too* eager to please, may we not? Some might say her dress is too mature for her, but I say a lady is wise to dress as suits her figure. Her dancing has improved, do you not think? She keeps time less awkwardly than she used to do, and I'm sure that if she continues to practice hard with a good dancing master, she'll bend her arms with better grace. But Mr. Crawford always makes his partners look well. Lord Flinton, too, I see. It's the mark of a good dancer, isn't it?"

This monologue went on at intervals, as the steps brought them together.

A poem came to Lisburne's mind — not one of Swanton's, but one Swanton liked to quote. One of Mrs. Abdy's comic creations. What was it? Something about a friend, and filled with similar backhanded compliments. Very likely Leonie would know the poem.

Lisburne remembered the way she'd acted out "The Second Son" at the Western Athenaeum. He tried to imagine what her rendition of the friendship poem would be like.

He became aware of Lady Alda's expectant gaze, and realized she was waiting for him to say she was grace personified, no matter who partnered her. In another time and place he would have said the right words without thinking. At present, for some reason, he couldn't put a sentence together, and the moment passed in an awkward silence.

"I'm so very glad on your account that the patronesses chose to overlook the dreadful scene at Vauxhall on Monday night," she said.

She'd used the silence, evidently, to gather her breath for another blast of ill wind.

"This is the last Almack's ball of the Season," he said. "It's hardly worth the effort to pitch out undesirables."

She protested that he was not *undesirable*. She tittered. He knew flirtation was expected. He liked flirting. It was one of his favorite things.

Yet his mind went blank, and the best he could manage was a politely amused thanks.

They went on dancing, mute for a time, then, "I notice that Lord Swanton has chosen to absent himself," she said. "It seems he declined to test the patronesses' forbearance."

"He's not the only one," Lisburne said. "I see no signs of Theaker. He was prominent in the Vauxhall performance, too."

"I'll admit I was amazed that his and Mr. Meffat's Almack's vouchers weren't withdrawn."

Lisburne raised his eyebrows.

"After their friend Lord Adderley's ghastly business last month with the French widow," she said. "Or whatever she was. I must say that something about her seemed not quite right." She looked up at him. "But I forget. You were not in London then."

"When was this?"

"A very short time before Lord Longmore married the dressmaker," she said. "That is to say, Miss Noirot. I'll admit that came as a shock. We'd all assumed something would come of the French widow. But she disappeared, and Lord Longmore recovered from his infatuation with astonishing speed. But I can't think why my mind wandered to that shocking episode. I only meant to say that some expected Lord Adderley's friends to be tainted by association. That seems to me not altogether fair. One ought not to judge a gentleman's friends by *his* behavior."

Lisburne didn't ask whether she applied the same rule to women. He could guess the answer. In any case, it was the other topic that awoke his curiosity. She didn't need much prodding to explain the "shocking episode."

The story didn't enlighten Lisburne much about Theaker and Meffat, and everything else she said only demonstrated her mastery of the oblique insult. On the other hand, the tale of the mysterious French lady was most interesting.

Wednesday, while not the worst day in Maison Noirot's history, would not qualify as one of Leonie's favorites. Only a handful of customers had entered the shop and they didn't come to buy anything. They fingered the hats and shawls, sneered at the mannequins, stage whispered insolent remarks, and stared the shopgirls out of countenance. Luckily, most of the girls, like Selina, had developed tough hides. Even so, tears were shed in the workroom. The girls feared for their futures.

Thursday proved marginally better. One of the shop's first important clients, Mrs. Sharp, remained loyal because she felt she had an image to uphold as a leader of fashion, at least among her set. While this group did not include the cream of the beau monde, it did comprise some of London's wealthiest families.

Her daughter Chloe had somehow snared one of London's most elusive bachelors. Since she'd soon become a countess, nothing but the best would do for bride clothes. Not that anything less would do, in any event. After all, the eldest Sharp daughter had recently married a prince, and her dress and those of her attendants had been the talk of London. Several ladies' magazines had described her wardrobe at length, thanks to Sophy.

"I told Mr. Sharp, it's either Maison Noirot or Paris," Mrs. Sharp said. "He drew the line at Paris, as I knew he would. He doesn't realize, as I do, that even Victorine cannot produce work superior to yours."

For all that she might disparage Paris's foremost modiste, Mrs. Sharp was furtive about Maison Noirot. She brought her daughter early in the day, while most of the fashionable world was still abed, and she asked Leonie to be discreet. Her princely son-in-law's family compensated for their lack of wealth with an excess of morality. Mrs. Sharp had no desire to hear her in-laws preach at her.

Keeping quiet about a large, costly order was not a good way to improve business prospects. Sophy would have been wild.

Meanwhile, Fenwick had been gone for most of the past two days. When he did turn up, shortly after Leonie closed the shop on Thursday night, his report was short: "Nuffin' yet. Better try Covent Garden."

He consumed two meat pies only at Leonie's insistence. He did this while protesting that he'd be too stuffed to eat when he got to Jack's Coffee House.

"You're not to eat anything in that place," Leonie said. "It's filthy."

The ancient coffee house in Covent Garden was as disgustingly unclean as it was disreputable. She'd rather he didn't go there, but she knew he'd promise not to and do it anyway. She told herself he'd survived London for this long, a feat not many unwanted children achieved, and one couldn't lock him up. She reminded herself that she'd survived the streets of Paris at much the same age.

"What do you expect to find there?" she said.

"Dunno," he said. "Lodgings thereabouts? I know a cove as goes there. He might know fings. *Th*ings."

"No word of the hackney driver, then," she said. "Charlie Judd."

Since they had the hackney coach's number, discovering the driver's name hadn't been difficult. Finding him was another matter. A hackney coachman had to accept anybody who wanted to hire him, at any time, no matter how many hours he'd already worked, and he might drive a fare ten miles into the country.

The boy shook his head. "He'll turn up, miss."

But when? For all the confidence she'd shown Lisburne, Leonie had known the search might take a great deal of time. They hadn't much left. In August, most of Fashionable Society left London for their country estates. July ended in eight days.

August was always a troublesome month financially. This year, it could be a fatal one, though Mrs. Sharp's ambitions and Mr. Sharp's money might allow the shop to scrape by.

Leonie was on her way to her office, to review expenses and decide where she might cut and which bills to pay first, when she heard the peremptory knock at the back door. Fenwick, who was on his way out, must have opened it, because she heard him talking, and a familiar voice answering.

Her heart sped up. She wanted to run to the door. She made herself pause in the corridor outside her office, don her politely amiable expression, and wait with what looked on the outside like absolute calm.

She watched Fenwick go out and Lisburne close and bolt the door after him.

Then he turned to her, and there was his perfectly sculpted face and the gold glimmering in his hair and in his green eyes, and the wicked mouth that had touched every inch of her skin, including the secret parts. Her heart turned over and over.

"I still don't understand a word he says," he said. "I barely recognized him. He's grown remarkably grubby."

"He can hardly prowl about the underworld in lavender and gold livery," she said.

"If he looks too pretty, somebody will steal him."

"Tell me something," he said. "When Sophy found him, was she pretending to be a French widow, or somebody else?"

Leonie was confused and happy and afraid all at the same time but she didn't blink. Even deranged by love, she remained a Noirot and a DeLucey. She knew how to play cards.

"I find it best not to inquire too closely into Sophy's doings," she said. "I hope you have some useful news for us."

He hadn't come in the dead of night, as he'd promised. She hadn't seen him since Tuesday afternoon. Not that she'd expected to. Naturally he'd make promises he wouldn't keep. A man who looked and sounded and made love the way he did could play by his own rules.

"Lady Alda believes there was something 'not quite right' about Longmore's French widow," he said. "After great efforts of cogitation — not easy while Lady Alda is shooting poison darts everywhere, in between trying to captivate and bewitch the unwary — a situation requiring a man to keep his wits about him." He frowned. "A task I find strangely difficult lately. I wonder why that is. Where was I?"

"I haven't the faintest idea," she said. "Whatever it is, it doesn't strike me as useful news." She walked into her office.

He followed. He closed the door.

She went to her desk and began putting papers in order. Bills. Two letters canceling orders.

"Now I remember," he said. "After a great labor of thinking, I brought forth an idea. Lady Longmore can't come back to London yet because some people might confuse her with Longmore's French widow and the great love affair from which he recovered with astounding rapidity."

"He's a man," Leonie said. "What was it Byron said about men versus women in love?"

"Byron? I thought you weren't literary."

"We read *Don Juan* because it was reputed to be naughty," she said.

" 'Man's love is of man's life a thing apart,' " he quoted. " ' 'Tis woman's whole existence.' Swanton worships *Don Juan*. And *Beppo*. He dotes on Tom Moore, too. And you have successfully diverted me from my objective." His voice deepened. "Come here."

"Certainly not," she said. "I need to add two and two and make it come out ten or twenty. I need to see whether one commission can be made to keep us solvent for all of August, and perhaps into September. I need —"

"I've missed you," he said.

At that moment, all sense flew out of her brain and all she needed was him.

Stupid, stupid, stupid. She hadn't time for this, for being ridiculous and irresponsible.

"It's been an age," he said. "The balls and assemblies don't end until dawn, and I know the seamstresses arrive at nine o'clock in the morning and the shop must open at ten, even though nobody comes at that inhuman hour. I knew I mustn't disturb your rest."

He didn't have to be here to do that.

"It's been scarcely more than two days since you were last here." She took out her pocket watch. "I make it to be about fifty-four hours."

"Can you not be more precise?" he said. "I love it when you're precise."

Her heart beat too fast. *Love.* But not love *you.* It was only a carelessly used word and it meant only that she amused him. Something she'd known from the beginning.

Man's love is of man's life a thing apart,
'Tis woman's whole existence.

367

Not hers. She had a life, a full, busy life. The life she'd had before he sauntered into it.

"Furthermore, customers do come at what your great ladies deem the crack of dawn," she said crisply. "They are not great ladies, but they pay their bills promptly. So bourgeois of them, I know, but —"

"I considered standing in the street beneath your window, and howling like a dog at the moon, the unreachable moon," he said. "But I didn't like to spoil your sleep. And perhaps people would throw shoes at me, or empty their chamber pots on my head. And I wasn't sure which was your bedroom window. We never reached it, you may recall."

She went hot all over.

"And so I went quietly home," he continued, "to my bed, and imagined you in your bed, your face a little flushed. Perhaps you'd thrown off the bedclothes, because the night was warm. Or perhaps you thought of me, and that made you overwarm. I pretended you thought of me, the way I was thinking of you . . ."

He trailed off, and she was amazed to see color climb his neck to his jaw and as far as his cheekbones. "Devil take him! That cousin of mine is contagious. What am I saying?"

"Poetry," she said. "Of a sort. Of the wooing sort."

As though he hadn't already wooed her and won with practically no effort at all. She'd been infatuated from the moment she'd looked away from the painting and up at him at the British Institution. From infatuation to falling in love . . . how absurdly easy it was, even for a sensible girl who kept her feet on the ground.

Or perhaps it was easy for her because she wasn't used to it.

Or maybe it was the sandwiches.

"I feared so," he said. "Is it working?"

"Not at all," she said. She turned her back to him and took up a bill and stared at it though the words and numbers might as well have been written in Greek or Arabic or Chinese.

She heard him cross the room. She didn't look up. She didn't need to. She could feel him behind her. The air became fraught — with the scent of a man and the tension between them or whatever it was he did to make the air seem to vibrate like harp strings.

"What have you got there?" he said softly. "A mercer's bill?"

She made herself focus. "I shall have to

speak to him. The quantities are odd, and I'm sure he's raised his prices since last week. Nine shillings sixpence for lutestring?"

"How much lutestring?" his voice deepened another degree.

She could feel his breath at the back of her neck. It was all she could do not to shiver. She swallowed. "Fifty-six yards. This must be Sophy's doing. She ever did —"

"Fifty-six yards of lutestring at nine and six per yard," he said, much in the same tone he used when she was in his arms.

"Yes," she said.

"What else?"

"What does it matter?"

"Read it to me," he said.

She could feel his voice in the pit of her stomach. He wasn't touching her, yet it seemed as though his hands were everywhere. His mouth, too.

"Ninety-eight ells of armoisin," she said. "At eleven shillings ninepence per ell."

"Per ell," he said.

"Yes."

"Go on."

"Sixteen yards of fine velvet at fifteen shillings threepence per yard."

"Mmm." His cheek brushed hers. "Don't stop."

"One hundred twelve yards —"

"One hundred twelve. So much." He kissed a sensitive place behind her ear.

She trembled.

"Don't stop," he said.

"One hundred twelve yards of black princetta at twelve shillings ninepence per yard."

She went on, reading the bill, while he went on kissing her, murmuring in her ear, encouraging her. "More numbers," he whispered. "More numbers."

He kissed the side of her neck while he moved his hands to the front of her dress and cupped her breasts. She went on reading, though her knees were dissolving.

Three hundred fifty-six yards of green Persian, twenty-seven yards of mode, and on and on, though she could barely see straight, because of his hands, his hands, everywhere.

"Leonie, Leonie," he murmured. "When you talk in numbers, you drive me mad."

He slid his hands lower, and fabric rustled as he drew up her skirts, and her eyes were crossing as she tried to read. She ought to stop him but she didn't want to. It was too wicked, and she wanted to find out where it would lead. She wasn't sure she could stop, even if she had to, because she was melting in his hands and under the spell of his voice.

She felt him lift her skirt and petticoat. Then he had his hands on her thighs, sliding over her drawers.

"Silk," he said. "Silk drawers, you naughty girl."

"White sarcenet, three shillings ninepence."

He was kissing the back of her neck. She heard sounds. She knew what they were. Buttons being undone, the whisper of wool against muslin.

He slid his hand between her legs and she moaned. "Keep counting," he said.

"Satin, nine shillings sixpence per yard. Genoa velvet, twenty-seven shillings sixpence per yard. *Oh.*"

He'd slid his fingers into the opening of her drawers. He was stroking her and she was shaking. Warmth flooded through her as though she swam in a pool, and hot mineral waters swirled about her.

"Mon Dieu!" A low, involuntary cry as pleasure raced through her and shot her straight up, into that place, that bursting joy.

He pushed inside her then and she braced herself on the desk. His cheek was against hers.

"Naughty, naughty girl." His voice was rough, his breath warm against her neck. "I missed you. Wicked thoughts while I lay in my bed, wishing I were in your bed, in your arms. I thought of so many interesting things we could do, so much I wanted to teach you, and all I might learn about you, all the secrets of your skin and your mouth and . . ." He withdrew a degree and pushed in again. "And here. Inside you. I wanted to be inside you."

And she wanted him there, inside her, though it was dangerous — perhaps *because* it was dangerous. She was who she was, and all the numbers in the world, lined up exactly in the proper columns and tallied correctly, couldn't change that. She was the sensible one, yet she was a Noirot and a DeLucey, and they'd been sinners for centuries.

He took her here, at her desk, and she took him, too, shamelessly, gladly, almost laughing as the heat and urgency built and built. She laughed even when she groaned. She laughed at their half-stifled cries of pleasure. She laughed at the foolish whispered words between them and at the naughtiness of it all.

It was a great joke, and a great joy, and she was happy, and happier still, and happier again, until there was no farther to go, and everything became absolutely perfect for one, glorious moment.

She savored that moment for the time it lasted, and remembered it when it was over. And she knew she'd remember it forever, long after he was gone and he'd forgotten her.

Later

What Lisburne had *meant* . . .

. . . when he still had a functioning mind . . .

. . . was to woo her — or seduce her — and by degrees lead her to bed or at least to the chaise longue upstairs.

But there she'd been, at her desk, frowning over a bill and reciting quantities and prices in her brisk, business-like voice. And his mind went dark, abandoning thinking to the other, very small brain, much lower down.

Then, after the sort of lovemaking more usually associated with courtesans and knowing country wenches — most certainly *not* recently initiated young women — she laughed.

There he was, still bent over her backside like a dog, trying to catch his breath and recover his reason, and she planted her elbows on the desk and her face in her hands and laughed.

And the sound caught at his heart and what was left of his brain and he laughed, too.

She turned and came up from the desk and took his face in her hands and kissed him. He felt the kiss to his toes and to the ends of his fingers and the roots and tips of his hair, as though he'd been struck by lightning.

Then she broke the kiss and said, "Come upstairs."

Later

Lisburne woke with a smooth, rounded backside pressed to his groin. From the silken shoulder where his face rested a delicious scent wafted to his nostrils: lavender and Leonie. His arm curved around her waist, his hand lay on her belly. Naked, entirely naked.

He didn't remember clearly the undressing, but when he opened his eyes, the bed curtains, not fully closed, revealed the aftermath of an orgy. The flickering light of a single candle illumined scattered pieces of clothing, some flung over chairs, some on the floor, some tangled about the bedposts.

Then he remembered.

A hurried undressing, and a long, slow time of lovemaking.

He smiled.

He kissed her shoulder and she turned in his arms, and her arms came up and went round his neck. He kissed her, and his heart began to race, he didn't know why. He ought to be content. Satiated. But the feeling wasn't recognizable. It was —

She broke the kiss. "What's that?" she said. She let go of him, and pulled herself up on the pillows. "Someone's at the door."

He had to strain to hear it, and mightn't have succeeded had the window not been open. From far below came several quick knocks in succession, echoing faintly in the court. Someone was at the shop's back door. Or at one of the doors facing the cramped court behind No. 56.

"It must be after midnight," he said. "Who the devil calls on you at this hour?"

Before he could collect his wits, she'd leapt from the bed. She hurried to the wardrobe, opened it, and pulled something out. A blue velvet dressing gown, very like a man's, embroidered with exotic flowers. It was nothing like the obscene wrapper she'd donned the other night. This was no wisp of a thing, but cut in a style that seemed oriental, and lined with silk. When she wrapped it about her, it concealed everything but her shape. For some reason, this struck him as lewder than the bit of gossamer.

He sat up. "You can't be meaning to answer the door," he said. "And not in *that*. Come back to bed. Let the servants deal with whomever it is. Unless you've another lover who calls in the dead of night."

"When do you imagine I have time for another lover?" she said. "I barely have time for you."

She hurried out.

He dragged himself out of bed and began hunting for his shirt. It took a while because he became distracted. He found her stockings and his, then her corset, and a garter. Only one garter. Where was its mate?

He couldn't leave her garments where he found them. He gathered them up as he'd done the other night, and sorted them into his and hers at the foot of the bed. By the time he'd found his shirt and pulled it over his head and was wondering where his trousers had got to, she was back.

"Make haste, make haste!" she said. "We've not a minute to lose."

He was still dazed. Her undergarments, draped at the foot of the bed, made his mind cloudy. He wasn't ready to make haste. He didn't want to. What he wanted to do was drag her back to bed. He wasn't done with her yet. He wasn't done with this night yet. He'd felt so comfortable. As though . . .

His mind shied away from completing the thought.

He said, "Who's come? Must I climb out of the window? Is the house afire?"

"Afire, indeed. Don't say that." She flung off the dressing gown and began rummaging in the wardrobe again.

Her back, her beautiful back . . . the sweet curve of her bottom . . .

He made himself think. "Leonie, who was at the door?"

She turned her head to look at him. Her hair was a riot of garnet curls, touched by streaks of fire where the candlelight caught it. Tendrils dangled at her temples and trailed down her neck . . . down her back, her beautiful back. The fog swept into his mind again, and he was starting toward her, forgetting everything else but the warmth of her body and the feel of her skin against his and —

"Isn't it obvious?" she said.

"What?" he said. "No."

"It's Fenwick," she said. "He's found her."

CHAPTER FOURTEEN

Are you struck with her figure and face?
How lucky you happened to meet
With none of the gossipping race
Who dwell in this horrible street!
They of slanderous hints never tire;
I love to approve and commend.
And the lady you so much admire.
Is my *very* particular friend!
— Mrs. Abdy, "My Very Particular Friend,"
1833

Environs of Tottenham Court Road
Small hours of Friday morning
Fenwick hadn't gone as far as Jack's disgusting coffee house, Leonie learned. He'd stopped at all the hackney stands on his way there — just in case, he said. This time he'd found his man. On discovering that Charlie Judd clearly remembered the fare in question, Fenwick decided he'd better not lose him again. He hired the driver to take him

to Maison Noirot and wait, in case Leonie wanted to interrogate him directly.

Since the coachman wasn't going anywhere, she'd hurried back upstairs to dress and to persuade a skeptical and uncooperative Lisburne to dress, too.

A few inquiries when they reached the vehicle were enough to change Lisburne's attitude. Though Judd had taken up the passengers in question on Monday night, and he'd ferried hundreds of passengers about London and its environs since, he clearly remembered the woman, child, and "gentleman."

"To and from Lambeth, wasn't it?" he said. "Only time I went to Vauxhall in this last week and more. And it weren't much of a tip he give me, was it?"

This told them they'd found the right trail. Before long, Leonie, Lisburne, and Fenwick were in the hackney coach and on their way.

Judd easily remembered the lodging house as well, because he stopped here frequently. Theatrical folk frequented the place, coming and going at odd hours. More than once he'd taken the performers' friends home after revelries.

This explained why the untidy maid who answered the door didn't blink at callers at such an hour, and why, after giving Leonie and Lisburne a quick assessment, she sent them up to the "widder on the second floor."

Clearly the "widder" was expecting somebody else. She flung open the door, her pale countenance expectant. Her eyes widened when she saw who it was, and she tried to shut them out. But Lisburne had already put his foot in the way, and Leonie said, "We came to help."

"I know you, Miss Noirot," the woman said. "You were at Vauxhall that night. Asking for money. For fallen women. Don't you know that helping them only encourages licentious behavior?" She gave a short laugh. But she backed away from the door and let them in. She closed it after them.

Leonie swiftly assessed her surroundings. The lodgings seemed to comprise two rooms. The one they stood in, relatively large and airy, was being used as a parlor. A door stood partly open, leading to what Leonie guessed was a smaller back room. Given the neighborhood and condition of the building, she estimated the rent at between seven and ten shillings a week.

The place was neat — neater than the maid, certainly — though it held little in the way of furnishings to keep clean, and these looked well used if not worn out. On a table near the door an open scrapbook lay, along with a handbill, a newspaper page, an open paste pot, and a pair of scissors.

Leonie moved to the table and read the handbill. It advertised a benefit night, the honoree's name printed large. "You're an actress," she said. "Dulcinea Williams, is it?"

The woman got in her way, threw newspaper and handbill into the scrapbook, closed it, and clutched it to her chest.

"I wondered whether you were a professional," Leonie said. "The graceful attitude of supplication, not to mention your dexterity in holding on to the child while pleading so beautifully with Lord Swanton."

Mrs. Williams's color heightened. She raised her chin. "The audience believed it."

Had Leonie obtained a closer or clearer view, she wouldn't have believed it. Now, even in a dimly lit room, the evidence was plain. All Noirots and DeLuceys were actors in some degree, and a few had even gone upon the stage. But family talent or no, Leonie had seen enough theatrical performances to recognize, in the way the woman carried herself and spoke, signs of one who'd trod the boards from an early age. Many actors couldn't shed their stage mannerisms altogether.

"Somebody paid you to perform," she said. "And you needed the money." She glanced at Lisburne, who stood guard by the door to the stairs, his pose deceptively casual, his face wearing the beautiful-but-stupid look.

Which showed how not stupid he was. He understood she was trying to win the woman's trust and he was doing what he could to appear harmless.

"I'd always been able to look after myself and my daughter," Mrs. Williams said. "I was with a good company. We toured the provinces. I had work, and nobody asked awkward questions about Bianca. Quite the contrary. She was a draw. The audiences love an infant prodigy."

Her gaze went to the back room. No doubt the child slept there.

"I was *Mrs.* Williams, in any event," she said, her voice lowered. "None of my fellow actors asked where Mr. Williams was. Bianca doesn't know. She thinks Papa is touring in America. The other night, when we were going to Vauxhall, I told her we'd be playacting. But we weren't, really."

Lisburne started to take a step away from the door, then subsided. His voice was mild when he said, "Not really playacting?"

Again the woman looked toward the room where her child slept.

"If you've been wronged," Leonie said, "Lord Swanton wants to make it right."

"But his lordship hasn't come, has he?" Mrs. Williams said.

"Do you want him to?" Leonie said.

Mrs. Williams looked from her to Lisburne. Then she moved away and gently closed the bedroom door.

When she returned to them, she returned the scrapbook to its place on the table. "If I ever imagined Bianca's father would carry me away on his white charger, I had my eyes opened when I told him I was expecting," she said.

"He offered no help at all?" Leonie said. This didn't sound like Swanton.

Mrs. Williams laughed. "I'd be helping him, more like. Maybe I'm not good enough for the great London theaters, but I'm good enough to find work easily elsewhere. Good enough not to be at any man's beck and call."

She threw Lisburne a defiant look. He only blinked stupidly, like the harmless aristocratic idiot he wasn't.

Mrs. Williams went on more rapidly, in the way people do when they've bottled up feelings for too long, "As I said, I'd joined a good company. Bianca and I did well. Then in May I fell ill and couldn't work. My colleagues helped as much as they could, but I seemed only to grow weaker and weaker, good for nothing. I had to let them go on without me. We were in Portsmouth then. I was running out of belongings to pawn. I used the little I had left to pay our way to London. Maybe I wasn't thinking clearly, but I couldn't think of anything else to do but appeal to Bianca's father."

"You wrote to him," Leonie said. "And he ignored you."

"Oh, no," the actress said. "I know about these *gentlemen* and their lawyers. I couldn't let him put me off by proxy, with affidavits and threats, could I? I went into a bookshop and found out his direction in *Boyle's Court Guide.* I went to his lodgings in the morning when I knew he'd be abed. I pretended to be a servant who'd brought a message to the wrong house. I was so prettily embarrassed. His servant flirted with me, and I flirted back, and found out where the master was going that day."

It was the same as Sophy would have done. Or Leonie. Or any Noirot or DeLucey. Pretend to be someone else. Play on others' weaknesses.

Her mind on her sisters, it took Leonie a

385

moment to notice the change in Lisburne, the way the tension went out of him. Then she realized: Whomever Bianca belonged to, it definitely wasn't Swanton. Among other clues, the poet didn't live in hired lodgings, but in the Marquess of Lisburne's villa in the Regent's Park.

"I lay in wait for him at the British Institution," Mrs. Williams said. "But I hadn't realized he'd be with a great crowd of people. I waited what seemed an eternity, trying to think of a way to get him alone, when he and his friend moved away from the others. By this time, you'd left, and Lord Swanton and the others had gone into the next room. You may be sure my two gentlemen whisked me out of sight of their fine friends. Then we had a long talk. He said he hadn't any money. I said he'd better get some, or I'd make scenes from one end of London to the other, haunting him like Banquo's ghost."

"But he might have had you arrested," Leonie said. The law was always on the side of the privileged. They weren't to be annoyed or harassed.

"I was desperate enough to risk it, Miss Noirot. He knows the kind of scene I'm capable of making. And I knew he didn't want anybody to know about me." Mrs. Williams smiled crookedly. "Not that my strength is up to haunting him as I threatened to do. But he doesn't know that. The trouble is, even the greatest Thespian can't get blood from a stone. I should have realized he'd be sponging off others and borrowing on expectations — of what, I can't say. His idea of a financial plan is waiting for the next tumble of dice."

By now it was clear who the culprits were: the same two men who'd spirited Mrs. Williams out of Vauxhall.

Leonie glanced at Lisburne, who merely looked about the room, apparently indifferent, though his posture told her otherwise.

"I saw how hopeless it was with him," Mrs. Williams went on. "I saw how foolish I was to think he'd help me. When his friend suggested I try a scene with the poet, what choice had I? He said Lord Lisburne would pay handsomely to make me go away."

"For somebody else's child?" he said. "If word got about, every unmarried mama in London would be at my door."

"For twenty pounds, I'll go away," she told him. She lifted her chin. "I would have left London by now if I could. I've had a stomach full of him and his friends and their brilliant ideas. He promised to arrange matters with you or the poet. But it's been days and I've had no word from him. I need to pay my rent, and my daughter and I must eat."

"I'll give you a hundred pounds," Lisburne said. "But strings are attached."

Mrs. Williams was a good actress, as she'd said. If she was frightened of exposure or arrest, she hid it well, from Lisburne, in any event. But she couldn't completely hide her shock when he offered a hundred pounds.

She'd thought twenty pounds was an immense amount. He knew some men paid no more than twenty shillings a year to support their bastards.

Lisburne said, "First, I want the father's name. We know it's one of two men."

He saw the struggle in her face, between need and fear. "If I tell you, I'll have no hold over him," she said. "They warned me —"

"They're bullies," Lisburne said. "Leave them to me."

"I can't risk exposing him," she said. "By law, the child belongs to the father. He could take her away." She bit her lip. "He cares nothing for her. He'd send Bianca to a charity school and forget about her."

"Let me deal with them," Lisburne said.

"Never mind," Leonie said. "It doesn't

matter which man it is."

Lisburne looked at her. He wasn't sure what she had in mind. He was sure she'd arrived at it through logic and calculation, though. "You're right," he said.

Her eyebrows went up.

"You could be right *once,*" he said. "Stranger things have happened."

Mrs. Williams was fixed on Leonie. "Miss Noirot, I'm sure you understand. I promise you, my conscience has plagued me ever since that night at Vauxhall. Poor Lord Swanton looked so bewildered. But they told me he'd pay me off and the matter would be hushed up." She wrung her hands. "And now I've got myself into a dreadful coil."

"We're going to uncoil it," Leonie said. "We don't need to know which of the two is the father. It's enough to know that they acted in concert to destroy Lord Swanton's good name as well as wreck others' reputations. All we need to do is prove this in a way the world will believe."

As she spoke, an image formed in Lisburne's mind. "I have an idea," he said.

She was looking at Mrs. Williams. "So have I."

The actress looked panicked.

"One hundred pounds, recollect," he said.

"But we need your help."

"I can't risk losing Bianca," she said. "Not for any amount of money."

"The Marquess of Lisburne outranks those two men," Leonie said. "Obviously he has a great deal more money. As well as an army of lawyers."

"If one of those men tries to take the child — which I very much doubt — I'll see him lawyered to death," Lisburne said. "But this matter wants discussion and a plan, and this isn't the time or place. Mrs. Williams, you seem to have been expecting company. The men in question, I suppose?"

"They promised to settle matters with Lord Swanton and bring me funds," the actress said. "All I got for my performance at Vauxhall was a few shillings to pay for this week's rent and food. I've been waiting for them for days."

"They won't help you now," Leonie said. "You've no hold over them. You can hardly make a scene about the real father after naming Lord Swanton in front of hundreds of witnesses."

Mrs. Williams stared at her for a moment. Her gaze returned to the bedroom door.

"We understand why you did it," Lisburne said gently. "But you've put yourself in a dangerous position. Those men could betray you and claim they had nothing to do with the scene at Vauxhall. They'd blacken your name as easily as they did Swanton's. While I know he won't press charges against you, I should imagine the scandal would make it difficult for you to find work."

Mrs. Williams tottered to a chair and slumped there. "I never thought . . ." She covered her face with her hands. It was a perfect attitude of despair, and she was an actress. All the same, Lisburne believed it. He believed her love for and fear of losing her child. Anybody who'd lost a loved one would believe.

"Bianca will be safe," he said. "I promise. The first step is to get you both out of here and to a place where nobody can trouble you."

It isn't easy to move a household in the dead of night or find a place to move them to on short notice.

But Mrs. Williams hadn't much of a household, thanks to her frequent visits to the pawnbrokers. Nearly all of her and her daughter's belongings fit in a large carpetbag. While Leonie helped them fill it, Lisburne went down to the landlady and paid the rent as well as something extra for her to send away any other visitors.

As to where to move them, that was obvious enough.

Leonie took them to Clevedon House.

She was well aware that Halliday, the Duke of Clevedon's house steward, was by now used to comings and goings at odd hours. Most usually it was Sophy coming and going, but Leonie's appearing before dawn wouldn't disturb his or anybody else's equilibrium. Her arriving with Lisburne, a strange young woman, and a child didn't leave Halliday at a loss. This wasn't the first time the duke's mansion in Charing Cross had provided refuge for pretty women in difficulties, and Halliday did not seem desirous of its being the last.

Equally important, being fully in the duke's confidence, he was aware that a search was on for a missing person. No one had to tell the house steward that the fair-haired woman in black, carrying a sleeping child, was this person. In short order, the housekeeper was escorting the strangers to the guest wing.

Meanwhile, His Grace, who'd returned a short time earlier from his own less successful investigations, was promptly apprised of the visitors. He summoned Leonie and Lisburne to his study.

Clevedon didn't ask annoying questions

392

about how Lisburne happened to be at hand at the odd hour when Fenwick arrived at Maison Noirot with his momentous news. He didn't try to throttle Lisburne, either. But every now and again the duke sent an unfriendly look in the marquess's direction. Lisburne met these with the pretty but stupid look.

"Leonie, you'd better stay the night," Clevedon said, after she'd summarized recent events. "Jeffreys can open the shop. It's not as though you'll be swamped with customers. You need to get some rest, and Marcelline will be anxious if she doesn't speak to you. I know she's been worried." Another thunderous look at Lisburne. "And I'm sure Lisburne will wish to return home and put his cousin's mind at ease as soon as may be."

Sometimes, when Clevedon became excessively ducal, as he was now, Leonie would entertain fantasies of choking him or hitting him in the head with one of the marble busts cluttering up the place. Since she couldn't injure her sister's husband — for one thing, he was too big and his head was too hard and thick — she would react by becoming obtuse and contrary. No Noirot took well to being ordered about.

But this night — morning — she hadn't

the wherewithal to argue with him. She'd sat in the hackney coach, watching Mrs. Williams lull her daughter back to sleep, and found herself brooding about what she'd do if she learned she was carrying Lisburne's child.

She knew he wouldn't turn his back on his offspring, as Theaker or Meffat had done. Since he had an honorable streak as well as a protective one, it wasn't farfetched to suppose he'd offer marriage.

She didn't want to be married to appease somebody's honor or sense of responsibility. She didn't want to be a married case of unrequited love.

Yet it would be the right thing to do for the child.

But the shop. The arguments she could make for Marcelline and Sophy's giving up the shop would apply to her as well.

It hurt, physically, to think of abandoning it. The shop was her link to Cousin Emma. She'd made them into a family and taught them how to have a real life, not one based on fraud and falseness. Every stitch was a stitch she'd taught them. Every design was based on principles she'd taught them. Everything was inspired by her, and by her great love — of the three girls she'd taken under her wing and of her work.

How could Leonie give that up? It would be like giving up some part of her heart.

She caught herself as her eyes filled. Juno, what was wrong with her? She didn't have time for weeping and grieving. She had important matters to put in order. Her trouble was, she was tired. Here at Clevedon House she'd be pampered. And she could confide in her sister. And after a good night's sleep and vast amounts of pampering, she'd sort it out.

Only a ninny would waste mind and time worrying about being pregnant until she was certain this was the case. Meanwhile, she had a problem to solve and a plan whose details needed working out. A clear head was wanted.

And so, for once, she disregarded Clevedon's acting like an overprotective brother. She only smiled and yawned and thanked him and said good night, leaving the men to do whatever it was men felt they had to do in these situations.

Lisburne House library
A short time later

"Not mine?" Swanton said. "You're sure?"

"The child was conceived and born in England," Lisburne said. "I don't know whether it was Theaker or Meffat who sired her, but it had to be one of them. I don't see their making any special effort to help friends out of difficulties of this sort. Their style is more in the nature of pointing fingers and laughing at fools who let themselves get caught."

Lisburne had found Swanton pacing the library. He hadn't been able to sleep, he said. A poem was forming in his mind, but when he tried to write it down, it slipped away.

"I feel sorry for Mrs. Williams and her daughter, then," Swanton said. "I like to think I'd be a good father. I should hope so. I had a good example."

"This is hardly your only opportunity to be a father," Lisburne said.

"I know that. I only meant . . ." Swanton sighed. "Actually, I'm not sure what I meant. My mind won't settle. That is to say, it wouldn't. But now that I know I'm not responsible, I expect I'll do better. Though I still don't know what's to be done."

"Miss Noirot has a plot of some kind simmering in her busy brain," Lisburne said. "So have I, and I was looking forward to fighting with her about it. But Clevedon chased me away and sent her to bed. And now, with your leave, I'll take myself to bed. It's been a tiring night."

As tired as he was, he didn't expect to sleep. He had too much in his mind. Hours of lovemaking with Leonie, and the strange happiness. And the confusion. He was too young to be easily tired or fuddled, yet this night swirled in his mind, images chasing one another. The little girl, asleep in her mother's lap as they traveled to Clevedon House . . . a child . . .

What if Leonie bore him a child? Answers tangled in his mind, going round and round, until fatigue swamped him, and he slept.

He awoke shortly after noon, which was when Polcaire presented him with a note in precise and dizzyingly feminine handwriting.

Lisburne read the message again and again. This was easy enough to do, since it was a work of most businesslike brevity: *Would his lordship be so good as to come to Clevedon House at half-past two o'clock sharp in reference to matters previously discussed.*

She'd signed it L.N.

That was all, a handful of no-nonsense words and her initials. Yet he studied it as though it had been some ancient text. He studied it the way Swanton had studied the *Spectacle* the other day. Looking for . . . what?

More, something more.

If only he had an inkling of what *more,* exactly, he sought.

The Regent's Park Zoological Gardens
Afternoon of Friday 24 July
"No, no, Clara, you mustn't vex yourself," Lady Gladys said. "Can't you see she's exactly like the poem?"

"Lady Alda Morris is no poem," Lady Clara said. "What she's like is a horrid novel."

"No, no, she's like Mrs. Abdy's poem. Only listen."

The two women stood in the shade of a thick stand of shrubbery. They were waiting for the rest of their group, who'd lagged behind to speak to a zookeeper.

Lady Gladys threw a mischievous look in the direction of the laggards, then fluttered her eyelashes and adopted a simpering smile and recited:

How charming she looks — her dark curls
   Really float with a *natural air.*
And the beads might be taken for pearls
   That are twined in that beautiful hair:
Then what tints her fair features
      o'erspread —
   That she uses *white paint some pretend;*

But believe me, she only wears *red,* —
  She's my very particular friend!

Then her voice how divine it appears
  While caroling "Rise gentle m-moo —"

"Moo?" Lady Clara said, stifling a giggle.

"If you could see the face you're making,"
Lady Gladys said. "Oh, you're too bad."

"I? How am I to help myself? You've
caught her mannerisms exactly. Who knew
what a clever mimic you were? It makes me
furious to think how long you hid your light
under a bushel."

"A bushel? At this size? I should have said
it wanted a hay barn, my dear."

"Oh, my goodness, you took the words
right out of her mouth."

Shrieks of laughter.

"Now you understand the trick of it."

"I do, but I couldn't do it half so well as
you. My mind isn't quick enough. I only
stand there wanting to scratch her eyes out."

"I never do anymore," Lady Gladys said.
"She affords me too much entertainment.
For instance, I've only to think of that
poem, and the fresh verses I could compose,
and it's impossible to be vexed. And best of
all — she has no idea how much she amuses
me."

"I wish I had your philosophy," Lady Clara said.

"Nonsense! You don't need philosophy. Everyone loves and admires you, as they ought to do. I, on the contrary, am as dreadful in my way as she."

"No, no, you're only the smallest fraction as dreadful." Lady Clara laughed. "One percent. Maybe one and a half."

"You wound me, cuz. You sadly underestimate my powers. I'm a Gorgon, a fearsome, dreadful thing. Men run at my approach. Which they can hear from a good distance away, like thundering herds of rhinocer— rhino— curse you, Clara. You put me out when you cross your eyes. What's the plural of rhinoceros?"

"Elephants."

The two women dissolved into laughter.

They went on in this fashion for another minute or two, then moved away from the shrubbery, arm in arm.

They had no idea that Lord Swanton stood on the other side of the shrubbery, hands clenched.

They never saw him hurry alongside the wall of greenery, trying to catch more of the conversation. They never saw his shoulders sag as they moved out of his hearing, and their companions rejoined them, and the group continued their tour of the Zoological Society's Gardens.

Saturday 25 July

My Dear John,

I beg you'll forgive this scrawl. My hands shake so, I can scarcely write. I was obliged to leave my lodgings in great haste. My landlady told me some strange men came yesterday, asking questions. She said she didn't want any trouble. I realized this was another way of telling me that she will answer the questions, depending on who gives her stronger reasons, in the form of coin. As you know, I've none to spare. All I could say was how sorry I was for the inconvenience.

You will hardly believe the speed with which she betrayed me. Not two hours later, she brought up a note from Lord Swanton's solicitor. I pretended not to understand what it was about, but I am terrified. It refers to a law about creating scandal against a peer, and threatens me with prison — and Bianca to share my cell! I hurried from my rooms, taking our daughter with me, and leaving most of my belongings behind, to prevent my landlady's knowing I'd absconded.

I write from Lambeth, to beseech your help. All I want is fare to Portsmouth and thence to America. From your silence of the past several days, I assume your applications to Lord Swanton have not been successful. On the contrary, I wonder if they've done more harm than good. I hope you have not betrayed me. <u>You know there are things I could tell certain people, not to your advantage.</u> It grieves me to press you like this, but time has run out.

A children's fête is held at Vauxhall this evening. The doors open early for the event, and there, with a child in hand, I shall pass unremarked. Certainly the scene of my last performance is the last place my pursuers will expect to see me. I have made arrangements for my departure. All that is wanting is funds, a small matter of five pounds. The same little theater will be empty until nine o'clock, and the acquaintance who allowed us discreet ingress the last time will do so again. I shall expect you promptly at eight o'clock. I shall await you immediately within the door through which I made my entrance last time. Do not fail me, else you will drive me to take measures I abhor.

Yours,
Dulcie

"The bitch," Theaker said, looking up from the letter his friend had handed him. "It's blackmail. Throw it on the fire."

"But we did promise," Meffat said. "We promised to speak to Swanton."

"Yes, eventually. After the furor's died down." Meaning, after Lisburne had had time to cool down. In the first heat of temper he tended not to behave rationally. An irrational Lisburne could easily make a man's life unexpectedly short or, at best, extremely painful.

When he was in a more reasonable frame of mind, they'd pay a visit. They'd say they'd worked on the lady, and she was willing, for a small sum, to let it go. She'd send a letter to the papers, absolving Swanton of blame. She'd claim it was a case of mistaken identity.

They had warned her, in no uncertain terms, not to use his name during the scene, else they'd find themselves in an exceedingly tight corner. But Dulcie Williams was no fool.

Unfortunately, she had turned out to be a great deal less of a fool than was quite convenient.

She didn't know — or did she? — how precarious their social position was at present, thanks to the scandal with Adderley. If she exposed them, their remaining friends would turn their backs.

Social ostracism would be catastrophic. Tradesmen preferred to extend credit to those who had full purses, prospects of same, or social connections from whom they could borrow.

"Five pounds," Meffat said. "You know they'll offer her more money to tattle on us, and you've seen what a fine liar she is. We'll have to raise it somehow. She has us at a stand."

"She had your cock at a stand, that's the trouble," Theaker said. "You couldn't find a stupid female? The world's overstocked with 'em."

"She *acted* stupid."

"Damn her to hell."

"What'll we do?"

"Hold your tongue. I'm *thinking.*"

CHAPTER FIFTEEN

The season — the season —
    It's nearly all over;
And spite of my schemings,
    I can't get a lover.
I've tried every method
    A husband to catch;
But at Hymen's bright flambeau
    I can't light a match.
                    — Miss Agnes Alicia****
The Court Journal, Saturday 25 July 1835

Vauxhall
Evening of Saturday 25 July
Theaker and Meffat found Dulcie Williams not immediately within the side door as she'd promised, but upon the stage, in front of the closed curtain. She was posed as she'd been when she played Rosalind in boy's guise in *As You Like It.* A carpetbag stood in for the fallen tree used in the performance, and she had her foot propped

on it in the same supposedly masculine way — the way that drove some men wild, since it showed her fine legs to excellent advantage. This evening, however, she wore a black frock, instead of the breeches Meffat had found so irresistibly enticing.

She looked up, surprised, when they entered.

"You're early," she said.

Theaker and Meffat had come early, hoping to catch her at any tricks she might be planning. They'd checked the main doors, and watched who was coming and going. Though they'd seen nothing suspicious, Theaker still felt something wasn't right.

"Forgot to wind my watch," he said.

"I was so sure you'd be late," she said. "Now you've caught me pretending I'm back where I belong. How I miss it! Still, as long as I'm here, shall I perform for you, gratis?"

"Not exactly gratis," Theaker grumbled. "Five pounds a bit steep even for the real thing, full length. Get down from there, will you? Never mind fooling about."

"John would like to hear my Rosalind, wouldn't you, John, one last time?"

"Rather see your legs," Meffat said.

"Don't be an idiot," Theaker said, looking uneasily about the dim theater. Outside, darkness wouldn't fall for a while yet. Within the theater, twilight prevailed.

"Not quite cured of me, John?" she said.

"For five pounds, we hope to be cured of you permanently," Theaker said. "Come down from there. We haven't time for games."

"How high-strung you gentlemen can be!" she said. "No one will disturb us for an hour at least. Did you notice the hordes of children and their mamas and papas? Nothing would lure them in here but jugglers and acrobats. Not that you know much about children, or want to know. But I promise you won't find a more private place in Vauxhall at present. The main door's locked, as you no doubt discovered when you checked. I heard you rattling it."

"To tell you the truth, Dulcie, he don't trust you much," Meffat said.

"The last time I came to this theater, he trusted me enough to do the acting he wanted," she said. "And then for only a few shillings, wasn't it?"

"A few!" Meffat said. "You know it was all the ready money we had."

"But you contrived to get more since you received my letter, I collect?" she said. "Because if you didn't, you'll place me in an awkward position."

What she meant was, she'd place Theaker and Meffat in the awkward position. Theaker wished he'd let Meffat give her money and send her on her way when she'd first cornered him at the British Institution. But as one with some experience in the blackmail line, Theaker had felt sure she'd come back and make a nuisance of herself.

He'd decided it was cleverer to kill two birds with one stone: Take the wind out of Swanton's sails and make Dulcie a partner in crime, so to speak. Who'd believe her, after she'd lied in front of all those people? She was an *actress.*

But he'd underestimated her audacity and her skill at double-dealing.

"You didn't give us much time to raise the ready," he said.

"I haven't much time to give," she said. "And no place to hide. In this" — she tapped the carpetbag with her foot — "is all we own, Bianca and I. Meanwhile I don't know when one of Lord Lisburne's detectives will knock at the door or spring out from an alley. Then it'll be the lawyers and writs. If you wanted more time, you ought to have managed matters better for me."

"If you'd been more discreet, you wouldn't have this problem," Theaker said.

"Were *you* discreet?" she said. "Did you

408

not promise me there'd be no trouble? Did you not tell me that Lord Lisburne —"

"Hush," Theaker said, looking about him. "That voice of yours carries, drat you."

"If you want me to whisper, you'll have to come nearer," she said.

"Stop playing about," Theaker said.

"Or what?" she said. "Would you be here if you knew a way to wiggle out of it? A little trickier, this, than wriggling out of what's owing to your child."

"Not mine," Theaker said. "And if it was, I wouldn't let anybody trick me into admitting it. Don't know how you never saw what a conniver she was," he told his friend. "But you couldn't see beyond her pretty arse— and still can't, by the looks of it."

"Dash it, Theaker, the chit looks like me!" Meffat said. "You said it yourself. My eyes. My nose. You were the one told me to keep away the other night. You're the one said all they needed to do was see me alongside the little gal and they'd never believe it was Swanton's."

"*Will* you hold your tongue!" Theaker said. "I vow, even now she turns you into a dithering idiot."

" 'Love is merely a madness; and, I tell you, deserves as well a dark house and a whip, as madmen do,' " she declaimed, becoming Rosalind again. " 'And the reason why they are not so punished and cured, is, that the lunacy is so ordinary, that the whippers are in love too.' Do you still love me, John?"

"Ah, no, no, it was never like that," he said. "You know it wasn't, Dulcie. I never said that, did I, nor made promises."

"He only wanted to bed you, and you knew it as well as he," Theaker said.

"I was scarcely seventeen years old!"

"More like nineteen and pretending otherwise," Theaker said. "Still, you're older and wiser now, aren't you?" He advanced to the stage and slapped down the coins. "There's your five pounds. Do we need to escort you to a hackney to make sure we see the back of you?"

"No, I'll take my daughter and be gone," she said. She moved to the edge of the stage, but didn't move to pick up the coins. "Only one thing —"

"Devil take you and the brat both!" Theaker said. "That's as much as we could raise. Will you pick our pockets?"

She only smiled. "I only want to satisfy my curiosity. Why, of all the men in London you might have paid me to accuse falsely —"

"As to that, who's to say who was the father?"

"But you know I wasn't in France when he —"

"You *might* have been."

"But I never was abroad. I've the handbills to prove it. In my scrapbook." Again she tapped the carpetbag with her foot.

The jade was playing her own deep game with them, beyond a doubt. More money wanted. Or something else? Theaker looked about him and listened. The trouble was, as she'd said, Vauxhall was very noisy this night. Even with the theater doors closed, he could hear children shrieking outside. Drums and music, too. The walls muted the sound, but couldn't shut it out altogether. The noise of the festivities outside made it difficult to distinguish untoward sounds inside the theater.

"Maybe we'd better see you on your way, after all," Theaker said.

She gave the carpetbag another tap. "Hoping for a look inside? But it's not in there. Not enough room. You're welcome to look. I know John won't mind peeping at my undergarments."

Theaker started toward the stage. He reached up for the carpetbag. She kicked it out of reach.

He swore.

"So sorry to disappoint you, my good sir," she said. "I find I'd rather you didn't paw through my clothes. But don't worry about the scrapbook. I gave it to a friend for safekeeping."

Theaker stepped back a pace, chilled. "What friend, damn you?"

"That would be me," came a woman's voice from behind the closed curtain. It moved slightly, and the redheaded dressmaker stepped out onto the stage. She held a large scrapbook.

"Was this what you were looking for, Sir Roger?" she said.

For an instant, the two men stood stock still, jaws dropped. Their expressions were so perfectly theatrical that Leonie had all she could do not to laugh. Meffat's face paled while Theaker's turned an ugly red. Meffat seemed to recover his wits first, making a dash for the door through which they'd entered, but that way out was closed now. One of tonight's performers, a circus strong man, guarded it.

"What're you running away from?" Theaker said. "A French milliner? Nothing she can do to you. Nothing she can say that

412

anybody'll believe. All the world knows she's a —"

"You might want to stop and think before you complete that sentence," Lisburne said as he stepped out from behind the curtain.

Theaker retreated a pace and looked about him. It was plain enough to see he had no easy way out. He could either surrender or brazen it out.

Leonie was betting on the latter. He was a bully, after all.

His color darkened another shade, and his voice grew louder. "You here, too, then? No surprise. Got you by the round, wrinkly ones, has she?"

Leonie shot Lisburne a glance, but he only smiled. Had Theaker a grain of sense, he'd hold his tongue, seeing that smile.

But no.

"Thinking of going the way of Clevedon and Longmore?" Theaker went on. "Might want to think again. Any idea who your pretty vixen is, really? Who any of them are, her and her scheming sisters?" He laughed. "What a joke! You see what this is, Meffat? Desperate measures. They've got nothing. What do you care about Dulcie's rubbishy scrapbook? How often do they print the year on a handbill? It's all a hoax, don't you see? Their word against yours."

Clevedon's voice came from behind the curtains. "Newspapers print the year." He stepped out from behind the curtains. "Mrs. Williams received laudatory reviews in the *Bath Chronicle and Weekly Gazette,* the *Bristol Mercury,* and other English newspapers during the years she was supposedly in France."

Theaker's color faded abruptly, as well it might, but he kept up the bluster. "You're in trouble now, Dulcie," he said. "Making scandal for an aristocrat. They'll throw you in a cell and forget you." He folded his arms. "If you were hoping to terrify me, Your Grace, you're headed for disappointment."

"We heard you admit to paying Mrs. Williams to accuse Lord Swanton of fathering and abandoning her child," Clevedon said. He nodded toward the others on stage. "All of us heard it."

"You heard. Hah. What did you hear or imagine you heard? A little playing about with Dulcie. The only proof you've got is that she lied."

"You admitted to paying her to lie about Lord Swanton," Leonie said.

"Did I? Don't recollect."

"You admitted it in the hearing of witnesses," Leonie said.

414

"Not the most reliable witnesses, I'd say," Theaker said. "You three have an interest in protecting Lord Swan-About. On the other side is everybody who saw Dulcie say it was him and no other who got the brat on her. If she lied then, she'll lie again. Probably don't know who the father is. She'll blame anybody."

He tipped his hat in a mocking salute. "Most entertaining, gentlemen, *ladies.*" He started toward Meffat. "But if there's nothing further, Meffat and I will be on our way . . ." He trailed off as he saw Meffat's expression change. The latter's eyes widened and his mouth fell open.

"What the devil are you gawking at?" Theaker said. He must have heard the sound behind him then, because he turned back to the stage.

The curtain slowly rose, revealing Lords Herringstone, Geddings, and Flinton, as well as Lord Valentine Fairfax, Messrs. Bates, Crawford, Hempton . . . and Tom Foxe, of *Foxe's Morning Spectacle.* The last had a shorthand notebook in his hand, in which he was busily scribbling.

Then Swanton came out from the wings. He stood a little apart from the others.

Mrs. Williams kicked the coins off the stage and onto the floor. "You'll need

those," she told Theaker. "To pay the lawyers."

"You filthy, lying slut," Theaker said. His
furious gaze went to Leonie. "The pair of
you. Blackmailing c—"

"You bastard!" Swanton roared. He
launched himself off the stage and onto
Theaker, knocking him down hard enough
to make Theaker's hat fly off.

Swanton grabbed him by the hair and
banged his head on the floor. "You two-
faced, bullying cheat! What did I ever do to
you?"

For a moment, everybody simply stood
dumbfounded.

Then Meffat ran back to aid his friend.
The others shook off their stupefaction, and
leapt off the stage and into the fray.

"Don't kill them!" Leonie cried. "No
blood! You promised!"

She wasn't sure anybody heard her.

Swanton was trying to choke the life out
of Theaker, and most of the other men were
urging him on or making bets. But Clevedon
pulled Meffat away and Lisburne pulled his
cousin off Theaker.

"By Jupiter," Leonie heard someone say.
"Didn't know Swanton had it in him."

Later

"That was better than any play," Crawford said.

"You could have knocked me over with a feather when Swanton went for him," said Hempton.

Lisburne doubted anybody was more shocked than he was.

Well, Theaker, possibly.

Lisburne smiled. "Swanton has un-plumbed depths," he said. "He's not as soft as he looks."

Not soft at all, Lisburne realized, except in his feelings, those tender sensibilities. In Tuscany hadn't the poet walked along rocky paths up and down mountains with Lis-burne? They'd crossed the Alps in miserable weather, and Swanton never faltered. He rode and fenced. He was fit, in any event, though not enough of a pugilist to floor Theaker in ordinary circumstances, as Swanton would be the first to admit.

At present, the men who'd joined them onstage now stood with Lisburne near Vauxhall's entrance. They were watching the Master of Ceremonies escort the not-nearly-battered-enough Theaker and Meffat from the Royal Gardens. This Mr. Simpson did with his usual courtesy. Without appearing to be ejecting anybody he smoothly led

417

them to the gate.

Some of the fête's earlier arrivals were watching, too, and word was already beginning to travel round the gardens.

Meffat made a shamefaced exit. Theaker swaggered out as though he hadn't a care in the world.

When they were out of sight, Clevedon said his goodbyes. He was eager to be home, Lisburne knew, to report the evening's events to his wife.

"I do wish Lady Gladys had been there to see it," said Flinton as they turned back toward the fête and its growing crowd. "She's always maintained there was something fishy about the business."

"There to see it!" Geddings said. "I should hope not. I blushed to hear some of Theaker's remarks. Shocking language. Unfit for mixed company."

"Doubt Lady Gladys'd turn a hair," Crawford said. "She's surely heard worse. Father a soldier and home like a military encampment, hasn't she said?"

"Lord Boulsworth can make a sailor blush," Hempton said. "That includes the King, or so I've been told."

The King had entered the Royal Navy as a midshipman and spent a segment of his early life at sea.

"Lady Gladys will hear about it soon enough," Bates said.

"Everybody will hear about it," Lisburne said. Even before Foxe's special edition appeared on Sunday morning, the Great World would be buzzing about the shocking disclosures, and the cruel way Theaker and Meffat had taken advantage of a young mother's desperation.

Swanton's display of outrage wouldn't do his reputation any harm, either.

"I'll wager five guineas those two will be on their way to Dover before dawn," Bates said.

"Before midnight," Hempton said.

A short period of betting ensued regarding precise times of departure — until Herringstone pointed out that it would be impossible to ascertain exactly what time the two would flee London.

That they would bolt for the Continent was not in dispute.

By Sunday, if not before, Theaker and Meffat would find all doors closed to them. Should they appear on the street, their former friends would cross it to avoid them. Wherever they went, they'd meet with the cut direct. They'd be fools to remain in London.

Despite Dulcie's taunt, no one needed

lawyers, as Leonie had pointed out early in the planning stages. She was, after all, a businesswoman, first, last, and always.

"Without friends, they've no credit," she'd argued. "Without credit, they can't remain in London. Every tradesman with a working brain keeps track of the bankruptcies and scandals. I certainly do. I like the idea of those two men spending time in a damp, dirty cell — but I think Lord Swanton would rather do without the publicity of a slander trial."

True enough. All the same, Lisburne was deeply sorry to see Theaker and Meffat go with all their teeth intact. Especially Theaker.

But it was done, and Leonie was satisfied, and she'd stood to lose most.

Lisburne looked about for her.

Bates followed his gaze. "Where's Swanton got to, I wonder?" he said. "You'd think he'd hang about to say bon voyage. Or throw bottles at their heads. Or at least rotten vegetables."

When Lisburne had last glimpsed his cousin, the two women were towing him through the side door. "Probably gone off to find a quiet place where he can compose an ode to redemption or revelation or the death of illusions or some such," he said.

"If I were Swanton, I'd hide," Valentine said. "When word of his wild avenger performance gets about, he'll have to fight off the women with a whip."

"There you're wrong," said Hempton. "It's his delicate sensibilities they love. Now he's shown he has ballocks like the rest of us, they'll have to take him down off the pedestal and treat him like anybody else."

"Stuff!" Crawford said. "If you think so, you know nothing about women. Did you forget that they cruelly abandoned him when he was falsely accused?"

"Not all of them," Flinton said. "Lady Gladys said it was a hoax or a madwoman."

"All but her, then," Crawford said. "But the others'll be back, all weepy and conscience-stricken — and if you think women mind a man having ballocks, you need to make yourself a reservation at the asylum."

Betting ensued.

Lisburne left them to it, and set out to find Leonie.

Darkness had fallen, and Vauxhall's thousands of lamps were lit. The orchestra played. Some visitors danced. Others ate. Most of the children had been herded to entertainments near the other end of the gardens, where they'd have a prime view of the fireworks.

While she would have liked watching Theaker and Meffat's ignominious departure, Leonie thought it best to get Mrs. Williams and Swanton away from the others. And if she was perfectly honest with herself, she didn't relish hanging about that lot of men, given what Theaker had said.

Swanton went with the two women meekly enough — or dazed, was more like it. Apparently, he was as astonished with himself as others were. He accompanied Leonie and Mrs. Williams without protest to a supper box, and only stared at the menu blankly until they gave up on him and ordered.

The thin ham brought to mind Lisburne's joke the other night. The wine was rather ordinary. But she was hungrier than she'd realized, and relieved, actually, to be with two people who required nothing from her, including attention.

Swanton ate what was put in front of him, though he did so in an abstracted manner.

Mrs. Williams reviewed her own recent performance, and imagined aloud the ways in which one might transform it into a play. The business at the end, when Lord Swanton leapt onto Theaker, would have an audience on its feet, she maintained.

"I wonder your lordship doesn't write for the stage," she said.

"I've tried," he said. "But I haven't the talent for plays. My mind's too plodding and studying. My touch is too heavy. But you, Mrs. Williams, ought to write. The rest of us needed only to stand silent like the Greek chorus. Clevedon had the most lines, but he's used to making speeches. But you — improvising as you went along . . ." He shook his head. "For a while I was so caught up in it that I forgot — plague take it! There's Lady Bartham and her daughters. I forgot that half the world would be here tonight."

For a moment, listening to her companions, Leonie had forgotten, too.

Not everything this night was playacting. The children's fête was genuine enough, and many of its sponsors would have begun arriving soon after the doors opened. Before long, news of Theaker and Meffat's disgrace would be making the rounds of the supper boxes and travel along the walks. Because of the charity fête, Vauxhall would hold a larger than usual proportion of the Upper Ten Thousand.

Mrs. Williams looked about her. "Do you know, in the circumstances, I think it politic to make myself scarce," she said, and quickly

423

suited action to words.

Meanwhile Lord Swanton summoned the waiter. As soon as he'd paid for their meal and offered a distracted farewell and thanks, the poet made himself scarce as well.

When they'd both moved out of sight, Leonie made her leisurely way toward the festivities. Lisburne, she knew, would be with the other men. Since her shop had been implicated in the scandal, people would understand her taking part in Theaker and Meffat's exposure.

But beyond that, she'd be most unwise to let herself be seen in Lisburne's company. After tonight's events, she could expect her customers to start returning. Best not to jeopardize that by arousing suspicions that her participation in the unmasking wasn't purely a business matter.

She had to trust Tom Foxe to resist printing Theaker's insinuations about Lisburne and her. But Foxe owed her a great favor. Rarely did he get to actually witness the beau monde's inner workings.

She supposed she ought to go home. But the last time she'd been to Vauxhall, she hadn't been able to enjoy it.

She could indulge herself for a little while. It was early yet, and since this was a charity event, at higher prices, the chances of encountering drunken riffraff . . .

The sound of familiar laughter broke her train of thought.

It came from nearby, but it was hard to pinpoint. She had paused near the orchestra, which was playing at the moment. Many people were dancing.

She saw Lady Gladys waltzing with Lord Flinton.

Leonie walked a little nearer to the dancing.

Her ladyship looked very well, in a shade of copper not all women could wear successfully. As she'd done time and again, Marcelline had created the illusion of a smaller waist, this time with judicious use of a V-line above and an upside-down V below, where the robe opened over the dress. Pretty embellishments softened the severity of the lines.

Equally important, though, was Lady Gladys's mien. She carried herself with confidence and good nature. Her face would never be pretty but her smile was, as was the sparkle in her eyes.

Lord Flinton seemed to be captivated.

Leonie had dressed elegantly, of course, for tonight's performance. Knowing she looked well always increased her confidence. More important, one must advertise the shop's wares whenever possible. But she'd never had a chance to watch her protégée at a social event. And so she made herself inconspicuous, in the way she and her sisters had learned to do, and slipped in among the bystanders to observe her and her sister's handiwork.

When the dance was over, Lord Flinton escorted Lady Gladys back to her chaperons — two matrons who seemed not much older than their charges — and others of their party.

Lady Alda was there, in an unbecoming puce gown that looked horribly like the work of Mrs. Downes's shop — also known as Dowdy's — which fancied itself a Maison Noirot rival. As Lady Gladys rejoined her group, Lady Alda made a remark, and Lady Gladys answered with uplifted eyebrow.

Leonie drew nearer, but she couldn't hear what they were saying. Then Lady Gladys laughed, and whatever she was saying caused the others to gather about her.

Leonie moved closer.

Lady Gladys was reciting a comic poem. She was acting it out, much in the way Leonie had done at the New Western Athenaeum with "The Second Son."

I have sung to a thousand;
    And danced with no fewer;
And sighed in the hearing
    Of hundreds, I'm sure.
But my sighs and my songs
    Have all failed most outrageously;
Nor have my poor toes
    Turned *out more advantageously;*
        And the season — the season —
        It's nearly all over;
        And spite of my schemings,
        I can't get a lover.
To archery meetings
    In green have I —
— have I —

She faltered and broke off as a gentleman advanced upon the group. He was a tall, slender gentleman who wore his flaxen hair overlong and dressed theatrically. The hair, as he swept off his hat, was tousled. His coat was a bit rumpled, and Leonie knew his trousers had a rip at the knee, thanks to colliding with the floor when he tackled Sir Roger Theaker.

The orchestra having paused, Leonie could make out some of the exchange, though Lord Swanton's voice didn't carry as clearly as Lady Gladys's did.

But Leonie had no trouble perceiving that

he was speaking and everybody else was behaving as though he was a snake charmer and they a basket of cobras. She saw his color rise as he spoke. Something about "do me the honor." Lady Gladys was blushing, too, the deep pink washing down over her well-displayed bosom.

The orchestra began playing again.

And Lord Swanton led her out into the dancing area.

And everybody who knew them simply stood watching in disbelief as Lord Swanton danced with Lady Gladys Fairfax. For a time the pair was silent. But at last her ladyship said something. His lordship looked at her for a moment. Then he laughed. The bystanders, their friends and family and acquaintances, looked at one another.

Then, by degrees, they made up pairs, and began to dance. All except Lady Alda, who walked away in a huff.

From behind Leonie came a low, familiar voice. "Well, it seems he knows how to further his acquaintance with a girl, after all."

Lisburne had watched Leonie much in the way he'd watched her at the British Institution. Then, though, she'd seemed to belong. At present, she stood on the fringes of the crowd, and it seemed to him that she stood on the outside looking in, like a shopgirl standing outside a great house where a party was in process.

No one seemed to notice her, which made no sense, even given the extraordinary sight of Swanton dancing with Gladys.

How could anybody fail to notice Leonie? Tonight she wore a blue gown of some silk as light as a cloud. Enormous sleeves as usual, and one of those vast shawl sorts of things that covered the tops of the sleeves and made women's shoulders seem enormous. It tucked into her belt, which, in contrast to the sleeves and skirt, seemed to circle a waist no bigger than a thimble. She'd tied a lacy thing about her neck, with a bow at her throat and tassels hanging from the corners of the lacy thing. Her coiffure rose in a fantastic arrangement of knots and braids adorned with ribbons and flowers.

A dizzying vision, and the more so because he knew what was underneath. He knew what she felt like under his hands. He knew what her skin smelled and tasted like . . .

But if he thought about that he wouldn't be able to think at all.

And it seemed he needed to.

Why wasn't she dancing with the others? She ought to be one of them. One sister

429

was a duchess. The other was a countess.

And she was . . . a lady.

How obvious that had been when she'd stood in the theater with Dulcie Williams.

Dulcie was a decent enough actress, and no doubt did a good job of playing ladies on the stage. She wasn't vulgar. On the contrary.

But she wasn't a lady.

Leonie was a lady.

It seemed so obvious now.

That pig Theaker.

Any idea who your pretty vixen is, really? Who any of them are, her and her sisters?

Lisburne had met only two of them but reason told him they must be three extraordinary women.

And this one had astounding self-control.

She didn't turn at the sound of his voice, and if he hadn't got into the habit of watching her so closely he wouldn't have discerned the slight change in her posture, the alertness.

"One can only hope her ladyship won't toy with his affections," she said.

"This doesn't mean you've won our wager," he said. "Swanton's been infatuated with Gladys's voice this age."

"Has he been, indeed?" Finally she looked up at him, her blue eyes wide and innocent.

"He falls in love with appalling frequency," he said. "If he hadn't been occupied with fending off admirers and writing new poetry to make them love him even more hopelessly — and possibly go into declines in droves — I daresay he'd have fallen in love a dozen times at least by now. But fame is distracting. I'm so relieved to see he's returned to normal."

"Was he always violent before, do you mean?"

"Violent emotions," he said.

"When was the last time he tried to kill a man?" she said.

A pause, though Lisburne didn't have to search his memory for the answer.

"Never," he said. "I didn't think he had it in him."

"I see a Botticelli in my future," she said.

"He's not going to offer for Gladys, if that's what you're thinking."

"One of them will," she said.

"Possibly," he said. "Eventually. But the Season is nearly over."

" 'The season — the season —/It's nearly all over;/and spite of my schemings,/I can't get a lover.' "

"You've got one," he said, dropping his voice.

"It's a poem," she said. "Lady Gladys was

431

reciting it, to the enraged confusion of Lady Alda — exactly as I suggested. Call me Pygmalion."

"Dance with me, Pygmalion," Lisburne said.

Her gaze went to the couples whirling about in front of the orchestra, then came back to him. "I can't," she said. "It's bad for business."

"It's Vauxhall," he said, "not Almack's. Once they spot you, all the other fellows will ask you, too. But I should like to be . . . first."

Again.

Always.

And that was when he realized how much trouble he was in.

Chapter Sixteen

We waltz! and behold her,
Her head on my shoulder,
Cheeks meeting, eyes greeting, hearts
    beating, and thus
I twist her and twirl her,
And whisk her and whirl her —
We whirl round the room till the room whirls
    round us!
                    — *The Athenaeum; or,*
    Spirit of the English Magazines, 1826

Lisburne made a bow so extravagantly beautiful, Leonie couldn't help laughing. In answer she gave him the extreme version of the famous Noirot curtsey. It was a theatrical performance of a curtsey, a flurry of silk and lace as she floated down, down, down like a ballerina, then rose up again "like Venus rising from the waves," someone had once said.

Then his arm went round her waist and

he whirled her into the crowd of dancers, and all her sensible thoughts flew away, up into the boughs of the trees among the colored lamps and up among the stars, to look down on her from afar.

She'd had more than one triumph tonight. She'd recovered her shop's and the Milliners' Society's reputation. She'd helped a potential tragedy of a girl become the belle of the ball, dancing with — unless Leonie had entirely lost her ability to read people — her heart's desire. She'd helped Dulcie Williams out of the trouble she'd got herself into.

Leonie was entitled to celebrate a little. She was entitled to forget her anxieties, at least for one dance.

"Such a trial you continue to be!" he said.

Startled, she looked up at him. But he was smiling.

"An enigma, or a puzzle at the very least," he said. "Where did a dressmaker learn to dance so well? Among other unlikely accomplishments, like Greek and Roman mythology and Byron's poetry. And when do you find time to practice?"

"I doubt any woman needs much practice to dance well with you," she said.

"Do you accuse me of making my partners look good?" he said.

"It's a waltz," she said. "A man takes hold of a girl and she must go where he takes her. You waltz in the same decisive way you do everything else. I'm certain you would never allow me to trip over your feet."

"And risk scuffing my boots' brilliant shine?"

"In spite of my profession, I'm overcome sometimes with the wild desire —"

"This sounds promising —"

"To scuff your boots and rumple your neckcloth and —"

"*Extremely* promising." His voice had deepened.

"But then I think of Polcaire," she said.

"To the devil with Polcaire," he said.

"And I can't do it in public, in any case," she said.

"An excellent point," he said. "Let's go somewhere private. Later. Soon, but after this. Because your dress was meant to be seen in motion. It was meant for waltzing, especially with me, because my attire complements it so well. For which we have Polcaire to thank."

"So I assumed," she said.

"You don't know the half of it," he said. "When he put out the blue waistcoat, I said, 'A certain lady remarked particularly on the touches of green, which complement her attire.' And he said, 'But my lord cannot wear green with that coat, and I have laid out the blue waistcoat.' Which only proves he is an oracle, because here you are in blue —"

"I think I rather love Polcaire," she said.

"I'd rather you didn't," he said. "I worry constantly that a woman will lead him astray or throw him into a state of careless desolation."

"I doubt he has it in him to be careless," she said. "I suspect he's an artistic genius like Marcelline. Why didn't he become a tailor? The hours are shorter, and with his artistic eye, he could make a great fortune."

"Because he never had the temperament to be a tailor's apprentice, I suppose," he said. "Or because so many tailors' customers attach so little importance to paying their bills. I believe the late King bankrupted several vendors. I know Beau Brummell was thousands of pounds in debt to his tailors. And that was nothing to what he owed his friends."

"That was a long time ago," she said. "A more innocent time. There are ways of making sure customers pay their bills. Or perhaps you need to have worked in Paris to learn the knack. Still, I'll admit it requires a degree of ruthlessness some artists can't stomach." Marcelline, for instance. Sophy. As ruthless and single-minded as they could be in other ways, they avoided all the nasty money issues.

"As I suspected, the waltz has aroused in you romantic feelings," he said.

She swallowed. "I'm not romantic."

"So you delude yourself," he said. "But when you speak of your ruthless ways with customers in arrears, my heart pounds."

She remembered the way he'd made her read the mercer's bill . . . and what had followed. Her skin took fire and the heat raced through her veins. It pooled in her belly and melted her brain.

And because her brain was melted, she lost track of words and had no clever answer. She was too aware of his hands, one so warm at her waist and the other clasping hers. She stared at his neckcloth and tried to be sensible. She tried to think of the shop and her real life.

But she was in his arms, and waltzing was so perilously like making love. She could see his chest rise and fall, and when he spoke she heard the quickened rate of his breathing. She was aware of the strength of his long legs as they brushed against her dress, as he led her, so surely and easily, round and round. She was aware of the place about them dissolving, as in a dream, to a blur of music and lights like colored stars, and in the midst of this, the shadow-like dark colors of the men's dress and the rainbow of women's summer dresses, a galaxy swirling about them.

She gave up fighting and let the night's sensual joys sweep her away. For this moment she would let herself be lost in the beauty of the fantasy world about her, set to music, real music.

Here she danced among men and women of the upper ranks as well as many of lesser importance. She wasn't dancing with one of her sisters or a seamstress but with a man who might be the prince in any girl's romantic fantasies. She danced with the man of her dreams. The man she'd fallen in love with, un-sensible she.

"In Paris," she said, "we danced. At La Chaumière and Montagne Belleville and the Prado and elsewhere. Even seamstresses learn how to dance. Certainly they ought to, and I take care to have my Milliners' Society girls learn. Dancing gives one grace and physical confidence. It's one of life's great pleasures, obtainable without great expense or difficulty. To dance, one doesn't need a special place or an orchestra. A piano will do. Or a guitar. Or one can sing or hum.

My sisters and I have danced to organ grinders in the street, playing Rossini."

He didn't answer right away, and that silence between them sounded louder than the music. Then he said so gently, "I think you dance so well because you love it. And because music appeals to your mathematical mind. And because . . ." He shook his head. "No, no more. I believe I was on the brink of poetry."

And she was on the brink of telling him too much, explaining herself, her past, the world she'd come from. Who she was, really. As though this night wasn't a dream, a momentary aberration in the real business of life. As though they had a future together.

She knew better. It was better to leave than to be left, and the longer she put it off, the harder the parting. Better to start as soon as possible, teaching herself how to fall out of love.

But she had these last few moments.

"Then let's just dance," she said.

Perhaps it was better not to talk.

When Leonie spoke of Paris, Lisburne's chest felt tight. He remembered her saying that of the three sisters she'd spent the greatest percentage of her life there. And this night he caught — along with the so-faint hint of Paris in her speech — the small, elusive note in minor key, of loss.

Any idea who your pretty vixen is, really?

Lisburne had thought he knew her, or knew all a man needed to know. She was pretty and shapely. She was clever and surprisingly well read, quick-witted and confident. He'd ended her virginity and discovered the sensuality and passion lurking under the businesslike exterior.

But this wasn't enough. He wanted to know the girl she'd been before she came to London. The girl Swanton had met in a shop in Paris.

He almost hated Swanton for having seen her when she was — what? Fifteen or sixteen, perhaps. She must have been more French than English then, a girl who laughed more, Lisburne was sure, than she did now, and in other ways, not only the low, intimate laughter that crept under a man's skin . . .

Whatever she'd done or said, she'd made an impression on Swanton, when scores of women hadn't.

In those days she must have smiled more easily and naturally, and talked entirely in French, and she must have been more lighthearted and less well armored.

Lisburne wanted that girl as well as the

woman in his arms.

He'd almost said that and everything that was in his mind.

He'd wanted to believe she danced so well at least partly because she danced with him, and they were meant to be together, and they'd met in front of the painting of Venus and Mars because they were meant to be lovers, too. It was Fate. Inevitable.

He became aware of her scent first, and realized he was leaning in too close, much too close for dancing in public. He felt her pull away slightly, in the instant before he did.

"They're all watching Swanton and Gladys," he said.

"And you think no one notices *you*?" she said. And laughed.

The music was ending, and more than one head nearby turned toward the sound of her low, rich laugh.

He had the presence of mind to release his hold of her. But not enough to control his tongue. "It's you they're looking at," he said softly. "The most beautiful girl in the place."

She looked up at him, her eyes shining.

"That's the perfect thing to say," she said. "A perfect ending."

"Ending?"

"Adieu, my lord."

She moved away, and he couldn't grab her and haul her back, with all the world looking on. In an instant she was gone, slipping into the crowd and disappearing, before his brain had caught up with what was happening. Had happened.

And while he stood there, bewildered and on the brink of anger, a familiar voice said, "Lisburne, if you do not save me I'll find a dastardly way to get even."

He looked to one side and not very far down, for it was his cousin Clara. She wasn't exactly an Amazon, although to some fellows she seemed so, but she was decidedly on the tallish side.

The habits of a lifetime came to his rescue. He collected his composure, his manners, and his powers of address.

"Of course I'll save you," he said. "Who needs a broken jaw, cuz, and why can't Val do it?"

"It's not that sort of thing. It's Sir Henry Jaspers."

She made a small movement of her head. Lisburne threw a discreet glance that way — enough to spot a young man of fair coloring and bull-sized proportions — before returning his attention to her.

"He's bearing down on me," she said,

"And I know that look in his eye. It means a lot of pretty poetry and admiration of my this and that and would I do him the honor of marrying him. He asks once a week, and even Mama cannot seem to dampen his ardor. He has a wonderful obliviousness. And one can't be cruel to him, because he's too sweet. But here! At Vauxhall of all places. He means no harm, I know, but if Gladys catches my eye, I'll never be able to keep in countenance, and one doesn't laugh at a gentleman in love, even if one doesn't want him. Oh, here he comes. Do be a darling, Simon, and dance with me, I beg."

He donned the right smile and said, "Nothing would give me greater pleasure."

Since resisting temptation wasn't in her nature, Leonie had to get herself out of its vicinity. Had she gone home to Maison Noirot and Lisburne followed her there, she'd never be able to maintain her resolve. She lacked the strength of character to send him away.

And so she went straight from Vauxhall to Clevedon House, where she often spent Saturday night.

This night she found Marcelline looking well, truly well, for the first time in weeks. Her Grace was in good spirits, too. This was partly because she felt better and partly because today Lucie hadn't clung to her like a limpet — as she'd done from the time Marcelline had first displayed symptoms of her pregnancy.

Lucie had stopped clinging because Bianca Williams had mysteriously arrived in the house in the middle of the night, "like a golden fairy princess," Lucie said.

"Bianca is the perfect playmate," Marcelline said after she and Leonie had withdrawn to the duchess's sitting room. "She'll sit still for hours on end while Lucie arranges her hair. She'll wear whatever outrageous ensemble Lucie concocts. Lucie treats her like a doll, and Bianca, like a good little actress, plays Doll. She'll play any other part, too. They made scenes from *The Arabian Nights* and went hunting as Red Indians. They played soldiers and had a tea party to celebrate the end of the battle. They've made costumes — and a fine wreck of the nursery, not to mention one of my gowns. Bianca hasn't Lucie's sewing skill, but she has strong ideas about proper costume. And props."

"I believe she was onstage from the time she could walk," Leonie said. "Or maybe before."

"She's been wonderful for Lucie," Marcelline said. "Clevedon says she was lonely here."

"But the servants dote on her," Leonie said.

"Lucie adores Clevedon and she likes being a princess in a grand house with servants, but it's not what she's used to," Marcelline said. "After all that happened in the spring . . ." She frowned. "He seems to understand her in a way I can't, and when he's about, she's calmer and happier. When he isn't about, she can be a little beast. But Bianca seems to have a positive effect. I'll be sorry to see Mrs. Williams go. Not that they'll be allowed to do so right away. She isn't quite as strong as she pretends. Clevedon is looking about for something suitable for her." She laughed. "But listen to me with my domestic tales!" She refilled Leonie's brandy glass. "What about you, my love? Have you something to tell me?"

There had been too much to do lately and Marcelline had been too ill when there was time. And so it was only now that Leonie could tell her the full story of the last two and a half weeks. She didn't cry. She'd never been one for weeping. But she'd almost wept at Vauxhall.

It's you they're looking at. The most beautiful girl in the place.

And her heart had broken then.

She and her sisters had looks, certainly, and they made the most of their assets, but they were not, strictly, beautiful. Leonie was the least beautiful of the three, with her crooked nose and too-sharp jaw and red hair.

But Lisburne had said she was the most beautiful girl in the place and he'd said it in a way that made one believe he believed it, which only a man besotted could do.

"Your taste, as it ought to be, is excellent," Marcelline said. "He's handsome to a painful degree." She patted Leonie's hand. "I was beginning to worry about you. I feared you'd hold out for a respectable professional man and save your virginity for the wedding night — and our ancestors would turn in their graves." She broke out into giggles then, and Leonie couldn't help giggling, too.

When they'd sobered, Marcelline said. "Clevedon didn't like it because he says Lisburne is *slippery.*"

"Slippery," Leonie said blankly.

Marcelline smiled. "I think he means that Lisburne is like the Noirots and the DeLuceys in one way. Charming but elusive. He treats women beautifully, Clevedon says, and stays with them long enough for them to believe he'll stay forever. Then he leaves them beautifully, with very expensive trinkets to help mend their broken hearts."

"That's nothing I hadn't worked out for myself," Leonie said. "I knew he was a charmer from the instant I met him. Completely irresistible. Entirely dangerous."

"That's why you're here," Marcelline said.

"Better to leave than to be left," Leonie said. "And I preferred to leave on a high note."

"Without the trinkets?" Marcelline said in mock astonishment. "Can you truly be a Noirot? Or did Gypsies take our real sister, and leave you on the doorstep as a consolation prize, as Sophy used to claim?"

"Oh, I'll get a trinket," Leonie said. "But better than jewelry, *chérie*. My goodbye gift from him will be priceless."

Lisburne House
On Sunday, a special edition of the *Spectacle* published Tom Foxe's blow-by-blow account of Theaker and Meffat's unmasking at Vauxhall. While dashes and asterisks stood in for names, nobody in Society remained in any doubt of Lord Swanton's innocence or his manly display when women bystanders were insulted, or the dastardly behavior of two men who had been, the *Spectacle* reminded its readers, intimate

friends of a recently disgraced member of the peerage.

In the entire edition, otherwise overflowing with gossip and innuendo, there appeared no sly insinuations about a certain dressmaker and a marquess. The children's fête received due attention, however, and in that context Miss Noirot's dress, along with those of Lady Gladys, Lady Clara, and other patrons of Maison Noirot were described in brain-freezing detail.

Swanton being late coming down to breakfast, Lisburne had more than sufficient time to read and reread the *Spectacle.* As though he'd find a clue there to explain what had happened between him and Leonie.

What had happened to him. When she left.

He'd stood blind and deaf and paralyzed until Clara had demanded his attention.

After a long, hard fight with his pride he'd gone to Maison Noirot. Leonie ought to have arrived long since, but she wasn't there. Fenwick had answered the door and said, "I fought she was wif you," or something to that effect.

A sound from the doorway brought Lisburne back to the moment.

Swanton entered, all aglow. He actually chirped a greeting. He hummed while filling his plate.

Lisburne wanted to throw the coffeepot at him.

Instead he flung the *Spectacle* across the table to Swanton's place. "You'll be happy to know you are once more an angelic being, whom all ladies must worship and adore," he said.

Swanton sat down. "Not happy to see you in a fit of the blue devils," he said. "My redemption is mainly your doing, after all."

"It's Miss Noirot's doing," Lisburne said. He felt a sharp ache in his chest. He ignored it. "If she hadn't had the wit to let that strange little boy loose on the streets of London, we might never have found Mrs. Williams. Or maybe we ought to thank her sister, for finding Fenwick in the first place."

"I saw you dancing with Miss Noirot," Swanton said. "You looked like a man in —"

"I saw you dancing with Gladys," Lisburne cut in.

"Yes." Swanton ducked his head and attended to his breakfast. Had Lisburne been paying attention, he'd have noticed the color creeping up his neck.

But Lisburne's mind was elsewhere. Swanton hadn't been Gladys's only partner at Vauxhall. She was never without a partner during all the time Lisburne had remained at Vauxhall — and a very long time it had seemed. After dancing with Clara, he'd danced and flirted with other young ladies. And why shouldn't he, when Leonie saw fit to abandon him? Not that he blamed her, after all, when she had just recovered her shop's reputation. He understood that shopkeepers, especially milliners, had to be careful about public perception of their morals, and she needed to be more than usually careful, because of the young women she sponsored. Still, she might at least . . .

"But I'll call tomorrow," Swanton was saying. "And I should like to borrow the curricle. I think, if I'm quick enough off the mark, she'll consent to drive with me."

"Yes, of course she will."

"Then it's all right?"

"What is?"

"For me to borrow the curricle," Swanton said. "Can't have the other fellows stealing a march on me."

"Certainly not. Help yourself."

Lisburne left the breakfast room and went upstairs to his room, where Polcaire waited, to dress his master for the day. The master dutifully played his part: He maintained an air of calm insouciance during this lengthy and critical procedure, and delivered the necessary bon mot for Polcaire to share with the other valets at their favorite drinking place.

Wednesday 29 July

Lisburne told himself he had nothing to be irate about. He had intended to seduce Leonie Noirot. He'd succeeded. She'd made his enforced stay in London very interesting, indeed. But he'd always known he'd return to the Continent, which meant that sooner or later they would part ways.

He hadn't expected to part ways quite so soon.

He told himself he ought to have expected it, since she wasn't a courtesan or a merry widow but a businesswoman with a shop to run, who couldn't afford to be seen as a demirep or the mistress of a nobleman. He understood this perfectly well. He better than many of his peers understood the way business worked. He viewed his own extensive holdings as business. Since he oversaw them from abroad, he was all the more careful and attentive to details.

He understood, truly he did.

And he was wretched and angry all the same, and it took only until midweek for him to break down and visit the shop.

He arrived shortly after opening time on Wednesday morning, when the ladies of the beau monde were least likely to appear.

But he hadn't reckoned on the wives of excessively rich barristers and their curst daughters who took it into their heads to become betrothed at the most inconvenient times and needed a thousand fittings for bride clothes.

He arrived, in short, ten minutes after Mrs. Sharp brought her second-eldest daughter in, when Madame couldn't possibly be spared.

"I am so sorry, my lord," Selina Jeffreys said, "but I can't say when Madame will be available. Mrs. Sharp was one of our first clients, and Madame must attend her personally. But perhaps in an hour — two at most — Madame will be free."

He went out and walked the few steps up and across St. James's Street to White's. There he loitered in the coffee room, listening to gossip and losing track of what people were saying. Then he decamped to the morning room, where he read the papers without knowing what he was reading.

He told himself he would not go back to the shop today. Tomorrow, perhaps. Or Friday. She would have to see him on Friday. It was the last day of July, the day of reckoning.

Judging by the newspaper gossip of the

last few days, the odds of his losing the Botticelli had improved. All that could save it was the failure so far of any of Gladys's numerous admirers to come up to scratch.

He supposed he had her father to thank. It would be one thing to get Gladys's consent. Quite another to face Boulsworth and the prospect of becoming his son-in-law.

That prospect was enough to make strong men quail.

And if Lisburne won the wager, he would get his two weeks with Leonie, and of course he'd be very discreet and devise a way of taking her away without causing any talk.

But if she didn't want to go?

Well, then, he was a gentleman, and he'd never forced a woman in his life. He'd offer an alternative, though there wasn't anything else he wanted and the thought of her not wishing to be with him made him feel . . . ill.

He flung down the newspaper he'd been staring at. He collected his hat and walking stick and started up the street to Piccadilly. He reached the corner, where he stood for a moment. Then he turned back and walked down St. James's Street and into Maison Noirot.

She stood near the door, arranging a hat on a mannequin's head. She wore an ivory color organdy dress, embroidered all over with little blue things. The sleeves might have doubled as hot air balloons, but instead of one of those pelerines that turned a woman's upper half into a wide inverted triangle, she wore a satin lace-trimmed scarf, knotted very much in the style favored some generations ago. Unlike so many other daytime fashions, it offered a glimpse of the velvety skin of her neck and throat . . . and he remembered the scent of her skin and the taste and feel of it under his mouth.

And though he'd been sure when he set out that he would offer her alternatives, his mind went to work devising seduction.

When she spied him, she smiled her polite professional smile and advanced. "My lord." She made a curtsey. Not *the* curtsey, but one suitably businesslike. "Jeffreys told me you'd stopped by. I was sorry I'd missed you."

"Were you really?" he said.

"Oh, yes," she said. "There are one or two business matters —"

The shop bell tinkled and what seemed like a herd of young women poured in.

But it was only Gladys and Clara and the other Morris girl — not Alda the adder, but the dark one — and Clara's bulldog of a maid, Davis.

"Lisburne," Gladys said, with a nod and a little smile.

"Simon," Clara said.

She turned to the Morris girl. "Lady Susan, I believe you know my cousin Lisburne."

She was dark and pretty and an agreeable sort of girl — rather a miracle, considering her mother and sister — and Lisburne wished her and his two cousins at the devil.

He said what was necessary, because it was habit, and required no thinking, which was just as well, since he was too angry and frustrated to think.

Gladys drew a little nearer, obliging Lady Susan to step back a pace.

"I do beg your pardon, Lisburne," Gladys said sotto voce. "I wouldn't interrupt your tête-à-tête for worlds. We can wander about the shop for a while, if you wish. Or we might walk down to the palace and try to stare the guards out of countenance."

"You needn't," he began. He found himself pausing to rethink his answer, because she tipped her head to one side and searched his face.

Though he was sure she could read nothing there, he felt exposed. And at the same time he had a sense of what some men saw in her: intelligent eyes, a fine complexion . . . and a surprising kindness in the way she looked at him.

"You're very good," he said. "But my business can easily wait for another day."

"We shouldn't have come so early," Gladys said. "But the party, you know. On Friday. All the world will be there, and now everybody wants a dress from Maison Noirot, and so we came early to avoid the mobs. Madame and her accomplices have made me yet another beautiful dress, and you'd think all they needed to do was fit it to the nearest barrel, but no, they're so fussy, and I must stand still and let them pin and trim and mutter."

"The party," he said blankly.

"Mama's party," Clara said. "Of course, you and Lord Swanton must be drowning in invitations, and I daresay it's slipped your mind. But Mama gives a grand ball every year at the end of the Season. The last day of July. An immense, elaborate affair, meant to make all the other hostesses gnash their teeth."

"This time it's to be quite shocking," Gladys said in a conspiratorial whisper. "For one thing, I'll be there." She laughed. "In bronze or sunset or whatever they call the

456

color. And I'll set the entire ballroom alight."

"And we're to have my new sister," Clara said. "Lady Longmore is coming. And the duchess will be there. And all we need do is persuade Leonie — and we'll be the talk of London!"

He looked at Leonie. He saw the very faint wash of color in her cheeks.

"Yes, yes, we'll discuss that later," she said. "But for the present, if your ladyships will be so kind as to proceed to the fitting room? We have a great deal to do, and not very much time in which to do it, yes? Come, come. No dawdling, if you please."

And in this imperious manner she shooed them on their way, and Jeffreys hurried along with them.

Once they'd passed through the door of the showroom and into the inner sanctum, Leonie said, "I can guess why you've come."

"Why should I not come?" he said. "Do you think I forget as easily as you do?"

She went still.

"I understand your reasons," he said. "I've understood it until I'm sick with understanding. Your business. I know. I must respect it else I don't respect you. But my pride is badly hurt and so I'm not behaving well. I should keep away, and not make any more talk. I should adjust the terms of our wager —"

"Which terms exactly?" she said, in a small, tight voice.

"No one's going to offer for her," he said, lowering his own voice. "Not soon, at any rate. Not because of her — you've performed miracles with her. Even I like her."

"I've dressed her," she said. "The rest she's done herself."

"With your guidance, I don't doubt. And whatever love potions you brew in the cellar. But anybody who offers for her must face her father, and I believe it will take considerable time and a wild, unthinking passion, to bring any of her current set of beaux to the point. I've no doubt that some of them have conceived an attachment — but unbridled passion, the kind that drives a man to enter a lion's den or undergo the labors of Hercules? That's another matter entirely."

"You don't think love is enough?" she said.

"It must be a potent love, indeed," he said.

She folded her hands at her waist. "Are you afraid I'll lose our wager?" she said.

"Yes, actually," he said. "True, you might win. Stranger things have happened. The transformation of Gladys, for instance. But in all likelihood, yes, you'll lose, and . . . ."

He paused.

"I shouldn't worry, if I were you," she said. "And I know exactly where I mean to hang the Botticelli."

It was a fine exit line and she started away, and he almost let her go, but, "Leonie."

She stopped and turned back to him, her expression inscrutable.

"Are you going to the ball?" he said.

She shook her head. "Lady Warford has resigned herself to Sophy and will put up with Marcelline mainly to aggravate her friends. But I haven't got a title and I'm still working in the shop and most of the ladies at the party will be ladies I've waited on this week. It's a ridiculous state of affairs."

He moved to her. "I'll tell you what's ridiculous," he said. "You've gone to incredible lengths to transform Gladys — and I know it can't have been easy, because I know Gladys. Or the Gladys she was, at any rate. This is a chance to see your handiwork."

"I saw it at Vauxhall," she said.

"Vauxhall is nothing," he said.

"Nothing," she said with a small smile.

"I was there, after you left. Gladys was the belle of a small party. But it was like a picnic. You've seen the dancing area. A small space, with trees in the middle. Mixed company, and a lot of gawking onlookers in the supper boxes. It's pretty and romantic, especially under the stars, when one dances with a beautiful girl. But it isn't a great ball at Warford House, with the crème de la crème of Society dressed in their finest, drinking champagne and dancing to London's most expensive musicians. You need to see your protégée in her proper milieu. And you ought to have, at least once, a proper milieu in which to show off one of your beautiful gowns."

He caught the look of longing in her eyes before she masked it. "I hear the voice of the serpent in the garden," she said. "You know I wasn't tempted, truly, until you mentioned showing off a gown."

"Advertising," he said. "When have you ever had such an opportunity?"

"Never," she said. "As you well know."

"And to make it even more irresistible, I promise to do you the great honor of dancing with you," he said.

She rolled her eyes and let out a theatrical sigh.

"Leonie."

"Oh, very well, if only to stop you plaguing me."

Then she turned away and flung up her

hand in a gesture of dismissal, and went out.

He wanted to lunge at her and drag her back.

He let her go.

CHAPTER SEVENTEEN

A partner, 'tis true, I would gladly command,
But that partner must boast of wealth,
   houses, and land;
I have looked round the ball-room, and, try
   what I can,
I fail to discover one Marrying Man!
   — Mrs. Abdy, "A Marrying Man," 1835

Friday 31 July
This had not been Lisburne's favorite day
of his life.

It had started with this morning's *Spectacle,* and Lisburne's spilling his coffee onto
his eggs as he read:

Was that a poet of late pugilistic renown
observed yesterday slipping into Rundell
and Bridge jewelers? And what was it the
clerk put into the little box, and the gentleman tucked into his waistcoat pocket?
But the world cannot be surprised, and

462

will not require more than one guess as to the identity of the lady for whom the little box's contents are intended.

We wish the gentleman well, in the *general* sense, as well as the specific acquisition of the hand of his fair one.

In case one was in any doubt, the pun on *general* was a sledgehammer reminder.

Swanton, meanwhile, had breakfasted early and gone out.

Then, at White's in the early afternoon, Lisburne encountered Longmore, who confessed that the news about Swanton and Gladys had floored him.

"When I first described Gladys to her, Sophy told me, only let Maison Noirot get their hands on her," Longmore said. "Well, what do I know about frocks, except that they're the very devil to get off these days? Not to mention I knew it'd take more than a frock to make Gladys tolerable. I vow, when I saw her, I couldn't believe it was the same girl. Thought they must have killed the original and put another in her place. But I hadn't seen her in ages, you know."

"I hadn't seen her in an age, either, until a few weeks ago," Lisburne said. "She didn't seem greatly improved then. Except for her complexion."

"What do you reckon?" Longmore said.

Lisburne shrugged. "It's a mystery to me."

This was not entirely true, but he hesitated to share his thoughts with Longmore, who was not a man of delicate feeling.

Perhaps all Gladys had wanted was pretty clothes to give her confidence, as well as some hints about, say, graceful deportment. Wasn't it possible she'd been ill-natured because she was self-conscious about her looks — and because her father made her life a misery? Lisburne recalled the girl he'd seen at his father's funeral. Maybe she'd known her father was trying to force her on a brokenhearted young man. A girl in her teens — already self-conscious — she must have been in agonies.

"But a *ring*," Longmore said. "Swanton must be made of sterner stuff than ever I guessed, if he means to face Boulsworth. Have you seen the betting book?

Thanks to today's *Spectacle,* Lisburne had finally looked into White's betting book. Swanton and Gladys featured in entry after entry.

Lisburne had read the *Spectacle* every morning. Until today he might as well have been reading gibberish. He'd passed the last few days in a haze, both literal and figurative. Since Wednesday, the skies had dripped and poured almost constantly, and when the rain stopped for a breather, the clouds loomed so black and heavy they seemed like mammoth stones crushing London.

Today's clearing skies must have cleared his brain, because he realized that Swanton must have confided in him at some point — perhaps several times — and Lisburne hadn't paid attention. Everything Swanton said had sounded like poetry, and Lisburne was sick to death of poetry.

And so he passed a wretched day.

Still, he had the Warfords' party to look forward to.

Where Leonie would be. He'd have his dance at the very least.

Warford House
That night

Given the occasion, the Noirot sisters were unlikely to slip in unobserved, though most of the ball's attendees would agree that, in their case, invisibility didn't fall within the realms of the probable.

For one thing, here they were making what constituted, in effect, their social debut — and under Lady Warford's auspices!

All the world knew that Lady Warford loathed the Duchess of Clevedon. Even though Her Grace had received royal recognition, Lady Warford had remained aloof. When her eldest son, Longmore, married the duchess's sister, her ladyship had taken a step closer to Sophy, but that was all.

Whatever mental revolution the marchioness had undergone had occurred promptly after the latest Vauxhall incident, and news of the scorned sisters being invited raced through London. No invitee still breathing would miss this for worlds. And since nobody wanted to miss a minute, the company arrived punctually.

The dressmakers timed it to a nicety, of course. The last to arrive, they paused at the ballroom entrance at the exact moment the musicians ended the overture from Rossini's *La Cenerentola*.

Brunette Lady Clevedon was dramatic in rose satin and black lace.

Blonde Lady Longmore, with her English rose coloring, wore a softer and warmer pink, with green and black embellishments.

And Leonie had chosen creamy white, a dress that seemed to be simplicity itself, if one overlooked the daring lines, the gold embroidery's exotic design, and the black lace scarf draped over her shoulders, a theatrical flourish.

For a moment a sound passed through the ballroom like the wind driving autumn

466

leaves: whispering that swelled and subsided and swelled again.

Then the three sisters curtseyed — *the* curtsey — the theatrical, ballerina performance that set their ruffles and bows aflutter and made the gaslight dance over their silk lace and embroidery and jewels.

The sight elicited a universal intake of breath. Then the room fell silent.

The sisters rose, in the same beautiful flurry of motion, and the ballroom began to hum — with speculation, admiration, envy, what-have-you.

Lisburne wasn't part of the hum. He stood mute and motionless. What happened to him happened inside, where his being seemed to thrum like the strings of a violoncello.

She was so beautiful he could have wept.

She was like a living poem.

She made love like poetry.

And they fit together like the lines of a perfect poem.

Not one of Swanton's.

But . . . well, Byron.

She walks in beauty, like the night
   Of cloudless climes and starry skies . . .

Images flashed in Lisburne's mind, of

Leonie standing before the Botticelli, of her briskly abandoning him in order to attend to Gladys, of her quarreling with him in Hyde Park and kissing him, kissing him, kissing him . . . the way she reached up for him and wrapped her arms about his neck . . . the way she laughed when they made love . . . the way she laughed . . . and teased . . . and the way she was . . . *too busy.*

"Drat you, Simon, what does a fellow have to do to get your attention?"

Lisburne looked away from the living poem, who seemed to be floating down the reception line while all the men in the room ogled her.

They all wanted her.

They all wanted to do to her — with her — what he had done.

A red haze enveloped his mind for a moment. He shook it off. "I think I'm —" He caught himself in the nick of time. He could not have been about to say what he thought he'd been about to say.

He met Swanton's amused gaze. "Kindly pay attention this time," Swanton said. "I won't have you complaining of being the last to know."

"I *am* the last to know," Lisburne said. "Living under the same roof, and kept in darkness while you creep furtively about

468

London."

"I've told you every morning what I was about," Swanton said. "And every morning you've said, 'Will you, indeed? Well, I'm sure it'll do admirably.' "

"I had things on my mind," Lisburne said.

"That much was obvious," Swanton said.

"The *Spectacle* claims you bought a ring yesterday," Lisburne said. "Doesn't that strike you as excessively sanguine?"

"If you'd been paying attention, you'd know all about it," Swanton said. "You'd know I've received encouragement. And I want you to pay close attention now, because a very short time ago, your cousin Lady Gladys Fairfax consented to make me the happiest of men." He blinked hard. "I'm sure you don't understand, and you think it's my sentiment, and I'm blinded by an excess of that article. You'll say we scarcely know each other. In terms of days and hours, that's true. Yet I feel as though I've known her all my life. From the first time I heard her voice, I knew we were kindred spirits."

Lisburne remembered what she'd said about the poetic temperament. He recalled the kindliness in her face. He suspected she'd had an extremely difficult girlhood, difficult enough to make her bitter and

469

venomous. But somehow she'd found the strength to rise above it. Certainly Leonie had had a good deal to do with Gladys's blossoming. But Leonie couldn't fight Gladys's battles for her. Gladys had found a way to fight — heroically, he thought, given the odds — and the battle had brought out the best in her.

"Pray don't sob," Lisburne said. "I wish you happy. I don't doubt you will be. She'll manage your affairs admirably and protect you from yourself. Or do you weep at the prospect of facing her father?"

Swanton swallowed. "Tears of happiness, that's all. As to her father — beyond a doubt he'll come thundering back to London the instant he gets my and Lord Warford's letters. But he authorized Lord Warford to act in loco parentis, and I have his consent."

"You know Boulsworth will do his best to destroy your will to live," Lisburne said. "Remember what you said about the enemy running away screaming at the sound of his voice?"

"Yes, but I'll have Gladys, no matter what he says," Swanton said. "And we've worked out strategies for confounding the enemy." He smiled. "She and I have tried out a dozen scenarios. She makes me laugh so and she teases me so — oh, never mind. I can see you grow ill listening to me."

Whatever Lisburne was at that moment, he wasn't ill. A little blinded, perhaps, by the light dawning.

"She makes you laugh," he said. "She teases. A kindred spirit, you said."

"Yes, all that and more," Swanton said. "But I've said enough. Now you know, and we may tell the rest of the world. Dash it, Simon, I never guessed it was possible to be so happy!"

After he'd bounced away, a thoughtful Lisburne went in search of Leonie, who'd disappeared into the crowd by that mysterious process she had of hiding in plain sight. His efforts were hampered by this one and that one who had to quiz him about Swanton or bother him about something or other.

Meanwhile, the Warfords wasted not a minute in making the news public. As the dancing was about to begin, a bemused Lord Warford announced the betrothal. Lady Warford was beaming.

A dead silence fell.

Then Lisburne clapped. He saw Gladys's gaze snap toward him. She smiled and in that moment was — no, not beautiful. But she was radiant, and in that moment it was easy enough to see what Swanton saw in her.

The other guests began clapping, too.

And the newly betrothed couple were asked to lead the first dance.

"Mama is in alt," Lady Clara told Leonie. "You have no idea what a coup this is for her. Lady Bartham has been perfectly vile with her *sympathy* because we've had to house Gladys and try to entertain her. Yet Lady Bartham can't marry off even one of her two pretty daughters, and here — in no time at all — is Gladys carrying off the man every girl wants."

"Not *every* girl," Leonie said.

"No, my dear, and I don't want him, either, though he is good-looking, rich, propertied, and rather sweet. But his poetry!" Lady Clara glanced about her and lowered her voice. "The sadder it is, the more I want to go off into whoops. But Gladys says he has a beautiful soul, and he — well, you've seen the way he looks at her."

"I shouldn't mind being looked at in that way," Leonie said. "One of these days it could happen, I daresay."

Clara drew her head back a bit, surprised. "Are you entirely blind? That's the way my cousin Lisburne looks at you."

But Lisburne had practiced that way of looking at a girl, or else he knew how to do it instinctively. Leonie could do it, too. She could gaze up into a man's eyes and make him believe he was the sun and the moon and the stars.

She didn't say this to Lady Clara. Her ladyship had suffered sufficient disillusionments lately as it was.

One day, though, a gentleman would gaze at this beautiful girl in the same love-struck way, and he'd mean it, all the way down to the secret places of his heart. And one day, it would be the right gentleman, and Lady Clara would reciprocate. And she'd be able to give her heart freely, because —

"I should have known I'd find you two lurking in a corner, conspiring," came a low male voice that made the back of Leonie's neck prickle.

"Simon," said Lady Clara. "We were talking about you. Were your ears burning?"

"If they were, it's no surprise I failed to notice, since everybody else was working them so hard," he said. "Every step I take, somebody must draw me aside to confide this or that or ask what I mean to do now or tell me how you could have knocked them over with a feather. If I'd had a feather, half the people in this house would be stretched out on the floor."

He looked at Leonie, his gaze softening in

a way that made her heart flutter like a schoolgirl's. "It's taken eons to find you. You promised me a dance."

"As I recall, you promised to do me the very great honor," she said.

"Well, then, here I am," he said. "I've been assured that the next is a waltz, and I believe your dress will show to great advantage in waltzing."

"I spy Lord Geddings looking for me," Lady Clara said. "I do want to see how this business between you comes out, but when one has promised a dance, one must keep the promise, except in cases of broken limbs — and then only if the fracture is multiple."

Away she went, a vision in lilac.

"You've won," he said.

"Yes," Leonie said. "Aren't you glad?"

"If that's meant to be a jest, it's a cruel one," he said. "A fortnight. I might have had a full two weeks alone with you, if only my fool cousin had waited one more day, curse him."

She looked for the teasing note in his eyes, his voice. But no.

He must have realized because he gave a short laugh. "That's being a bad sport, and I thought I wasn't. But everything is . . ."
He trailed off and shook his head. "There, the music is starting. I'll have my dance —

and I'll see what more I can accomplish."

"If you make yourself very alluring," she said, "I might grant you two dances." She oughtn't to, she knew. But she didn't know how to resist temptation when it stood right in front of her.

He smiled. "Come here, you wicked girl. You're too beautiful this night. Almost unbearably so. I can't sustain my ill temper."

"Come here?" she said indignantly.

But he only laughed softly and drew her into his arms and then out onto the floor among the other dancing couples.

And then . . .

And then . . .

Magic.

It was as he'd told her. Compared to this brilliant gathering, Vauxhall was a single glowworm on a moonless night.

A grand company filled the splendid ballroom. Above their heads three great chandeliers hung from shallow domes, their myriad crystals shooting rainbow sparks. Below the glittering lights floated gowns in every variety of muslin and silk, in every shade of white and every color in nature. As at Vauxhall, the men were the chiaroscuro, with colors swirling about them. But this place offered more of every sight and sound and feeling. This was truly beautiful.

Instead of dozens, scores of dancers whirled about her. On this night the multi-colored lights were precious jewels. Pearls and diamonds and sapphires and rubies and emeralds and every other color of stone sparkled in the ladies' hair and at their ears and necks, upon their wrists and fingers, and over their gowns.

The music was heavenly, and under it flowed a sound like summer breezes and whispered secrets: the sibilance of muslin and silk in motion. Dancing this night was like dreaming, and the sound at times seemed like the rustle of bedclothes.

One of Lisburne's gloved hands clasped her waist, the other her hand, and she moved into another realm of being. She'd danced with other men this evening, but it wasn't the same. It could never be the same. She'd been aware of him from the first time she'd met him, potently, physically aware, and the awareness had only grown stronger, until it seemed to course in her veins and beat in her heart.

He'd made her his, and now she belonged to him, it seemed. Her intellect might claim otherwise, but her body wouldn't listen. Her heart wouldn't listen.

While they danced, he drew her nearer. If she were capable of listening to intellect, she'd have drawn a proper distance away. But she wanted to go where he led. She ached to twine herself with him, to feel his mouth on hers, his hands on her skin.

Never had he seemed more like a Roman god than now. He glittered as gods ought to do, the sparkling lights dancing about his head and shimmering in his green-gold eyes. When she dropped her gaze, because studying his face made her foolish and too unforgivably fanciful — he was only a man, after all — the emerald in his neckcloth twinkled at her.

She was distantly aware of Lady Gladys dancing with Lord Swanton, but they might as well have been in another world. Though guests filled the ballroom and spilled into adjoining rooms, they all seemed to be far away, far below her. Their feet remained solidly on the ground while she soared among the stars. Her heart was broken, and yet she couldn't remember when last she'd been so happy.

Ah, yes, the last time she was in his arms.

"When you entered the ballroom, you took my breath away," he said.

"All three of us at once is more than some minds can sustain with any degree of balance," she said.

"I meant you," he said. "The others might

as well have been the curtains framing the window display."

"Oh, very well," she said. "You take my breath away, too. There isn't a man here whose attire sets off my dress so well."

"Actually, it's I who set you off," he said.

"Don't underestimate your waistcoat," she said.

He released a theatrical sigh. "Curse that Polcaire! And bless him! When I saw this white waistcoat I said, 'Are you mad? *Ivory and gold?* Tonight?' and he said he had a horror of my clashing. With whom, he didn't say, but I reckon he knows, as he knows everything, being an oracle. Come out with me to garden."

"Certainly not," she said. "I know what happens in gardens during balls. Girls take leave of their senses. And their virtue."

Not that she owned any of the last article. Yet some sense remained. If she gave herself to him again, she'd have to start all over again, trying to take herself back.

"You voice my fondest hopes," he said. "Come. The dance is ending, the place is stifling, and half the company has slipped out for a breath of air. You must give me a chance to worm myself back into your good graces or . . . or I'll run mad, Leonie."

The music had stopped, but he held her hand.

"Whatever ails you, I promise you'll recover," she said, heart pounding.

"You of all women ought to know better than to judge by appearances," he said. "You don't believe I'm a desperate man because Polcaire won't let my feelings show. Left to my own inclinations, I should not be so point-device. My hose should be ungartered, my sleeve unbuttoned, my shoe untied, and everything about me demonstrating a careless desolation. But I can't, because my valet won't allow it. All I can do — plague take the man, he can't be meaning to dance with you!"

Lord Flinton was walking determinedly toward them.

"He's had a terrific disappointment," she said. "He's trying the dance-with-every-girl-in-the-room cure."

"Then by all means let's get you out of the room," Lisburne said.

His gloved hand clasping hers was warm, his hold firm.

She knew he'd let go if she resisted, but she was still in love.

And it was all very romantic, a night she'd remember, probably forever.

And she was, after all, a Noirot.

■ ■ ■ ■

Leonie made herself as invisible as possible — not easy with Lisburne in close proximity — but he seemed to know, too, how to pass smoothly through a crowd, acknowledging acquaintances, speaking to this one and that one, yet never really calling attention to himself or pausing for long on their way out of the ballroom. In any case, the house was in motion, guests coming to and from various rooms in search of refreshments or card games or even quiet conversation. She walked with him through the next room, small but spectacular. It was the work, he told her, of "Athenian" Stuart. The theme, Lisburne told her, was the Triumph of Love. She wanted to linger and gape at the gold-topped Corinthian columns and the copies of ancient paintings. A moment ago, she'd wanted to throw caution to the winds. A moment ago, she couldn't wait to be alone with him.

But as soon as they'd entered this room, something changed. He stared for a long time at the chimneypiece frieze, a wedding scene.

Yet she continued with him down the stairs and out into the garden. Guests filled the terrace above and some wandered in the garden. It wasn't large, not a fraction the size of the grounds of Clevedon House, though that stood in Charing Cross in the midst of warehouses and shops. The Warfords' small green space contained an open oval area, within which glistened an ornamental pool. The area, squeezed between the imposing house and the Green Park's border, was well lit for the festivities.

Still, sheltering trees and shrubbery screened it from public view, and in a path through the greenery Lisburne found a private place, and a pretty one, where a marble nymph hovered by a stone bench.

He sat beside her and took her hand again.

At that moment, every instinct told her she'd made a mistake. He hadn't drawn her away for dalliance and sin.

She broke into a sweat and her heart raced, and she wanted to run away. Which was silly and cowardly. She told herself her imagination was running away with her, on account of the shock of finding herself among London's haut ton and for once not waiting on them or measuring them.

She looked up at the marble figure. "A nymph," she said, and her voice sounded unsteady.

"Yes. Leonie . . ."

Oh, there was a tone, a strange tone to his voice and it wasn't steady, either.

"Or is she meant to be a muse?" she said lightly. "Isn't it wonderful that the ancient Greeks had deities they'd summon for inspiration?" She lifted an imploring hand to the nymph.

> Muse make the man thy theme, for
> shrewdness famed
> And genius versatile, who far and wide
> A Wand'rer, after Ilium overthrown,
> Discover'd various cities, and the mind
> And manners learn'd of men, in lands
> remote.
> He numerous woes . . .

". . . numerous woes . . ." She racked her brain, trying to remember the next lines, but there was only noise in her skull.

"Good gad, Leonie, how do you know these things?" he said.

She wanted to go on, about Jove and Calypso and . . . who else? But she couldn't remember. She wasn't calm enough, not calm at all, because he was . . . because this was . . . not what she'd supposed. Not the romantic interlude she'd envisioned — though she couldn't say what this was or how she knew it, only that every Noirot

482

instinct was on the alert, and urging her to run.

"I read a book once," she said, fighting the urge to pull her hand away.

"Once," he said. "How many dressmakers can quote from *The Odyssey*?"

"I had an education," she said. "I read books. Not in Latin and Greek. Translations. Because I wanted something in my mind that wasn't dressmaking or business. Something . . . beautiful." And to her horror, her throat closed up.

"Like the Botticelli," he said.

She nodded, afraid to speak because she was going to cry, which was so stupid. What had she to cry about, on this triumphant night of all nights?

"It's yours," he said. "And so am I. Entirely. I lo—"

"No!" She pulled away and jumped up, covering her ears. "No, no, no."

"Leonie."

"No, no, no." She shook her head, her hands on her ears, like a child.

He took her hands from her ears and said, "Leonie, I love you."

"No," she said. "How can you? Oh, don't do this. It's not to be borne. I only wanted you for your body. And — and your handsome face. And, no really, it was only the

Botticelli I wanted all along, and I'd have done anything or said anything —"

"I don't care," he said. "Marry me."

She went cold all over. Then hot. She pulled away. "Are you completely insane?"

"I'll recite poetry to you," he said. "Even Homer. 'Alike desirous, in her hollow grots/ Calypso, Goddess beautiful detained/ Wooing him to her arms.' "

"No! No!"

"I'll recite even — heaven help me — Swanton," he said. "Whatever you want. And you'll have beautiful things. All the beautiful things you could want, my love, and I should be so happy to give them to you."

He was going to make her weak. She'd melt into his arms. She'd lose her reason. She started away. He caught her arm.

"Listen to me," he said.

"I can't!" she said. "Don't you understand? I can't listen to you. You're like — like the Sirens. I have responsibilities. You'll make me forget them. We've lost Marcelline and Sophy. I'm all that's left. If I leave, there's nobody to hold it together."

"The shop?" he said. "This is about the shop? Dammit, Leonie, don't tell me it's *business.*"

"It's business!" she said. She waved her

hands. "That's who I am and what I am. It's always been business. Lady Gladys and you and — and everybody. And I love my business. We all do. Nobody understands, especially not the men — and now . . ."

She couldn't go on. The tears she refused to shed were choking her.

"I see," he said, more quietly. "Of course. You can't give up the shop."

"Even for you," she said, her voice clogged. "Even if I love you more than you could ever love me or anybody."

"Even if," he said.

She waved impatiently. "Oh, very well. I do love you. You must be blind and stupid if you don't know. But maybe you're so used to girls falling in love with you that you don't even notice anymore."

"Well, actually, I forgot what it was like, because they all started falling in love with Swanton," he said. "To my very great chagrin."

She looked up at him.

"Shall I take you home?" he said.

The look she gave him was almost comical.

He might have found it fully comical if he hadn't been holding on to his composure by a thread.

"Unless you'd prefer to return to the

party," he said very calmly.

She shook her head. "No. I'll have to pretend, and . . . Oh, Gemini, I've been screaming, haven't I — and everybody will have heard. Wonderful. My first time in Society and I make a spectacle of myself."

She covered her cheeks. He supposed they were hot. He wanted to put his hands there. Not only there. But he was desperate, not unintelligent.

He said, "Nobody can hear us over the music and chatter. And the chatter grows louder as the guests grow drunker. It's a wonder they can hear themselves think. No one minds us. I can leave a message with one of the footmen when I send for my carriage."

She took her hands from her cheeks. "Maison Noirot is only around the corner," she said. "We can walk."

"In these shoes?" he said. "Polcaire will kill me."

She looked down at his dancing pumps. "I can walk by myself," she said.

"Not in that dress," he said. "But never mind. My shoes be damned. I'll carry you."

"You will n—oof! Lisburne!" she cried as he swooped her up into his arms.

"Be quiet," he said. "You've crushed all my hopes and dreams. If you will be so good as to submit with good grace to being carried, I shall manfully resist the temptation to throw you into Lord Warford's ornamental pond."

The last time he'd carried Leonie to the shop had presented no hardship. She was no pocket Venus, but he was a good deal stronger than he looked. In any event, he would have carried her to the moon, if necessary. This wasn't necessary. He had only to walk downhill. And talk, to distract her.

He was successful but not for long. "Lisburne, are you drunk?" she said. "The shop is the other way."

"But the hackney stand is this way," he said.

"Oh, am I too heavy for you?" she said. "Put me down, and I'll walk."

"No," he said.

A taut pause then, "Where are you taking me?" she said.

"Home," he said.

"It's only up the street a few paces."

"I didn't say whose home," he said.

How could she have been so stupid, to believe he'd give in so easily?

He was an aristocrat. Once they got an

idea in their heads, all the horses in the Augean stables, pulling at once, couldn't drag it out.

"This is not the Dark Ages," she said. "You can't carry me to your lair."

"Watch me," he said.

She struggled. "Put me down!"

His grip only tightened.

"Put me down or I'll scream," she said.

"I have an idea how to stop the screaming," he said.

He would kiss her and she'd melt and give in and abandon everybody who depended on her. She'd abandon herself.

She wriggled and punched and pushed and made such a frenzy that he had to let her down. But before she could start up the street, he picked her up and threw her over his shoulder and marched down toward St. James's Palace.

"Lisburne, put me down!" she said.

"Simon," he said.

"I will never call you that, *my lord*! Put me down you — you —"

"Brute," he said. "*Brute* is a good word. A bit clichéd, but clichés are apt, else they wouldn't be clichés. Ah, here we are." He stopped at the first hackney in line, and wrenched open the door.

"I'm being abducted!" she called. "Help me!"

Lisburne threw her inside. "My wife," he told the driver. "Drunk, I'm afraid. Gets lively." He tossed a coin to the driver. It was probably a guinea, curse him.

"The Regent's Park," he said.

Chapter Eighteen

We looked in vain for many fashionists belonging to the higher order of society, who had gradually disappeared; and though the town cannot yet be called empty, it is very visibly thinned; and the few stragglers that still remain, are hastening from us, to overtake their modish contemporaries at the different summer recesses.

— *La Belle Assemblée,* August 1823

The night being warm, previous passengers had let down the coach window. Knowing she could reach the door handle without much trouble, Leonie pretended to slump in a corner of the seat while Lisburne settled into the seat opposite. But when she jumped up to open the door, he was up, too, and pulling her back.

She remembered the swiftness with which he'd caught her when she tripped at the

British Institution. Of all the men in the world to carry her off, she had to have the one with impossibly quick reflexes.

"Faster!" he called to the coachman. Then Lisburne put the window up more than halfway. "A fine abduction this would be, if you escaped when we'd hardly set out," he said as he settled back into his seat.

At this hour St. James's Street was not congested, and the coachman made speed. Even if she succeeded in getting the window down quickly enough, if she tried to jump out she'd break her neck.

She was in a panic. She was not suicidal.

She sat back and folded her arms. *Think,* she told herself. She was a Noirot. And a DeLucey. She could get out of this.

But she needed to be calm to think, and she couldn't make herself calm. She tried estimating the number of guests at the ball, the proportion of men to women, and the percentage of ladies who were not wearing Maison Noirot creations. It didn't work. She tried planning instead.

The coach traveled Piccadilly and turned into the Quadrant while plan after plan presented itself, only to be discarded as impossible or insane. She was at a loss, a state of mind she hated. Tears started to her eyes, which only made her angrier. The farther they progressed from St. James's Street the more difficult it would be for her to get home. She had no money for another hackney. The return walk was growing longer by the minute, and the gaslights couldn't drive away the darkness altogether. Lit or not, even Regent Street held danger for a woman alone at this hour.

For the average woman, perhaps, but not Leonie Noirot. Hadn't she traveled alone in far less salubrious neighborhoods in Paris and other cities?

But then she'd been a child, a young girl, dressed so as not to attract attention. In those days she'd never worn such finery or such expensive jewelry. Marcelline had insisted on lending her pearls, and the ones about Leonie's throat were monstrous. Even if she concealed the jewelry . . .

Stupid. Futile. Walking alone was out of the question.

"I hate you," she said.

"Come, madame, you can do better than that."

"I detest you," she said. "You're loathsome to me. You are *no gentleman.*"

"That's more like it."

She felt stupid and helpless, and she wanted to throw herself into his arms and cry like the child she wasn't. She was a grown woman who ran a business, possibly London's most successful dressmaking shop. She'd seen more of life than gently bred ladies twice her age. She'd been in far worse situations than this.

But she was falling to pieces.

And so she made herself angrier, and launched into French, the better to scourge him with. Bitter words came more easily to her in French, and she hadn't yet run out of execrations when the hackney stopped at the door of Lisburne's villa in the Regent's Park.

He alit and held his hand out to her.

What could she do? Run? Whatever else she was, she wasn't a coward. He'd brought her here to exploit her weaknesses, that was all.

Her weakness for him, certainly. Which meant seduction was on the menu. Physical and financial. He'd show her his splendid house — and this was only one of several — and make her realize how ridiculous she was, to refuse to marry him.

Everybody in the world would think her ridiculous. Or mad.

Because nobody else could understand.

Very well. Let him do his worst. She'd survived Paris during the cholera epidemic. She'd survive this.

She lifted her chin, took his hand, and let him help her out of the hackney.

She looked up at the front of the house — a modern house, not ten years old, she estimated. With its classical-style portico and austere, elegant lines conjuring Greek and Roman temples, it was a residence eminently suited to a Roman god.

He glanced up, too. "It's Burton's work, like so many other handsome modern structures in London. My father built it. He loved this house. A shame he had so little time to enjoy it."

She caught the odd, taut note in his voice and looked at him, but his face had closed.

Had she put that shuttered look there?

Had she hurt him, truly?

Guilt flooded her, and she was ashamed of herself, so ashamed.

She had her own troubles, and they loomed large. Yet he hadn't hurt her. Never once, in all the time she'd known him, had Lisburne been unkind. Annoying, yes, but never hurtful.

What was wrong with her that she should hurt him?

"Are you quite, quite sure," she said, "you don't want to toss me into the hackney and send me back?"

"The temptation is nearly overpowering,"

he said. "But I'm determined to resist. Ah, here's my house steward, Edkins, who does us the inestimable honor of opening the door himself. No doubt one of the servants spying at the windows has informed him of his master's arriving with a beautiful young woman in tow, identity unknown. I hope he doesn't faint. I never bring beautiful young women home. Yet I daresay he's up to this or any other occasion, are you not, Edkins?"

"Your lordship pleases to jest," Edkins said. "I have not fainted in several days."

By this time Lisburne had handed over his hat and gloves. "Send refreshments to my study, as soon as you may," he said over his shoulder as he headed toward a great staircase.

Leonie followed blindly for a moment, then stopped short. "Your study?"

He paused and turned to regard her with upraised eyebrow. "Did you think I'd take you to my bedchamber, after the way you've behaved?" he said in an undertone. "No, the study it will be, and I've half a mind to use it as my father used to do the one at our town house, to deliver a lecture and a birching." He looked her up and down. "Maybe more than half a mind." His voice dropping further, he added, "I should bend you over the desk, and lift your skirts and petticoats, and then . . ." He trailed off and shook his head. "I'm unbearably tempted, for you've used me abominably. But we've business to attend to."

He continued up a splendid staircase and into a corridor and she followed, her mind tangling with lifted skirts and petticoats and . . . spankings? She was hot everywhere.

He stopped in front of a doorway and opened the door.

She looked in. Bookshelves filled with books. A desk and a few chairs. A fine rug. Everything expensive and comfortable and without question the furnishings of a study.

"You brought me all this way for . . . business," she said.

"You can't think I brought you here for pleasure? After what you said in the hackney —"

"About that, Lisburne —"

"I didn't even know some of those words," he said. He opened the door and ushered her inside.

He walked behind the desk and drew out the chair but did not sit down. He opened a desk drawer and took out three pieces of writing paper. He tapped them on the desk to align the sides exactly. He moved the inkstand within easy reach. He brought out from another drawer three sharp pencils and laid them neatly next to the inkstand, ends precisely aligned. He took out a ruler, and set it down alongside the paper. Then he moved the ruler one inch farther to the right. He straightened the inkstand to make it exactly parallel to the paper.

"There," he said. "Or do you want me to rule the sheets for you?"

She stared at the stationery items he'd laid out. "What game are you playing? Did you bring me here to do your accounts? I thought your secretary —"

"Don't be nonsensical," he said. "I brought you here to explain to me, in a logical and concise manner, why you won't marry me. You may wish to draw two columns, one listing the pros and one listing the cons. If you need anything, ring the bell over there." He indicated a bellpull near the chimneypiece. "Or open the door and tell the footman outside what you require. His name is John."

He walked to the door and paused. "I could send Uttridge to you with a list of my assets and liabilities, but I'm sure you've a fair estimate of my financial worth."

She found her voice, "Oh, Lisburne, as though I cared about that!"

"That's emotion speaking," he said. "If I were an investment you were looking into,

you'd care. View this as a question of investment — of your life."

And he went out, closing the door behind
him.

Lisburne waited as long as he could, but
when two hours had passed, his willpower
ran out.

He opened the door to the study. The tray
of refreshments looked decimated. So did
she.

She sat, head resting on one hand, the
other holding the pen, which inched along
the paper. Her lower lip trembled.

She looked up. Her eyes brimmed. "Oh,
Simon!" She leapt up from the chair and
threw herself at him. His arms went round
her.

Simon. At last.

"I love you," she said against his neckcloth. "How does one write that in a column? Two yards of this and six ells of that.
How do I measure love, or what makes it?
You know how it happens. That beastly little
boy — Cupid or Eros, or whoever he is. He
shoots his arrow and you're done for. Love
won't be weighed and measured. It isn't so
much of this silk and so much of that, this
quantity of bows and this embroidery pattern. What do I put under pros? His beauti-

ful eyes. The sound of his voice. The scent of his skin. The way he ties his neckcloth. I wrote it all down, but it doesn't add up."

The knot in his chest eased.

"You might add to your list," he said, "his willingness to move heaven and earth to make you happy." He kissed the top of her head, careful to avoid impaling his eye on one of the decorative sprouting things. "I hope you included my assets."

"All of them," she said on a sob. "Including the ones we don't mention in public."

He laughed. He couldn't help it. He didn't know why he loved her or how or when, exactly, he'd come to fall in love with her. That was all as she said: One couldn't add it up or point to precisely this or that. But she made him laugh and she taxed his intellect and he'd not felt truly happy until he found her. He hadn't thought it possible to be truly happy again.

"Well, then, I forgive you," he said, "for all those ghastly things you said in the carriage."

"I was overwrought."

"Do you think so? Leonie Noirot, in Lord Warford's garden, covering her ears, like a child, and shrieking to drown me out. It was so out of character that I became truly alarmed."

She drew away a bit and looked up at him. "Is that why you took me away in that high-handed manner?"

"Somebody had to keep his feet on the ground," he said. "And somebody had to help you get yours back down there as well."

She closed her eyes. "That's why you sat me down with sharp pencils and a ruler and paper."

"If that didn't work, I planned to dose you with laudanum. The trouble is, one has to be very careful with dosing. I wasn't thrilled with the prospect of enacting a tragedy. *Romeo and Juliet* is all very well on the stage, but in real life, one wonders at their stupidity."

She opened her eyes, a deep twilight blue by lamplight. "I believe they were quite young," she said. "During a certain phase of youth, everything is tragic."

"Thus my cousin's popularity," he said. "And it's so typical of Swanton to find his true love and win her in a matter of days, while I work and slave for weeks, and cannot bring my girl to the sticking point."

She shook her head. "I'm sorry. It's embarrassing to be tragic. But I've written them down. The cons. And if you mean to move heaven and earth, you'll have your work cut out for you."

She straightened her posture and squared her shoulders and slipped out of his arms. She returned to the desk and picked up the three sheets of paper. She'd filled them, both sides, with her curiously precise and inescapably feminine script. She gave them to him and walked to the window and looked out into the darkness.

He scanned them quickly. "This is rather . . . overwhelming," he said.

"I warned you it was complicated," she said.

"Yes," he said. "I feel a strong desire to lie down. And have my brow bathed in lavender water."

She turned away from the window. "I can do that," she said.

Where else should Lisburne lie down but in his bed? And if Leonie didn't get far with bathing his fevered brow in lavender water, that was only because he pulled her down into his arms when she'd scarcely begun, and kissed her, and she dropped the cloth onto the floor. The papers he'd had in his hand, the papers she'd labored over, flew about before floating to the floor as well. In another moment he and she were making love, urgently, too impatient to trouble with undressing. And that was an experience, all the silk and lace foaming about them, and the pearls knocking him in the head until he swore, and stopped wrestling with her petticoat to take them off.

It was not the most elegant coupling of his life. Her carefully assembled coiffure nearly blinded him, but he persevered. A simple enough matter of unfastening his trousers and lifting her skirts and petticoat. Then it was elegant enough, this night, to be inside her, to watch her face as they moved together, to hear her voice — a soft moan, a sigh, murmured French — and to watch her open her great blue eyes and to see pleasure there, and love, and wicked laughter.

"I love you," he said. "I love you."

He told her over and over, like an incantation, while he watched her face and the way it changed, because in bed she hid nothing. He watched until he saw her nearing the peak. Then he let go of self-control, and gave himself up to the onrush of pleasure, and heard her give a little cry at the same moment he spent himself inside her.

Saturday 1 August
The first bout of lovemaking hadn't been the last. Eventually, their clothes had come off. And eventually, exhausted, they'd fallen

502

asleep in each other's arms.

For this reason, Leonie wasn't completely surprised when she woke, to see sunlight pouring through the lantern. She was surprised, however, to discern how far it had risen. It must be past noon. This was an aristocrat's idea of early morning, not hers. No matter how late she went to bed, she always rose at the same time on workdays, at half-past seven, to allow time for bathing, dressing, and breakfast before the seamstresses arrived at nine.

For a moment she wondered if Lisburne had given her laudanum after all.

But no. Relief must have sent her into so deep a sleep. Relief because she'd made some sort of peace with him and with herself. And it had been a relief and a joy to make love with complete abandon, not fretting about his needing to depart before daylight, before any of his friends could see him leaving Maison Noirot. Small wonder she'd slept as she hadn't done in at least a week, even though she'd solved none of her problems.

She'd slept in his arms this time. When she turned in the night, he was there, and knowing he was beside her eased her heart.

He wasn't beside her now.

But she was too content to worry. She

stretched lazily, then sat up, drawing up the bedclothes to cover her nakedness, in case of strange servants popping through the door without warning.

Actually, she could use a servant, strange or not, at the moment. She was in the habit of dressing herself, but that was everyday clothing. Her evening dress was far more challenging to manage single-handed.

After listening for footsteps outside, she climbed cautiously from the bed, unearthed her chemise from the haphazardly folded garments on a chair, and threw it on. She looked at her stays and sighed. It was one of her most beautiful corsets and she'd designed it to be self-fastening, but Lisburne had undone the strings completely, which defeated the purpose.

She picked it up and put it down again. Somewhere nearby must be his dressing room, and surely he owned dressing gowns.

She was heading toward a likely looking door, when she heard a sound behind her.

"I'm in the nick of time, I see," Lisburne said. "Another minute and you'd have entered my dressing room and touched something, and Polcaire would go into a decline. Will you come down to breakfast?"

"In what?" she said. "My chemise?"

"In this."

She'd been so occupied in gazing dreamily at his beautiful face that she'd failed to notice he had something draped over his arm.

He approached. "I found one of my mother's morning gowns. It's a decade out of date, but easier to get into, I reckon, than your gorgeous ball dress."

She took it from him and held it up. It was a deep green, made of twilled sarcenet, and closely fitted to the body. "How narrow it is!" she said.

"Women used to show off their shape more," he said. "I hope you don't mind. It's the best I could come up with on short notice. Bachelor place, you know. I hadn't any women servants to help me, except from the kitchen, and I doubted they'd be au courant with ladies' fashion."

"It's exquisite," she said. "Beautifully made. Your mother has impeccable taste."

"Yes, I think you'll like her."

"Oh, Lisburne."

"Simon," he corrected. "You must be starved for breakfast. I'll help you dress."

The dress felt very strange, snug along the arms and hips and, because she'd had to forgo her corded petticoat — it was too wide and the wrong shape — falling straight to the floor. She did not feel fully dressed.

Which would not have been any great problem, had she not had to face a series of servants.

And then, when she entered the breakfast room, she found her sisters there with their husbands.

She stood for a moment, debating whether to race to the sideboard, snatch a knife, and stab Lisburne.

But that was the sort of thing Sophy would do. Leonie Noirot wasn't dramatic. In any case, she refused to show any signs of being taken aback, let alone in a state of murderous rage.

How *could* he?

Did he think this was going to work? Advertising his conquest? Did he think her brothers-in-law would make her marry him?

As if they could.

She smiled. "What a lovely surprise, Lord Lisburne. How sweet of you to think of inviting my family for breakfast."

"It's a business breakfast," he said. "That's why they're all here."

He took out from the pocket of his waist-coat the three sheets of paper, rather the worse for wear.

"I went at a somewhat indecently early hour to Clevedon House to consult with the duke," he said. "And he sent for Long-more. And after we'd argued back and forth, we came to something like agreement."

"They did not, I ought to point out, consult with us," Marcelline said. "Nor have they confided in us. You can't blame Sophy and me for anything but curiosity. Speaking of which, what an interesting dress that is." She rose and approached to take a closer look.

She stood for a moment, frowning. Then she took Leonie's hand and examined the sleeve and said, "But my dear, that's an Emmeline dress. Come here, Sophy. Don't you recognize the satin rouleaus? That's from Cousin Emma's shop, I should stake my life. Good heavens, I believe I sewed those satin bands myself! Wherever did you get this?"

"Cousin Emma's?" Leonie said. "This was Cousin Emma's work?" Her eyes filled and her throat closed and she found the nearest empty chair and sat down.

"Cousin Emma?" Lisburne said.

She made herself speak. "Emmeline was the shop in Paris. Where Lord Swanton met me. The cholera took our cousin Emma and decimated Paris. It killed our seamstresses and our customers. It destroyed our business. There were riots. The shop was looted. We had a sick child, and we feared the mob would hear of it and set fire to the shop with us in it. We left Paris with nothing. Not a scrap of muslin. Not a silk ribbon. We had nothing left of all Emma had done. All her beautiful work. That's what I was trying to explain." She nodded toward the papers in his hand. "What it meant to us. What opening our own shop meant. It's very hard to describe, let alone put into neat columns. But my heart is there, in the shop. Marcelline and Sophy — they're artists. They can be artists in other ways. I can't. I'm a businesswoman."

"My love," Marcelline began, so gently, the way she used to do, when their parents had abandoned them for the hundredth time.

"Don't," Leonie said, holding up her hand. "I like numbers. I like reviewing the merchants' bills. I like negotiating with tradesmen. I like managing a shop. It makes me happy. I wish you and Sophy were still there —"

"We haven't left."

"But you will. You must. It's completely ridiculous. A duchess can't wait on customers, Marcelline! Do use your head. And a countess can't, either, Sophy, so you may

508

put that fantasy out of your fevered brain. The shop will go on, but not with you. It's too disruptive. I need to know I can count on you and I can't anymore. The next I know, Sophy will be pregnant, too, and running away to be sick."

"And what about you?" Marcelline said. "Have you and Lisburne been writing in ledgers and only holding hands? Or do you imagine you're immune to the laws of nature?"

"Right," Lisburne said. "If we might return to business? I have a business proposal to make to the proprietresses of Maison Noirot."

Leonie looked up at him. In truth, he did look businesslike. It was the waistcoat, certainly — Polcaire truly was a genius — but Lisburne held himself with an air of authority, and he'd made his beautiful face very stern.

It was rather adorable.

She said, "Marcelline and Sophy, pray sit down. I'm only going to throw some food on my plate, and I'll attend you directly, Lisburne. But really, I can't bear any more emotion on an empty stomach."

"Ma pauvre!" Marcelline said. "Don't stir. I'll get you something to eat."

She heaped food on a plate and set it

down in front of Leonie.

She oughtn't to have had any appetite.

But Lisburne looked so imposing that one couldn't feel anxious about anything. Perhaps she was deluded, but for now she felt less worried than she'd done in months. She took up her cutlery and ate.

Though Lisburne had made notes on her sheets of paper, he had it all in his head. He'd only needed to speak to Clevedon for a short time this morning before the pieces began to fit together.

He said, "Firstly, we address the question of vocation. Three highly talented women, passionate about their work, whom one cannot expect will find contentment in idleness. The Duke of Clevedon proposes a magazine —"

"Oh, Clevedon," the duchess said. "The magazine again? It's a lovely idea, but —"

"If you would be patient, my dear, and let Lisburne say his piece," the duke said. He looked round the table. "I know he can be deuced annoying, and he likes to pretend he's an idiot. The truth is, he's far more astute than he lets on. Perhaps we might all listen quietly and raise objections at the end." He nodded at Lisburne. "Pray continue."

"An expensive magazine, containing a large number of color plates," Lisburne continued. "An emphasis on women's fashion. Her Grace to provide the designs for dresses and Lady Longmore to provide a selection of hats and bonnets as well as descriptions, anecdotes, and stories in her own inimitable style. Miss Noirot to manage the enterprise entirely."

He paused. The three sisters' expressions remained inscrutable. He made a private note never to play cards with them — or not all three at once.

He went on. "Secondly, the shop. The three proprietresses to retain ownership as well as continuing to provide designs for apparel in their different areas of expertise, with the aim of keeping Maison Noirot at the very forefront of ladies' fashion. The day-to-day work of the shop, however, to be under the supervision of the eminently qualified Selina Jeffreys. Furthermore, to be staffed by the most talented professionals available as well as provide training for qualified indigent females proposed by the Milliners' Society. As regards qualified professionals, His Grace and I take the liberty of recommending one Dulcinea Williams to the ladies' attention. It is our belief that Mrs. Williams can sell anything to anybody."

The three sisters' faces remained politely amiable, no more, yet he sensed an intensifying of attention. For one thing, Leonie plied her cutlery more slowly.

"The changes will allow the proprietresses to devote more time to the Milliners' Society," he went on. "For example, in using their social position to increase sponsorship and donations, which will lead, we trust, to the building of a larger facility, a project they will supervise."

Leonie put down her cutlery. She and her sisters looked at each other, still giving nothing away.

"As this may offer insufficient use of Miss Noirot's business skills," he said, "I offer her the position of Marchioness of Lisburne and the management of my several properties and business interests."

He folded up the pieces of paper and stuffed them into a pocket. Polcaire would give him martyred looks, but never mind.

Lisburne waited through a fierce silence while the three women digested his summary and while at least one of them tried to work out the implications and consequences, writing out ledger pages in her mind, he had no doubt.

After a time, the duchess glanced at her sisters and said they needed to go into another room to discuss it. They rose as one and went out.

They were gone a very long while.

After half an hour had passed, a bored Longmore went out to take a walk. Clevedon went to the library.

An hour after leaving the breakfast room, the ladies returned. The men were summoned to hear their decision.

The three women moved to stand in front of the chimneypiece, where the afternoon light flowed becomingly over their dresses.

"As the eldest, I've been deputed to speak for the others," the duchess said. "We find your proposal generally satisfactory and have agreed to accept it."

"All of it?" Lisburne said. "Duchess, there's one item, I believe, about which you can't speak for one party. Miss Noirot, do you agree to become my wife?"

"That depends," she said. "Will the Botticelli still be mine?"

Thanks to Clevedon, Lisburne had to wait a full week for the wedding.

Lisburne had raced to Doctors Commons the same day Leonie had at last consented. He'd waited there for what seemed an eternity, after which he was obliged to pay out a great deal of money for the piece of paper he wanted. Then he had to wait some more.

But special license or no special license, Clevedon wouldn't allow his sister-in-law to be wed until he plagued Lisburne with lawyers, and the lawyers fought with each other and finally came to a truce, at which point Lisburne signed the marriage settlements.

The Botticelli was to be included as a bridal gift, which made it Leonie's own property. All provisions were made for offspring and in case of illness and death and bankruptcy and whatnot. She must have pin money and a dower house.

It was all very well, Clevedon said, to promise a girl the moon, but the law was not very protective of women, especially wives, and he was damned if he wouldn't protect his wife's sister's future security, since he'd been unable to protect her virtue.

And then His Grace invited his aunts to the wedding! Which meant that Leonie was obliged to stay at Clevedon House, so as not to shock them.

But the Friday came at last, and they were married at Clevedon House rather quietly, with only what seemed like hundreds of

Clevedon's aunts and thousands of Fair-faxes, and Swanton and Gladys, and all the gentlemen who'd assisted at Vauxhall, because without them as witnesses, Lisburne might have rescued his cousin, but not Maison Noirot's and the Milliners' Society's reputations.

But at last the celebrations were over, and he and Leonie retired to his villa, where the servants made a little party for them, and Polcaire bore up manfully under the prospect of a mistress of the house and the inevitable lady's maids disturbing his perfectly ordered world.

Then it only remained for Lisburne to bed his bride, which he did at first with feverish impatience and at second at a more leisurely rate. Then, as they lay in bed, quieting, she said, "You never said about the last item."

He puzzled over this for a moment. "What last item?"

"In the cons column," she said.

He thought. Ah, yes. The last item had been Dreadful DeLucey, underlined twice.
Dreadful DeLucey.
He smiled.

"You said nothing," she said.

"Neither did you," he said. "I covered every other item, but you never asked what I meant to do about that."

"I forgot," she said. "I was so busy making sense of all the rest, and so taken up with it that I forgot. And I never thought of it again until today when we stood before the minister, and that seemed an awkward time to bring it up."

"Yes, well, as to that." He came up onto his elbow and looked down at her. "I've not been altogether honest with you."

"Not honest? You mean pretending to be stupid when you're not? Claiming you leave all your business to Uttridge? Leading me out into a dark garden, not to use me in wicked ways, but to propose matrimony? Those sorts of deceptive practices?"

"And you?" he said. "Claiming you're not literary and know nothing of poetry —"

"I've already admitted I'm not to be trusted. But you're not entirely what you seem, by any means. In fact, sometimes I've wondered if you're a Noirot — because they're the French edition of the Dreadful DeLuceys, you know. And you —"

"My maternal great-grandmother was Annette DeLucey," he said. "When my great-grandfather married her, his father threatened to kill him so that he couldn't inherit. But Annette won her father-in-law over, eventually."

She sat up. "I knew it!"

"Of course you did. It takes a thief to catch a thief."

"We're not thieves, exactly," she said. She settled back down, and looked up at him. "That is to say, not all of us. But we are rather underhanded and not overly scrupulous . . . no wonder I've always felt so comfortable with you!"

"Comfortable!" he said indignantly. "Like an old shoe?"

"Because you understand me," she said. "And because you use your DeLucey powers for good, mainly, and for very nice naughtiness."

"Very nice," he said. "Is that the best you can do?"

She laughed and reached for him in the way that made his heart seem to curl in his chest. "My realm is numbers, sir. If you want me to rise to great literary heights, you must inspire me."

"Like the muse," he said as he lowered his face to hers.

"Yes, like the muse," she said.

"This could take time," he said. "But as long as you're not too *busy* . . ."

EPILOGUE

But by special licence or dispensation from the Archbishop of Canterbury, Marriages, especially of persons of quality, are frequently in their own houses, out of canonical hours, in the evening, and often solemnized by others in other churches than where one of the parties lives, and out of time of divine service, &c.

— *The Law Dictionary,* 1810

Bedford Square
Saturday 15 August
Madame Ecrivier, forewoman of Downes's dressmaking shop, frowned at the short, round man who'd swaggered into the shop. "I do not comprehend your meaning," she said.

"I beg you won't fret yourself, my mamerzelle," he said. "I only want to see your mistress, if it isn't too much trouble."

The man held an official-looking paper.

In Madame Ecrivier's experience, official papers were trouble. Especially when greasy men in red neckerchiefs and too-tight green coats delivered them.

Mrs. Downes paid two men, Farley and Payton, to deal with annoyances of all kinds. As her forewoman debated whether to summon them, another man entered the shop. He was tall and stooped, dressed in black.

"Here, now," he said. "Otherwise engaged, is she?"

"Don't know," said the other man.

"See here, miss," the tall man said. "We want to see your mistress. Important business. You take my card to her —" He held out a thick, dirty card, which Madame, seeing no alternative, collected with the tips of her fingers. "And tell her we can still settle matters agreeable to all parties."

Madame hurried from the showroom. She ran into the workroom, and learned none of the seamstresses had seen Farley or Payton all day. She ran up the stairs to Mrs. Downes's private quarters. The footman told her that the mistress had gone out two hours earlier. To dinner, he believed.

Madame, who'd lived in Paris during terrible times, could put two and two together — in this case men carrying official documents and an employer who'd gone out without informing her forewoman. She made her way to Mrs. Downes's bedroom. No clothes. No cosmetics. No bandboxes, valises, or trunks.

She hunted down Mrs. Downes's maid, whom she found packing her bags.

"Sent me out, she did, on about a hundred errands today," the maid said. "That was to keep me away." After jamming aprons, chemises, stockings, and so on into a valise, she started stripping as much of her little room's contents as she could stuff into her bags. "Owed me since Midsummer Quarter Day, didn't she? Don't you look at me like that. You'll be grabbing what you can, too. You don't think she left wages for you, do you?"

"There are men downstairs," Madame Ecrivier said. She still couldn't take it in. She'd worked so hard to build a new clientele, and retain the few older customers who still patronized the shop. She'd fought for higher wages, in order to attract more skilled help. She'd mounted an attack on inefficiency and shoddiness, and she was seeing — slowly, admittedly — signs of improvement. It only wanted patience. And time.

"They've come with a writ of execution, I don't doubt," the maid said.

Madame clutched her throat.

The girl gave an exasperated snort. "It don't mean the guillotine, you noddy. It means they'll take an inventory, then more men will come and take whatever isn't nailed down. The missus borrowed a lot of money from somebody, and never paid it back."

"But this is not possible!" Madame cried. "What of all my customers? What of all my orders?"

"Well, she must've spent whatever you earned for her, don't you think? On her fine carriage and dinner parties and a box at the opera and who knows what else. What I do know is, we haven't none of us seen any money lately. I recommend you take what you can, and slip out the back way before them men realize she's bolted."

Madame Ecrivier had come from Paris to London to make a fresh start. It hadn't taken her long to realize she'd chosen her employer unwisely. At the time, however, she'd been desperate for work, and Mrs. Downes had offered a position of responsibility and higher wages than the seamstresses made.

Madame Ecrivier felt desperate now. She'd saved what she could, but London was expensive, and her wages did not go far.

This day she'd receive no wages.

Still, she wasn't a thief.

She returned to the showroom and told the unpleasant men that Mrs. Downes had run away. Then Madame Ecrivier told the seamstresses they were unemployed. She did her best to comfort them and offer advice.

Then she collected her hat and shawl and set out for Maison Noirot.

Warford House
Wednesday 26 August

"Italy, indeed!" Lord Boulsworth boomed. "Whoever heard such nonsense?"

He strode back and forth across Lord Warford's study carpet, in the manner of one inspecting unsatisfactory troops. These comprised his daughter and Lord Swanton.

Though Lord Boulsworth had delegated his cousin Warford to act in loco parentis, the latter knew better than to allow the wedding to proceed without Boulsworth there to bless the proceedings. Lord Warford's wife provided more than sufficient displays of temperament. He did not want to give Boulsworth reason to storm into Warford House and roar at everybody. Not that

Boulsworth needed a reason.

"I've a house standing empty outside Manchester and a lot of idle servants in dire need of discipline," the general went on. "Since duty calls me elsewhere, I look upon you as the next ranking officer. Your father acted bravely at Waterloo. Long past time you lived up to him, instead of writing rhymes for silly girls and gadding about the Continent. You and Gladys will take up residence in Lancashire."

"Lancashire?" Swanton echoed. And fainted.

"What the devil?" cried the general.

Gladys knelt beside her lover and lifted his head and held it against her bountiful bosom. She looked up at her father, eyes blazing. "How could you, papa!"

"I? What the devil did I do? What sort of milksop have you given your hand to?"

"This *milksop* nearly killed a man with his bare hands!"

Lord Boulsworth eyed the fallen hero dubiously. "I suppose he had bricks in them at the time. Otherwise —"

"Gladys." The poet's eyes fluttered open. "My dear girl. Please forgive me. The shock overcame me. But only for a moment. Let me rise." Gently he put her helping hands

523

away and pushed himself up and onto his feet.

He squared his shoulders and jutted out his chin. "Sir, you seem to be laboring under a misapprehension. In three days' time Gladys will be my wife. We will travel to Italy, where I shall continue to write poetry — better poetry, I hope, with her as my muse —"

"Muse! Ballocks! I won't have her traipsing about the Continent on the whim of a fellow who faints at trifles."

"The shock of your presuming to command both myself and the lady who is to be my wife left me temporarily deprived of my senses," Swanton said. "I could scarcely believe my ears. Your lordship seems to forget that Gladys will swear a sacred vow to love and obey her *husband*. Will you have her violate sacred vows? Will you have me violate mine? Am I not bound to love and honor her? Does not this love require my respecting her wishes for me to continue in my vocation?"

The general stared at him, his face a shade of red inferior officers had learned to dread.

Swanton only smiled with angelic patience and said, "Whether you will or not, makes no matter. I shall do whatever is necessary to make Gladys my wife."

Lord Boulsworth had fought and won too many battles to accept defeat easily. He sputtered and argued and threatened. Swanton bore it like a stoic, only reiterating his intention of being the head of his own family. He might have continued forbearing but Gladys, who knew how obstinately domineering her father could be, sank into a chair and began to cry.

Swanton looked at her and at her father. He clenched his hands and set his jaw. "Very well," he said. "I've tried to fight fair. But I won't have Gladys distressed."

Then he began to recite:

We fled a far but happier clime,
　From kindred's pow'r and foeman's hate;
Our crime was love — if love be crime,
　She was my hope, my fate.

The poem went on for an infinite number of stanzas.

At the end, Lord Boulsworth, in tears — of rage or desperation or possibly even sentiment — surrendered.

On 29 August, Lord Swanton and Lady Gladys Fairfax were married by special license in the room of Warford House containing the wedding scene.

According to *Foxe's Morning Spectacle,* "The bride wore a dress of white satin, with a close-fitting corsage en pointe, a richly embroidered pelerine over short sleeves, and embroidered crepe flounce. Her hair was ornamented with flowers, and an arrow from which descended on each side a blond lappet."

The following day, Lady Warford wrote to Lisburne's mother, reporting that the wedding had gone off without a hitch the previous day. The general, she said, appeared strangely subdued.

"Gladys looked very well, indeed," Lady Warford wrote.

She glowed with happiness, and I'm sure I'm happy for her. I know she will look after your nephew Swanton, and he has been surprisingly protective of her. In any event, you'll see them soon enough, and can judge for yourself. But oh, my dear, what is to be done about Clara? I fear that if she keeps on as she does, the gentlemen will give up on her. Who would have thought that such a beautiful girl should remain unwed all this time? Sophy claims the only trouble is that no one is worthy of her, but you know Clara has always had a rebellious streak, like her father's mother.

She has had more than one narrow escape and I fear — I greatly fear — that she'll err again, and this time no one will be able to get her out of the scrape, and she'll be disgraced forever, or else married to a Monster like That Man with whose name I will not sully my pen. (We have confirmation, by the way, that his confederates, those scoundrels Theaker and Meffat, have followed his lead and fled their creditors as well as disgrace, to wander penniless about the Continent, I sincerely hope.)

But Clara is safe from them, in any event, and I desperately hope she has learned something from that Mrs. Williams's horrible experience. I know it is useless to press my daughter about marrying. She gets her back up and then won't listen to a word — but my dear Enid, I am at my wits' end. I wish you would look about you for a gentleman of maturity and backbone, for she will need a strong hand. And truly, I no longer care whether he is of the highest rank, if only he can keep her comfortably.

Oh, but what do I ask? Never mind, my dear. I begin to think my eldest daughter a lost cause. It would be wiser, you will tell me, to put my energies into the others.

Thence followed domestic matters, of little interest to those but the correspondents.

In February, the Duchess of Clevedon gave birth to a healthy little boy. His sister and her best friend, Bianca Williams, made his christening bonnet.

AUTHOR'S NOTE

Next, o'er his Books his eyes began to roll,
In pleasing memory of all he stole,
How here he sipp'd, how there he
    plunder'd snug,
And suck'd all o'er, like an industrious
    Bug.
— Alexander Pope, *The Dunciad,* Book I

For starters, I stole the art, making the Botticelli *Venus and Mars* (also known in some quarters as *Mars and Venus*) part of my fictional Lord Lisburne's art collection as well as giving the work its modern title. The subject matter has been in dispute, and it may not even have had an English title until it came to England in the 1850s (anachronism ahoy!). London's National Gallery purchased it in 1874, and there it remains on glorious view. Botticelli's unpopularity at the time of the story, however, is not a figment of my fevered imagination. He fell out of favor after his death and didn't recover until the second half of the nineteenth century.

Veronese's *Virtue and Vice,* on the other hand, really was on view during the British Institution's 1835 Summer Exhibition.

All the poetry is stolen, mainly from early nineteenth-century ladies' magazines, in keeping with their own grand tradition of stealing from one another. Ask Charles Dickens about copyright infringement and watch him tear out his hair and gnash his teeth.

"Never warn me, my dear, to take care of my heart," is from Mrs. Abdy's "A Marrying Man," which appeared in *The Comic Offering; or Ladies' Melange of Literary Mirth,* edited by Louisa Henrietta Sheridan.

http://www.google.com/books?id=9G4 FAAAAQAAJ&pg=PA145#v=onepage&q &f= false

Mrs. Abdy's poem "The Second Son" appeared in the same periodical.

http://www.google.com/books?id=9G4 FAAAAQAAJ&pg=PA259#v=onepage&q &f= false

"The Dead Robin" appeared in the *Lady's Magazine and Museum,* Vol. VI, 1835, ascribed to a frequent poetry contributor who called himself/herself "Tacet."

http://books.google.com/books?id=wUc FAAAAQAAJ&pg=PA65#v=onepage&q &f=false

The poem with the gushing torrents came from No. IV of a series of poems entitled, "Lays of the Affections," in the 1830 *Lady's Magazine*.

http://www.google.com/books?id=K3EE AAAQAAJ&pg=RA1-PA136#v=onepage &q&f=false

"Oh! late I view'd her move along, the idol of the crowd" is the ending of a poem titled "Ethelinda," which appeared in *La Belle Assemblée*, 1826, and was attributed to "D.L.T." http://books.google.com/books? id=8E ExAQAAMAAJ&pg=PA71#v=one page&q&f=false

"A thousand faults in man we find" appears repeatedly in periodicals from the Regency era into the 1830s (and possibly later) under various titles, and with different authors, e.g., A.A., Tom P., or no author at all — a great example of the rampant piracy of the time. I gave it the earliest attribution I was able to find via Google Books.

"My Very Particular Friend" is another of Mrs. Abdy's poems, which I found quoted in a review of *The Comic Offering; or, Ladies' Melange of Literary Mirth for 1834*. The review appeared in the *London Literary Gazette and Journal of Belles Lettres, Arts, Sciences, Etc.,* 1833.

http://books.google.com/books?id=54d HAAAAYAAJ &pg=PA658#v=onepage&q &f=false

Louisa Henrietta Sheridan, writer and editor of *The Comic Offering,* wrote her own version, also titled "My Very Particular Friend," meant to be sung. This multitalented lady wrote the music herself. It appeared in the *New Monthly Belle Assemblée,* 1836.

http://books.google.com/books?id=y90 PAAAAMAAJ&pg=PA10#v=onepage&q &f=false

"We waltz and behold her" is from "Mynheer Werter's First Interview with Charlotte, Versified," which appeared in *The Athenaeum; or, Spirit of the English Magazines,* 1826.

http://books.google.com/books?id=I2 cAAAAAYAAJ&pg=RA1-PA447#v=one page&q&f=false

The quotation from *The Odyssey* is from the William Cowper translation.

http://www.gutenberg.org/files/24269/ 24269-h/24269-h.htm#BOOK_I

"We fled a far but happier clime" is from "The Wreck," by W.L.R., which appeared in the *Magazine of the Beau Monde* in August 1835.

http://google.com/books?id=Gh4AAAA QAAJ&pg=PA186-IA190#v=onepage&q &f=false

Another Pesky Anachronism

Since the Hans Christian Andersen tales in which "The Emperor's New Clothes" first appeared weren't published until 1837, it's not likely anybody in England would be using it as a reference in 1835. So that one's a stretch, but nothing else I could come up with worked so well.

And Speaking of Clothes . . .

Once upon a time, all we had were natural fabrics, made of cotton, linen, wool, silk, and blends of these. Silk, for instance, came in varieties whose names are no longer familiar. The definitions below come from Louis Harmuth's *Dictionary of Textiles,* 1920 edition. The information in brackets is courtesy the milliners and mantua makers of Colonial Williamsburg. My comments are in parentheses.

Armoisin: light and thin silk taffeta for lining; made in Italy and France with stripes, geometrical designs or dots. Heavier a. with ribs was made for curtains and bed covers. Nowadays, East India produces two kinds of a., one called damaras, with flower patterns, and arains, with stripes or checks.

Genoa velvet: 1. Very fine thick, all-silk velvet brocade on satin ground, having large patterns: made in Genoa, Italy, centuries ago; 2. A weft pile cotton velvet, having a one-and-two twill ground. [— from Italy, could be cotton velvet but most likely was silk. It was the best silk velvet on the market, and copied by the rest of Europe.]

Green Persian: Very light silk lining, printed with large flowers, used in England in the XVIII century. (Author's note: Here Harmuth is far from satisfactory. The term "green Persian" appears frequently in nineteenth-century novels, including works by Dickens.) [Persians are lightweight, China-like silks. There are six grades, and they're used primarily for linings. They come from Turkey and Persia.

Lutestring: fine, warp ribbed silk dress goods of high finish. [Fine silk with a bit of stiffness, like today's taffeta.]

Mode: (Author's note: Harmuth is even more disappointing here, since he doesn't list it, at least not by this name.) [Another lightweight silk that came primarily in either black or white, and was used mostly for outdoor cloaks, though also for linings.]

534

Princetta: An English worsted fabric in the 19th century, made with silk warp and worsted filling; originally made of pure worsted.

Sarcenet (sometimes spelled sarsenet or sarsnet): obsolete, light, soft and thin silk fabric, used as lining in England. [Thin, clingy silk.]

The detailed fashion descriptions (not those written from a man's point of view) are taken/adapted from ladies' fashion magazines of the time. The women's clothes are based on fashion plates.

Who Are These People?

As the third in a series, *Vixen in Velvet* brings in characters from the first two books. For Marcelline's story, please see *Silk Is for Seduction*. Sophy is the star of *Scandal Wears Satin*. Lord Lovedon and Chloe Sharp's story is told in "Lord Lovedon's Duel," a short story in the anthology *Royal Bridesmaids*.